PENGUIN BOOKS

THE CONTINUING SILENCE OF A POET

A. B. Yehoshua, one of Israel's foremost writers, has achieved international renown. His highly acclaimed works have been published in many languages and include *Five Seasons*, *A Late Divorce*, *The Lover*, *Early in the Summer of 1970*, *Three Days and a Child*, and *Between Right and Right*. Mr. Yehoshua lives in Haifa with his wife and children.

The Continuing Silence of a Poet:

THE COLLECTED STORIES OF A. B. YEHOSHUA

PENGUIN BOOKS

PENGUIN BOOKS
Published by the Penguin Group
Viking Penguin, a division of Penguin Books USA Inc.,
375 Hudson Street, New York, New York 10014, U.S.A.
Penguin Books Ltd, 27 Wrights Lane, London W8 5TZ, England
Penguin Books Australia Ltd, Ringwood, Victoria, Australia
Penguin Books Canada Ltd, 2801 John Street,
Markham, Ontario, Canada L3R 1B4
Penguin Books (N.Z.) Ltd, 182–190 Wairau Road,
Auckland 10, New Zealand

Penguin Books Ltd, Registered Offices:
Harmondsworth, Middlesex, England

This edition reprinted by arrangement with Doubleday,
a division of Bantam Doubleday Dell Publishing Group, Inc.
Published in Penguin Books 1991

1   3   5   7   9   10   8   6   4   2

LIBRARY OF CONGRESS CATALOGING IN PUBLICATION DATA
Yehoshua, Abraham B.
[Short stories. English]
The continuing silence of a poet: the collected stories of A. B.
Yehoshua.
p.   cm.
Contents: The continuing silence of a poet—Three days and a
child—A long hot day, his despair, his wife, and his daughter—
The Yatir evening express—Galia's wedding—Flood tide—Facing
the forests—The last commander—Early in the summer of 1970—
Missile base 612.
ISBN 0 14 01.4844 2
1. Yehoshua, Abraham B.—Translations, English.   I. Title.
PJ5054.Y42   1991
892.4'36—dc20   90–43253

Printed in the United States of America

CONTENTS

The Continuing Silence of a Poet

HE was late again last night, and when he did come in he
made no effort to enter quietly. As though my own sleep did
not matter. His steps echoed through the empty apartment for a
long time. He kept the lights in the hall on and fussed about
endlessly with papers. At last he fell silent. I groped my way back
towards the light, vague sleep of old age. And then, the rain. For
three weeks now this persistent rain, sheets of water grinding down
the panes.

Where does he go at night? I do not know. I once managed to
follow him through several streets, but an old acquaintance, an
incorrigible prose writer, button-holed me at a street corner and
meanwhile the boy disappeared.

The rains are turning this plain into a morass of asphalt, sand
and water. Tel Aviv in winter—town without drainage, no outlets,
spawning lakes. And the sea beyond, murky and unclean, rumbling
as though in retreat from the sprawling town, sea become background.

Not five yet but the windows are turning grey. What was it? He
appeared in my dream, stood there in full view before me, not far
from the seashore, I think, dark birds were in his lap, and he
quelled their fluttering. His smile amazed me. He stood and faced
me, looked hard at me and gave a feeble smile.

Now the faint sound of snoring reaches me from his room and I
know I shall sleep no more. Another boat sails tomorrow or the day
after and I expect I shall board it at last. This anguish will dissolve,
I know. I have only to preserve my dignity till the moment of
parting. Another twenty hours or so, only.

Though I do not see him now, I know he is asleep, hands over
heart, eyes shut, mouth open, his breathing clear.

I must describe him first. What he looks like. I can do that for,
though not yet seventeen, his features appear to have settled. I have
long regarded him as unchanging, as one who will never change.

His slightly stooping figure, fierce frame craned forwards in submission. His flat skull. His face—coarse, thick, obtuse. The pimples sprouting on his cheeks and forehead. The black beginnings of a beard. His close-cropped hair. His spectacles.

I know very well—will even proclaim in advance—that people think he is feeble-minded; it is the general opinion, and my daughters share it. As for myself, I am ready to concede the fact, for it contains nothing to betray *me*, after all, nor to reflect upon the soundness of my senses. I have read scientific literature on the subject and I assure you: it is a mere accident. Moreover, he does not resemble me in the least, and barring a certain ferocity, we two have nothing in common. I am completely unafraid therefore, and yet for all that I insist he is a borderline case. He hovers on the border. The proof? His eyes. I am the only person to have frequent occasion for looking into his eyes and I say at times (though rarely, I admit), something lights up in them, a dark penetrating vitality.

And not his eyes alone.

And yet . . .

He was born late in my life. Born accidentally, by mistake, by some accursed miracle, for we were both, his mother and I, on the threshold of old age by then.

I have a vivid recollection of that time, the time before he was born. A gentle spring, very long, very wonderful. And I, a poet with five published volumes of verse behind me, resolved to stop writing, resolved with absolute, irrevocable conviction, out of utter despair. For it was only during that spring that I had come to admit to myself that I ought to keep silent.

I had lost the melody.

My closest friends had already started to taunt and to discourage me, dismissing everything I wrote. The young poets and their new poetry bewildered, maddened me. I tried to imitate them secretly and managed to produce the worst I ever wrote. "Well then," I said, "I shall keep silent from now on . . ." and what of it? As a result of this silence, however, our daily routine was disrupted. Sometimes we would go to bed in the early hours of the evening, at others spend half the night in crowded cafés, useless lectures or at gatherings of aged artists gasping for honours at death's door.

That long, wonderful spring, filled with gentle breezes, bursting with blossoms. And I, roaming the streets, up and down, swept by excitement and despair, feeling doomed. Vainly I tried to get drunk, proclaim my vow of silence to all, repudiating poetry, jesting about poems computed by machines, scornful, defiant, laughing a great

2

deal, chattering, making confessions. And at night writing letters to the papers about trivial matters (public transportation, etc.), polishing my phrases, taking infinite pains with them.

Then, suddenly, this unexpected pregnancy.

This disgrace.

We found out about it in early summer. At first we walked a great deal, then shut ourselves up at home, finally becoming apologetic. First we apologized to the girls, who watched the swelling figure of their elderly mother with horror, then to the relatives come to cast silent looks at the newborn infant.

(The birth occurred one freezing day in midwinter. The tufts of grass in our garden were white with frost.)

We were imprisoned with the baby now. (The girls would not lift a finger for him and deliberately went out more than ever.) We two wanted to speak, tell each other: What a wonderful thing, this birth. But our hearts were not in it, quite clearly. Those sleep-drunken night trips once more, the shadow of the tree streaking the walls, damp, heavy nappies hanging up through all the rooms, all of it depressing. We dragged our feet.

Slowly, sluggishly it grew, the child, late in everything, sunk in a kind of stupor. Looking back now I see him as a grey fledgling, twitching his weak limbs in the cot by my bed.

The first suspicion arose as late as the third year of his life. It was the girls who broached it, not I. He was retarded in his movements, he was stuttering badly, unprepossessing—hence the girls declared him feeble-minded. And friends would come and scan his face, looking for signs to confirm what we dared not utter.

I do not remember that period in his life very well. His mother's illness took up most of my time. She was fading fast. Nothing had remained of her after that late birth but her shell. We had to look on while she withdrew from us into the desert, forced to wander alone among barren, arid hills and vanish in the twilight.

Each day marked its change in her.

The child was six when his mother died. Heavy, awkward, not attached to anyone in the household, withdrawn into himself but never lost in dreams—anything but a dreamy child. Tense, always, and restless. He trembled if I ran my fingers through his hair.

If I could say with pity: an orphan. But the word sticks in my throat. His mother's dying left no impression, even though, due to my own distraction, he trailed behind us to her funeral. He never asked about her, as though he understood that her going was final.

3

Some months after her death, moreover, every one of her photographs disappeared, and when we discovered the loss a few days later it did not occur to us to question him. When we did, finally, it was too late. The light was fading when he led us to the burial place; in a far corner of the garden, beneath the poplar, among the traces of an old abandoned lime pit, wrapped in an old rag—the slashed pictures.

He stood there in front of us a long time, stuttering fiercely, his small eyes scurrying.

Yet nothing was explained . . .

For the first time our eyes opened and we saw before us a little human being.

I could not restrain myself and I beat him, for the first time since he was born. I seized his wrist and slapped him hard in the face. Then the girls beat him. (Why did they beat him?)

He did not understand . . .

He was startled by the beating. Afterwards he flung himself down and wept. We pulled him to his feet and dragged him home.

I had never realized before how well he knew the house, how thoroughly he had possessed himself of every corner. He had collected his mother's pictures out of obsolete albums, had invaded old envelopes. He had even found a secret spot in the garden that I did not know of. We had lived in this house for many years and I had spent many troubled nights pacing up and down this small garden, but I had never noticed the old extinguished lime—pale, tufted with grey lichen.

Were these the first signs? I do not know. None of us, neither I nor the girls, were prepared to understand at the time. All we feared was the shame or scandal he might bring down on us. Hiding him was impossible, but we wanted at least to protect him.

You see—the girls were single still . . .

In September I entered him in the first year of a school in the suburbs; and during his first week at school I left work early in order to wait for him at the school gate. I was afraid the children would make fun of him.

Noon, and he would be trudging by my side under the searing September sky, his hand in mine. The new satchel lashed to his back, cap low over his forehead, lips slightly parted, the faint mutter of his breathing, his eyes looking at the world nakedly, without detachment, never shifting the angle of his inner vision.

Acquaintances waved their hats at me, came over, shook my

hand, bent over him, took his little hand, pressed it. They tried to smile. His dull upward glance froze them. Imbecile, utter imbecile.

After a week I let him come home by himself. My fears had been uncalled for. The children did not need to take the trouble to isolate him—he was isolated to begin with.

The girls were married that year. On the same day, hastily, as though urged on to it, as though they wished to flee the house. And they were so young still.

A year of turmoil. Not a week went by without some sort of revelry in the house. With tears in their eyes the girls would demand that I hide him, and weakness made me comply. I would take him out and we would wander through streets, fields, along the beach.

We did not talk. We watched sunsets, the first stars; rather, I watched and he would stand by my side, motionless, his eyes on the ground. But then the rains came and turned the fields into mud and we were forced to stay indoors. The two suitors had appeared on our horizon, followed by their friends and by their friends' friends, and the whole house went up in smoke and laughter. We tried hiding him in the maid's room, but when he could not sleep we would sneak him into the kitchen. There he would sit in his pyjamas and watch people coming and going, then get up and wipe the cutlery; just the spoons at first, then they let him do the knives as well.

Gradually he gained access to the drawing room, the centre of commotion. Serving sweets or biscuits to begin with, then filling glasses and offering lighted matches. First, people would draw back at the sight of him. A brief hush would fall upon the room, a kind of sweet horror. One of the suitors would start up angrily from his seat to go and stand by the dark window, seeking refuge in the gloom. Nothing would be audible in the silent room but the child's excited breathing as he moved from one to another with a hard, painful solemnity, his tray held out before him. No one ever refused to take a sweet or a biscuit.

People became used to him in time. The girls softened towards him and tolerated his presence. His small services became indispensable. And when, late in the evening, everybody would be overcome with lassitude, his own face would assume a new light. One of the guests, flushed with drink, might show a sudden interest in him, pull him close and talk to him at length. The child would go rigid in his grip, his eyes dumb. Then he would go to empty ashtrays.

By the end of that summer we two were alone in the house.

The girls were married one afternoon in mid-August. A large canopy was put up in our garden beneath a deep blue sky. Desiccated thorns rustled beneath the feet of dozens of friends who had gathered there. For some reason I was suffocating with emotion. Something had snapped within me. I was tearful, hugging, kissing everybody. The child was not present at the wedding. Someone, one of the bridegrooms perhaps, had seen to it that he be absent, and he was brought back late in the evening. The last of my friends were tearing themselves from my embrace when my eye suddenly caught sight of him. He was sitting by one of the long tables, dressed in his everyday clothes except for a red tie that someone had put around his neck. A huge slice of cake had been thrust into his hand, the soiled tablecloth had slipped down over his knees. He was chewing listlessly, his eyes on the yellow moon tangled in the branches of our tree.

I went over and gently touched his head.

Flustered, he dropped the cake.

I said: "That moon . . . To be sure, a beautiful moon . . ."

He looked up at the moon as though he had not seen it before.

Thus our life together began, side by side in the quiet house with flasks of perfume and torn handkerchiefs still strewn about. I—a poet fallen silent, he—a feeble-minded, lonely child.

Because it was that, his loneliness, that he faced me with.

I understand that now.

The fact that he was lonely at school goes without saying. During his very first week at school he had retreated to the bench at the back of the classroom, huddling in a corner, a place where he would stay for good, cut off from the rest of his class, the teachers already having considered him hopeless.

All his report cards were inscribed "no evaluation possible", with the hesitant scrawl of a teacher's signature trailing at the bottom of the sheet. I still wonder how they let him graduate from one class to the next. For though occasionally he would be kept back in a class for a second or even a third year, he still crawled forwards, at the slow pace they set him. Perhaps they were indulging me. Perhaps there were some teachers there who liked my old poems.

Mostly I tried to avoid them.

They did their best to avoid me too.

I do not blame them.

If we were nevertheless forced to meet, on parents' day, I always preferred to come late, to come last, with the school building wrapped in darkness and the weary teachers collapsing on their chairs in front of empty classrooms strewn like battlefields and illuminated by naked bulbs.

Then I would appear stealthily at the door, my felt hat crumpled in my hand. My long white mane (for I had kept my mane) would cause any parent still there—a young father or mother—to rise from their seat and leave. The teachers would glance up at me, hold out a limp hand and offer a feeble smile.

I would sit down and face them.

What could they tell me that I did not know?

Sometimes they forgot who I was.

"Yes sir, whose father please?"

And I would say the name, a sudden throb contracting my chest.

They would leaf through their papers, pull out his blank card and, closing their eyes, head on hand, would demand severely: "How long?"

Meaning, how long could they keep him since it was a hopeless case.

I would say nothing.

They would grow angry. Perhaps the darkness outside would increase their impatience. They insist I take him off their hands. Where to? They do not know. Somewhere else.

An institution perhaps . . .

But gradually their indignation would subside. They admit he is not dangerous. Not disturbing in the least. No, on the contrary, he is always rapt, always listens with a singularly grave attention, his gaze fixed on the teacher's eyes. Apparently, he even tries to do his homework.

I crumple my hat to a pulp. I steal a look at the classroom, floor littered with peel, torn pages, pencil shavings. On the blackboard— madmen's drawings. Minute tears prick my eyes. In plain words I promise to help the child, to work with him every evening. Because we must not give up hope. Because the child is a borderline case, after all.

But in the evenings at home I yield to despair. I spend hours with him in front of the open book and get nowhere. He sits rigidly by my side, never stirring, but my words float like oil on the waves. When I let him go at last he returns to his room and spends about half an hour doing his homework by himself. Then he shuts his exercise books, places them in his schoolbag and locks it.

Sometimes of a morning when he is still asleep I open the bag and pry into his exercise books. I look aghast at the answers he supplies—remote fantasies, am startled by his sums—outlandish marks traced with zeal and beyond all logic.

But I say nothing. I do not complain about him. As long as he gets up each morning to go mutely to school, to sit on the bench at the back of the classroom.

He would tell me nothing about his day at school. Nor would I ask. He comes and goes, unspeaking. There was a brief period, during his fifth or sixth year at school, I think, when the children bullied him. It was as though they had suddenly discovered him and promptly they began to torment him. All the children of his class, the girls not excepted, would gather around him during break and pinch his limbs as though wishing to satisfy themselves that he really existed, flesh and blood, no spectre. He continued going to school all the same, as indeed I insisted that he do.

After a few weeks they gave it up and left him alone once more.

One day he came home from school excited. His hands were dusted with chalk. I assumed he had been called to the blackboard but he said no. That evening he came to me on his own and told me he had been appointed class monitor.

A few days went by. I inquired whether he was still monitor and he said yes. A fortnight later he was still holding the post. I asked whether he enjoyed his duties or whether he found them troublesome. He was perfectly content. His eyes had lit up, his expression became more intent. In my morning searches of his bag I would discover, next to bizarre homework, bits of chalk and a rag or two.

I have an idea that from then on he remained monitor till his last day at school, and a close relationship developed between him and the school's caretaker. In later years they even struck up some sort of friendship. From time to time the caretaker would call him into his cubicle and favour him with a cup of tea left by one of the teachers. It is unlikely that they ever held a real conversation, but a contact of sorts was established.

One summer evening I happened to find myself in the neighbourhood of his school and I felt an impulse to go and get acquainted with this caretaker. The gate was shut and I wormed my way through a gap in the fence. I wandered along the dark empty corridors till I came at last upon the caretaker's cubicle, tucked away under the stairs. I went down the few steps and saw him.

He was sitting on a bunk, his legs gathered under him, darkness around. A very short, swarthy person deftly polishing the copper tray on his knees.

I took off my hat, edged my way into the cubicle, mumbled the child's name. He did not move, did not appear surprised, as though he had taken it for granted that I would come one night. He looked up at me and then, suddenly, without a word he began to smile. A quiet smile, spreading all over his face.

I said: "You know my son."

He nodded, the smile still flickering over his face. His hands continued their work on the tray.

I asked: "How is he? A good boy . . ."

His smile froze, his hands drooped. He muttered something and pointed at his head.

"Poor kid . . . crazy . . ."

And resumed his calm scrutiny of my face.

I stood before him in silence, my heart gone cold. Never before had I been so disappointed, never lost hope so. He returned to his polishing. I backed out without a word.

None of this means to imply that I was already obsessed by the child as far back as that, already entangled with him. Rather the opposite, perhaps. I would be distant with him, absent-minded, thinking of other things.

Thinking of myself.

Never had I been so wrapped up in myself.

In the first place, my silence. This, my ultimate silence. Well, I had maintained it. And it had been so easy. Not a line had I written. True, an obscure yearning might well up in me sometimes. A desire. I whispered to myself, for instance: autumn. And again, autumn.

But that is all.

Friends tackled me. Impossible, they said . . . You are hatching something in secret . . . You have a surprise up your sleeve.

And, strangely excited, I would smile and insist: "No, nothing of the kind. I have written all I want to."

First they doubted, at last they believed me. And my silence was accepted—in silence. It was mentioned only once. Somebody (a young person) published some sort of résumé in the paper. He mentioned me *en passant*, disparagingly, calling my silence sterility. Twice in the same paragraph he called me that—sterile.

Then he let me off.

But I did not care. I felt placid.

This wasteland around me . . .

Dry desert . . .

Rocks and refuse . . .

In the second place, old age was overtaking me. I never imagined that it would come to this. As long as I move about town I feel at ease. But in the evenings after supper I slump into my armchair, a book or paper clutched in my lap, and in a while I feel myself lying there as though paralyzed, half dead. I rise, torture myself out of my clothes, receive the recurring shock of my ageing legs, drag myself to bed and bundle up my body in the clothes, scattering the detective novels that I have begun to read avidly of late.

The house breathes silence. A lost, exhausted tune drifts up from the radio. I read. Slowly, unwittingly, I turn into a large moss-covered rock. Midnight, the radio falls silent, and after midnight the books slip off my knees. I must switch the silent radio off and rid myself of the light burning in the room. It is then that my hour comes, my fearful hour. I drop off the bed like a lifeless body; bent over, racked by pain, staggering I reach for the switches with my last strength.

One night, at midnight, I heard his steps in the hall. I must mention here that he was a restless sleeper. He used to be haunted by bad dreams that he was never able to relate. He had a night light by his bed, therefore, and when he woke he would go straight for the kitchen tap and gulp enormous quantities of water, which would calm his fears.

That night, after he had finished drinking and was making his way back to bed, I called him to my room and told him to turn off the light and the radio. I still remember his shadow outlined at the darkened doorway. All of a sudden it seemed to me that he had grown a lot, gained flesh. The light behind him silhouetted his mouth, slightly agape.

I thanked him.

The following night he started prowling through the house again about midnight. I lay in wait for his steps and called him to put out the light once more.

And every night thereafter . . .

Thus his services began to surround me. I became dependent upon them. It started with the light and sound that he would rid me of at midnight and was followed by other things. How old was he? Thirteen, I think . . .

Yes, I remember now. His thirteenth birthday occurred about

that time and I made up my mind to celebrate it, for up till then I had passed over all his birthdays in silence. I had planned it to be a real party, generous, gay. I called up his class teacher myself and contacted the other teachers as well. I invited everybody. I sent invitations in his name to all his classmates.

True, all the children in his class were younger than he. Hardly eleven yet.

On the appointed Saturday, in the late morning, after a long and mortifying wait, a small band of ten sniggering boys showed up at our place waving small parcels wrapped in white paper. Not a single teacher had troubled himself to come. None of the girls had dared.

They all shook hands with me, very much embarrassed, very much amazed at the sight of my white hair (one of them asked in a whisper: "That his grandfather?"), and entered timidly into the house which none of them had visited before. They scrutinized me with great thoroughness and were relieved when they found me apparently sane.

The presents were unwrapped.

It emerged that everyone had brought the same: a cheap pencil-case worth a few pennies at most. All except one curly-headed, rather pale boy, a poetic type, who came up brazenly with an old, rusted pocket-knife—albeit a big one with many blades—which for some reason excited general admiration.

All the presents were accompanied by more or less uniform, conventional notes of congratulation. The little poet of the pocket-knife had added a few pleasing rhymes.

He accepted his presents silently, terribly tense.

It surprised me that no one had brought a book.

As though they had feared he might not be able to read it . . .

I waited on them myself, taking great pains with each. I served sandwiches, cake, sweets and lemonade, then ice cream. They sat scattered around the drawing room, embedded in armchairs and couches, munching sweets, not speaking. Their eyes roved around the room incessantly, examining the place as though suspicious of it. Occasionally tittering among themselves for no good reason.

My boy was sitting forlornly in a corner of the room, more like a visitor than the guest of honour at his own party. He was munching too, but his eyes were lowered.

I thought my presence might be hampering the children and left them. And indeed, soon after I had gone, the tension relaxed. Laughter began to bubble up in the room. When I returned after a while I found them all with their shoes off, romping on the carpet, jumping up and down on the couch. He was not among them. I went to look for him and found him on the kitchen balcony, cleaning their shoes.

He said: "I am the monitor."

Thus ended his birthday party. Their clothes in wild disarray, stifling their laughter, they put on their shoes, then rose to face me, shook my hand once more and were off, leaving nine pencil-cases behind them. As for the old pocket-knife that had aroused so much admiration, the little poet who had brought it asked there and then to borrow it for a week and apparently never returned it.

It is in self-defence that I offer these details, since before a fortnight had passed he was polishing my shoes as well. I simply left them on the balcony and found them polished. He did it willingly, without demur. And it became a custom—his and mine. Other customs followed.

Taking my shoes off, for instance. I come back from work late in the afternoon, sink down on the bench in the hall to open my mail. He appears from one of the rooms, squats at my feet, unties the laces, pulls off my shoes and replaces them with slippers.

And that relieves me to some extent.

I suddenly discover there is strength in his arms, compared with the ebbing strength in mine. Whenever I fumble with the lid of a jar, fail to extricate a nail from the wall, I call upon him. I tell him: "You are young and strong and I am growing weaker. Soon I'll die."

But I must not joke with him. He does not digest banter. He stands aghast, his face blank.

He is used to emptying the rubbish bin, has done it since he was eight. He runs my errands readily, fetches cigarettes, buys a paper. He has time at his disposal. He spends no more than half an hour on his homework. He has no friends, reads no books, slouches for hours in a chair gazing at the wall or at me. We live in a solid, quiet neighbourhood. All one sees through the window are trees and a fence. A peaceful street. What is there for him to do? Animals repel him. I brought him a puppy once and a week later he lost it. Just lost it and showed no regret. What is there for him to do? I teach him to tidy up the house, show him where everything belongs. He catches on slowly but eventually he learns to arrange my clothes in the cupboard, gather up the papers and books strewn over the floor. In the mornings I would leave my bedclothes rumpled and when I returned at night everything would be in order, strictly in order.

Sometimes I fancy that everything is in readiness for a journey. That there is nothing to be done but open a suitcase, place the curiously folded clothes inside, and go forth. One day I had to go on a short trip up north, and within half an hour of informing him he had a packed suitcase standing by the door with my walking stick on top.

Yes, I have got myself a stick lately. And I take it along with me wherever I go, even though I have no need of it yet. When I stop to talk with people in the street I insert it in the nearest available crack and put my whole weight on its handle. He sharpens the point from time to time to facilitate the process.

To such lengths does he go in his care of me.

At about that time he also learned to cook. The elderly cleaning woman who used to come in now and then taught him. At first he would cook for himself and eat alone before I came back from work, but in time he would prepare a meal for me too. A limited, monotonous menu, somewhat lacking in flavour, but properly served. He had unearthed a china service in the attic. It had been a wedding present, an elaborate set containing an assortment of golden-edged plates decorated with flowers, cherubs and butterflies. He put it into use. He would place five different-sized plates one on top of the other in front of me, add a quantity of knives and forks, and wait upon me with an air of blunt insistence.

Where had he learned all that?

It transpired that a story about a king's banquet had been read in class.

I am roused.

"What king?"

He does not remember the name.

"Other heroes?"

He doesn't remember.

I ask him to tell the story, at least.

He starts, and stops again at once. It has become muddled in his head.

His eyes cloud over. The first pimples have sprouted on his cheeks.

A thought strikes me: viewed from a different angle he might fill one with terror.

At night he assists me in my bath. I call him in to soap my back and he enters on tiptoe, awed by my nakedness in the water, picks up the sponge and passes it warily over my neck.

When I wish to reciprocate and wait upon him in turn, nothing comes of it. Arriving home I announce: tonight I am going to prepare supper! It appears supper is served already. I wish to help him in his bath, and it appears he has bathed already.

I therefore take him with me at night to meetings with friends, to artists' conventions, for I still belong to all the societies and unions. I have accustomed people to his presence and they notice him no more, much as I do not notice their shadow.

He always sits in the last row, opening doors for latecomers, helping them out of their coats, hanging them up. People take him for one of the attendants, and indeed, he is inclined to attach himself to these. I find him standing near a group of ushers, listening grim-eyed to their talk. At times I find him exchanging words with the charwoman who stands leaning on her broom.

What does he say to her? I am never able to guess.

Does he love me? How can one tell. Something in my behaviour seems to frighten him. Perhaps it is my age, perhaps my silence. Whatever it is, he carries himself in my presence as one expecting a blow.

Strange, for there is peace between us. The days pass tranquilly, and I imagined this tranquillity would last out our life together, till the day I would have to part from him, that is. I thought, how fortunate that in this silence of mine I am confronted by a boy of such feeble brains, on the border, and far from me.

True, I am sometimes overcome by restlessness, possessed by a desire to cling to somebody. Then I rush off to Jerusalem and surprise my daughters with a visit of an hour or two.

They receive me affectionately, hang on to my neck and hug me hard. And while we stand there in a clinging embrace their husbands look on, a faint expression of contempt in their eyes. Afterwards we sit down and chat, bandying about the kind of word play and witticisms that irritate the husbands. Still, they utter no word of complaint, knowing full well that I won't stay, that if I come like a whirlwind—so I go. After an hour or two I rouse myself for a speedy departure, still harbouring the dregs of my passion. They all urge me to prolong my visit, stay, spend the night, but I never do. I must go home to the boy, I argue, as though his entire existence depended upon me. More kissing and hugging follows; then the husbands take me to the station. We rarely speak during the short ride. We have nothing to say to each other. Besides, I am still suspect in their eyes. This white mane flowing down my neck, the stick jiggling in my hand. I am still some sort of a poet to them. The volumes of my poetry, I know, have a place of honour in their drawing-room bookcase. I cannot prevent that.

At such a time I prefer the child's dumb look.

In the winter there are times when I draw the bolts at six. What do I do in the hours left till bedtime? I read the papers, listen to the radio, thumb the pages of books. Time passes and I make my bargain with boredom in private.

In the summer I often walk back and forth along the beach or aimlessly through the streets. I am likely to stand in front of a building under construction for hours on end, lost in thought.

Trivial thoughts . . .

Years ago I would carry little notebooks with me wherever I went. Working myself up into a fever, fanning the flame of creation; rhyming, turning words over and over. Nowadays, not even a pang.

Where is he?

I look through the window and see him in the garden, under a bleak autumn sky. He is pruning the bushes and trees with a savage violence. Lopping off whole branches, tearing at leaves. He has it in for the old poplar in particular, cuts away with zeal the new shoots that have sprouted at its base, climbs up into the foliage and saws relentlessly. The tree bends and groans.

Sometimes my eyes stay riveted upon him for hours and I cannot bring myself to look away. His intent gravity, his rage. Shadows play over his face, his face which has taken on an absurdly studious quality owing to the thick spectacles he has begun to wear. He was found to be short-sighted.

I know he is trimming off more than is necessary, that he pulls up plants, roots and all, in his vehemence. Still, I do not interfere and go on standing mutely by the window. I would tell myself: what survives will flower in the spring and make up for the damage.

When was the first time? That he found out about my being a poet, I mean. This madness that has taken a hold over us the past year, I mean.

Towards the end of last winter I fell ill and kept him home to nurse me. For several days we were together the whole day long, and he did not move from my side. This was something that had never happened before, for as a rule not a day would pass when I did not go out, wandering, sitting in cafés, visiting people.

I was feverish and confined to bed, dozing fitfully, eyes
fluttering. He moved about the house or sat by the door of my
room, his head turned in my direction. Occasionally I would ask for
tea, and he would rouse himself, go to the kitchen and return with a
steaming cup.

The light was dying slowly, grey sky flattening the windows. We
did not turn on the lights for my illness had made my eyes sensitive.

The silence lay large between us. Could I hold a conversation
with him?

I asked whether he had prepared his homework.

He nodded his head from his corner of the room.

What could I talk to him about?

I asked about his monitorship. He replied with yes and no and
with shakes of his head.

At last I grew tired. I let my head drop back on the pillow and
closed my eyes. The room grew darker. Outside it began to drizzle.
During those days of illness my mind had started to wander with
fantasies. Fantasies about the bed. I would imagine it to be a white,
violent country of sweeping mountains and streaming rivers, and me
exploring it.

Then such utter calm. The warmth of the bed enveloping each
cell in my body.

I started at the sound of his harsh voice, sudden in the trickling
silence.

"What do you do?"

I opened my eyes. He was sitting by the door, his eyes on my
face.

I raised myself a little, astonished.

"What? What do you mean? Now? Well, what? I'm dozing . . ."

"No, in general . . ." and he turned away as though sorry he had
asked.

In a while I understood. He was asking about my profession.

Had they been discussing "professions" in class?

He did not know . . .

I tell him what my profession is (I am employed by a
newspaper-clipping bureau), but he finds it difficult to understand.
I explain at length. Suddenly he has understood. There is no
reaction. He seems a little disappointed. Hard to say why. He
cannot have formed the idea in his feeble mind that I am a pilot or a
sailor, can he? Did he think I was a pilot or a sailor?

No.

What did he think?

He didn't think.

Silence again. He sits forlorn in the corner, a sad, sombre figure. His spectacles gleam in the twilight. It rains harder now, the old poplar huddles in the garden, wet with tears. Suddenly I cannot bear his grief. I sit up in bed, eyes open in the dark, and tell him in a low voice that, as a matter of fact, I used to have another occupation. I wrote poetry. You see, father used to be a poet. They must have learned about poets in class. And I get out of bed in a fever of excitement, cross the dark room in my bare feet, light a small lamp, cross back to the bookcase, pluck my books one by one from the shelves.

He watches me in silence, his spectacles slightly askew, hands limp on the arms of his chair.

I grasp his wrist, pull him up and stand him before me.

Dry-handed I open my books in their hard covers. The small, untouched pages move with a faint crackle. Black lines of print on pale paper flit before my eyes. Words like: *autumn, rain, gourd.*

He remains unmoved, does not stir, his eyes are cast down, motionless. An absolute moron.

I sent him out of the room. I gathered my books and took them with me to bed. The light stayed on in my room till dawn. All night I lay groping for the sweet pain passionately poured into ancient poems. Words like: *bread, path, ignominy.*

The next day my fever had abated somewhat and I sent him off to school. My books I thrust back among the others. I was convinced he had understood nothing. A few days later, though, discovering all five volumes ranged neatly side by side, I realized something had penetrated. But it was little as yet.

That was his final school year, though the fact marked no change in his habits. He still spent about half an hour a day on his homework, wrote whatever it was he wrote, closed his exercise books, locked his bag and turned to his household chores. In class he kept to his remote corner, but his attendance at lessons had dwindled. The caretaker would call upon him time and again. To help store away stoves in the attic or repair damaged furniture in the cellar.

When he was present in class he would sit there rapt as ever, his eyes, unwavering, on the teacher.

The final days of the school year, their slack atmosphere . . .

Two or three weeks before the end of term a poem of mine was taught in class. The last pages of the textbook contained a collection of many different poems, some sort of anthology for every season, for a free period or such. An old poem of mine, written dozens of years ago, was among them. I had not aimed it at youth, but people mistook its intention.

The teacher read it out to the class. Then she explained the difficult words and finally let one of the pupils read it. And that was all there was to it. My son might have paid no attention to the occurrence from his bench had the teacher not pointed him out to say: "But yes, that is his father . . ."

The remark did nothing to improve the child's standing in class, let alone enhance the poem's distinction. In any case, by the end of the lesson both poem and poet were no doubt forgotten.

Apparently, however, the boy did not forget; he remained aglow. Possibly he wandered by himself through the empty classroom, picking up peel, wiping the blackboard, excited.

Coming back from work that evening I found the house in darkness. I opened the front door and saw him waiting in the unlit hall. He could not contain his passion. He threw himself at me, bursting into a kind of savage wail, nearly suffocating me. And without letting me take off my jacket, undo my tie, he dragged me by the hand into one of the rooms, switched on the light, opened the textbook and began reading my poem in a hoarse voice. Mispronouncing vowels, slurring words, bungling the stresses.

I was stunned in the face of this turbulent emotion. Compassion welled up in me. I pulled him close and stroked his hair. It was evident that he had still not grasped what the poem was about, even though it was not rich in meaning.

He held my sleeve in a hard grip and asked when had I written the poem.

I told him.

He asked to see other poems.

I pointed at my volumes.

He wanted to know whether that was all.

Smiling I showed him a drawer of my bureau stuffed with a jumble of poems and fragments, little notebooks I used to carry on my person and have with me always.

He asked whether I had written any new poems today. Now I burst out laughing. His blunt face raised up to me in adoration, this evening hour, and I still in my jacket and tie.

I told him that I had stopped writing before he was born and that the contents of that drawer should have been thrown out long ago.

I took off my jacket, loosened my tie, sat down to unlace my shoes.

He fetched my slippers.

His expression was despondent.

As though he had received fearful tidings.

I burst into laughter again.

I made a grab for his clipped hair and jerked his head with a harsh affection.

I, who would shrink from touching him.

A few days later I found the drawer wrenched open, empty. Not one scrap of paper left. I caught him in the garden weeding the patch beneath the tree with a hoe. Why had he done it? He thought I did not need them. He was just cleaning out. And hadn't I said myself I wasn't writing any more.

Where were all the papers?

He had thrown out the written ones, and the little notebooks he had sold to a hawker.

I beat him. For the second time in my life, and again in the garden, by the poplar. With all the force of my old hands I slapped his rough cheeks with their soft black down.

He trembled all over . . .

His fists closed white-knuckled and desperate over the hoe. He could have hit back. He was strong enough to knock me down.

But then, abruptly, my anger died. The entire affair ceased to be important. Relics of old poems, lost long ago. Why the trembling? Why, with my silence sealed?

Once more I believed the affair ended. I never imagined it was but the beginning.

Long summer days. Invariably blue. Once in a while a tiny cloud sails on its sleepy journey from one horizon to the other. All day flocks of birds flop down upon our poplar, screaming, beating the foliage.

Evenings—a dark devouring red.

The child's last day at school.

A day later: the graduation ceremony and presentation of diplomas.

He did not receive one, of course. He ascended the platform with the other pupils nonetheless, dressed in a white shirt and khaki trousers (he was about seventeen years old). And sat in the full, heavy afternoon light listening gravely to the speeches. When it was the turn of the caretaker to be thanked he lifted his eyes and began a heavy, painstaking examination of the audience to search him out.

I kept myself concealed at the back of the hall behind a pile of chairs, my hat on my knees. The speeches ended and a short artistic programme began.

Two plump girls mounted the stage and announced in voices shrill with emotion that they would play a sonata by an anonymous composer who lived hundreds of years ago. They then seated themselves behind a creaking piano and beat out some melancholy chords with four hands.

Stormy applause from enraptured parents.

A small boy with pretty curls dragged an enormous cello on to the stage and he, too, played a piece by an anonymous composer (a different one, apparently).

I closed my eyes.

I liked the idea of all this anonymity.

A storm of applause from enraptured parents.

Suddenly I became aware of someone's eyes upon me. Glancing around I saw, a few steps away, the caretaker, sprawled on a chair, dressed in his overalls. He made a gentle gesture with his head.

Two girls and two boys came on stage and began reciting. A story, a humorous sketch, two or three poems.

At the first sound of rhymes my boy rose suddenly from his place and began a frantic search for me. The audience did not understand what that spectacled, dumb-faced boy standing up at the back of the stage might possibly be looking for. His fellow pupils tried to pull him down, but in vain. He was seeking me, his eyes hunting through the hall. The rhymes rang in his ears, swaying him. He wanted to shout. But he could not find me. I had dug myself in too well behind the chairs, hunched low.

As soon as the ceremony was over I fled. He arrived home in the evening. It turned out he had been helping the caretaker arrange the chairs in the hall.

The time had come to decide his fate. I reiterate: he verges on the border. A borderline child. Haven't I let the time slip by? Do I still possess my hold over him?

For the time being he stayed at home with me, took care of his father and began to occupy himself with poems.

Yes, he turned his hand to poetry.

It turned out that those poetry remnants of mine, the little notebooks, thin little pages, were still in his possession. Neither thrown out nor sold. He had lied to me there by the poplar.

I did not find out all at once. At first he contrived to keep them hidden from me. But gradually I became aware of them. Scraps of paper began to flit about the house, edges sticking out of his trouser pockets, his bedclothes. He introduced a new habit. Whenever I sent him on an errand he took out a piece of paper and wrote down the nature of the errand in his slow, elaborate, childish script full of spelling mistakes.

"Oblivion o'ercomes me," he suddenly informed me one day.

My walking stick had split and I had asked him to take it for repair. At once he extracted a little notebook, one of those old notebooks I used to cherish, used to carry in my pocket in order to scribble the first draft of a poem, a line, the scrap of an idea.

I felt my throat contract, sweat break out. My hand reached for the notebook as of itself. He surrendered it instantly. I leafed through with a feeble hand. White pages, the ragged remains of many others torn out. Then a single, disjointed line in my hurried scrawl: *"Oblivion o'ercomes me."* And then more empty pages, their edges crumpled.

Peace returned to me. He wished to leave the little notebook in my hands but I insisted that he take it back.

He went off.

Up in his room I rifled through his desk but found nothing. Then I took my mind off the whole thing. In the evening I found a yellowed piece of paper on my bureau and written on it in my indecipherable script: *This azure sky's the match of man.*

And the words "azure sky" crossed out with a faint line.

I swept up to his room and there he sat, huddled in a corner, waiting for me in dull anticipation. I folded the paper in front of his eyes, placed it on his desk and left the room. The following evening, after supper, I once again found two forgotten lines on my bureau.

Futile again before thee.

This long slow winter.

And this one I had already torn up.

And the day after, a slanting line in tortuous script: *My lunacy in my pale seed.*

And harsh, violent erasures around the words.

And beside the torn-out page a red carnation from the garden in a small vase.

Here now, I must tell about the flowers.

For the house became filled with flowers. Old, forgotten vases came down from shelves and storeroom and were filled with flowers. He would gather buttercups on his way, pick them between the houses, steal into parks for carnations and pilfer roses from private gardens. The apartment filled with a hot, heavy scent. Yellow stamens scattered over tables, crumbled on carpets.

Sheets of paper were always lying on my bureau; sharpened pencils across.

In this way, with the obstinacy of his feeble mind he tried to tempt me back to writing poems.

At first I was amused. I would pick up the little pages, read, and tear them up; would smell the flowers. With the sharpened pencils I would draw dotted lines and sign my name a thousand times in the little notebooks.

But soon this mania of his became overwhelming.

Those pages uprooted from my notebooks would pursue me all over the house. I never knew there had been so much I had wanted to write. He placed them between the pages of books I read, in my briefcase, beneath my bedside lamp, beside the morning paper, between the cup and saucer, near the toothpaste. When I pulled out my wallet a scrap of paper would flutter down.

I read and tore up and threw out.

As yet I made no protest. I was intrigued, curious to read what went through my mind in those far-off days. And there was bound to be an end to those little pages. For this much I knew: there *was* an end to them.

Late at night, when I had long been buried under my bedclothes, I would hear his bare feet paddling through the house. Planting pages filled with my personal untidy scrawl. Twisted, entangled letters, scattered words thickly underscored.

We maintained our wonted silence. And day after day he collected the torn-up scraps from ashtrays and wastepaper baskets.

Except that the flow of notes was ebbing. One morning I found a page on my desk with a line written in his handwriting striving to imitate mine. Next morning it was his hand again, stumbling awkwardly over the clean page.

And the flowers filling every room . . .

And the sky filling with clouds . . .

My patience gave out. I rebelled. I burst into his room and found him sitting and copying the self-same line. I swept up the remains of all the little notebooks and tore them up before his eyes. I plucked the flowers out of all the vases, piled them up on the doorstep and ordered him to take them away.

I told him: "These games are over."

He took the flowers, went to bury them in the nearby field and did not return. He stayed away three days. On the second I ransacked the town in a silent search. (The house filled with dust in the meantime. Dishes piled up in the sink.)

In the afternoon of the third day he came back, sun-tanned, an outdoor smell in his clothes.

I suppressed my anger, sat him down in front of me.

Where had he been? What done? Why had he run away?

He had slept in the nearby field, not far from home. Whenever I went out he would return and hide in his room. Once I had come in unexpectedly, but had not caught him. Why had he run away? He could not explain. He had thought I wished him out of the way. That I wished to write poetry in lonely seclusion. For that was what they had said at school about poets, about their loneliness . . .

Those accursed teachers.

Or could it be some heavy, some new piece of cunning.

I must decide his fate. He is beginning to waver on the border.

I armed myself with patience, talked to him at length. Well, now what do you want, I said. For I, I have done with writing. I have written my fill. Then what do you want?

He covered his eyes with his palms. Blurted out some hot, stuttering words again. It was hard to follow him. At last I gathered from his confused jumble of words that he believed me unhappy.

You should have seen him.

This feeble-brained boy, boy on the border, his spectacles slipping slowly down his nose. Big. Nearly eighteen.

Late afternoon, an autumn sun roving leisurely about the rooms. Music is coming from the house next door. Someone is practising scales on a violin. The same exercise, many times over, and out of tune. Only in one key the melody goes off every time into some sort of melancholy whine.

Suddenly I am certain of my death. I can conceive how the grass will go on rustling in this garden.

I look at him and see him as he is. An unfinished piece of sculpture.

Smiling, I whisper, "See, I am tired. Perhaps you could write for me."

He is dumbfounded. He takes off his spectacles, wipes them on his shirt, puts them back.

"I can't," he in a whisper too.

Such despair. Of course he can't. I must cut loose. Ties, tangles. Long years of mortification. One could cry. They left me alone with him. And again that dissonant whine.

"You'll help me," he whispers at me now, as though we were comrades.

"I will not help you."

A great weariness came over me. I stood up, took my hat and went out, walked twice around the scales player's house and went into town.

In the evening I came back and found him gone. I was obliged to prepare my own supper again and when I was slicing bread the knife slipped. It has been many years since I bled so.

I believed he had run off again, but he returned late at night, my room already dark. He began to prowl about the house, measure it with his steps, back and forth, much as I used to in former days when words would start to struggle up in me.

I fell asleep to the sound of his tread.

Next day he emptied out his room. All his schoolbooks, encyclopaedias received as presents, copybooks, everything went out. The sheets of paper and sharpened pencils he transferred to his own desk.

The sky turned dim with autumn.

I began to play with the idea of retirement. Something in the romantic fashion. To give up work, sell the house, collect the money and escape, far away. Settle in some remote, decaying port. From there to an attic in a big city. In short, plans, follies. I went to travel agencies and was deluged with colourful pamphlets. I affixed a notice to the fence: For Sale.

A light rain fell.

One Friday I went to Jerusalem to see my daughters and spend the Sabbath there.

I received a great welcome. They even lighted candles in my honour and filled the house with flowers. My grandchildren played with the walking stick. I realized I had been neglecting everybody. At dinner they placed me at the head of the table.

I talked all evening about him, obsessively. I did not change the subject, refused to drop it. I demanded a solution for him, insisted he be found some occupation. I announced my plans for going abroad, wandering about the world for a bit. Someone must take charge of him. He can be made use of, too. He may serve someone else. As long as he was taken off my hands. I want my release, at last. He was approaching manhood.

I did not say a word about the poems.

For once the husbands gave me their full attention. The girls were puzzled. What has passed between you two? We rose from the table and transferred to armchairs for coffee. The grandchildren came to say good-night in their pyjamas. Gesturing with their little hands they recited two verses by a poetess who had died not long ago. Thereupon they put their lips to my face, licked me and went to bed. I went on talking about him. Impossible to divert me. They were all tired by now, their heads nodding as they listened. From time to time they exchanged glances, as though it were I who had gone mad.

Then they suddenly left me. Promising nothing, leading me gently to bed. They kissed me and went away.

Only then did I discover that a storm had been rising outside all evening. A young tree beat against the window with its many boughs. Thumping on the glass, prodding around the frame. All night it tried to force an entry, to come into my bed. When I woke up in the morning all was calm. A sky of sun and clouds. The young tree stood still, facing the sun. Nothing but a few torn leaves, bright green leaves that trembled on my window-sill.

I went home in the afternoon. My sons-in-law had promised to find him employment. My daughters talked about a semi-closed institution.

Winter erupted from the soil. Puddles were forming between pavements and road. My reflection rippled and broke into a thousand fragments.

He was not at home. His room was locked. I went out into the yard and peered through the window. The window stood wide open and the room appeared tidy beyond it. The sheets of paper glimmered white on his desk. Something was written on them, surely. I went back into the house and tried to force the door but it would not yield. Back in the yard again I rolled a stone to the wall beneath his window and tried to climb on top of it but failed. My legs began to tremble. I was no longer young. Suddenly I thought: What is he to me? I went in, changed my tie, and went out in search of friends in cafés.

Saturday night. The streets loud. We are crowded in a corner of the café, old, embittered artists, burnt-out volcanoes wrapped in coats. Wheezing smoke, crumbling in our withered hands the world sprung up since last Saturday. Vapours rise from the ground and shroud the large glass front of the café. I sprawl inert on my chair, puffing at a cigarette butt, dancing my stick on the stone floor between my feet. I know. This town is built on sand, dumb and impervious. Under the flimsy layer of houses and pavements—a smothered desert of sand.

Suddenly a crowd of unkempt, hairy bohemians swarm by. A crowd of young fools. We scowl, squint at them. And there is my boy trailing after them, a few paces behind the crowd, his cheeks flushed.

They fling themselves on the chairs of a next-door café. Most of them are drunk. My boy stays on their fringes, huddled in a chair. Some sort of blustering conversation goes on. I do not take my eyes off him. Someone rises, takes a piece of paper out of his pocket and begins reading a poem. No one is listening to him except my boy. The reader stops in the middle, moves from one to the other, finally hovers intently over the clipped head of my son. A few of them laugh. Someone leans over the boy, pats his cheek . . .

I am certain: nobody knows his name, nor that of his father.

Some minutes later I sit up, take my stick and go to the beach to look at the dark sea. Then home. I lie on the couch, take the paper and begin turning its pages. I linger over the literary supplement, read a line or two of a poem, a paragraph in a story—and stop. Literature bores me to tears. Abruptly I fall asleep, as I am, in my clothes. Dream I am taken away for an operation. Being anaesthetized and operated on, painlessly. Wakened, anaesthetized again, the still flesh dissected. At last I understand: it is the light shining in my face.

I wake, rise, shivering with cold, clothes rumpled. A soft rain outside. I go to the kitchen, put a kettle on and wait for the water to boil. Piles of dirty dishes tower over me.

A big dilapidated motor car, its headlights off, crawls into our little street at a remarkably slow pace. At last it brakes to a creaking stop in front of our house, beside the lamppost. Loud whooping and howling from inside. A long pause. A door opens and someone is discharged, pale, confused. It is my son. His features are petrified, no shadow of a smile. Another door opens. Someone else scrambles out, staggers into the middle of the road, dead-drunk. He goes over to the boy, grasps his hands and pumps them up and down

26

affectionately. Then squeezes his way back into the car.

More yells and screams from the imprisoned human mass. A long pause. Then a jerk and a roar, and the blind battered wreck reverses and like some black turtle inches its way backwards out of the street.

My son is standing by the lamppost, at the precise spot where he has been unloaded. For a long time he stands there unmoving, his body slightly bowed. Suddenly he doubles up and vomits. He wipes his mouth with the palm of his hand and strides towards the house. Passes by the kitchen without noticing me, enters his room and shuts the door. A faint cloud of alcohol floats through the hall.

Winter. With the first touch of rain these lowlands strive to revert to swamp.

An old half-blind poet, who publishes a steady stream of naive, pitiful poems and woos young poets, meets me in the street, links his arm through mine and walks me round and round under a grey sky, through wet streets. Finally, he informs me with something like a wink that he has met my son in the company of young artists.

"A fine young man. Does he write?"

Rumours reach me from all sides. Some say they torment him. Others say that on the contrary, those degenerate creatures accept him gladly. It isn't every day that they get hold of such a tongue-tied moron. Meanwhile he has become one young poet's minion, and messenger boy to the editor of a literary magazine.

I reproach him with harsh words but he does not listen. Abstract-minded, his eyes flitting over the cloud-hung world, he does not even see me. His face has paled a little over the past few weeks, his blunt features taken on an ascetic, somehow spiritual look. I know: one incautious word on my part, and he will break loose, roam about the streets and disgrace me. Already he has neglected the house completely. He takes his meals outside. The garden is running to seed. And I had imagined that he felt some tenderness towards the plants.

When at home he shuts himself up in his room and throws himself into writing. We have not seen a single poem yet. But I know beyond question: he writes.

I come up against him in the hall, catch him by the sleeve and ask mockingly: "Monsieur writes? Yes?"

He wriggles under my hand. My language startles him. He does not understand and looks at me in horror, as though I were beyond hope.

He is capable of staying locked up in his room for hours on end, wonderfully concentrated. Occasionally he enters the drawing-room, goes to the bookcase, takes out a volume of poetry or some other book and stands a long time poring over it. As a rule he never turns over the page. Then he puts the book down quietly and goes out. Of late he has begun referring frequently to the dictionary, digging into it, turning its leaves incessantly like a blind man. I doubt whether he knows how to use it.

I finally come over and ask him what he wants.

He wants to know how to write the sky.

"The sky?"

"The word 'sky' . . ."

"How? What do you mean, how? Just the way it sounds."

That does not help him much. He stands in front of me, fearfully grave.

"With an 'e' after the 'y' or without . . ." he whispers.

"With an 'e'?" I say thunderstruck. "What on earth for?"

He bites his lips.

"With an 'e'?" I repeat, my voice shrilling to a yell, "And, anyway, what do you want with the sky?"

This one remains unanswered. The dictionary closes softly between his hands. He returns to his room. A while later he steals back to the bookcase, takes the dictionary and starts hunting through it. I jump up.

"What now?"

"Independence . . ." he stammers.

"Independence? Well?"

". . . ance or . . . ence?"

Once again this inexplicable fury. The more so as all of a sudden I do not know myself how to spell independence. I pounce upon him, grab the dictionary out of his hands, search feverishly. . .

Meanwhile my retirement plans are taking shape. From time to time people come to inspect the house put up for sale. I show them over the rooms, let them intrude into every corner, take them down to the cellar, around the yard, into the garden and back to the balcony. In a low voice I recite its merits, this house that I have lived in for thirty years. Then, coolly, I state the price. Before they depart I take down their name and spell out mine in exchange. They bend over the piece of paper and write my name with complete equanimity. Not the faintest ripple of recognition. Haven't they ever read poetry in their lives? I shall apparently leave these regions in complete anonymity.

The garden, however, leaves a bad impression with the buyers. Weeds and mires. The boy refuses to touch a spade. I therefore take up the gardening tools myself and every day I weed out some of the boldest specimens and cover the puddles with them.

A farewell party at the office in my honour. All the office employees assembled an hour before closing time. Cakes were served, glasses raised. I was eulogized at great length. I even saw tears in some eyes. No one mentioned my poetry, as though to avoid hurting my feelings. Finally, a parting gift: an oil painting, a murky sea.

I start packing my bags. Much vacillation in front of the bookcase. What shall I take, what leave? I send off urgent letters to my sons-in-law regarding the boy's fate. I engage them in telephone conversations, prevail upon them to act. Finally they make an appointment to meet me at a small café in town. Sitting round a small table they unfold their plans. They have made inquiries and finally have found an old artisan in a Jerusalem suburb, a book-binder who has consented to take on the boy as an apprentice. He will be provided with his meals and sleeping quarters. The man used to have just such a child himself, and it died of an illness. He has, however, laid down one condition: should the boy fall ill he will be returned at once. Like a seizure or some such case . . . On this point they were inexorable: they will not care for him in sickness.

The sons-in-law have therefore made further investigations and found a lone old woman, a few houses away from the bookbinder, who will be prepared to accept him when ill. Against a remuneration, of course . . . Well, and that is all. I must put my signature to both.

And they come out with papers.

I sign at once. Yet a rage flares up in me while I do.

"As far as seizures and sickness are concerned, your trouble was unnecessary. You know he isn't one of those . . . He is a borderline child . . . I have said as much a thousand times . . . But you won't begin to understand . . . Oh well let it go."

My sons-in-law collect the documents, barring one copy which they leave with me. They gulp the last of their coffee, give me a kindly smile.

"See, and you thought we weren't looking after you . . ."

The day after I sign again, this time to transfer the house to a buyer found at last. When all is said and done, I have received a reasonable sum for it, and that just for the land, since the house itself is going to be demolished.

The furniture was included in the price. Three workmen appeared one day at dusk and began clearing the house. Everything was taken except two mattresses. They even pulled the desk from under him while he sat writing at it. He was outraged. He prowled about the house, his papers fluttering white in his arms. A few slipped to the floor and, by the time he noticed, one of the workmen was already picking them up to wrap the lamp shades in. He threw himself at the man with all the strength of his heavy bulk. Tried to get his teeth into him.

It has struck me that dusk is a time when his senses are overcome by a heavy stupor.

Banknotes fill my drawer. I obtain no more than a quarter of the things' value, but even so the money piles up. I wish to sell everything, and what I can't sell I give away. I have been forcing loads of books on my friends. Were the boy a little less occupied he would sell to his hawkers what I throw out.

We have even been making incursions into the cellar and have dredged up old clothes, brooms, more books, manuscripts—my own and others'—trivia, simulacrums and crumbs and fables. A cloud of dust hovered on the cellar steps for three whole days.

I told my café friends: "Here, this is how a man cuts his bonds."

In addition I still pay regular visits to the tiny harbour of this big town in order to whip up a wanderlust. Wrapped in my overcoat, umbrella in hand, I wander among the cranes, sniffing salt and rust, trying to strike up a conversation with the sailors. I am still deliberating where to go. At first I had considered Europe as my destination, then thought of the Greek islands. I had already entered into negotiations with a Turkish ship captain regarding the Bosphorus when I went and bought, for a ridiculous price, a round-trip ticket on a freighter sailing the sea between this country and Cyprus. I went on board the ship myself and rapped my stick against the door of my prospective cabin.

This journey will be something of a prelude. Afterwards we shall sail away again, further away.

My son writes on throughout, writes standing as though in prayer. His papers are scattered on the window-sill which serves him as a desk. Beside them lies a small dictionary which he has rescued from the debacle. When I look at his form the thought strikes me: Why thus, just as he is, he may go and sleep with a woman. And who knows? Perhaps he already has. He has not yet taken in the fact of my retirement, my impending departure. He is intent on his own. It was difficult enough to tear him away, one afternoon, and make him accompany me to Jerusalem to see the old book-binder.

It was a gentle winter day, cloudy but no real rain. In Jerusalem we found the old book-binder waiting for us at the bus station with a run-down commercial van, unbound books slithering about in the back. He took us to a suburb of the town, to the slope of a narrow, tree-tangled wadi very close to the border. He motioned us into the house in silence, and in silence his wife received us. Tea and cakes were served and we were made to sit by the table.

I was very pleased with them. They scrutinized the boy carefully. Hard to say that he pleased them, but they were visibly relieved, having expected worse. Slowly, hesitantly, conversation began to flow between us. I learned to my surprise that the book-binder had heard of my name and was, moreover, certain that he had read something by me (for some reason he thought I wrote prose). But that had been so long ago, nearly twenty years.

Truth to tell, I was gratified.

Wind rustled outside. A samovar murmured on the table (such quaint habits). There was a large tree in the book-binder's garden too, older even than ours, its trunk gnarled. Winter twilight was fading beyond the window, grey tinged by a flaming sunset. Intimations of borderland. He was sitting frozen by my side, an oversized adolescent, the cup of tea full in front of him, the cake beside it untouched. Sitting there hunched, his eyes on the darkening window. Not listening to our talk. Suddenly he pulls out of his pocket a sheet of paper, black with lines of lettering, smooths it out in front of him, slowly writes a single word, and folds it up again.

Our conversation breaks off. The book-binder and his wife look at him in amazement.

With half a smile I say, "He writes . . ."

They do not understand.

"He is a poet."

"A poet . . ." they whisper.

Just then it began to rain and the sunset kindled the room. He was sitting near the window, his hair aflame.

They stare at me with growing disbelief. And he, pen dropping between his fingers, passes his eyes over us in a pensive glance.

I say to the book-binder: "He'll publish a book of poetry. You can bind it for him."

The book-binder is completely at a loss. Am I making fun of him? At last a doubtful smile appears on his face.

"Sure. He'll publish a book. We'll bind it here, together we will."

"For nothing?" I continue the joke.

"For nothing."

I stand up.

"All right, it's a bargain. D'you hear?"

But he hasn't.

(On our way out the book-binder and his wife pulled me into a corner of the hall and reminded me in a whisper of that part about sickness, or seizures . . . reminded me of their non-responsibility in such case. I put their minds at rest.)

We went out. The book-binder could not take us back to the station because the headlights of his old car did not function. We therefore took our leave of him and of his wife and started walking along the road under a soundlessly dripping sky. He was in a state of complete torpor, almost insensible. Dragging his feet over the asphalt. We arrived at the bus stop, stood between the iron railings, the iron roof over us. Housing projects all about, bare rocks, russet soil. A hybrid of town and wasteland. Jerusalem at its saddest, forever destroyed. However much it is built, Jerusalem will always be marked by the memory of its destruction.

I turned to him and the words came out of my mouth pure and clear.

"The book-binder and his wife are very good people. But you will have to behave yourself."

He kept silent. Someone rode past on a bicycle, caught sight of the boy's face and turned his head back at once.

Full darkness now. Lights went on in the building projects. We were standing under the awning, the two of us utterly alone. Suddenly I said: "I had a glimpse of that page and saw—there's a poem there. See, you were able to write by yourself. You did not need me."

He raised his eyes to me, and remained silent.

I drew nearer to him, very near.

"Show me the poem."

"No."

"Why?"

"You'll tear it up . . ."

"No, no, of course I won't . . ."

And I stretched out my hand to take the page. But he shrank back. I meant to use force but he raised his arms to defend himself. This time he would have hit me.

Again someone passed on a bicycle. From the distance came the rumble of the bus.

It had been the last word of his poem.

I did not know.

That was three days ago.

So terrible this season. The windows are covered with mist or frost. I cannot recall such a hard winter before. This lasting leaden grey, day and night, deepening yet towards dawn. Who's that in the mirror? Still I. A furrowed stone. Only the eyes stand out, glittering, amazingly alive.

I am about to leave. I have missed one boat, another is awaiting me. I have only to stuff the last things into the cases, fold the towels, pick up the money and be off. We have been living here on mattresses a full fortnight now; and the new owner comes and looks at us every day. The man is reaching the end of his patience. He hovers about me in despair, waiting for me to be gone. Yesterday he even threatened me with a lawsuit. He has bought the house with his last pennies. He has his dreams.

Indeed, I must linger no more. I must send the boy to Jerusalem, to the old book-binder waiting for him by the border. There must be no more lingering. For the boy is forever roaming about these nights. He has stopped writing. Yesterday I waited up for him till after midnight and still he had not come. He returned shortly before the break of dawn. His steps woke me.

The balcony door creaks under my fingers. The floor is wet, strewn with broken leaves and branches, the aftermath of the storm. A cold hopeless sky. A silent drizzle and the first light. This large and so familiar universe silently dripping here before me. The leaves in the tree rustling.

Was there no wish in me to write? Did I not long to write? But what is there left to write about? What more is there to say? I tell you: it is all a fraud. Look, even our poplar is crumbling. Its bark is coming off in strips. The colours of the garden have faded, the stones are gathering moss.

To be driven like a slow arrow to the sky. To sprawl on the

cotton clouds, supine, back to earth, face turned to the unchanging blue.

Pensioned-off poet that I am. It is pouring now. Drops splash over me. I dislodge myself and retrace my steps. A bleak silence over the house, the faint wheeze of a snore drifts through it. I go up to his room, night-clothes trailing behind me. My shadow heavy on shut doors.

He is sleeping on a mattress too. His night light is on the floor by his head. He still cannot fall asleep without his eternal light. The slats of his shutter are slicing constant wafers of dawn light.

I look down silently upon the sleeper at my feet. When I turn to leave the room I suddenly notice some newspaper sheets strewn on the floor by his mattress. Terror grips me. I bend down at once, gather them up. The pages are still damp, the fresh ink comes off on my fingers. I go over to the window, to the faint first light.

A supplement of one of the light, impudent tabloids. And the date—today's, this day about to break. I turn the pages with dead hands. Near the margin of one I discover the poem: crazy, without metre, twisted, lines needlessly cut off, baffling repetitions, arbitrary punctuation.

Suddenly the silence deepens. The sound of breathing has died. He opens his eyes, heavy and red with sleep. His hand fumbles for the spectacles by his mattress. He puts them on looks at me—me by the window. And a soft, appealing smile, a little sad, lights up his face.

Only now I notice. It is my name plastered across the top of the poem, in battered print.

Three Days and a Child

Awakening

I had thought I would have to apologize; somehow it turned out the other way.

The three-year-old son of the woman I had once loved was delivered into my charge in the last three days of the holiday, in the first days of autumn, in Jerusalem.

First I pondered over the child, then I wanted to kill him. I did not accomplish that, however. I must still discover what prevented me. Anyway, the time and place were ripe.

The time: end of summer, hot desert winds blowing over the land, clouds and blue sky tangling, vain watching for rain. The longing and melancholy of a new year.

The place: Jerusalem, which is a quiet town.

The beginning of summer had been different. I mean, desires were born. I had even thought of getting married this summer holiday. At least Yael, my girl friend let fall some hints in that direction. Then we both forgot about it, overcome by lassitude. The land became covered with thistles and thorns, and Yael began disappearing to the various regions; uprooting bulbs, drying out stalks, crumbling tufts between her fingers, making soil tests; the final chapters of her botany thesis, which is entitled "Thistles of Our Country".

My own thesis in mathematics, on the other hand, is still far from finished, for I must write it by myself, without soil or sky. I have been stuck, ever since the spring, within a self-made labyrinth, laid open to a suddenly discovered logical contradiction. I need inspiration, a special kind of light. As though I were writing a novel. Every step in working out an equation becomes a painful burden.

And now the desert wind blows steadily over Jerusalem. The flowers that Yael has planted in my yard have turned to brittle straw.

Then all of a sudden, after years of silence, she; she and her husband. In the middle of the holidays I received a letter from them, followed by another. They want my advice, my help if possible. Because they know no one else in Jerusalem. You see, they have decided to leave their kibbutz in Galilee (they did not bother to tell me why), and they want to come and study at the university, the two of them. Will I be so kind as . . . could I obtain the registration papers . . . find out particulars . . . fill in question-naires. . .

The letters, awkwardly styled, were written by her husband. As though I meant something to him, a friend. As though I owe him something.

I told myself: what are they to me? But anything connected with her name rouses an emotion.

Five years have passed since I left the kibbutz, three years since I saw her, and still I believe myself in love with her.

I did all they asked me. Quickly, efficiently, soundly. I can be very useful, at times.

I went to the Faculty of Humanities, and though not versed in its rules and regulations I found out all they needed. I was told they must pass entrance examinations, was even given a timetable. I bundled together questionnaires and the timetable, and added a note of explanation written in a matter-of-fact tone. Let them know I can be relied upon.

I addressed the letter to both of them.

I sent it by express post.

They did not even write a line of thanks.

I am familiar with her lack of courtesy and her carelessness. But the husband, who isn't so young, might have shown some politeness.

Yael came back from Galilee tanned, with dust and scratches all over her. She emptied a rucksack full of thistles in my kitchen and left again the next morning for new regions, to pick new thistles.

Our sweaty bedding, in the twilight.

I did not tell her about the two newcomers. It's none of her affair. The more so as I'm not married to her yet.

The holidays were drawing to a close. Jerusalemites, sun and salt-baked, were beginning to return to their city. The sky clouds over suddenly and it looks like rain. People rouse themselves and go, as of habit, to buy new exercise books, calendars, pencils. And I—the two prospective students have nearly slipped from my mind. But then, an urgent letter.

The Faculty has informed them that the date of their entrance examinations has been moved forward. They are therefore in a hurry to come to Jerusalem. They will have to spend two or three days in the university libraries in order to prepare for the examinations, get some idea of their subjects. The child, though . . . Where can they leave their small son? (They do not want him to stay behind on the kibbutz, for some reason.) Would I be prepared to look after him for those few days. They just don't know anyone else in Jerusalem. . .

They undertake to bear all the expenses. They will be very grateful, too.

I am still on holiday, aren't I?

Once again, they are so sorry to bother me, but they don't know anyone else in Jerusalem, do they?

I said all right. . .

Not that any new hopes were born in me. I am not naïve, after all. Five years ago I had fallen in love with her, fallen hard, agonizingly, lost in advance. But I gave her up long ago; sometimes I think I gave her up in advance.

I am not stubborn, nor am I violent. And after all one cannot dabble in one love affair forever. I ran away from the kibbutz, enrolled at the university, studied mathematics for five years and even passed the difficult final examinations. If I am still stuck with my thesis, that is nothing but an accident.

What I have achieved till now no man can take away from me.

It is out of laziness, no doubt, that I still consider myself in love with her. For I do not even remember the contours of her face. I may need to debate with myself at length in order to recall the colour of her eyes, the way she carries herself, her voice.

It is out of laziness, no doubt, that I still consider myself in love.

First Call

Three days later, in the afternoon, my neighbours from the first floor called me down to take a telephone call.

The dull heavy voice of her husband.

"Hello. We're here."

"Good. Fine. Have you brought the child?"

"Yes . . ." (A slight hesitation.) "We took your word for it and brought him along."

"Yes, I said I'd take him and I will. Hope he isn't too naughty. . ."

Silence at the other end of the line. A readiness to judge the matter with an open mind. Finally, the answer.

"No, he isn't naughty. A lively child, but not wild. You'll easily control him."

I say nothing; a feeling of sadness, weariness overcomes me. What are they to do with me anyway?

Waves of anxiety reach me from the other end in response to my silence. The husband's voice wavers.

"It's just that . . . we wanted to know . . . when can we bring him?"

"Oh, any time you like."

"Tomorrow? Tomorrow morning?"

"All right."

"Early in the morning?"

"As you like. . ." (I am getting tired of the whole thing.)

"Really, we're terribly grateful. I can't say how . . ."

"Oh, never mind."

"Well, goodbye then. See you tomorrow . . ."

"Goodbye . . ." (Now *my* voice wavers.) "Give my regards to Haya."

"She's here, right next to me. She sends her regards too."

The Child

I had imagined they meant eight in the morning. But they had been thinking of dawn, sunrise and morning dew. They woke me out of my sleep, of course. Her husband and his son. He rang the bell furiously, and since I did not open the door at once he twisted the handle hard. He all but burst into the house. The transition from kibbutz to town had completely unsettled him. He seemed determined to throw himself at his studies as though they were a patch of thistles he'd been told to weed.

And before I had time to collect myself there was a suitcase in my room and a child of three sitting on top of it. A pale little bundle dressed in blue. And I, sour-faced, heavy, hairy, eyes gluey, bent helplessly over the child to examine his face.

He was bathed in rays of light streaming in from the east.

The child's resemblance to his mother was amazing, frightening, exhilarating. The same features, the same wide, ever-thirsty mouth. And the eyes, deep-set, the same. I wandered about drowsily but already excited, all my love already flying out to him. I elicit basic information.

What does he eat? What does he drink? How do I wash him? When does he sleep? What do I do with him?

And I receive plain answers.

He eats and drinks everything but shouldn't be forced. I can take him anywhere, and if he complains that his legs hurt I needn't believe him. He just likes to be carried. He had better not sleep during the day, else he may make trouble at night. At this point the father stoops, tips his son off the suitcase, turns it over and searches through its contents till he comes to a rubber sheet. With a shamefaced smile he explains that I must put this under the sheet, because the child still wets the bed.

I am exultant. I jest at the expense of kibbutz child-rearing, but accept the instruction enthusiastically. Joy lights up in me. Already I am impatient to be left alone with the child. His father, though, regards me with misgiving. Indeed, in this early hour of the morning I do not exactly inspire trust. A bulky bachelor warm from bed, going about in crumpled pyjamas, his room in a mess.

I therefore proceed to send the father off at once. The child follows us like a puppy. His father stops, bends over his son, hugs him hard, caresses him, takes a comb out of his pocket and passes it through the boy's curls. He issues instructions :

That he behave himself—

That he be no trouble—

That he not pester me with demands.

Because, see, it's not as though anybody wants to abandon him. But if he misbehaves, who will come to fetch him and take him back?

We move towards the door, but the child, grave and stubborn, clings to his father. The father has no choice but to turn on his heels, rummage through the suitcase again and scatter a collection of typical kibbutz toys over the floor: clumsy wooden tractors, ploughs, mowers, tiny figures of agricultural labourers frozen in ridiculous attitudes.

The child attacks this booty, and meanwhile we slip away in the direction of the front door, establish ways of getting in touch (phone calls, that is all). All at once I realize with a shock that it is their firm intention to leave the child with me for three whole days. There is nothing I can do but wish them success with their examinations, add some advice from my own rich experience, then say goodbye. But now, suddenly, the man hesitates, brooding, reluctant to hand over his son. In a low voice he tells me that last night, upon arrival in Jerusalem, they had seemed to detect symptoms of illness in the child. Haya had even wanted to keep him at the hotel, try and study despite his presence. But he, the father, had been firm. Illness? Rubbish. The boy is just confused from the trip.

I run my eyes over his bony face, the shaved, dingy skin. Sunlight flickers and splits between his strong teeth. My windows glow in the bright light. We are in for a hot day.

I close the door gently behind the man's back, sending him straight off to the hills rising beyond our street.

Coming back into the room I roll at once on to the still warm bed, exhausted by this early rising. I look at the child, who has hitched a plough to one of his tractors and is now proceeding to cultivate my floor tiles. I had not counted on such an utter resemblance. It is as though nature were playing a trick on me. How could she thus impose her image on her son.

The child ploughs. Occasionally he steals a glance at me.

I tell him to come over to the bed. He abandons his toys at once, straightens up and comes to me. Such sweet obedience. He, too, has apparently grasped the fact that his parents have deserted him and that there is no one left in this big new town but me. He stands by my bed. His face is pale, ascetic almost. Happily, wonderingly, I look into his eyes—her eyes in all their glory. Green, the same dreamy green. Lightly I smooth his hair, then with an abrupt gesture, harsh and clumsy (too clumsy), I grab and hug him, hold him close; and while he is struggling in my arms I kiss his eyes, his cheeks.

Then I let him go and ask him his name.

He is called Yahli.

The Pregnancy

Three years ago, in winter, in the rainy season, friends left a young Alsatian pup in my care for a few days. Every evening on my return from the university I would put the dog on its lead, go out into the rain-swept street and walk it under the dim wet lights, from lamppost to lamppost, tree to tree. One evening I found under one of them, sheltering from the drizzle, one Arieh G., member of the kibbutz, a big, bearded, middle-aged bachelor wrapped in a filthy sheepskin coat. Though he had not belonged to my own group at the kibbutz, I stopped to talk to him. The dog seemed interested too, sprawled at Arieh's feet and licking his boots.

Sworn bachelor that he was, the fellow would from time to time swoop down upon one of the large cities to find himself women.

We engaged in some perfunctory gossip, leisurely, between showers. At last I plucked up courage and asked about her. He told me she was pregnant.

All night I tossed in bed, excited by this news. Next day I locked the dog in the kitchen with some food, put on khaki trousers and set out to see her. I thought I would find her in the first months of her pregnancy. She was in her last.

Her belly was huge.

A stormy day. All day the rain beat down upon the roads. The soil was turning into a soggy mush. The bus windows were clouded with grey steam.

By afternoon the bus dropped me by the roadside, and I travelled the four miles from the main road to the kibbutz on foot. A mud track between mountains, grey dripping sky ahead.

The dining hall was cold and empty. Five o'clock in the afternoon, a silent time at the kibbutz. I wandered about the large hall, among the bare tables, trying vainly to get dry. My shoes were heavy with mud, the cuffs of my trousers soiled. Suddenly I was overcome by embarrassment. What was I doing here? None of my group had remained at the settlement except she and one unfriendly couple. I went out into the corridor, stood by the notice board and read with great zeal through the week's Working Arrangements, the plans and programmes of the Cultural Committee, a message from the Central Executive of Communal Settlements. Someone came and stood close behind me and started reading too. Inadvertently, our bodies touched.

I turned and saw her.

She was reading with that dreamy concentration typical of her. Her sweet, slim legs stuck into heavy rubber boots. A huge, fearful belly thrust between us. She noticed me and smiled, casually, as though it were a matter of course that I should be here in front of her on a rainy day, two years after I had left the kibbutz for good.

She asked what I was doing now. I told her about the university in Jerusalem. I kept my account brief, in order not to bore her. My eyes kept roving over her belly. What else had I come for?

I dragged behind her to her room. A pregnant woman, soft, beautiful, booted, trudging through the mud, over the paths of a rain-drenched mountain kibbutz whose members were hiding.

Her man was dozing in the dark room. She approached him quietly and he woke with a start, jumping off the bed as though frightened by her.

We introduced ourselves: "Ze'ev."

"Dov."

We drank coffee and nibbled biscuits hard as rock. Then we put out feelers to discover common acquaintances and nibbled at them too. Nothing was left for me but to speak about algebraic equations, which are beyond all grief.

The room grew dark. (For some reason they failed to switch the light on.) Silence. She was sprawled in a chair, her feet bare, her beauty dimmed, her enormous belly floating in space. A hard rain began to fall outside. Hail beat against the windows. Everything dimmed, drooped. Mist covered the roofs of the small kibbutz houses. Languor came over us. Even the halting discussion about the future of the kibbutz movement faded out. Suddenly I rose, seized with a sense of urgency, eager to go, to retreat. She in her chair was moving her head in a parting nod (this talent of hers to treat people as if they were objects); but Ze'ev, her husband, held me back.

"In this weather?" he demanded. "Who'll you get to pick you up on the main road?"

I went with them to the dining hall for supper. People came over to our table, slapped my back, uttered some trivialities. Everyone realized that I had come to see her.

We returned to their room, the three of us, and sat down to smoke. They were stuck with me. An unwieldy guest, stubborn, in love. Her husband would not leave me alone, kept moving around by my side, his body tense, eyes anxious.

Suddenly we were speaking of the coming birth. I said: "It's going to be a girl, you'll see." Her husband was inclined to agree. But she was certain that it was a son she was carrying inside her. She would not let us argue.

Afterwards we listened to some records . . .

I was close to tears . . .

I was to sleep in a room next to theirs. She fetched sheets and blankets and made my bed. Suddenly we were alone together in the room. I sat on a chair, tensely watching her light movements; the way she spread a sheet, a blanket, dropped a white pillow into place. Her serenity that drove other people out of their minds. Her bare feet, smooth flesh. I speak mainly of the flesh, of her body, in order to be understood. She fixed her gaze on me. As though she had noticed my presence only now.

"What's wrong?" she whispered.

I shivered.

Her husband came and took her away.

I extinguished the light, undressed, slipped between the freezing bedclothes. I could not sleep. I rose in the dark and opened the window. The world—awash and teeming with growth. Shoots were springing out of the spongy soil, climbing in the dark. Trees branching out over roofs, casting roots into the moist depths. Lawns were bursting forth tumultuously. Fields sprouting far and wide.

The smell of wind and rain swept my face.

I tiptoed over to the wall dividing my room from theirs, placed my ear against the thin partition to hear what they were saying, what they were doing. Their room was silent. I heard the rustle of their clothes dropping. At last her quiet, slightly hoarse voice.

"It's now three days since the child's moved. He doesn't kick . . . nothing. . ."

The light went out in their room. They did not mention me. As though I hadn't come, as though I had never been.

At dawn I was gone.

Three months later, when I heard she had given birth to a son, I was already up to my eyes in examinations, closed in by graphs and tables.

Plans

How ridiculous. For the last fifteen minutes I have been trying to elicit the child's real name, but without success. My logical deductions: Yuval, Eyal or Eliezer are rejected with an emphatic shake of his little head. I can't find out anything from him. No one has taken the trouble to teach him his real name. I ask for his name in a thousand ways, and in a thousand ways he answers: Yahli.

At last he stops answering altogether.

The sun shines in our eyes . . .

He stands before me unspeaking, inspecting me with grave eyes. A small child, ostensibly human. No telling whether this is a defined personality or perhaps just a shape. Silence between us. I smile at him, pull a face. His look remains grave. I place a pillow on top of my head. A smile lights up his face. I crawl into a corner of the bed, wrap myself up in the blanket, become a dark, growling lump.

43

He bursts into loud laughter.

Now the barriers are down. Without any inducement he begins to tell me, in crude baby talk, some pointless tales that have no apparent connection with each other. Something about a tractor that went up a rock and down again, something about some child's father getting injured, and something about a "terribly dangerous" snake that was crawling near the grown-ups' dining hall.

Many of the words I fail to grasp. The effort to understand him tires and bores me. His stories are rather queer. They have neither an ending nor a moral. Just a string of facts. At last he falls silent. Then he asks for water.

We go to the kitchen and I inquire whether he would like iced water. This offer amazes him. He hesitates and finally decides to accept. I pour some water into a glass, extract a few ice cubes from the refrigerator tray and drop them in.

He holds the glass with two hands, takes a cautious sip, licks at the floating ice cubes. He is startled. The cold prickles his tongue. He doesn't give in, though, but sends me a conspiratorial smile. At last he sets the glass down, fishes out an ice cube and starts nibbling at it.

By the time I have finished washing, shaving, dressing and having my coffee, the kid has finished off five ice cubes.

Not that I think they are wholesome, but I have already made up my mind early in the proceedings that his health is none of my responsibility.

He can have whatever he wants.

I am free to spoil him.

He seems sad, a sad child.

And had they given a beloved woman to my charge, would I have granted her her every wish?

Now, the room tidied, I sit him on my knee and proceed to map out the various wonders of our day.

To begin with: the zoo—lions, monkeys, bears and wolves.

Second: an ice cream.

Third: the swimming pool.

Fourth: more ice cream.

Fifth: a tank that we shall go and buy for him. A tank to defend his tractors.

Sixth: the stories we shall tell him at bedtime.

Seventh: we may find a swing.

He listens to my plans in utter serenity, then slips off my lap and stands up. His posture is the same as hers, a slight rounding of the soft, frail shoulder blades. Loose, somewhat struggling limbs. Her pensive face.

I draw his head close, take a comb and pass it through his hair. Suddenly he throws his arms around my middle in a childish hug. He must be convinced by now that his parents have forsaken him and there is nobody but me.

I am moved. No, wildly excited. I toss him high in the air, kiss his eyes again.

It was perhaps at that moment that the agreeable fact came home to me that I would actually have the child in my possession for three whole days.

At last I release him. I feel a slight nausea rising in me. I put on sunglasses, cast a glance in the mirror, open the door. A mighty sun and a world ablaze.

The two of us go out to wander about a Jerusalem stewing in its silence.

In Dispraise of Jerusalem

One has to take a clear stand about Jerusalem. One cannot pass through in silence. I claim that Jerusalem is a hard town. A harsh town, sometimes. Don't trust its modesty, its gentleness that isn't gentle. Look at its sealed stone houses.

People extol the sweetness of its air. Yes, I know about that. But the empty nights. Pass through any of its quarters after nine in the evening and you will be walking through a city of the dead. No car will ever stop at your call. Jerusalem, its calm is feigned.

Its people are always tense, always anxious, as though they might be besieged at any moment, their houses shelled, their water despoiled.

Their worried Jerusalemite eyes, their caustic humour. The frenzied greed for mail, devouring of newspapers. The endless pursuit of endless honours.

I am speaking of the real Jerusalemite.

If you walk through the centre of town, across the little triangle where the main streets meet, you are bound to see everybody. You will be caught, avoid no one; not the little professors who stop you eagerly in order to sound their latest innovation in your ears, only to drop you again because they have suddenly spotted someone more important on the other pavement.

And the neologisms.

All day they're fussing about language, dabbling in words. Even Jerusalemite lecturers in mathematics try their hand at coining new words.

Because everyone is bent upon symbols. In their zeal for symbols Jerusalemites are inclined to consider themselves symbols. Hence they use symbolic language, walk and talk symbolically, and meet each other symbolically speaking. At times, when the mood is on them, they look upon the sun, the wind, the sky stretched over their city as nothing but symbols that require study.

I leave my flat in Neveh-Harim, my quarter, skip and slide among rocks, along the familiar paths twisting down into the Valley of the Cross. The child toddles behind me, a stranger, her image, her symbol. His light burning eyes follow me. He imitates all my movements.

I break off a stalk, he breaks off a stalk too. I hit rocks with my stalk, he hits rocks too. I bend to tie a loose shoelace, he bends and fumbles with his shoe. I slip off to urinate behind a tree, he too stops behind a tree.

You see, I can consider myself a symbol too.

The Jerusalem Zoo

In a way, our visit to the zoo was a waste of time. Yahli was too young, and though I tried to stir up some enthusiasm he did not show any interest in the caged animals. He surveyed the giraffes and elephants dispassionately; I think he did not see them whole. The lions, bears and wolves bored him. The screaming pack of monkeys meant nothing to him. The peanuts I had given him to feed them with he threw into a ditch. But near a cage containing ordinary chickens he lingered for a long time, and he showed great interest in a puppy dragged along by some woman. The crushed carcass of a turtle lying on the path excited him.

We wandered about the place for all of three hours. I had not been to the zoo since childhood, and in a way I was curious about it. We did not skip a single cage, therefore, but went all the way round from Libyan Adder to Negev Deer; we even went and peered at the Yellow Wagtail. Many of the animals lay hidden in their lairs because of the searing heat. Much as I shouted to rouse them they refused to appear. Relations between the child and me had suddenly turned dull, laborious. Perhaps it was my fault, due to my impatience, my boredom. Yet he isn't friendly either, is silent much of the time, like his mother.

At last I grew weary of the zoo. I found myself a pleasant little retreat behind one of the cages, in the shade of some pine trees, near the enclosure of an ancient buffalo. I sat down on a bench and Yahli began pottering about by my side, searching among the pine needles and along the hedges for whatever he might find. Then he asked for my permission to go and explore a patch sloping down in front of us. I agreed, on condition that he stay in sight.

Promptly he went off and out of sight. I rose and ran to catch him. I grabbed his hand hard and led him back to the bench. He kept silent. He picked up some scrap of metal bearing a faint resemblance to a car and began steering it around and around the bench. I discovered a day-old newspaper stuck between the bars of my bench and started reading it.

This dry heat. The waste of time.

My head lolled wearily. The child was beginning to fidget, steal an occasional glance at me. He longed to go a bit farther, explore that patch or some nearby wall. Now I made no sign. Let him wander about. What can happen to him, after all. The animals are locked up in their cages, the grounds are fenced in. I have a firm faith in the Authorities. There is no reason why anything should go wrong, is there? The newspaper bored me. I realized I'd read it the day before. The heat made me drowsy. No need to speak again of my early rising. My hands flagged by my sides. A tiny fly had fallen asleep on one of my eyelids and I felt too exhausted to wake it.

I must have slept for a few minutes. I woke and the child wasn't there.

I did not stir, only searched for him with my eyes. I found him at once. Three children were walking along the top of a slanting wall, and Yahli was walking behind them.

(A description of the wall: grey, rough-hewn rocks. The wall grew higher as it went, sloping down the hillside. At its base—a tangle of thorns and briers. A long history of thorns. Here and there—crumbled bricks, empty tins. Futile attempts at burying litter.)

Yahli had quietly been trailing behind three street kids older than himself, who had climbed on to the wall in order to walk along its top. He had no doubt been watching them for quite a while already, though they had not even noticed his existence.

The three figures crept slowly along, carefully balancing

themselves, their heads bent down to the rocks moving under their feet. Yahli was coming some way behind, moving doggedly, with a kind of sleep-walker's perseverance.

I followed him out of the corner of my eye.

His body stoops, the shoulder blades stick out beneath his thin shirt. His movements are gawky too, but now there is terror in them. Slowly he crawls forward, his steps hardly noticeable. The street kids have got way ahead of him and are now sliding precariously down the far end of the wall. Their daring venture is over. Yahli halts, looks about him. One incautious movement and he'll be lying on the ground with a broken neck. But I didn't care.

On the contrary, I was excited!

See, the sun is burning overhead, a grey hot autumn day, and the child I am supposed to watch is walking along a wall that he isn't up to. There is no one about, the animals are nodding in their cages. I lie sprawled on a bench, watching him. I thought: if the child were to fall now, she would remember me all right. I would be engraved in one of the pictures of her mind, if only as a figure dozing on a bench at the side.

The child takes another few steps, and then he stops for good, for the wall is growing higher and higher under his feet. He is terrified, starts to whimper.

I picked up yesterday's paper and spread it over my eyes. I was well-satisfied with myself. This feigned calm, not at all like me.

The child called me.

I did not bat an eyelid. Motionless on my bench, I thought of the barefoot woman I had not seen for three years.

The child screamed.

Then, abruptly, silence. Light shimmering among the pine branches flickers on my eyes. Someone has rushed to pluck him off the wall. They have taken him down now, and have asked him his name, for I hear his voice between sobs: "Yahli."

Some minor commotion is afoot around him. Even the old buffalo lifts its head. A couple of zoo attendants come over and ask: "Where's your daddy, where's your mummy?"

At this point I must intervene, before they take him away from me. I get up from my bench, fold the paper, approach the group and pick up the child. Saying nothing, not a word of thanks.

We leave the zoo and I lift him off my shoulders and throw him high up in the air, catch him, swing him, sit him on my head. He laughs. In his eyes the tears still shine, and he is already laughing.

A Reflection

It is a simple case. A woman and a man have left a kibbutz (a common affair, that) and have come to Jerusalem. They have a small son, and there is nothing wrong with that. Since they were required to pass an examination and since they had not touched a book for a long time, they shut themselves up in libraries and left their little boy in my care. I am no friend of theirs, but I know they have no one else in Jerusalem to turn to.

I fell in love with a woman years ago, fell hard, painfully, silently. Since she is a heedless woman, pensive, losing herself in reveries, she forgot my love, and sent her husband at dawn to wake me and hand her child, her only son, her image, over to me. And it was hot, an end-of-summer heat wave, and it was Jerusalem, a harsh town.

First I kissed the child, then I listened to his pointless stories. Finally I took him to the Jerusalem zoo, because he was beginning to get bored, because I was getting bored myself. I dozed off on a bench in a corner, and meanwhile the child slipped away and climbed on to a battered wall that rose higher and higher.

His life had been in the balance.

Amazing that I stayed calm, that I could still have wished to sleep.

Lunch

Yahli's lunch was spoiled by the large portion of ice cream I bought him on leaving the zoo.

At all events, I did the best I could to make him eat. I took him to a decent restaurant, sat him on a chair, tied a napkin around his neck and gave him the printed menu, then read the whole thing out to him. He listened patiently and even studied the list in his hand with great solemnity. The waitress coming over to our table cupped his chin in her hand voluptuously. For Yahli, to tell the truth, is a captivating child, with his beauty, his shining eyes, his hot, tawny skin.

We held a little conference. But Yahli took no notice of our decision, reached after much ado. He did not touch the food placed before him. He had no appetite whatever and just sat there toying with his fork. The disappointed waitress kept fussing about him, making signs for me to coax him, to try and force him. But I refused.

Why should I? Force him? Me?

People at nearby tables looked at me suspiciously. As though I had kidnapped the child somewhere and were going to sell him into slavery.

I finished off my food, pulled his plate towards me and finished off his, then took out a cigarette and settled down to smoke. And through the curling smoke I stared in silence at the open window near my table, at the bluish Hills of Edom in the distance. The hot wind blew. The child nodded sleepily opposite me.

I stubbed out the cigarette, got the child up from his chair, paid and went out into the street. We stopped again beside an ice-cream seller. I bought two cones, for him and for me. After he had finished his portion I bought him some cold lemonade. His huge thirst surprised me. It was as though he needed to extinguish a fire burning within his little body.

He dragged his feet. All at once he suggested that we go to bed. But I said: Why no, we still have a long way ahead of us. He begged me to carry him, because his legs hurt. I picked him up, put him on my shoulders. After a while I put him down.

Jerusalem lay hushed. We sauntered along slowly, in the wake of some fat pigeons which Yahli vainly tried to catch. The asphalt is soft under our feet. By and by we arrived at the Municipal Garden with its white paths and ugly flowers. A harsh sun trembled overhead. I led him on aimlessly, through the heat, straying over the desolate park. He lagged behind, flushed with heat and fatigue. I left the park, crossed a little patch of thistles and approached the old Moslem graveyard. Yahli, swallowed by the tall weeds, plodded steadily behind. The graveyard is fenced in, but I discovered a gap in the fence and entered, the child on my heels, into a tangle of olive trees, among large tombstones.

The Gap

Between the end of high school and the beginning of our army service we had gone to work at a kibbutz, and shortly afterwards another youth-movement group arrived and joined us there. How happy we were to mingle with such a rich variety of new people. In time we became aware of her, her loose, slouching walk, her rare beauty. We were like children, and like children we fell in love with her. There were about a hundred people in our group and we did not think ourselves lonely. Nevertheless, we were.

I kept silent, of course, mocking those others who tried to approach her. But at night I would wander around the hut where she lived. She used to go barefoot, in work clothes. Even at Friday evening parties she would appear with her feet bare, as though she had been born in the fields. Always my eyes would travel down to her feet, her flawless feet, filthy and pure at the same time.

Except for some commonplace and idle generalities we never exchanged a word.

Yes, we had one long encounter though, once. It happened in the vineyard, at the end of summer, a few days before we boys were to go to the induction centre. A large number of us were sent to gather grapes. And after lunch, when the sky was clouding over, the kibbutz member in charge paired us off together.

We began to work at either side of a serried row of vines.

The sudden darkening of the sky, the wind sweeping through the wadi, autumn, the impending draft, her sudden presence, so close to me—everything surged in me.

She was a swift, skilful worker and I strained every nerve not to fall behind.

A dam burst in me.

I never stopped talking to her, told her everything that came into my mind. I talked about the kibbutz, about some of our group, about startling new ideas in mathematics.

Although she kept silent, she seemed to be listening. I could not see her face. It was hidden by vine leaves. I heard only the soft rustle of her movements on the other side, between the branches. She worked, as always, barefoot. And her slender, mud-covered feet would slip into view close to my heavy boots, among the thin twisting stems of vine.

What with the furious speed of our work we soon were far ahead of the others, thrusting on towards new rows heavy with grapes, drenched with water, tangled with weed and grasses. Empty crates were scattered here and there over the muddy earth and we filled them to the brim with the ripe fruit. My hands were daubed with the sticky dark sap. Actually, we ought to have gone back to help those who hadn't finished their own rows yet.

The end of the working day was drawing near.

I talked on and on. At times I even erupted into brief, impassioned lectures. I felt more at ease not seeing her face, my silent listener.

But at last a wide gap appeared in our row. Four vines lay

crushed to the ground. All at once we faced each other, exposed. She was sitting on a crate, the shears trailing in one hand. A wind came and brushed our faces.

She was so plainly unattainable, so airy, thin, slouching. I did not say anything of importance, but she rested her cheek against the palm of her free hand, attentive.

I remember that my gaze strayed to her feet sunk in the mud, and remained fixed there. It hurt, seeing them like that. I began to lose the train of my thoughts, my speech became halting, faded out. A withered bunch of small, unripe grapes was dangling near the ground, grazing her bare foot. I stopped talking and bent, shears in hand, to cut it off.

The world around us was not silent. The wind, the voices of the others murmuring among the tall vines, sounds coming over from the workshops in the distance, in the settlement white against the dark mountain.

Still bent, close to the ground, I stretched out a hand and scraped with my fingers at the mud drying on her feet, peeling off a layer till I felt the smooth skin.

She kept silent all the while. She sat as though in pain, did not move, did not draw her feet in. And when I straightened up, in despair, she sat still, the shears trailing in her hand, her eyes wide.

In the distance, by the packing house, the end-of-work bell rang. We went back, dragging our feet, back to where we had started. And still we weren't silent, went on talking. A dark puddle lay in the middle of the road and she waded through it deliberately, the mud staining her feet.

The Pool

Yahli scrambled on top of one of the large tombstones, stretched out his little legs and lay down. I found a place nearby among the trees, shaded by their foliage. I sat lost in thought and smoked three cigarettes one after the other. Then I went over to the child, examined his flushed face, tried to take his pulse, felt a queer, irregular, jerky beat under my fingers.

Amazing that Yahli has still not asked about his parents, as though they had died or disappeared, and not a word from him.

I offered to play hide-and-seek with him.

I would burrow my head in the crook of a tombstone and he would go and hide. He wouldn't move more than a few paces away, to go and stand behind the nearest tombstone. If I put on a show of looking for him, and passed him by pretending not to see him, he would at once come out of hiding and present himself.

When it was my turn, on the other hand, I took great pains to conceal myself thoroughly from view. I discovered a ditch between two trees, dug myself in and covered myself with underbrush. For ten minutes he searched for me. He shouted, pleaded, wept.

He was calling me: "Mister! Mister!"

At last I crept out of hiding and found him wandering about white-faced. I told him my name was Dov. He wanted to know where I had been hiding. I showed him my ditch. He cast a worried glance into it, then scrambled down to try it out himself.

Afterwards we pretended that we were back at the kibbutz. Moslem tombs are shaped rather like small, roofed houses, and we proceeded to give them names. In silence we walked, among the rustling trees, from the grown-ups' dining hall to the kids' dining hall, from the nursery to the tractor shed, from there to the carpentry shop and back again. I tried telling him about the dead people buried beneath the soil, but he did not understand.

The keeper of the graveyard, wakened from his siesta, discovered us and began to shout, curse and throw stones at us. We escaped through the gap. Yahli kept glancing at me anxiously.

Jerusalem lay sweltering still.

We got on to a bus and went to the swimming pool. Yahli was stripped of his clothes and thrown into the water. He screamed with the cold and the pleasure. I dropped into a deck chair at the edge of the children's pool, took off my shoes and watched Yahli splashing about in the water.

He was the smallest child there.

A vendor selling sugar-coated almonds passed, an odd sort of flag blew in the wind. Some boys were holding a dare-devil swimming match among themselves. Suddenly there emerged a swarm of teenagers from around a corner, all pupils of mine, all wearing bathing suits. When they noticed me they stopped, spoke in whispers. Then they came over one by one with a twittering, "Good afternoon, teacher!"

None of them missed this opportunity to hail me.

I sat there with lowered eyes, forcing my face into a smile, beleaguered. Most of them were girls.

Making conversation, they ask how I am, how I have spent the holidays, whether I didn't miss them, and why didn't I swim (with glances toward the child). Most important, will I be teaching them again this term?

A few clouds appeared in the sky.

The more impertinent among them cast an amused glance at the pale, hairy feet sticking out of my trouser legs.

It appears that the entire fifth year has come to the pool *en masse* to mourn the dying holiday.

They can have their fun for all I care. I do not fear them. What sometimes amazes me is the ease with which they lie, the ease with which they believe their own lies.

A light breeze ruffles my hair. Absent-mindedly I unbutton my shirt, bare my chest before my pupils, bury my hands in my lap. They throng around me, hemming me in, suffocating me with their curiosity, their fawning and flattery. They want to find out all the particulars of the coming school year. I am evasive, try to fend them off with jokes, vague generalities. But little by little they squeeze all they want to know out of me.

Two of the girls go so far as to enter the pool, converge upon Yahli, pet him, ask his name.

The whole lot of them are burning with curiosity about the child. He isn't mine, then whose is he?

Finally they go away, all of them together, the little males caught up among a solid knot of girls. They disappear.

I am bored as usual.

Yahli is busy floating a piece of stick in the deserted pool. A languid, sickly sun. People are drying themselves, dressing, leaving. We are among the last left. Yahli comes to tell me he is cold. He shivers, has gooseflesh. But I send him back to the water.

A solitary woman rouses my desire, shamefully. I lie on the chair, devoured by lust, hopeless, my head thrown back, watching the sky prepare to celebrate the sun's departure.

Before the Classes

I teach mathematics to two fifth year classes majoring in literature. Students who had tried to avoid the subject were caught in the net and forced to do sums and solve problems. No, they never ventured to provoke me into fury, and yet the room was always astir with a slow commotion, an endless murmur of calculations.

Being a new, young teacher, I was obliged to take the last hours of the school day. I would have a dull, spent classroom on my hands, most of them girls who would prop their breasts on top of the desk and gaze at me with sleepy, troubled eyes. The few weakly, bespectacled boys trapped among them would take out sharp pocket-knives and during the whole hour would use them to scratch into every available surface: chairs, desks, pencil cases. At nearly every lesson one of them would stand up happily, point in triumph at his bleeding fingers and ask permission to go and get them bandaged.

Nevertheless, they learned mathematics.

They did tolerably well, on average, though they were never inspired with any enthusiasm in the working out of a problem. They would think mechanically with their literary brains.

Large windows faced my platform in both classes.

A few moments after I had entered the room the sun, too, would enter through the window. The light would glare in my eyes. It was pure torment. I asked the management for curtains but the budget did not seem to allow for them. Ridiculous. Packages of chalk lay around by the hundreds in the teachers' room. I could have started a trade in them and no one would have been any the wiser.

I stand in front of the class and presently the sun explodes into my eyes. As soon as I turn to the blackboard I am blinded. I scrawl distorted figures, triangles that do not close, make blunders in simple sums of addition.

Then a hush falls on the room, and one of the girls bestirs herself and remarks upon my error. Sometimes I might hear a giggle, and it might be charged with yearning.

As for their yearning, it would flow towards me in vain, flow far and beyond.

They had their dreams, no doubt, their longings, perhaps, but I was over the river and out of reach beside a blackboard abounding with quadratic equations of the first degree, my eyes full of sun.

And sometimes during examinations, when they all sat silently racking their brains over the perfectly easy questions, my heart would contract. I would climb my platform, crouch behind my desk, alone, lonely, head on fist, thinking suddenly of my love, trying to imagine, for instance, what she was doing now.

The Borderline

When we left the pool, Yahli and I, we were surprised to discover traces of autumn outside. Clouds, leaves drifting, a grey tint in the air and the sharp cold of Jerusalem's mountains enveloping us, caressing our cheeks. Yahli began to shiver. His kibbutz clothes (briefest of shorts and thin shirt) did not protect him against the cold. I touched his forehead and felt it burning. His hair was still wet, and from time to time a drop of water would well out and trickle down his face.

Then he stopped and began to cough. In the face of a grey world, grey Jerusalem, he stood there and coughed painfully, from the depth of his lungs. I stood beside him, hands in pockets and regarded him attentively. Passersby threw us a glance.

You cannot deny that he is a sweet kid.

A beauty? Maybe.

He stood in the middle of the street and coughed like a little old man.

And I stood and looked.

At last he stopped. He wiped his mouth, raised his eyes at me as though wishing to say something. I smiled down at him, then bent to hear what he had to say.

He asked whether he could go and see Deborah now.

Naturally I inquired who Deborah might be.

"Deborah . . . Deborah . . ." he clung to the name, insistent.

She was a little girl his age whom he had left behind at the kibbutz. His little sweetheart, perhaps.

I pretended to be thinking it over. Then I informed him resolutely that no, he could not see Deborah. I spoke to him as to an adult, firm and straightforward, not trying to sugar my voice.

I wanted to shatter his hopes.

He listened and kept silent. He still hadn't mentioned his parents.

Lost in thought, we strayed into a forlorn Jerusalem alley, its pavement cracked, its houses shuttered, some of them in ruins. Through a break between two houses sagging towards each other there was a glimpse of the border—a line of hills and a few straggling olive trees. A section of the belt of menace encircling Jerusalem. For a moment I considered stealing towards the border and leaving him there, among the olive trees, among rocks and thistles. Except that the child's steps faltered suddenly, as though he had read my mind. We stopped, looked at each other unspeaking.

I bent down to him and asked whether he wouldn't very much like now to be rocked on a swing.

56

Yael

I met Yael on a hike of the Nature Lovers' Society. Once, during my first year at the university, I happened to join a Nature Lovers' hike. I only understood my mistake when it was too late. I had imagined theirs to be something like a youth-movement trip, but it turned out to be an entirely different kind of thing. To begin with, nature lovers go along at a snail's pace, all but creeping over the ground. Secondly, they examine every detail of their surroundings. They do this out of a sacred principle. I don't say that the countryside (west of Jerusalem) isn't beautiful, but I had been accustomed to the youth-movement pace, the rapid marching, the breathless climbing up a good high mountain, the looking for half an hour over a marvellous and historically significant landscape, then climbing down again.

Anything less than two far mountains and a wide horizon we wouldn't call nature.

Yael belonged to the Nature Lovers, was one of them, a member of the breed. For nature lovers are a collection of archaeologists, zoologists, botanists, vegetarians, naive prose poets. They and their fat "flora" clasped in their hands like prayer books. I know them from the "Introduction to Mathematics" course. And though to all intents and purposes they belong to the Faculty of Natural Sciences, they are actually terrified of figures.

About every hundred yards they stop, to crouch over mosses, clasp reptiles, cast a hush over the universe in order to hear a bird chirp. Everyone except me was interested in something, was collecting plants, fossils, scorpions, soil strata.

Yael, for instance, was taken up with thorns. And a hard job it was that she had chosen herself. She would disappear into a wilderness of thistles, uproot her choice with bare hands, then sally forth again waving an anonymous thistle over her head.

I was getting sick and tired of this slow tramping.

I started to walk ahead of the tribe, crushing important mosses, squeezing the life out of rare insects, throwing stones at birds. Close upon twilight I started to hang about the thistle girl, to walk by her side and sneer. I would stand with my hands in my pockets and look on while she struggled with an unyielding plant.

In the evening the nature lovers set up camp and gathered to sing. Yael had spread herself a little to the side, near a rock, surrounded by her thistles, for she hadn't finished sorting them yet or extracting their pappus.

She isn't pretty. Tall, thin, brisk. Her hair is dry and straggly, her hands rough, her legs permanently scratched.

They all sang and she sat and worked. I lay on the ground between the singers and her. Not that I was waiting for her, but I wanted to see when she would finish her task. She had undoubtedly noticed me there but pretended to be absorbed in her work. She was biting her lips with absorption.

At last she rose and with a single match set fire to the whole harvest of thorns about her. A sudden flame leaped up. The singers stopped their singing and shouted, "Hey, you!" But she smiled, and her lean body was lit up.

Perhaps my desire was already aroused, perhaps it was only some warmth I wanted, to arm myself for the long cold night ahead. Whatever the case, in a little while I had penetrated beyond the flames, and by the time its last cinders were dying out we were already close to each other, within reach of the sweet flesh.

We cleaved together in the depth of night, the nature lovers scattered around us snoring softly and mumbling the names of favourite plants and insects in their sleep.

Because we had started at the end, we had to turn in our tracks next morning and walk the tedious way back to the beginning; talk about the scenery, search for common acquaintances, help her dig up thorns, hear her explain, attend. . .

Since then we have been friends.

Though love between us there is none, there is a vast understanding. Look, we may chance to meet in a crowded Jerusalem street, on the afternoon of a weary day. And only last night we lay locked and now, as if by agreement, we ignore each other. Our eyes meet, and then we have passed each other by without a word. So great is the pity we sometimes bear each other.

The Old People

Yael lives close to the swimming pool, in that former Arab quarter in the south of Jerusalem where splendour and penury mingle. Her house, a single storey, lies in the centre of a sizeable patch of land, untilled but properly fenced in. Week after week building contractors come to see Yael's old parents, to hold out tempting offers. They are willing to pay a fortune for the grounds in order to raze the little house. But the old people hold on. And what do I care, after all. But their obstinacy drives me mad. Like Yael's. We may be going to the cinema, for instance, and suddenly she discovers a thorn growing from a crack between road and pavement. She may stay hovering about it for a long time, while I stand and wait till she has calmed down. If at least she were my love. But she isn't.

Ancient pine trees surround the little house, shielding it. Her Jerusalemite parents are like two seedy old foxes in their burrow. They throw nothing away. Their small backyard is a jumble of rusted paraphernalia and the clothes of three generations. Even Yael's doll's pram is buried there.

Planted in the middle of their wild, barren front yard there is a magnificent swing. It was the former owner, fled over the border long ago, who put it there. Once, in a mellow moment when we were talking, Yael and I, about our marriage, to the point of even making a list of what we would need, the old woman told us in all seriousness: "A swing, at any rate, you already have."

The old ones do not like me. They have never invited me to a meal in their house. They have said to Yael, "But he doesn't love you . . ." One time I felt like swinging on their swing, but they wouldn't let me for fear I would break it.

I lifted Yahli to let him press the bell.

Their bell button is attached to a gate in the fence. This arrangement is intended to give the old people time to prepare for visitors, hide their underwear flung about the living-room, wash the dishes, arrange the bureaus. Anyone ringing at the outer gate does not hear the sound of the bell, only sees the dusty, shrivelled tops of pine trees swaying in reply. Yahli was disappointed. He pressed the button for a long time without letting go. He believed it to be his fault that no ring would come. Meanwhile, the old people were frightened out of their wits.

At last the old woman turned up—sour-faced, agitated, her housecoat in disarray—and stopped behind the gate. When she saw me she scowled.

"But Yael's away . . ."

From behind the bars I told her that I knew, but that the child here with me would like to swing.

"Child?"

The old man came scurrying out of the house as well, doing up the last buttons of his trousers. Grudgingly they opened the gate, glaring at Yahli who had hesitantly crossed the threshold. I told them briefly about his parents but they did not hear, fluttering their eyelids suspiciously. They must think the child is mine, born to me in secret.

I led him to the swing, lifted him, sat him down, lashed him in. His body is burning, he is feather-light. I start pushing him, gently, aad the old couple stand at a little distance, looking on resentfully. Yahli holds on tight, for I am quickening the pace. He starts to laugh with increasing panic. I remind him of the monkeys at the zoo but he doesn't remember. He clings to the ropes with all his might, flies through the air in long sweeps, laughing till he cries; he screams, begins to whimper.

The old ones take a small step forward.

Furiously I push the swing. The child has closed his eyes, his features blur, his whimper is stifled.

The two foxes swing their tails lightly, their eyes narrow into slits.

Nothing but the creak of the swing, the wind rustling.

At last I take my hands off the swing. Slowly it comes to a halt. His eyes shut, pale, faint, the child collapses into my arms. I put him down. Such a kid. Without looking at the old people I lead him to the house, take him into the living room. The old people follow quietly. I order the old woman to give him a sweet. Shocked she goes over to the sideboard and rummages through it for a long time till she finally comes up with a mouldy piece of toffee. Never taking his clear eyes off the old people, the child unwraps the toffee and puts it in his mouth. A stupefied silence. The toffee sticks to his tongue. Through the window the pines look darkly in at us. The old man is fascinated by the child, watching him in alarm. The child retreats one step in my direction. The toffee is still lying whole on his tongue. I grab him by the nape of his neck, mumble goodbye. The old ones come to with a start and sigh. Suddenly the child spits the toffee out onto the floor and looks at it attentively. Then he takes a step towards it and vomits, moves over desperately to the old man and vomits over his clothes. A hush. Gently the pines swing by the window. The old woman utters a stifled shriek.

The First Evening

Once more I was forced to escape with him. We took the first bus that came along. Oddly, people vacated a place for me, as though they sensed the child was ill. I took him on my knees and huddled against the window.

He did not cry. He did not even wish to cry. He had no reason for crying, after all. I had given him whatever he had asked for, and what he had never thought of asking for as well. Had he begun to form a picture of me?

His eyes were closed.

He propped his head on his hand as though he had a headache, or was thinking.

How old was he after all. Three, and a few months.

In fact, why didn't he cry? If he had, I would have released him. I am not overly patient.

At last he opened his eyes. I smiled at him, whispered, "Yahli." As I said, his eyes are like hers, as though wrenched wide.

On the way home we entered a toy shop and I bought him a grey-green tank with a cannon mounted on top. The tank was in a little box and given to him to carry. Then we were crossing fields, descending slopes, walking in the face of the sunset. Worn out we climbed the steps to my flat. Between one landing and the next he stopped, handed me the tank, took hold of the railing, bent over and was sick again. I picked him up in my arms and swiftly climbed up the rest of the way. In the already darkening flat I wiped his mouth with a little towel discovered among his things. I washed his face. I was like a nursemaid to him.

He relaxed and sank exhausted into the armchair. I knelt in front of him and undid the little parcel. He took the tank and, his face very pale, very grave, he aimed the gun straight between my eyes and fired.

I dropped dead on to the rug. But he did not laugh.

I did not switch the light on. The room was dim in the dying sun and I left it that way.

I undressed the child, washed his body, dried it, dressed him in the funny little multi-coloured nightgown that I found in the suitcase. I combed his hair. Then I went into the kitchen to prepare his supper. I made him a soft-boiled egg, warmed some milk and made cocoa, cut thin slices of bread and butter and cut a tomato into small sections. I arranged it all neatly, cleanly, tastefully.

He didn't eat a crumb. He just messed it all up. He poured the egg over the tomato, dipped the bread in the cocoa then tore it to pieces and dropped it all on the floor.

But I did not press him. Calmly I threw everything into the rubbish bin and cleaned up after his would-be meal. He asked for water and I gave him milk. But he wanted water. Slowly and steadily he drained off three whole glasses of water. He refused the chocolate I offered him. He had become refractory, silent and stubborn.

I made his bed, my own big one. I tucked in the rubber sheet, smoothed a clean sheet over it, placed my own large pillow at the head of the bed. Meanwhile he was crawling on all fours, steering the tank awkwardly about the room and shooting at everything in sight. At last he abandoned the tank, went out on to the balcony, pushed a chair up against the railing all by himself and climbed up on it the better to see the world.

Silently I went and stood behind him. He did not turn his head but continued standing with half his body arched over the railing, passionately absorbed in the sight of buses collecting down the road at their terminus. The drivers, talking among themselves, now and then kicking against the big inflated tyres, excited him. His head was craned far out over the railing, his eyes were hungry. No wonder, for it is from some out-of-the-way kibbutz in Galilee that he has strayed here, and though Jerusalem is a quiet town, a little stir and bustle will always come into it at this hour of twilight.

I grabbed his gown with both hands, for he had become carried away now, seemingly eager to cling to the engines dying out and starting again, to hug the steering wheel with the few travellers getting on and off in the last grey light.

Quietly, carefully, I could have dropped the child into the darkening street. I wasn't a paid keeper and wouldn't be called to account.

Except that a dark drop fell on one of the leaves of a bush that Yael had planted by my house, and then another drop and a third on the same leaf. Dark spots. I leaned over and saw blood dripping out of the child's nostrils.

One last, lost patch of light in the sky now.

Yahli wiped at the blood with his hand. He did not even glance at his stained fingers for the buses down at the station had just put on tiny lights, and he was excited.

"No," I whispered suddenly, swept him off the chair and felt my way through the dark room to the bed.

I was surprised that he did not resist; that he was so hot, shattered, already dreaming perhaps.

Carefully I laid him on my bed, mopped up the blood with the little towel (it stopped flowing at once), covered him with a blanket and arranged chairs around the bed so that he wouldn't roll off.

Then I closed the balcony door, let down the shutters, drew the curtains.

I shall have to do without bedtime stories, it seems.

Loneliness

Now my loneliness was undoubtedly greater than his.

A Ring at the Door

A ring at the door. Long and loud, aggressive. I froze in my place. The flat was in darkness. I thought: Ze'ev has come to see his son. And soundlessly I crept into the kitchen.

Silence.

Another ring, followed by two short ones. I thought: So much the better. Let them break down the door, I won't make a move. I sat down by the kitchen table and in the dark, softly, I trickled some honey on to a slice of bread and began to chew.

Half a minute passed and then another ring, drawn out and desperate. I shrink into my chair. The sweet bread crumbles between my teeth. Another ring. Such obstinacy. And another. My caller descends the stairs (the sound of his sandals), comes back, tries to write something (rustle of paper), rings. He tears off the page.

A long silence follows.

Suddenly, a light knock on the door, once, and then again. A final desperate attempt. An obscure scraping of feet. Then, truly, silence.

I thought he had gone away. I waited a long time, then went to the door and opened it cautiously to see if he had left me a message.

Hunched on the staircase, his long delicate legs thrust through the railing bars, his flaxen head in his hands, waiting there is Zvi.

Aware that the door has opened, he straightens his long limbs, picks up a cardboard box at his side. His glasses glint in the light of the rising moon.

"Is that you there?" I whisper.

"Is Yael there?" he asks.

Zvi

Zvi, too, belongs to the Nature Lovers, whose marks of identification are khaki shorts, worn sandals, and thighs covered with sun-blond down. He is in love with Yael, a grim, dogged love.

I do not know what he sees in her, but I am glad that he loves her so much. I have an idea that some time in the past, before I appeared on the scene, he slept with her once or twice, and has been filled with longing ever since.

He is a zoologist and his pockets are always full of vermin that he picks up on the highways and by-ways of Jerusalem. Once he left in my charge two poisonous scorpions, who pranced about in a glass jar for a whole fortnight before they died. He catches spiders with his nimble fingers without squeezing them. Tiny grasshoppers slumber in his palm. His love and compassion for every living thing are amazing. He even loves snakes.

I am fond of him.

He is a gifted fellow. He studies at the university on a scholarship and gets an allowance to boot. Unlike most nature lovers, he is not at all intimidated by mathematics. He happened once to glance at my thesis, and afterwards shyly suggested that I cut ten stages out of some demonstration.

Really, I am very fond of him.

There are many things that I can discuss with him. The eventual explosion of the sun, the energy of light, the elusive relativity of time. He knows a lot, and if I talk about subjects that are unfamiliar to him he catches on quickly. On his side he tells me amusing anecdotes about the ways of insects. His vision is imperfect, however. His light, clear eyes are all but blind. The double-lensed glasses he wears are hardly a help for his ravaged eyes. When Yael and I go to the cinema with him we must sit in the front row, and even then he cranes forward.

Sometimes I steal his glasses, move away and ask: What do you see of the world? And he says: A stain. The world is a stain. And Yael and I laugh.

Such a true friend.

I do not know whether he likes me or not. At any rate, he cannot avoid meeting me because he is always after Yael, follows her like a shadow, hoping still. Sometimes the three of us spend an evening together in my room, talking late into the night. Yael is always tired, though, being an early riser. She starts yawning and, against my will, insists on staying the night, sleeping in my only bed. Deep in my large armchair, Zvi declares that he, too, is going to stay, and it is plainly impossible to throw him out. Go to bed, you, go to bed, he says, I'll sleep right here.

I have no choice.

We extinguish all the lights in the flat, remove Zvi's glasses from his eyes and conceal them in a drawer. Yael undresses and slips into my bed.

Sometimes we fall asleep at once, but more often we do not let go of each other, and Zvi is nearby, quiet, almost blind, the dark caressing his face. In the morning he is gone without us knowing when. And between the twisted sheets, weary, heavy-lidded, we wonder how in the world he found his hidden glasses.

The Snake

Though I state explicitly that Yael isn't there, Zvi nevertheless insinuates himself into the flat. Cardboard box under one arm, tall and lanky, his slender limbs thrust forward, he feels his way through the dark passage, missing door openings, upsetting chairs. I am forced to lead him if I do not want him to wake the child or wreck the place. I push him into my little kitchen and there, crowded close together, we remain standing.

"Where's Yael?" he asks again.

"She's gone. She's off on a trip. I told you, didn't I?"

He lowers his head.

"When'll she be back?"

"Who knows? Not tonight anyway."

He removes his glasses, wipes them quickly, puts them back.

"And you here in the dark. What's happened? A short circuit? I'll fix it for you in a minute. . . ."

"No, it isn't that," I answer curtly.

"Is there somebody with you?" he whispers.

"Somebody?" I say questioningly.

"I thought . . ." he mutters and falls silent.

I do not want to get talking with him or he'll find an excuse to stay. All I want now is to be left alone. He keeps silent. He knows he ought to go. But he doesn't want to go, or he can't. Sadly he bites his lips. Then he reaches out with his long-fingered hand, scrapes together all the crumbs that are on the table, puts them carefully into his mouth.

I send him a furious look.

He doesn't notice my fury, though. He is peering around, trance-like, for a slice of bread.

"Haven't you . . . Maybe you have a slice of bread."

I still have not switched the light on. The moon coming through the window is enough for me.

I cut him some slices of bread, pour honey over them. I shove the cardboard box aside (it is empty, apparently), and place the bread in front of him. Slowly he folds himself into a chair, picks up a slice shyly and politely, raises it to his sombre mouth. I stand over him, watch him.

And he says:

"What a heat today, eh?"

And takes a small bite.

"The days are growing shorter though."

And with his mouth full:

"It's the last of the heat. See if it isn't."

And swallows:

"The birds are already going south."

And softly:

"You know something, Dov. I rather like this darkness of yours."

And still I do not utter a word.

"By the way, careful with that box. There's a snake inside."

I draw back a little.

A serpent coils between us in the dark. I glance at the box, touch it lightly. Yes, something rustles within.

"Not venomous, is it?"

"It is. It's a little viper."

And at once he pours forth the whole story.

He had found it slumbering, curled up on the path. Here, on the hillside, quite near to my place. It must have lost its parents. That had been half an hour ago. Silently Zvi had approached it, expertly—it wouldn't be the first time he'd caught a viper. As a matter of fact, he might well have let it go on twisting among the thorns, except that two girls at the laboratory had implored him to get them snakes.

Though he had approached it quietly, he had missed. The reason was, his eyes. The retinas. He had been to his doctor that very afternoon and the man had prescribed an urgent operation, the day after tomorrow. That was why he had come to see Yael. To say goodbye. He would have to stay in bed for a month with his eyes bandaged.

His wonderful, stubborn love for Yael—

The snake had woken, slithered off the path, and stopped. Zvi had gone in pursuit, and again he had missed. There had still been some afterglow in the sky. The snake had moved again, twisting over the bare rocks. Zvi had grabbed its tail. The snake had tried to sting but had failed. Though mind you, it does have poison. The time it had taken him to find a box for it. Dear God, his eyes are dimming. . .

I still do not put on the light.

A faint sigh reaches us from the room.

Zvi jumps up.

"Yael . . ."

I tell him about the child—

(Yes, he does know something about my old love.)

He wants to see it—

Suddenly he becomes insistent—

I take him to the room. It is stifling. I draw the curtains apart, open the shutters. The child on the bed is breathing heavily. Moonlight pours over his face, reveals the little tank lying on its side by the pillow, caresses his little hands flung out defenceless beside his body. Zvi must bend low over the little figure to make it out. He peers intently, as though it were an insect on a slide.

At last he straightens up, remains stock-still, his chin stuck out.

I admit:

"Yes, the child's a bit ill."

And then:

"God knows what's wrong with him."

And lightly I catch Zvi by the arm.

"Maybe I'd better take his temperature after all."

Zvi keeps silent still. I fetch the thermometer and stick it gently in the sleeping child's armpit. After five minutes I remove it, push Zvi out of the room, shut the door and return to the kitchen.

One hundred and three.

Where can I hide my joy?

To my surprise Zvi says:

"That's not too bad. Temperatures can rise very quickly with kids."

I have heard something like that myself.

And I sit down.

I smile at Zvi. He smiles back and sits down opposite me. He has brightened up now that he realizes I do not intend to throw him out.

We forget the child's existence.

We settle down by the kitchen table. I light a cigarette (Zvi doesn't smoke, naturally) and listen sober and wide-awake now to a new selection of anecdotes about the life and habits of the snake.

Second Call

At half-past ten there is a telephone call for me at the neighbours.

My neighbours, who are not so young, had already gone to bed, and since they keep the telephone in their bedroom they were forced to get up and leave the room. She, in a nightgown, retires to the kitchen; he, in striped pyjamas, prowls like a panther in the passage. I enter their room, shut the door behind me, edge in between the two rumpled beds.

My neighbours bear me good will because I have spent many evenings baby-sitting with their infant when they wanted to see a movie.

I pick up the receiver, hear her slightly hoarse voice.

"That Dov?"

(Excited) "Yes. Dov here. Haya?"

"Still alive?" (I was silent. My heart throbbed.)

(Then softly) "Who?"

"You, of course."

"Yes, of course."

"And Yahli? Behaving himself?"

"Nice kid. Bearing up like a hero. He won't eat a thing, though."

"Never mind that."

"I've washed him. He's asleep now. We've been to the zoo, and afterwards to the swimming pool . . ."

I enter into particulars. She doesn't listen. She attaches no importance to all that.

"And you, aren't you horribly bored?" she whispers suddenly.

"No, not at all. Being with him is kind of a test. One must . . ."

"A test?"

"No. Never mind. (A silence.) By the way, he didn't mention you once all day."

"Obviously. He's convinced we are lost forever."

Her laugh. My laugh. My silence.

"And how's the library?"

"Strange. It's been so long since we pored over books like that. We'd meant to come and see you two, but Ze'ev was cramming. Examination fever's got him. It's after ten now and we've only just left the reading room. We were the last."

"And how's Jerusalem?"

"Odd. Such a scholarly town."

"You won't be able to walk around barefoot here."

Her laugh. Silence.

(Very low) "You know, the child looks like you. All his features. When I saw him this morning I was moved. . ."

Her silence.

"D'you hear me?"

"Yes."

Her face tilted back. Her feet. The beautiful deep-set eyes. Her desire to cut this conversation short. The neighbours in the passage, waiting to go back to their beds. The stars in the sky through the window. The feverish child upstairs. This genius of mine to make a nuisance of myself, to drag out this conversation with her only so that I may not lose her. To ask pointless questions, mystifying her. The neighbour bursting into the room at last, turning and twisting about me like an animal in despair; the call cut off.

A Stroll in the Night

I do not return to the flat but go out and up the hill. I cross a pile of building equipment, scramble up a sand heap, veer around a lime pit, climb the steep track till I arrive at a clearing where heavy tractors and bulldozers stand in a frozen jumble. I am standing in front of the silent scaffolding of the Jerusalem museum.

I am the unseen architect, the nightly architect of the Jerusalem museum. Nearly every night I come for an inspection, to check on its progress.

Regretfully I must admit: progress is rather slow.

Swiftly I climb the ladder of the big crane. My feet race up the iron bars, nimbly I swing myself into the mechanic's cabin, slide into his seat.

My night post, confronting Jerusalem.

Pencils of light at the university, the National Convention Centre in gloom. The urge of the heavy blocks of government offices on their hillside to career down the slope and into the road. The houses of Jerusalem scattered over the hills, fading out one by one. My own quarter, Neveh-Harim, is asleep too. All its houses are dark. There is my house, in darkness, the window of my room, the hall window, the window of the kitchen where Zvi sits and thinks.

The museum watchman and his puny, bandy-legged dog saunter

across the clearing. They halt. The watchman yawns out loud. Would it occur to him that high over his head, now, at this hour of the night, someone is watching him?

Moonlight turns the soft breeze into poetry.

I am getting bored—

I try to pinpoint the lodgings of Haya and Ze'ev. Slowly, thoroughly, I attempt to reconstruct their neighbourhood, guided by the street lamps. I discover darkness. Perhaps they have already gone to bed. If they knew their little boy was burning with fever they wouldn't sleep with such wanton abandonment.

Bad habits those kibbutz people have—to cast their children off on others and sleep in peace.

One hundred and three. He won't die. What children did a few hundred years back, Yahli can do as well. Struggle through by himself. Me, I'm not a doctor.

This fool moon dangling over Jerusalem like a yellow stone. It floods the sky, floats towards me, fills me with sweet sadness.

A final glance at my quarter. Suddenly to discover that the whole flat is lit up, the windows wide open.

Has Zvi gone out of his mind?

Quickly I slide down the ladder, sneak past the watchman dozing beside a tractor, look at the dog who is looking at me, startled.

Down, sprinting over the track, tearing up the stairs, hurtling through the door.

It is true. The flat is bathed in light and Zvi is kneeling on the floor.

The child is still asleep, despite the bright light.

He has only turned over on his side and kicked the blanket on to the floor. His breathing comes with a kind of wheezy snore now, pervading the whole flat.

Good Lord! What's happened? I stoop over Zvi with the last of my patience for him.

The serpent has escaped.

Escape

White-faced, Zvi stands before me as one condemned to death.

In his boredom and solitude, in the darkness I had imposed on him, he had begun to fool with the box. He had wanted to take a peep and see whether this serpent of his didn't by any chance belong to some rare species. He found it coiled in a corner of its

70

prison, and identified it regretfully as nothing but a plain and common viper. Owing to his feeble eyesight he hadn't closed the box properly. He had shoved it aside and then heard a rustle, and had spied the snake wriggling on its way out of the kitchen.

Now he is looking for it—

We are both looking for it—

What a number of nooks and crannies there are in such a small flat as mine.

We continue with our search till after midnight, in vain. I even woke up Yahli and held him in my arms, sleepy and hot, while Zvi ransacked the bed.

My legs succumb.

Anyway, the snake may well have escaped through one of the windows.

Zvi searches on, with his failing eyes, his blindness.

I am nodding off on the couch, though only after having inspected it a thousand times.

Amazingly, Yahli isn't awakened by the light and noise. When he does wake and asks for water, it is only due to his high fever. (I took his temperature again: it was a little over one hundred and three.)

At two o'clock I say the hell with it, and go to sleep beside the child.

Zvi falls asleep as well.

I leave all the lights burning.

A Dream

I had a dream and saw a field in dazzling light, and tiny drops of rain like a vapour moving upon its face. And I, in working clothes, walking in a straight line along the open furrows. Beside me, astride the seat of an old rattling tractor, there is Arieh wrapped in his filthy sheepskin coat.

Slowly the tractor lumbers along.

"You back at the kibbutz?" yells Arieh, trying to make himself heard above the roar of the engine.

"Yes."

"Yeah? Couldn't make it at the university?"

"What do you mean?" I say indignantly. "I've come back to finish my thesis. I can't get any peace in town. My place has become an open house."

He does not reply, is bent over the wheel of the tractor, his damp coat glistening in the radiant light.

Amazing, this full sun bathing the whole field in light. A sun facing us, directing our progress.

"Ever since Haya's death . . ." I whisper to myself and am filled with sadness.

"Yes, poor Yahli," he shouts to me.

"Still, I fail to understand why they have attached him to me. Why have they made me his guardian? I agreed to take him for three days and I've already had him for three months. I'm like a nursemaid to him."

Arieh does not answer, or maybe he doesn't hear.

The field lies streaked with furrows. The tractor rises and descends like a ship at sea. Thorns sprout among the furrows, hairy, juicy thorns soaring and blooming, queer, heavy with greyish fronds.

I say to Arieh: "What now? Have they stopped harrowing the soil around this kibbutz?"

"But we grow thorns now."

"Grow thorns?"

"Sure. The townsfolk are getting interested in thorns, don't you know. They plant them in their backyards, put them in vases."

I stop, worn out by the trudging over ploughed furrows. Absent-mindedly I bend over a thorn to look at it more closely. I wonder whether Yael has studied this genus. The tractor stops too. Arieh slips down, extinguishes the engine and comes over to have a look.

Such instant silence. Nothing but the whisper of the mist.

I stammer: "I know something about thorns. I had a girl once who specialized in them. . ."

Now Arieh applies himself to the thorn as well, and suddenly he picks up a short stick; he prods it among the grey fronds sparkling with tiny drops of mist. He crushes the leaves with his stick, and a yellowish sap oozes from the cuts. All at once it seems as though the leaves are shaking, the plant is agitated, something stirs the sun.

I jump up.

"A snake! Be careful!"

Arieh smashed the snake's head with a single blow. He lifted the twisting carcass on his stick and raised it in in the sun.

"A viper," he said calmly, and without even looking at me he cast the bloody carcass against my clothes. And laughed. "So what? It's dead isn't it?"

Morning

At last I wake up. I open my eyes. It is unbearably hot, a heat wave. The room is in chaos, the windows wide open. The pale electric light evokes the memory of last night. Yahli is sitting on the rug in his laundry-frayed nightgown, playing laboriously. He has arranged all his tractors in a line, and from time to time he pushes them an inch or two forwards. The tank is stationed in front of the procession with its gun aiming straight at the tractors. Instead of defending, it threatens.

I jump up from the bed, bend over him, look silently at his train of tractors. He lowers his head. His face is puffy, his eyes screwed up and heavy lidded, yellow gum collected in the corners. I touch his forehead with my lips. No doubt about it, he still has a fever. I tell him to open his mouth.

A swollen throat.

I ask him whether he is hungry.

He shakes his head.

"A soft egg at least, and a slice of bread?"

He shakes his head.

"Do you have a pain somewhere?"

No reply.

"Isn't your throat sore?"

No reply.

"Yahli!"

He raises his eyes.

He looks like a little hedgehog with those screwed-up eyes. The pinkish calves of his legs are exposed under that funny nightgown of his.

I say: "If I should tell Haya and Ze'ev about the way you're behaving they'll refuse to take you back. Then what'll we do with you? We'll have to leave you on the street with the street kids."

I have poured oil on the flames of his silence. The more so as my words do not make any impression on him. The street does not frighten him, and he is longing to be with other children. He bites his lips.

"A drink at least."

No reaction.

"I'm getting you a glass of milk."

"No!"

At last. One word.

"What then?"

"Water," he whispers.

I am losing my temper. I have done my duty, haven't I? I throw him a severe look and order him back to bed.

Mutely he obeys, leaves his tractors and climbs back into bed, rolls himself up in the blanket.

The bedclothes smell of urine and sweat. Here and there the sheet is stained dark with blood.

I hold out a glass of water at arm's length.

He sits up, takes the glass and, gripping it in one hand, he gulps. The water trickles on to his gown, the bed, the floor. The place is like a bear garden. Clothes strewn everywhere, chairs overturned, toys littering the floor, getting underfoot. The floor is filthy. The light is still on.

To extinguish the light, at least . . .

Such heat. The dry air parching the nostrils. I walk around, bitter, barefoot, lightly dressed. But for the child I'd go about naked.

I ought to wake Zvi.

I open the kitchen door and find Zvi gone. He must have escaped through the balcony door and down the tree. And left a mess behind. He has made himself breakfast and added to the pile of dirty dishes in the sink. The door of the refrigerator stands open. He has left me a note, written on the marble slab beside the sink: "Sorry about the mess. Have gone to health-insurance office to arrange things. Haven't found the snake. Must have left for the wide open spaces by now. If Yael comes tell her not to forget me. Tell her to come and see me. I may come by again tonight to see if she's back."

How on earth did he manage to disappear without me noticing.

I touch what is left of the bread. To judge by the dried surface he must have left at dawn.

Third Call

The woman downstairs calls me to the telephone.

I enter a bright, spotless flat, go to the bedroom smelling of talcum and scent. Their baby, immaculate in white, regards me severely from under his canopy, looking like a high priest.

I pick up the receiver.

"Yes?"

"That Dov?"

"Yes. Hallo, Ze'ev."

"How did you pass the night?"

"Fine."

"And where's Yahli?"

"Upstairs. Playing with his toys."

"How is he?"

"Fine. Bearing up like a hero."

"Not crying for us?"

"No. No. What gives you that idea? Would you like to talk to him?"

"If it isn't too much trouble."

"Of course not."

I lay the receiver down, cast a stern look at the infant who is watching my movements, troubled. Softly I leave the flat, climb the stairs, pick Yahli up from the bed and, just the way he is, hot, a bit sleepy, I carry him down.

"Your daddy wants to talk to you."

He raises a pair of weary eyes to my face. He feels heavy in my arms. With one hand I hold him, with the other I pick up the receiver and place it against his little ear.

"Here's Daddy now," I say.

Yahli listens. Then he emits a long-drawn-out "Ze—ev."

And is silent.

The faraway father mumbles into the silence. I do not understand a single word, and I doubt whether Yahli does. All the same he listens, his lashes drooping over his eyes. Apparently they are asking him, there in the distance how he is, what he's been doing how he's behaving. Yahli does not utter a syllable. His father's mumble begins to sound cross. He repeats the same question again and again. And then Yahli replies with a kind of curious composure: "Yes."

And a short time later he says softly: "All right."

And removes the receiver from his ear.

I believe he has difficulty speaking. His throat is sore, blocked, for otherwise he would have shouted at his faraway father, would have screamed for help.

I take the dangling receiver. The child is still in my arms.

"Not much of a talker, is he?" I laugh.

"No . . . no," a worried, nervous cackle. "You must have a way with children. Such peace and self-command, Yahli's . . ."

"And you, how are you? How's the midnight oil?"

"Piles of books. We're never going to make it. It's a good thing Haya's still keeping her nerve. I gave up hope long ago."

I try to console, encourage him.

"And you needn't trouble to call if you're busy."

The man grows confused.

"It's that we feel uneasy about it. To be exploiting you so. Just abandoning him to you. . ."

"Would you call that 'abandoning'?" I answer unperturbed.

"Oh, no, I didn't mean . . . We're very grateful to you. We'll come and fetch him tomorrow, right after the examinations."

"No. That isn't necessary. I'll bring him myself."

(Tomorrow evening I shall be walking over the hills of Jerusalem by myself. I shall come to them and I shall say: The child is no longer.)

"Thanks, Dov. Thanks a lot, really."

Yahli is asleep in my arms. I return the receiver to its cradle, leave the room quietly, smiling on my way out at the baby who is like a high priest. The baby is startled, and without any reason it bursts into a piercing wail.

The mother comes running, folds back the canopy, lifts the baby and hugs it against her chest. We stand there confronting each other, each with an infant in our arms.

I whisper: "Thank you."

She nods, looks inquisitively at the child in my arms. She is quite obviously eager to be told a little about him.

And so, standing there like that, I tell her about his parents, their examinations, his illness.

"Did you tell his parents?"

"No."

"That's the spirit. No need to have them worry. Do you want any medicines?"

"No, thanks. I have a drawer full of them at home. I'm not going to miss a chance to get rid of them."

She chuckles. Her baby starts screaming again. I take my leave. Slowly I climb the stairs.

In the Dim Flat

From where this peace of mine?

I resolve to fight the heat. I make the flat airtight, close the shutters, the doors, the windows, darken the place, stuff up cracks and crevices. I suppose the viper must have departed by now. I rake up all the tractors, the ploughs, the misshapen peasants, and dump them in a corner, introduce some order into the gloom. I light the desk lamp, lay out my thesis and try to concentrate.

But what can I do? The logical contradiction lies exposed before me, plain and unmistakable.

I bite my nails in despair, feel an urge to cry. Then I sweep the papers away, take off shirt and vest, place some sheets of blank paper before me and, half-naked, running with sweat, I start preparing test papers for my pupils.

It is my habit to hold a test regularly once a week. And I am already laying in a store for the coming term.

I work rapidly. First I write down the answers, and only then do I match them with questions and exercises. How many anxious hours my pupils will have to go through, tensely chewing their pencils, grappling with problems that I create here with a single stroke of the pen, in the half light, to the rhythm of the child's harsh breathing.

At noon I am pierced by a furious hunger. I go to see what is left in the refrigerator and find the shelves bare. I pull on a shirt, take a basket, glance at Yahli who has buried his face in the pillow, and go out into the fierce yellow day, its incandescent air dancing before my face.

The thorns covering the hill near my house do not stir, stay frozen in their ugliness.

Once I told Yael: "If you'd only tear out and study the thorns by my house. . ."

But she replied gravely: "What is there to study? They're all common Syrian briers."

And because they are common, because they are thick over every path, my legs, dragging to the grocer's, get scratched.

The streets are lifeless. The men are at work, the women and children hiding from the heat. Cats lie prostrate on the doorsteps, looking as though poisoned.

The rumour that I have a sick child on my hands has already circulated as far as the grocery store.

"Such kindheartedness," says the woman at the store. "And when'll we have the pleasure of seeing you with one of your own?"

I buy five bottles of fruit juice, milk, bread and honey, and I leave.

Outside it is an absolute wasteland. The cats, too, have now disappeared. Again I walk between houses, over thorny paths. The sky is reduced to a turbid haze. A blast of heat comes from the sweltering mountains.

And then for an instant, as I am plodding up the track, there is a breeze. A Jerusalemite breeze, cool, coming out of nowhere, ruffling my shirt, fanning my brow.

I stand rooted to the spot, every limb frozen, till the breeze is past and gone.

I enter my twilight flat, prepare myself a meal, drink incessantly, inane thoughts coming into my head there by the table. Afterwards I go and look at Yahli who is holding the slipping blanket tight in his little fists.

If at least I could figure out this disease, I could play my cards then. Yet I have no illusions. He is not dangerously ill. No doubt it is only one of those wayward children's diseases.

In any case, I am waiting . . .

I rouse him from his sleep and steer him—a cross, unwieldy body—to the lavatory. He stands for a long time in front of the bowl till at last he produces a thin squirt. Then he returns to bed. I force a spoonful of honey into his mouth and cover him up.

My heart leaps with bliss when I see his burning face, smooth, shaped like hers, her face of old, as though falling in love again. Pacing the hot room, my movements soften, my heart beats hard. I strip myself of my sour-smelling clothes, fill a glass with ice cubes, drag the big armchair over to the bed, find some trashy book and sit down. Occasionally I run my eyes over the printed lines, now and then I sip a few drops that have melted in the glass.

Whenever he wakes I say: "Some cold water, Yahli?"

And gently I raise my cool glass to his lips.

And if the strong and clear daylight clamours at me with little daggers through the cracks in the shutter then I, in my darkness, am ready to yield an account at any hour, and be it the very worst, and be it demanded of me through a telephone call.

A Possible Call

"Yes?"

"Hallo, Dov. How are things? See, we have found a minute to call you after all."

"Things are rough."

"What's the matter? Grown tired of it?"

"No. Worse. The child's fallen ill."

"The child? Ill? You don't say! What's wrong with him? Why didn't you tell us?"

"I didn't want to bother you."

"What do you mean! What's wrong with him?"

"You've thrust a sick child on me. He was ill to start with. You didn't warn me. I'm not used to children, after all . . . I'm not his father. It seems he had diphtheria or something. . ."

"Diphtheria? Dov, that can't be true. The doctor must have made a mistake. Why didn't you call us?"

"It all happened so fast. I was thinking of the child, not of you. Besides, I had to get him to a hospital fast."

"Hospital? Dov, is he in a hospital? What's it all about Dov? What happened? This is terrible! Why didn't you say something? And what if we hadn't called. . ."

"But I was just about to go and look for you."

"Dov, are you out of your mind? He is our child. . . We were here all the time. . ."

"I thought it was nothing serious. I thought, a cold or something. I didn't want to keep you from your studies."

"Keep us from our studies? How can you say such a thing, Dov? He is our son! Where is he?"

"But he isn't . . . He is . . . Don't you see . . . Gone . . ."

"How gone? How gone, Dov? Dov . . ."

"But he is . . . I'm terribly miserable myself."

"Gone . . . Dov, Dov!" (The pleading, the clinging to my name as though it were God's.) "In God's name . . . Dov, what do you mean? Dov—Dov—What—what happened? How's it possible?"

And half an hour later . . .

The bursting into hospital, assailing the nurses, the doctors.

The meeting face to face.

Her wonderful, crushed beauty.

They at my feet, I at theirs. Clinging to each other. The large hospital windows open to the wind. Jerusalem which shall be quiet and peaceful. Which shall be witness.

The wonder of their not letting me go, of their never being able to let me go now. They would cleave to me then, surround me, as though their child were in me, of me.

Would take me for their son.

Because love—of love I have despaired.

A Flood of Tears

The child mumbles something, wakes. He sits up in bed, wipes his red eyes, licks his dry lips. The sheets are damp. A faint smell of urine floats through the room. The day is beginning to fade. Suddenly he bursts out crying, stops, gathers strength, stands up in bed and starts crying again in earnest. From the depth of his heart he wails, inconsolable. He asks for his father, his mother. He remembers them all now. His face is swollen, his eyes smudged, his voice raucous.

He calls out into the twilight.

He has dashed the tank I bought him to the floor, and the gun has come off. He leaves the bed and starts walking about the room in his bare feet, hot, weeping. He kicks his tractors. He wants his mother. His mother and no one else. Where is Mummy? He refuses to let me touch him. When I do, he screams. Floods of tears well out of his eyes, on and on. He is a bundle of misery and grief. He hurts all over. His throat aches, and so does his little finger, here, this one. (Why his finger of all things?) He wants to go back to the kibbutz. He wants to go home. Passionately, right now, he wants to go, to take home his bitterness and pain. He goes to the front door, which is locked. He cannot reach the lock. He comes back into the room and without looking at me he drags a chair towards it with the last of his strength. He climbs up and starts rattling the handle. He wants to run away from here, run straight for the kibbutz, just the way he is, with his illness, his fever and his funny nightgown.

When he realizes that the door here is locked he climbs off the chair and starts kicking it with his bare toes.

And I, sole witness of the scene, sit low in my chair, my head in my hands, motionless, listening, sad in the darkness, waiting for the child to calm down, for his strength to fail him. I hear the last sobs changing to a whimper, see him returning to bed, climbing in, wrapping himself into his ravaged blanket; sense the drowsy note that creeps into his whine.

Then I rise softly from my chair to restore order. I remove the chair from against the door and return it to its place. Carefully I adjust the blanket over the child, who lies watching me with tranquil eyes. I bend down, gather the tractors strewn over the floor, pick up the little tank and even go around looking for the detached gun that has gone astray somewhere, under the bed perhaps.

Something gleams in the dark, flashes past me, whisks across the rug and vanishes beneath the wardrobe.

Zvi's viper.

Still here?

At once I tear all the shutters open, the windows, the doors. The last rays of the sun break over me, set me afire. A slow wave of heat fills the room.

Zvi, Once Again

At ten o'clock in the evening Zvi appeared, walked over the threshold and was standing by my side before I had noticed him. He looked tired, worn, his shoulders sagging, a sheaf of crumpled health insurance forms in his hand. All day he had shuttled from one office to another. Before he had time to open his mouth I pounced upon him, choking with fury. "Your snake . . . It's still here . . ." He was not surprised. On the contrary, his lips crinkled into a smile, as at the memory of some nice little creature. But I seized him by the shirt, savagely, tearing it almost. I preached him a furious sermon, not mincing words. About his selfishness I spoke, about his serenity that drove me mad. He'll be resting in hospital while I have a serpent rampaging through my flat. Because I won't be able to find it, I won't even look for it. Because here he and Yael are turning my flat into a field, she with her thistles and he with his snakes. If they want to love nature, let them go and love it where it belongs— outside. I complained about my thesis which had run aground, because I had no peace. They were trampling it underfoot. I came to live in a quiet neighbourhood, on a bare hillside, and they all use it as a transit station. And each passing guest takes the trouble to leave me something: a thorn, a grasshopper, a child, a serpent or some other animal. . . All that time Zvi stayed motionless, afraid his shirt would come off in my hand. When he saw that I was through he gave me a sad smile. Haltingly he promised to find the little viper right away. It only wanted to find a snug corner for the winter. And, anyway, it wasn't that dangerous. All those terrifying things you heard were nothing but fairy tales. A snake will never attack you. Only if you step on it, or try to catch it, only then will it rear its head to sting. And by the way, its sting wasn't fatal. A serum was discovered long ago, and he was prepared to write out its formula on a piece of paper, if he had one, because for several days now he had been going around without a scrap of paper on him, whereas his pockets were full of pens. Look, this very morning he couldn't find a piece of paper to write me a note on and had been forced to write on the marble. And oh yes, about that note, have I seen Yael? He had called the lab five times and hadn't found her in. How come she wasn't yet back? Wasn't I worried?

He shivered suddenly.

Slowly I released him, my hand dropped to my side. I sat down, folded my arms, gave him a hopeless look.

Amazing how he ignores the child's presence, as though it did not exist. He turns to the bed as though it were empty, hunts through it sniffing for traces as though he were in a forest. All his senses are roused, tensed. Yet his eyes betray him. Does he see anything? Can he distinguish between objects?

Now and then he raises his fair, vigilant face, fixes his gaze on me to say quietly: "Look, I'll find him. Just make yourself easy and go about your affairs, just work away peacefully at your thesis, I won't disturb you."

And with a sleepwalker's thoroughness he goes about turning up and turning over everything that is still standing.

After an hour of that I make him some coffee to fortify him a little. I also cut him some slices of bread and honey, certain that he has not eaten all day. ("Yes," he smiles guiltily, "I simply forgot.") He has not yet grasped the rules of health-insurance officialdom. He feels as though he has been floundering in a jungle all day.

Once more we sit facing each other in the little kitchen, over the empty coffee cups. We sit in the dark, for the light hurts his eyes. He tries to engage me in conversation, rouse my interest; tries to explain, for instance, in popular terms, how they are going to operate upon his eyes tomorrow. I am perfectly aware that he hasn't the energy, hasn't the will, to go on searching for the little snake.

He is so tired . . .

Despite the coffee he is already half asleep, and still he promises that right away, in a minute, he will go and search, and even if he does not find the little snake now, then tomorrow he will rise at the break of dawn and catch it. Because he won't kill it. Certainly not, there isn't any need to kill it.

Only let me not forget to tell Yael about him. Let her please come to visit him in hospital. He must tell her. . .

His drowsiness makes me drowsy too.

The flat is wide open. Even the front door stands ajar, ready to admit the night. Yet the air is stagnant, not a breath stirring.

The moon is down and the windows reveal a harsh darkness against fierce stars. The pale university buildings have come to rest beyond the wadi.

Zvi is lost in silence. He has removed his glasses and placed his fingers over his eyes. Suddenly: "The heat wave's over."

And is silent again.

And looking out I see a high tuft of cloud.

I rise and go to bed.

Another Dream

Another dream. Without women. A heavy, dim, tangled dream. I have, on my own initiative, taken the two classes on a hike through the streets of Jerusalem, along the border.

They are ambling slowly, desultorily along, pausing beside shops, straying into doorways, disappearing down alleys, crossing the border. By the time I arrive at the centre of town only a few remain with me.

There is a river flowing through Jerusalem. Instead of the main thoroughfare there is a river: green, wide, slow moving, its banks overgrown.

The river swells and I and the few left with me trudge along the muddy banks, picking our way among the tall rushes. A powerful sun shines down upon us.

Suddenly they are waving at me from the other bank, waving and yelling. All the pupils who were lost in the alleyways are assembled there into one merry crowd. They have found the right way.

I have gone astray, apparently.

They continue shouting.

The few that were with me tear off their clothes and spring into the water, swim across the river. I alone remain on the shore, hesitating, timid, slowly shedding various articles of dress, tortured, taking off my shoes.

And they, all of them on the other shore, are rudely cheering me on, jeering, for the sun is setting, darkness descends, the river is growing black in the gathering shade. . .

Dawn

Morning? And who's here? And this terrible uproar in the flat? It's as though the kitchen's being broken up and a shiver runs down my spine; and Zvi, gaunt, lanky, is walking about in his underclothes and gestures at me: Hush!

The dawn is wreathing a lattice on the window.

In the hall the little snake lies coiled, watchful, its tiny eyes glittering like pinheads. From time to time it raises its head, twists from one wall to the other.

I whisper at Zvi, furious with rage: "Kill it. . . . Damn you . . . What're you waiting for?"

But Zvi defies me, does not even listen. Tensely, stubbornly, he applies himself to the problem of the snake, blocks its path, stretches out his long arms. But at the last moment the snake slips away, glides swiftly past my feet, twists into the room, streaks from wall to wall.

Zvi swears.

I swear at Zvi.

Quietly, softly in his bare feet, Zvi pursues the snake. He moves around bent, half blind, throws both arms at the snake, grabs its tail and lifts it. But the snake slips between his fingers, drops on to the slim feet and fawns upon them, laps them and bites. Zvi recoils, winces with pain. With an impulse beyond his control his heel comes down upon the little skull and crushes it. A few drops of blood ooze on to the rug.

Out on the Road

Zvi is shaken.

Though he must know the formula of the poison that the dead viper has injected into his blood, he is overwrought. His face has drained of colour. He bends over and examines the spot where he was bitten with a probing finger, mumbles to himself, "What've I done?" and tries to squeeze some blood out of the shallow wound. But the blood does not come. It is as though no blood flows through his body at this early morning hour.

"Must go up the road . . . find a car. . ."

He thinks aloud, his face breaking out in sweat. He bows over the viper's carcass, fumbles with its crushed skull. Then he stands up, goes to the kitchen to put his trousers on, drapes his shirt carelessly over his shoulders and turns to go. He encounters me and his eyes narrow with an unknown hatred.

"But you could have caught it . . . You . . . It passed right by you."

He binds his handkerchief tight around his ankle in order to halt the poison coursing through his body, and then he is up and feeling his barefoot way to the door.

I look at him in silence, completely enervated. Wonderingly, my eyes linger on the windows suffused with grey light. I am wrapped up in myself, musing still lost in the night's dreams.

Zvi slips out without a word. I follow him to the front door and breathe in the fresh air, return absent-mindedly to the kitchen and trip over his sandals. I pick them up. Long, frayed sandals, road-weary.

In this still hour it seems as though I am alone in all the world.

At last I rouse myself and go out, still in my night clothes and slippers, take the short cut across the hill, climb rapidly in pursuit of the tall figure limping among the rocks. I touch his back.

"Your sandals . . ."

He seats himself on the nearest rock, throws the sandals on the ground before him and tries to edge his feet into them. He fails. He is so weak.

I kneel down in front of him, take his bare feet and push them one by one into the sandals, fasten the straps. The health-insurance papers have slipped out of his pocket, a white patch on the earth. I gather them up and hand them to him.

Without a word he continues on his way. I do not know why he limps. I saw nothing but two reddish spots and a faint swelling on his foot.

A breeze, and I shiver; nowhere but in Jerusalem could a man dressed in pyjamas and slippers saunter casually over a bare hill in the middle of town.

At last we arrive at the road.

Zvi stretches down at once upon the hard surface of the road, spreads his arms wide, bends his head back in pain, lies looking at the sky. I approach him, stand over him, look down at his eyes twitching near my feet. A line of hills closes us in.

What on earth would a car be doing, travelling around Jerusalem at this hour?

I ask him how he feels.

He speaks of nausea rising in his throat.

He's grown squeamish apparently.

He bites his lips, beads of perspiration appear over his upper lip. Suddenly he shuts his eyes, sits up, vomits over the dusty side of the road which is sparkling with dew. Well, what can I do for him?

Now, in this town of the dead. The nearest public telephone is a mile away, and it is out of order at that.

I tell him, softly but definitely: "You know you are not going to die, Zvi."

There is no reaction from him.

The museum stands out gloomily, its empty windows gaping. How long does the thing take to build?

On Zvi's request I undo the handkerchief and tighten the knot. His foot is pale, bloodless.

Suddenly, tears in his eyes, in his so clear eyes.

Dear me, is that behaviour fit for a Nature Lover?

I squat beside him, the hem of my pyjama trousers trailing in the dust. I believe the time is ripe for a little moralizing: "So that's the end of playing around with vermin, snakes, scorpions."

He is silent, does not listen, looks through me as though I were air, as though I didn't exist. But the tears dry in his eyes, he turns over on his stomach, presses his body against the road, his fingers claw at the asphalt, he whispers to himself.

". . . and it's years since I slept with a woman . . ."

I am confounded, stand frozen to the spot. I look at the figure burrowing its face in the road. Slowly I straighten up, acting as though I had not heard. I start walking along the roadside, praying for a car.

At last, the distant drone of a car from beyond the hills.

I rush to stand in the middle of the road.

A military van bearing down upon us. I wave my arms like mad, my whole body yearning in its direction.

The van squeals to a stop, nearly overturning. The driver jumps down from his cabin and is revealed as a little soldier, pale and sad-eyed, his faded uniform hanging loose on his body.

I tell him . . .

He drinks in my words, all of him agog to be the good Samaritan.

Meanwhile Zvi has already scrambled up, heaved himself into the back of the van and lain down flat on its floor, his head on his crossed wrists.

The little soldier watches him respectfully. A moment of silence. Then he bolts for his cabin, starts the engine, and before I have time to say a word to Zvi the van has disappeared beyond a turn in the road.

I drag myself back across the road, down the mud track.

And Jerusalem, behind me and ahead, is silent once more.

Down the Hill

I lack a feeling for nature, claims Yael, and perhaps she is right. Nature in detail bores me. Before I have turned to watch I am past it, have already crushed it underfoot. I am incapable of loitering. It seems senseless to me. I have offered my opinion of nature lovers.

Yet now, having sent off Zvi, walking down the hill, across the short cut that leads from the road to my house, at the break of day, the light misty, now I cannot hurry, must linger. Simply because I am still in my slippers, because I am excited, because I am reaching out to touch bare soil.

And slowly as I slip from rock to rock, dewdrops trickle over my hands, thistle buds open before my eyes, flowers caress, moisten my skin. How then can I avoid noticing the rustling insects, the tiny winged things, the whisper of a million miniature cells quickening into life, the joy of the delicate grass and lichen at gaining back their green extinguished by the night.

And all this on the hill by my house.

And the sky thawing before my eyes. Streaks of light rising and fusing its blackness into a soft grey.

Jerusalem in its bareness, its rocks, its secret fertility.

And all this in slippers, on the hillside, with light wandering steps, wide eyes, with the shiver of the tiny wet thorn prickles. Yes, the cool of a morning in autumn. Autumn has come today. Autumn.

Only in this hushed world can I say it. Yes, I slept with Haya once. Once in autumn. Some time after we had started our army service I was granted a sudden, unasked-for leave. Someone's mistake. Alone I left the camp, I alone of all my group. I spent many hours travelling to the kibbutz, and when I arrived it was already dusk. A cold wind swept the fields. I drifted among the kibbutz houses, a sad-eyed soldier, a new recruit in his ill-fitting uniform. On one path, between lawns, she met me and took hold of me suddenly; frightened, in need. I have said so: it was autumn. We went and lay on a bed in a room whose door stood open, people passing to and fro continuously.

But I cannot speak of it. Tears are choking me.

The Stories

I found Yahli awake, bent over the snake's carcass. Curiosity had won out over fear. He was looking at the crushed skull straight into the little dead eyes.

I have an idea that in time he'll grow up to be a nature lover.

I fetched a broom and swept the carcass out of the house and up against a rock. Wherever I went, Yahli followed. Nothing remained but a dull bloodstain encrusted in my rug.

The crisis had passed. The puffiness of Yahli's face had abated, the redness in his throat dwindled to a single spot, his temperature dropped. His appetite had come back.

He ate two slices of bread and honey, munched some chocolate, drank tea, then went back to sleep.

I sat down at my desk, spread out my thesis papers. In this deep morning silence, I thought, I might achieve something.

At last I fell asleep.

Two hours later we were both woken by the roar of a tractor that had lurched down the hill and began nibbling at some nearby rocks.

Yahli had forgotten about the snake by now. He was hungry again. I gave him two more slices of bread and honey, boiled an egg, sliced a tomato, and dissolved an aspirin into some cocoa to get his temperature back to normal.

Not a crumb left on his plate.

The amazing thing is that I, who never skip a meal, have lost my appetite completely. An ominous burning throbs in my throat.

Little by little the morning passes, a wind-blown morning. Yahli stays in bed, wrapped in his blanket, sleeping and waking, pushing a tractor over the pillow.

I sit at my desk, thumbing through my wretched thesis which is stranded on such an obvious logical contradiction. I have gone over the formulae a thousand times in order to find the mistake, and no mistake has come to light.

Beneath my window the neighbourhood women are singing the praises of autumn.

Yahli is perspiring. The tablets I made him swallow have brought down his temperature completely. His lips are cool, his limbs light and weak. Whenever he drops a tractor to the floor I have to go and pick it up. Relations between us have shifted into a realm of silence. It is as though we had both woken from a shared dream. We need only a few words, brief phrases. Except that I know we shall part tonight, while he believes this is but one more day in our eternity together.

Anyway, I must cure him fast, obliterate all traces of disease. As to mine, each time I give Yahli his medicine I swallow a double dose myself.

Jerusalem is growing overcast. I must switch on the lights in my flat. If I weren't a Jerusalemite born and bred I would say: we are going to have rain.

To be exact, at this very time Haya and Ze'ev are writing their examinations. This selfsame breeze is cooling their bodies, is blowing through the windows of the examination room where bored supervisors are pacing up and down. I imagine Ze'ev biting his pen, all of him bent upon success. Haya is writing leisurely, pensively, sloppily. She relaxes in her chair, her tousled head tilts backwards.

If I were one of those supervisors I would go and stand opposite and keep a severe eye on her.

At noon I prepare a lunch that only Yahli enjoys eating. The dull ache in my throat persists. I have difficulty swallowing, even honey stings my throat.

After lunch I go out (Yahli trailing behind me in his nightgown) to inquire into the destiny of the dead snake. I discover that a swarm of enterprising ants have already hauled most of it away and are now reassembled for a conference over its heavy skull.

I go and ask the tractor driver why he has come to gnaw at my hill. He explains that one wing of the museum complex is going to be erected here. He thinks it will be devoted to the natural sciences—dried plants, fossils, stuffed beasts.

I shall not move out all the same. I am attached to this neighbourhood.

Strangely, I do not think of Zvi but of other matters. Here in the open, in the autumn wind, beside the relics of the snake, I suddenly imagine that the logical contradiction in my thesis isn't all that logical.

I rush home and start rummaging through my papers. Yahli drifts out on to the balcony. What is he looking at? At the clouds. A chain of clouds coming in from the sea.

Still poring over my contradiction, which may not be logical, I am suddenly approached by Yahli, who brings me some books that have been placed among his toys. He hasn't forgotten my erstwhile promise to read him stories.

I put down my papers, take the books, leaf through the pages, look at the pictures, open one at the first page and start reading aloud.

But we run into difficulties almost at once. To begin with, the story is downright stupid. Next, the hard words. On top of that, I do not read properly. Apparently I am supposed to intone the story in a specific manner, one that Yahli is used to. The proper way turns out to be a kind of singsong, each sentence to be chanted on a rising note, up to the final word which not I but Yahli must say, and in a triumphant voice.

As though we were praying . . .

Finally I give up.

I say: "This book is not for us," and fling it straight out of the window. He laughs, delighted by my deed. He fetches the other books, climbs on a chair and throws them all to the autumn winds.

Now I begin a story of my own. I begin a tale of adventure embroiling all the beasts of the forest: a stocky bachelor bear, two old foxes, a wolf, a long-legged deer—they and their wives and children. They go prowling through the forest, eating and drinking and sleeping and waging desperate battles. The majority die all manner of horrible and fearful deaths, and those that survive do not deserve to.

Yahli listens raptly, excitedly, his eyes wide open, swallowing my every word, even the most halting.

Never has he heard such a long and wonderful story.

Not a single chance detail is lost on him. If I have left a wounded animal on one of the forest paths he reminds me of it, that I may tell him what became of it. At several points in the story tears shine in his eyes. His heart goes out in particular to the little wolf cubs doomed to drown in the river, to the rabbits devoured by the fox.

I introduce the vegetable kingdom into the picture too.

Gnarled trees argue with the animals. The rushes anoint a king over them, then rise up in a body to search for water; thorns put their heads together to hatch an insidious plot.

Whenever I pause in my narrative to catch my breath, I feel the child may faint, so great is his suspense.

"Do you like the story? Like it?" I ask him from time to time.

He nods his head, swallows. Unwittingly he has placed his hand on my shoulder, is stroking my hair gingerly. He's positively fallen for me. I put out a feeler to see whether he remembers his parents still.

Yes, he does, but they no longer matter.

It seems to me that he is growing flushed again. I therefore avail myself of his engrossed submissiveness to force down another pill and pour a spoonful of some old and bitter medicine down his throat.

After that I continue. I make up my mind to exterminate every living creature and plant, save one little wolf cub.

Return

At an hour when Jerusalem was hovering between daylight and dark I stripped the child of his nightgown and dressed him in the clothes he had come in. His face was still pale, his eyes sunken and cool. It was as though he had grown up in his three days with me.

It was cold. A great wind blew over the town. Fat clouds hustled each other, merged. Jerusalem changes moods like a snake shedding its skin.

I took Yahli on my shoulders, picked up the suitcase and walked to the bus stop. Perched on his mount, Yahli was straining his eyes at the sky, searching it for stars. When he had found them he said, "Stars," and I realized that in the three days I had learned to make out his childish lisp.

Slowly the bus crept up the hill of the Military Cemetery. Black gravestones lay still in the dusky light, the town flowed backwards, houses dipped and vanished down gullies.

Between gravestones I slumbered, and when I looked up I saw Yahli's eyes fixed on my face. I bade him kiss me. He offered his cheek. I kissed him limply. He talked, something about the stars again. A soft glow lit up the edges of the bus windows when we got off.

Our road lay in darkness. I walked, always with the child on my shoulders, the suitcase in my hand. He held on tightly to my hair, dishevelling it. I strode on rapidly, crossly humming a tune under my breath. Two shadowy figures stopped me suddenly, dislodged the child from my shoulder, took the suitcase. Hands patted me.

"He's sleepwalking already. Yahli's done for him," came Ze'ev's laugh.

I was shattered. The child was in their hands now. I had failed.

She stood beside me, light, thin, open to the night. A jersey flung casually across her shoulders, her feet in sandals. Her clear eyes wide, smiling. Her serenity. She held the child clasped in her arms, his head on her breast.

"How did the examinations go?" I asked with the last of my strength.

He began explaining at length, about the nature of the questions, about their chances. I did not listen. I wanted them to fail, to leave the town.

They dragged me along to their hotel, pressed me into a chair. Then I saw their faces, a bit pale from studying at night. But they were looking at me and at the child in shocked amazement. What did you do to him, what he to you? I rose and glanced in the mirror and saw a haggard face, I touched the bristles on my cheeks. The child was following me with his eyes, still mute.

Now comes the turn of the stories.

I told them, briefly, curtly, rapping out my words. I invented incidents that never were, muddled up the days. I breathed no word of his illness. Yahli sat calmly listening to my lies, cradled in his mother's lap. This little creature without any sense of time who had lain light-headed with fever in my room, what could he do to me? Tell them I'm lying?

I finished. A brief silence followed.

All at once Yahli slipped off his mother's lap, stood up and declared in the face of the world, in a voice clear and sweet: "I was sick."

With a smile I explained about his having vomited, admitted to a slight illness, became mixed up in my timetables. She listened attentively. Ze'ev aghast. I never imagined he loved his son so.

They asked me to stay for supper, they all but beseeched me. But I refused. Yael is expecting me, I lied. Whenever I want to back out of something I place an impatient Yael at a street corner waiting for me.

Though it is early evening still, we are all tired.

I rise to go. They thank me. Their hearts are overflowing. Where would they have been without me. Even she, the never-changing, thanks me in a few brief, dreamy, desultory phrases. Her deep eyes shine with a fleeting compassion. Ze'ev pulls out a banknote uncertainly, wishes to compensate for some of the damage, the expenses, the tank, maybe. I let the note flutter contemptuously to the floor. What? Are they crazy?

At last I make my departure. The street is empty. On the drive back the bus lurches wildly down the steep incline. Gravestones creep, houses pop up on the hills. My eyes close. I all but fumble my way home. There is a light on in the flat? Have I forgotten the light?

It turns out that Yael has come back. She is waiting for me, grey upon my turbulent bed; bruised, her dry hands scratched, reading a book that I left open. Piles of thistles, defined and undefined, are scattered on the floor.

She, too, is startled by my appearance.

"Their child," I whispered, "vomited over your parents."

She smiles, shuts the book, adjusts the pillow, and comes across a little towel stained with the child's blood.

"Blood?" she wondered, yet smiling still.

She will never be beautiful, I thought in despair. I got into bed and lay in my clothes beside her, flung an arm over my eyes and slept.

When I opened my eyes she was no longer in the room. Midnight. The light she had left on hit my eyes. A note by my bed. "Tomorrow at noon." Perhaps she had understood. I undressed and extinguished the light. The child's smell emanated from the pillow; vomit, blood and soap. I inhaled deeply like a father intoxicated with his first child.

Now I remembered having forgotten to find out Yahli's real name.

I did not fall asleep at once. My hand flitting over the dark floor struck a thorn. Once in a mellow moment I had allowed Yael to teach me to identify flora. I tried it out now. Carefully I trailed my finger over the stem till it reached the downy tuft of the pappus. I counted the stamens. It cannot be a safflower, the *Carthamus tinctorius,* since Yael would never take the trouble to pick such a common plant. Nevertheless, in the dark, it felt like a safflower, to wit: "A honey plant, swarming with bees from the early morning hours till noon. Its seeds are ovated, the central ones attached to a pappus that disseminates them far and wide. The peripheral seeds are without pappus, and it is their function to ensure the plant's propagation in its native soil."

A Long Hot Day, his Despair,
his Wife and his Daughter

ANOTHER hot day, he thinks in his sleep and is suddenly filled with anguish. He turns over, burrows his face in the pillow, flings his arms wide and becomes a limp lifeless cross. And without waking he thinks a wordless curse on the sun ploughing the back of his neck with a broad furrow of light.

It is eleven o'clock in the morning.

His wife is long gone. Left the house at six to catch the first bus to Jerusalem for a full day at the university. Like a light bird she has flitted without leaving a trace. Her bed is made, nightdress folded, even the sound of her steps is gone from his mind.

His daughter had blustered about the house at half-past seven, the sweetest time, hour of his true sleep. She had wakened with the ring of an alarm clock, had turned on endless taps, dropped a frying pan in the kitchen, opened and shut the refrigerator again and again. At last, when he had imagined her gone for good, the door of the room had opened softly and she had entered on tiptoe in her school uniform—blue shirt and too-short skirt—to pick up the schoolbooks that he takes from her room to while away his insomnia. Silently she had collected the books and crammed them into her schoolbag. He had lain watching her noiseless movements out of the corner of his eye, impatient to be asleep. Except that suddenly, with that absent-mindedness that comes over her so often, she had begun to hum a tune. Furiously he had stirred between his sheets and she had fled the room at once, shut the door carelessly and vanished.

Their street, a blind alley, is very quiet. He had managed to curl back into sleep again but presently, with the light gaining strength, he had begun to swelter in his bed.

A man like him—forty-two years old, robust, hairy, an engineer with the Water Company. Convalescing and hence idle, sleeping badly at night, by his bed—glasses of water, medicine phials, a few scattered pills. A sweating man who, slowly and with eyes shut, gets rid of the last of his covering. Jacket, trousers and sheet spill about him; naked and bare he wakes.

A few weeks ago his mission to Africa had been cut short due to a false alarm. For nine months he had been employed as a foreign engineer on the construction of a dam some hundred miles south of Nairobi, in a mountain region of mists and forests strewn with green huts. An Israeli and a Dutch company had jointly obtained the technical supervision of the project. The dam, going up at the meeting point of two river beds, was designed to hold back the flood waters and create a reservoir. The National Water Company, with which he had been connected for many years, had offered him the job and he had responded at once, enthusiastically. Besides the promotion gained by supervision over such a large project and the release from a round of futile drills in the Negev, he would come in for a considerable rise in salary, enough to trade in his old car by the end of a two-year contract. Naturally he had not been allowed to take his family along, but what would he have done with Tamara anyway in that bleak mountain region. He had therefore hesitated for a while whether to accept, but Ruth had dismissed all his doubts. His trip would lend new life to old plans: another year at the Jerusalem University in her endless round of studies.

He and the Dutch engineer, a fat and rather lazy bachelor of about thirty-five, had been the only white men in the working village erected on the site. All the rest had been Africans, two or three thousand of them (their number kept changing). There had been a great deal of work and it had had to be done in something of a hurry. Several stages would have to be completed before the wet season set in.

He had found his niche at once.

His store of broken English had been enough to keep up a limited contact with the native foremen and engineers. The rest of his work had been a matter of maps, blueprints and calculations. Because he had been excited about his job and had lived in fear of disasters like the sudden collapse of a construction, he had never allowed a nail to be driven in without preparing a sketch first. The Dutchman used to scoff at such formality, but he had been insistent. In addition, he had always tried to stay within reach of the site and whenever he had been forced to go to Nairobi to order tools or a spare part he had risen at dawn in order to get through his errands in time to be back the same night. He would leave Nairobi when it was dark, speed along a highway that would presently turn into a wide and empty dirt track, tear past sleepy villages, scare unidentified wild animals with the headlights of his jeep and, when reaching the camp late at night, he would not go to bed before he had slipped down to the dam and there, among silent scaffolding and concrete mixers, by the light of a torch and the stars of a tropical sky, inspected the work done that day.

Apart from that he lived in solitude, conceived by him as freedom. His wages were sent directly to Ruth and he would reserve only a small amount of pocket money for himself, since his needs were all supplied on the spot. From time to time the Embassy would send him a parcel of Israeli newspapers, which would lose their sting in a region bordering on the famous jungles.

And, of course, a short letter from Ruth now and then and half a page from Tamara. He, too, wrote seldom. What was there to tell? Each time he would apologize, though no apology was asked for. Sometimes, instead of a letter, he would send a blurred snapshot of himself, down at the dam, on top of the scaffolding, or bent over his plate. One old native labourer used to bring a heavy square English camera to work with him and would photograph everybody, whether they wanted him to or not, then sell them the pictures.

Everything would have gone well, except that one night, back in camp from a little native celebration at one of the villages in the area, he had wakened with a feeling of being strangled. It was as if someone were wedged on top of him and squeezing his throat. It was the same on following nights. Sometimes, without any warning he would wake in pain, lose consciousness for a few seconds, and come to again exhausted, as though rising from the dead. He, who had never been ill.

He had thought the weather was to blame, the winds at night that had suddenly grown cold, heavy with fog. As his temperature stayed normal and in daytime he felt only slight bouts of dizziness, he had waited for it all to blow over. A few days later he had, nevertheless, gone to the African medic and told him. The man had listened full of interest, attentive, had seemed embarrassed, and had at once broadcast the news of his illness through the entire camp. The natives had been puzzled, a little worried, had seemed to take an oddly grave view of the matter. They began to inquire about his welfare, dozens of labourers crowded around him to shake his hand and, with queer grins on their faces, to wish him health. They had liked him, apparently. The Dutchman had suggested that he see a doctor and at last he had indeed gone to Nairobi and seen one, an English doctor. He had been baffled by the English words needed to define the subtlety of his sensations. The Englishman had made light of the whole thing and had prescribed a series of sedatives, which had made him feel drowsy.

The pains had eased somewhat, but his work suffered. He began to rise late and was forced to go back to his hut for a rest after the midday meal. The native medic began to dog his steps, visit him daily, bring him his meals, crouch on the floor by his bed, his first-aid kit at hand, watching him for hours on end. Labourers would stand and peek at him through the windows. One evening the medic had brought along the old man with the camera, dressed in gay working clothes, jeans and faded red shirt. After lengthy explanations it appeared that the old labourer was a former village witch doctor. He had refused to be examined, of course, had laughed. But the old man had not come to examine him at all. He had stood hesitating on the doorstep, looking at him from afar as though afraid of contagion, then had taken a scrap of dried leather from the pocket of his shirt, placed it on the table among the blueprints, and slipped out. That same night, after midnight, he had detected dark spots in his groin. He had been alarmed, had gone to wake the Dutchman, had lost his head. Next morning, wrapped in an army blanket, placed in the back of a van, his suitcases by his side, he had been borne away to a hospital in Nairobi. The hospital, however, proved to be a small old-fashioned outfit, its equipment dating back to the Second World War and suited mainly for the treatment of injuries. They failed to diagnose his case and the Embassy people had advised transferring him south by plane to Dar-es-Salaam, to a new hospital built under the supervision of Chinese experts and inaugurated—a blend of barracks and pagoda —but a few months back.

After several hours of fastidious registration at the reception office, an African doctor had come and taken him under his wing. He was a young man, bespectacled, calm, serious-looking. Though the hospital was only half occupied the doctor had allocated him a bed next to an old dying native.

For three whole days that doctor had not let go of him, had kept at him even at night. He had him undergo dozens of examinations and tests, probed at him with every conceivable instrument, as though having been asked to break in the new equipment. For hours on end he had lain naked on a stretcher, had been tossed about, strong lights directed at him, his wrists tied with electrodes. During the course of lengthy examinations the doctor subjected him to political arguments. He had shown himself to hold extremist views, to hate anything Western, to hate particularly anything to do with whites. Actually he had not argued about his views but had preached them, and in fluent English, detached, unsmiling, as though all this contact with the white body under his hands was a kind of compulsion for him. He considered all white experts dangerous parasites, he grieved for Africa. Of Israel he had never heard, nor wanted to.

The engineer had wished to avoid a dispute. Now and then he tried, with his awkward English, with a puckered smile, to come to the defence of the Western world.

Never had loneliness been so hard to bear. Without a newspaper, a letter, another human being; in a half-empty hospital smelling of new paint, by the bed of a dying African, wheeled across long dim corridors, between landings; the dumb contact with native nurses who spoke no English. The spots, by the way, had vanished, his pains had abated; only a dull fleeting echo at night.

Then the examinations were over. At dusk the doctor entered his room, dressed in a grey jacket, without his white coat and with a somewhat formal air about him, to say that he had been found to be suffering from cancer and that the disease was in an advanced stage. Tomorrow at dawn he would operate upon him. He even showed him a small coloured sketch to explain the nature of the operation. There was no trace of sympathy in his voice, it was just information, flatly delivered. A light rain was falling outside, an unexpected tropical rain. Near them, a soft rattle came from the old man's throat. He heard the doctor out calmly, taking deep breaths. The doctor drew nearer his bed, very dark, very quiet, agile. Outside the darkness began to move in on the windows.

The engineer replied, feverishly, that he refused absolutely to accept the diagnosis. They had made a muddle somewhere. He didn't have cancer, he was convinced of that, and he certainly didn't intend to get on any operating table here. If die he must, he would die at home.

The doctor was stunned, deeply offended. Uncertainly he removed his glasses and began to wipe them, the whites of his eyes showing large. Then he collected himself, spat out a venomous rebuttal, jeered at his conviction, turned, and left the room.

The engineer got up at once, dressed, packed his suitcases and placed them on the bed, went down the staircase and, after a little wandering, found a way out through the garage and escaped into the street. That same evening he sent two long telegrams to Israel—one to the Water Company to ask for a replacement, the other to Ruth to announce his return. To Ruth he wired a whole letter, as she did not even know of his transfer to Dar-es-Salaam. He gave an account of the findings, asked that a bed be made ready for him in hospital, added a long involved love message, and all of it in Hebrew spelled out in Latin script. It cost him eighty dollars but he did not care. The astonished clerk at the post office, awed by such a large sum, had risen to accompany him to the door, shaken his hand, thanked him warmly, as though the post office were a private concern of his. He drifted through the town, found a hotel and took a room. He lay in his clothes, his shoes, without taking off the bedspread, doubled up all night, not moving, not sleeping, freezing with cold. In the morning he returned to the hospital and slipped in with the first shift of nurses. He had thought they wouldn't notice him, but he was stopped at the information desk. It turned out that his refusal to get on the operating table and his subsequent escape at night, which had been discovered when his old African neighbour had died, had raised a scandal. He turned a deaf ear to what they said, to the lecture they wanted to read him. He settled his account and picked up his suitcases. There was nothing now but this longing to go home.

Soon after midday he had his flight ticket to Israel via Addis Ababa in his wallet. He wired the flight number to Ruth and returned to the Embassy to wait around in one of the corridors by a table overflowing with old Israeli magazines. He began digging among the pile, and presently it began to slide and totter towards him, as if trying to snow him under. Suddenly he remembered that he had seen nothing of the town and that soon he would be leaving Africa for good. He got up, deposited his suitcases at the airport, and began exploring the town as though in search of something. As it was he took in nothing. When his eye caught a glimmer of the sea, the Indian Ocean beyond the houses, he began walking towards it in a dream, attracted to the beach, dragging his legs among native huts, a mixture of housing-estate boxes, Arabic arches, minarets of new mosques. Here and there he absent-mindedly entered a courtyard, walked past doors, wrapped in thought, meaning to see how the people lived and then left. After a while he gained a following of children, a flock of starlings trailing in his wake.

Adults, too, came out to watch him. Someone even approached to ask what he wanted but he did not answer and pushed the man away. They were alarmed and the children were warned to stay away from him. A gang of young men, a flock of crows, began to follow him. He drew away from the houses, began walking along the shore, near the water line. He remembers a dun-coloured sea, glazing over with yellow towards nightfall. A light drizzle came down for a few minutes, and then he had also cried a little, an eerie wail forced out of him. The young men closed in on him, peered into his face, made some obscure threat, then left him.

He realized at last that he had long left the town behind. Fields stretched around him and a desert far ahead. He stopped an old lorry driven by a native who for a fee agreed to take him back to civilization, to the airport.

At Addis Ababa there was a telegram from Ruth: "Expecting you. Hospital bed ready. Chin up." For about half an hour he wandered round the lounge, past booths selling cigarettes and drinks. Suddenly it occurred to him that he hadn't bought any presents to bring back from Africa. He crossed over to one of the counters and bought ten identical statuettes: little figurines of a grave African warrior bearing a red-painted shield and sword. Its face looked familiar. Before boarding the plane he managed to send a postcard to the Dutchman, in English: "Unbelievable, but it seems that I have cancer. I return therefore to my land. Regards to our dam. Yours . . ."

His plane touched down at Lydda Airport at half-past three in the morning. He had not slept a wink during the long flight, had sat with his face pressed to the window among shreds of cloud and summer stars. He had been away for nine months.

The airport was completely deserted, only a weary figure moving here and there, a policeman. Ruth and Tamara waved at him from afar. He was surprised to see how Tamara had grown, a whole head. She had grown thinner, too, and prettier, and though only fifteen she was as tall as Ruth. Ruth was in slacks, her hair cut short, her eyes behind new glasses. Yes, they were frightened and unable to hide it. He approached. The customs official did not even turn to him, let him by without a word. They embraced. Actually he did not embrace either of them but pressed them both together against him. And suddenly Tamara burst into tears, a wild ominous wailing that echoed around the empty lounge. A sleepy policeman rose from his seat and ran towards them. It took them a long time to calm

Tamara. At last, abruptly, she was quiet, began even to smile through her tears. Meanwhile a porter had picked up his suitcases. He thought there had been some muddle, but it appeared that Ruth had hired him.

An Israeli night, a summer night flooded with moon. The smell of earth which for months had tasted no rain. They walked to the old car and he insisted on driving, even though utterly exhausted after almost forty-eight hours without sleep. Ruth gave in. He drove slowly, more slowly than he ever had. A faint smell of petrol was seeping through the car, poisonous, intoxicating. Through the windshield the moon seemed about to drop to the horizon, huge and oppressive, just as it had looked on long nights of guard duty when he had been strained to the edge of wakefulness. He thought of words, prepared himself to come to the point at once. But Ruth was trying to divert his attention, prevailing upon Tamara to talk, and the child, sunk into the back seat, at peace now, began a laborious tale of a play at school in which she had acted an important part. He did not hear, was intent upon unfamiliar ill-boding noises in the engine.

Home. Everything was as he had left it. Though it was after four now, they did not go to bed but sat around the table to drink tea. Tamara's chatter lapsed into an obscure mumble. Her head drooped. They sent her to bed, only a child after all. He went into her room to switch off the light and found her curled up in her blankets, her room as always in wild disorder, books and papers littering the desk. He bent to kiss her. She said: "It'll turn out to be nothing, you'll see." But there was fear in her eyes and she drew back from him as though afraid of contagion. Her eyes closed. His heart contracted. His glance flitted over the books. Her *Young People's Encyclopaedia* lay open at the entry "Cancer". In the centre of the page enlargements of cell tissue. He shut the book, extinguished the light.

A quiet Ruth was waiting for him beside a fresh cup of tea. A deep silence over all. Now he wanted to start to tell her about the hospital, but she checked him at once. Not now. Tomorrow. If he must talk, let him talk about something else, about the dam, say. It was nearly five in the morning. He was quite ready to talk about the dam, was wonderfully, burningly awake.

At last they went to their room, prepared for bed. A light morning breeze blew outside. The orange tree stirred beyond the familiar rectangle of the window, laden with shrivelled fruit left unpicked during the winter of his absence.

He said: "Tamara has grown tall, pretty." She said: "She's got suitors already. Once she made me read a note she got from some Danny or Gaddy. We had such a laugh."

"And you with glasses," he whispered suddenly and collapsed on the bed.

Mechanically her hand went up to the frame of her spectacles.

"But you love me like this too."

He put his arms about her. In spite of his abysmal tiredness he intended to be with her, to make love to her if only to prove himself still alive. But she pushed him away lightly, kissed the top of his head, slipped out of her clothes, put on a nightdress, got into her bed. He tried to insist. Perhaps it was the so-familiar room that had kindled his desire, perhaps her bare feet. At last he let go. Anyway, there had been trouble even before his African journey. And now, after two days without sleep, at five in the morning, before entering hospital? He gave in.

She fell asleep at once. He could not sleep. At six he saw the morning at the window. With staring eyes, desperate, he touched his wife: "I'm not sleeping." She woke at once, talked to him with closed eyes: "What's wrong? Pains?"

"Not pains. I can't sleep."

"Your illness?"

"Not just that."

She was silent. Suddenly she sat up, eyes closed, felt for her slippers, went like a sleepwalker to the bathroom, returned with a glass of water and sleeping pills, put them down beside him, fell into bed, curled up and went to sleep. He sipped at the water, left the pills untouched, and did not sleep. Light came bursting through the window, a hot summer day.

Tamara woke at ten. Ruth gave her a note for the teacher: "Dear Sir . . . Tamara's father . . . etc." He was still writhing between the sheets. Not until eleven did the sounds die down and he fell asleep. He slept like the dead for twenty hours. They had to postpone his admission to the hospital by a full day.

Again he underwent the same examinations, though this time the pace was a little hurried. Gangs of doctors and nurses kept coming in and out of his room. An Israeli kind of bustle mingled with the hard light. One of the doctors turned out to be an old acquaintance from his war days who kept scoffing at him and his mysterious aches. "What's all this nonsense," he would grumble and would handle him with pointed irony, as though this whole illness wasn't worth notice. Nevertheless it proved a long affair. They had him in the X-ray room for hours on end, anaesthetized him, were even obliged to perform a "teeny little" operation. To everyone on the staff, to the doctors and nurses, he would say again and again: "Look, I'm not afraid of the truth . . ." But they all made light of his illness. Some queer kind of blood poisoning. One doctor spoke of an ancient African disease mentioned in the travel books. Gradually his mind was set at ease. His friends from the Water Company began to come in droves, ply him with flowers. He would recount the whole story, at length, over and over, would curse the African doctor. Cancer, of all things. Why had the fellow taken it into his head that I have cancer?

When they gave him permission to smoke he was convinced.

"Of course, no cancer," he wrote from his bed, on a postcard in simple English, dripping with sweat, one hot afternoon, to the Dutchman who had stayed by the dam.

He left the hospital after a fortnight. Ruth arrived in the afternoon, shuttled back and forth between office rooms for hours, collected a huge parcel of documents, test results, and his suitcase. She was in a great hurry. Tamara was at her music lesson.

The sudden encounter with the street tumult made him feel weak. He let her drive, sank into the seat beside her, picked up the parcel of documents and began searching through them, silently, feverishly, ripping envelope after envelope, rifling pages and trying to decipher the doctors' wild handwriting; examining X-rays, urine tests, blood tests. At last he gave up, swore loudly that Tamara would have to go and study medicine whether she wanted to or not. From now on he would need an attendant physician. Then he began listening to the engine, fixing his eyes on the world streaming towards them, which Ruth was pushing through with arrogant manoeuvres.

"How the hell are you driving?" he fumed. "They ought to have put you behind bars long ago." But she smiled and absently rushed through a red light. Pedestrians swore at her.

Not far from home, near a barber where he used to go for his haircut, she stopped the car suddenly and bundled him off.

"Get yourself a haircut, my lad. You look like an animal. And with Africa we're finished and done with."

He glanced into the little mirror floating above the wheel. It was true. A huge wild head, hair like a tangle of forest framing a dusky, deep-coloured face. A long mane at the back, adding a softness to his eyes, as though he were an artist. All at once he was sorry to part with his hat.

Ruth herself continued towards the centre of town, hurrying to buy something for supper before the shops closed.

At the barber's he was given a great reception. He told about Nairobi, about the Indian Ocean, about the dam, the Negroes. He had begun to follow a pattern by now, stock tales, leitmotifs. Meanwhile they cut off his locks. Twice they had to sweep around his chair. They cut his hair short, a crew cut "American fashion", as the proprietor himself assured him. Then, a slight unpleasantness when he wanted to pay and found himself without Israeli currency, not even small change, nothing but a few Kenyan shillings. They all laughed. No problem at all. He could pay next time. He was here for good now, wasn't he?

By the time he left it was already dark outside. Winds blew round his cropped head. He approached and found the house in darkness. Ruth hadn't arrived yet, nor Tamara. He did not yet have a key. He tried breaking in through the back door, but everything was locked. He squatted on the porch step. A smell of new-mown grass came from the neighbour's garden. In the street, close by the fence of their own yard, a figure was outlined, a young man, waiting, waiting for Tamara perhaps, moving about nervously. Perhaps belonging to the house across the road, dark as his own.

At last the car appeared with Ruth. And he, concealed by darkness, immobile, watched the woman labouring under two heavy shopping bags. She gave a start of fright when she came up against him in the dark, on the step. For a moment she failed to recognize him. Then she laughed, dropped the bags at her feet, stroked the stubble on his skull.

"They've mown off your last touch of exoticism."

And suddenly she was angry. How could a man let them do such a thing to his head.

The bags yielded an abundance of delicacies. Exquisite cheeses, expensive salami, the best she could lay her extravagant hands on. Except that she had forgotten to buy bread. He helped lay the table, very hungry. They waited a long time for Tamara. At last, tired of waiting, he was going to start by himself when suddenly they heard Tamara's voice floating outside. He went out and saw her sitting on the curb, against a tree, her bicycle sprawled on the road, a guitar beside it, and standing over her the same young male he had seen loitering about before, his arm around the tree now and making it sway gently. From the doorway he whispered: "Tamara?" The boy, startled, said a hasty goodbye. Tamara jumped up, grabbed the guitar, propped her bicycle against the fence and came in.

She looked flushed glowing with excitement.

Before he could reproach her she had burst into loud laughter at the sight of his cropped head. She sat down at the table and began to eat. Ruth made both of them get up and sent them to wash their hands. In the narrow bathroom, crowded together over the wash-basin, he noticed the thin straps of a brassière outlined through the taut material of her shirt.

"Who's that kid?"

"Kid?"

"I mean, that young fellow."

"Oh, just someone from the play."

"What's his name?"

"What's it matter?"

"Come on . . ."

"Gaddy."

"Gaddy who?"

"You don't know him. He's from the top year. He's being conscripted tomorrow."

The guitar became the topic over supper. He plied her with questions: Why had she switched to a guitar all of a sudden, it had been the piano before his trip to Africa, hadn't it? Since when does one learn to play the guitar? What's there to *learn* about it anyway?

What does he mean? Half the class is taking guitar lessons.

Following which, Tamara gave him a lecture, all about the guitar, and towards the end of the meal she even jumped up from her chair to strum out a little tune, which did nothing to prove any of her profound theories. For all that, he was pleased to sit and sip coffee while his daughter, in her school uniform, eyes sparkling, sat playing for him. They exchanged some banter. Ruth was quiet, withdrawn, a little sad. The glint of her glasses was unfamiliar. She was fetching plates, clearing them away. At last, since she planned to go to Jerusalem the following morning for a long day at the university, she shut herself up in the kitchen to cook a chicken for them both. Tamara suddenly remembered her homework and made a dash for her room. He sank into an armchair for another go at the documents, this time with the help of a foreign dictionary. He came up with a blank, or with plain absurdities.

At half-past eleven they went to bed. He took off his clothes, and a sharp hospital smell rose from his bare body, fumes of ether or iodine or something. He lay down naked on the bed, waiting to show Ruth his new scar, relic of the "teeny" operation. When she still did not come he picked up a newspaper, skimmed its pages, grew tired, sleepy. At last Ruth came, saw the scar, undressed, put on a nightdress, glanced through the paper trailing over the bed. He put on pyjamas, Ruth extinguished the light. Everything was so much as usual it never occurred to him that once again he would be unable to fall asleep; at half-past two, desperate in the dark house, he wandered about softly, watching Tamara and Ruth who were sleeping like the dead, very much alike in their sleep. He heard crickets, babies crying, the sound of distant cars. In the sky before his eyes a giant moon was born, faint with its own radiance. He did not dare wake Ruth again. This is ridiculous, I'm going to fall asleep any moment now, he said aloud and turned over and over in bed.

When he woke up it was past ten and he had wakened into a house filled with midmorning silence, into a hot day.

Naked he paces through the house, enters each room and closes shutters and windows against the heat. By every mirror he lingers to examine himself and where there is no mirror he searches for his image in window-panes. His hair has grown, little by little he is returning to the way he was three weeks ago. He brushes his teeth lazily, enters a sun-drenched kitchen and tumbles straight into the chaos left by his daughter. The butter is melting on the table, the milk going sour in the heat, the door of the refrigerator isn't shut properly, jam is dripping over a dry slice of bread, a piece of nibbled cheese is on top of a load of dirty dishes—it's as though a band of hoodlums had had their breakfast here instead of one thin, straggly child. The dishes include a whole series of plates, sieves and spoons with which she has tried to get rid of the skin on her milk—in vain. Squeezed between the dishes there is a page covered with figures and formulae, a last-minute attempt at cramming for a test in mathematics set for today. He puts the kettle to boil, moves the entire pile of dirty dishes to the sink, and starts chewing at the slice of bread left by her. He eats slowly, without relish, slumped in his chair, sighing once, suddenly. Bread crumbs collect in the tangle of hair on his chest.

Silence. He telephones, in the darkness, naked, to the Water Company offices. Once every three or four days he gives them a call. He is passed from one secretary to the next. He is looking for a certain department head who has promised him an answer concerning allocation to a new assignment. The fellow isn't there. He talks, therefore, to the secretary, who inquires first of all after his health. He informs her that everything is fine, asks what has been concluded. She goes in search of the file. A long time. The receiver, meanwhile, spills voices, giggles, telephones ringing. Back comes the secretary armed with the file and she announces that he has been granted additional sick leave. Another two months.

He does not understand, is smitten. Additional sick leave? What for?

She doesn't know, of course. She will ask her boss. There's a certain measure of unemployment about, maybe it's that. Anyway, the boss'll be back, as she said, in a week.

They chat. She is full of patience (if she only knew that he is in the dark, completely naked). He questions her about his replacement in Africa, a young engineer whom he doesn't know. Has he written to them yet?

"Sure. He's been sending picture postcards to everyone in the office."

"What does he say?"

"He's having a high time."

"A high time." His heart contracts. "Meaning what?"

"He likes it awfully there. Raves about the scenery. He's been driving around a lot, writes about interesting little villages, about folklore. The other day someone at the office even said: 'What the hell? Did we send them an engineer or did we send them a poet?'"

He laughs, bubbles over with laughter: a poet . . . great . . .

"And the dam?"

"The dam . . ." She considers, "The dam's all right, I guess. But it's not going to be finished in a hurry. They've already written to us from the Kenyan Labour Department, asking to renew the contract. They've plans to extend the dam to another river."

He is aroused.

"Another river? Which one?"

"Don't know . . . I know nothing about this kind of thing."

"The one south?"

"Dunno."

Suddenly his voice breaks. "Sorry to be such a nuisance. But you know, don't you, about this muddle. Such a horribly stupid thing. I was supposed to stay on there."

Yes, she has heard all about it. Those doctors. And what a way to tell a man just like that, right in his face: You've got cancer.

"Especially when one hasn't," he cuts in with a hoarse laugh.

"Sure. Specially when one hasn't," she seizes at his words, agitated, her voice shrill. A grey little secretary. He remembers her.

And suddenly she has lost her patience. Someone has burst into the room over there, a door is slammed, sun let in. A concrete mixer trembles, a shout comes.

"Excuse me, I've somebody here now."

"Just, please, don't forget about this job . . . this leave . . ."

"Sure, I won't forget. Just let my boss come back . . . first thing . . ."

"Me too, I'll look in at the office again one of these days."

"Why bother in this heat?"

"I don't mind."

Then again he is pacing softly, barefoot, like a giant cat. Goes to Tamara's room, takes the guitar out of a corner, strips it of its cover, sinks down on the bed and starts plucking single notes.

The guitar—a folly, a dull affair. What after all can he play—slowly, haltingly, groping for every note: a children's song, the national anthem, an old dirge? After five or ten minutes he would grow bored, abandon the guitar, and go in pursuit of fresh occupations. During the first days after his return from hospital he would rummage through drawers, spy into everything. He reread all the letters he had sent from Africa, inspected the blurred snapshots. After that he started to ransack bundles of old letters: his own letters from the war, before their marriage, his queer confessions of love, his passionate, clamourous wooing of a hesitant Ruth. Letters written to her by others in the same period. Numerous letters from girl friends; involved, facetious styles and tiny script. Among them, a whole collection of poems composed by a girl who had obviously been in love with Ruth.

Apart from all these—documents. Ruth's school reports by the dozens, her military insignia (she had been an officer), their marriage certificate, her birth certificate, Tamara's (where's his?), the title deed to their house. Every scrap of paper connected with her past was deposited here. He wanted to tidy up, wondered what he could destroy. After a long deliberation he threw away the envelopes.

Strange, these mornings suffused with drowsiness and heat. He would wake between ten and eleven in a house invaded by a hard sun, the windows wide open. At once he would stuff up every crack, attack each ray of light. Then he would wander naked through the illusory darkness, alone among beds, chairs, illustrated magazines. Odd, this silence, new to him. The house without Ruth. It's as though they weren't living together anyway. Four days a week she would make the trip to Jerusalem, spend the day at the university from morning till night, between lectures and reading rooms. A not-so-young woman moving among the young. In the two days left she would go looking for work, visiting office after office. Apart from that—her shopping. In the evenings—in the kitchen or studying for her exams. And on the Sabbath, after washing her underwear, she suddenly discovers the abysmal depths of her fatigue, collects newspapers into a pile, sinks into them, drowses on the couch, or in the sun, prostrate on the little square of lawn left in their yard. Her body exposed, naked almost, greased with lotion, not wearing her glasses and hence squinting, a small transistor radio playing between her legs. For hours and hours. There is no knowing whether she is conscious or not. Once in a while she exchanges a few words with her old, silent parents who come to see them regularly every Saturday, sitting very still on the balcony and awaiting the favours of Tamara, who would on Saturdays run to particularly giddy moods, tearing like a whirlwind through the house, making endless telephone calls, seeming to rally whole crowds to meetings.

And just on these Saturdays, amid this unaccustomed stir, he would find himself full of animation. He would come up with schemes, would suggest going to the beach, to the woods, to Eilat, Jerusalem, to the Syrian border. In vain would he appeal to the glistening limbs, the slim, somewhat boyish but already deeply furrowed body. His wife swooning fervently under a heavy sun.

After her parents have left he flings himself down by her, silences the radio, tries to sleep by her side. But he ends up studying her at length, he passes his hand over her hair, tries to rouse her with new ideas that he whispers at her: for instance, that they have another child together.

Then she murmurs: She knows. It's Saturday. But he can see for himself, she is deadly tired. And a merciless week is ahead. Yes, a crazy spell. Just let her get through with her studies and the exams and then they will go not just to the Syrian border but beyond it. For the time being, why doesn't he go to see friends. Where are all his friends? Pity that he's neglected friendship . . .

They have not made love, not since his return.

When she apologizes:

True, he is right, impossible to go on like this. But he hasn't quite recovered yet, has he. And she, oh well, he can see, is ready to drop. He's right. It's wrong. There's no excuse. It's all evasions. What's to be done? And if he were to pretend he isn't back yet? He came back by mistake, didn't he. What would he have done if he'd stayed on in Africa?

And at night, she gropes for his head, she kisses his eyes, tries to take him in her arms, and gradually falls asleep, and he still responding.

Those mornings of drowsiness and heat. His new solitude, his superfluous thoughts. The feverish hunt for spots on his skin. Above all, the deep hush reigning in their street. It is a marvel to him. No children's voices, not a human being. Now and then the sound of a car. Such mornings he seems to be the only one left. In sudden agony he slips on some light clothes and goes out to wander among the small semi-detached houses, along hedges, avoiding the battering sun as much as possible. Cats peer at him out of bushes, follow his movements anxiously as though he were an actor tramping a bare stage, against a painted backdrop of sky.

He escapes to the small orange grove that seals the street; it is all that is left of the vast plantation that used to cover this whole area. And there, between rows of trees choking off light, he drifts through a warm green haze, from shadow to shadow. At last he seats himself on an upturned crate, near a puddle fed from a dripping tap. With a dry twig he starts scratching at the loose soil, carves a little ditch, diverts the water to a slope, directs it to a basin, casts in pebbles, and builds a dam. Then he rigs up a bridge of leaves. He rises, wipes it all out with his shoe and clears off through an old gap in the fence.

By the letter-box in front of his house he lingers, looks at his watch, opens the box, closes it. Since his return from the hospital he has began loitering by the letter-box. Here, every day towards noon, he intercepts letters addressed to Tamara. That kid, youngster, soldier, that Gaddy, is apparently falling in love with the child. And in his torment, his longing, his hope, he sends her a letter a day.

The child: yes. Grown slimmer, taller, prettier, learned to play the guitar: but she has also become independent, breaking loose, slipping his authority.

She would return from school at irregular hours. Sometimes he would wait till four in the afternoon. When she appears she is always "dead beat", flushed and excited for obscure reasons. She drops her schoolbag at the door as though it were beyond her strength to carry it another yard, slips out of her sandals and leaves them beside it, and barefoot, blindly, she makes her way to the refrigerator, clasps the cold-drink bottles. Then she attacks the morning paper. Meanwhile he warms up dinner, which as a rule will not be to her liking. She picks a bit here and there, chews listlessly, leaves the main dish untouched, pronounces herself not hungry, and makes a dash for the telephone to talk to girl friends she has just parted from. Breathless whispers, giggles, veiled confessions, inanities.

If she happens to have a guitar lesson she shuts herself up in her room, practices for about half an hour, then vanishes with her bicycle.

If she doesn't have a lesson she takes off her school uniform, puts on a light blouse and the briefest of shorts, spreads herself on the couch and plunges into illustrated magazines or a love story. When he talks to her she replies in grunts.

Only when the sky begins to fade a little does she bestir herself to find out what homework there is to be done. She drags the schoolbag to her room as though it were a heavy cross, heaps a plate with grapes or cherries, spreads all her books and copybooks across the eternal confusion of her desk, starts losing things, despairs.

She calms down for a while, till all of a sudden she discovers that actually she doesn't know what the teachers want of her. Back to the telephone, long discussions, clarifications.

She comes back, sits still awhile, and now she gets up to buy a new exercise book. Not a day has passed since his return from hospital that she did not need a new exercise book. She takes some change from the pile on the cupboard (the last of his African salary) and returns after a long absence, laden with good things: bars of chocolate, sweets, two dripping ice-cream cones, an evening paper. Sometimes the one thing she would forget to buy would be the exercise book.

She would make him join her "party", eat the ice-cream, share the chocolate with her, nibble the sweets. Afterwards they would both get absorbed in the evening paper, wordlessly swapping pages.

The hard light would break.

The sky would lose its colour.

Suddenly, without reason, she would be gripped with anxiety, would fling down the paper, fly to her room.

She would always embark on her English lessons first, one hand plucking grapes, and in shouts across the whole house, she would dump obscure words in his lap, demanding explanations. Words from poems by Byron, Wordsworth, Shelley, words from tragedies of Shakespeare: names of plants, clouds, subtleties of light, distant scenery, castles, and English lords.

Words of whose meaning he had no idea.

He would try evasion, would ask to hear the full sentence, then the word spelled out, and all of it in loud cries, shouts trumpeted across the rooms. At last he would jump up, go to her room, bend over the open book, glance at the difficult word, read whole verses of the poem, consult the poet's biography, study his portrait, scratch his head and offer assumptions that would at once be proved wrong.

Extremely annoyed at being shown up in his weakness, he would retreat.

Well, what the hell are dictionaries for?

But the dictionary reduces Tamara to gloom.

In the end she hangs her arms around his neck, implores him, pleads for her life, cajoles, heaps words on him, sits him on her bed, brings him a newspaper, settles a pillow behind his head, presses grapes on him, invites him to more chocolate. Finally she lays the dictionary on his chest.

He shall do the looking up for her.

Well, has he anything better to do?

Idler that he is.

Outside the sun is beginning to set.

The poems one and all seem to be nothing but a string of hard words. He curses the poets. At slack intervals he will delve into other textbooks, read a bit about Africa in her geography book (what do they know about Kenya?), leaf through biology books, study the human body.

Sometimes the telephone rings and Tamara leaves him for a long time and only his threat that he will abandon the dictionary then and there will bring her back. Occasionally, girl friends come to see her, two fat girls materializing suddenly on the threshold of the room, having crept in softly, without ringing, through the open doors. They find him sprawling on the bed, the dictionary lowered on his belly, books scattered about him, the evening paper fluttering around his head. The pair of them, acutely embarrassed, greet him, inquire nervously after his health. He knew already that on the day his African wire had arrived Tamara had wept in school, had moreover informed the teacher and the entire class of the exact diagnosis. This had brought on a storm of emotion. Everyone had wished to share her grief. During break, in a corner of the playground, bosom friends had huddled around to weep with her.

Perhaps these very girls had wept for him, he thinks, and watches motionless how the two gather the hems of their skirts, sit down nearby, fix their eyes on the floor in a silent, polite stare.

He, his chest naked, bare feet stuck out in front of him and planted on the window ledge, smiles at them.

He would wonder if Tamara had taken the trouble to say that the whole thing had been a mistake.

Through the open window leaves are trembling in the warm twilight breeze. The edges of the curtain glow a soft pink. He remembers the dam near Nairobi, chokes with the misery, the longing. He thinks of the Africans, smiles secretly to himself. Hadn't thousands swarmed around him there, foremen followed him about?

Tamara does not mind his staying among them, listening from her bed to their conversation. The two girls, though, are ill at ease, but eventually they recover, forget his existence and open out, telling stories, cursing the teachers, gossiping about the boys: first about the boys in their class, then about strange boys, young men from the older classes, from other schools. He listens with half his mind, grows bored. His eyes close, he nods a little, emits a light snore. Out of the corner of his eye he discovers his feet wandering away from him, sticking high into the heart of the darkening sky.

Occasionally he ventures to join in the conversation. Feebly he defends the teachers.

Tamara shakes with laughter, whereas the girls turn to him and, very politely, backing up one another, they prove to him how wrong he is. It's a fact: all teachers are bastards.

At last he gets up and goes to the balcony to wait for Ruth.

The English gets done somehow, followed by the rest of the homework. Afterwards—supper, chitchat, idling around. He would be waiting for his hour, hour of the lessons in mathematics, for Tamara's glaring weakness in that subject had come to light. The many rehearsals for the famous school play, it seemed, had regularly been held during the mathematics hour, and Ruth, ever absent, had been neglecting the matter.

Tamara had appeared to be lacking the first rudiments. She was already called upon to solve equations of three unknown factors and she still had no idea of how to do division in fractions. It had therefore been decided, without the least spark of zeal on Tamara's part, that each night before going to bed they would sit down together to work out problems.

She would try to wriggle out of it in a hundred ways, put off this hour until far into the evening. When at last he would be called to her room, after all the other homework had been done, at the close of a hot day, he would find her dull, listless, unable to concentrate, her head nodding. Her room would be a shambles, her desk littered with books and exercise books, crumpled pages, chocolate wrappers, the skeleton of a bunch of grapes, the statuette of the brave African warrior toppled from its base. Through the open window the blind stirring of night, pierced by hot stars.

He would fetch a second lamp from the living room, join another chair to hers, attach the wires, cast a strong light, pull out white pages, ruler and compasses, and be set for battle. And she, barefoot, light, brittle, huddling her frail shoulders, nervously biting her pen and already in despair, shrouded herself in a fog of stupidity.

Those hours would become an endless source of wrangles between them. In no time he would have lost his temper, started scoffing, despising her; and she, put in the wrong, defiant, catty, would begin to argue about every number.

Presently they will have worked up a bitter hostility between them.

It sometimes happens that the lesson ends with Tamara in a fit of sobbing; and Ruth, exhausted after a hard day, rushes to part them.

She's just a baby, he would think, pacing in the garden on hot nights, round and round between trees, car, hedge and strip of lawn; watching the lights go out one by one in the little houses, in his own house. And as though the telephone calls, the girl friends, the chocolate and the newspapers weren't enough there still would be clamouring for her, here in the letter box, day after day, love letters. If he did not dam their tide, they would flood her altogether.

And, anyway, she would never have been able to decipher his handwriting, the words, the dreams, the lovesick harangues. Yes, and she would have gone and bothered Ruth with the letters, asked for advice. And at night she would yet have sat and composed replies, prepared envelopes, licked stamps; and perhaps fallen in love herself, in a fit of absent-mindedness . . .

And he, here, alone, racked, drifting under a sultry fan.

He would run his eyes over Gaddy's letters cursorily, standing there, right by the letter box, exposed to the sun. Then he would fold them and stow them away in the car's toolbox. Never did the letters cross the doorstep. Nights when he could not sleep he would sometimes go out to the car, and there, by the light of a small electric torch, would leaf through the letters again. The pages were getting shuffled, the days confused. For the youngster, in love as he obviously was, would write to Tamara every single day.

He had opened the first letter by mistake. Home a few days from hospital, still new to the morning hush, wrung by the dry desert heat. Between a telephone bill and a municipal bulletin there had been an envelope with a military postmark. He had torn open the envelope, slid out the pages, run his eyes over the writing unable to make anything of it, and then he had discovered that the letter was addressed to Tamara and had wished to return it to its envelope at once. Eschewing the torn envelope, he had folded up the lot and thrust it into his pocket. He had meant to hand the whole thing over to Ruth, except that she had returned near midnight, and by then he had forgotten all about it. At night, when he remembered, she had been asleep. He had got up, read the letter, and wanted to destroy it at once, then decided to stow it in the car. And what if the letter had got lost? Such a letter would only have made Tamara laugh anyway.

Gaddy himself had written as much:

You may be surprised getting a letter from me. It'll probably make you laugh.

That talk by the fence that your father interrupted.

Of course, you may not answer.

Me, I shall go on writing.

Actually, your silence makes it easier for me.

And so, day after day, he would send letters and the father would waylay them all, around noon of each hushed morning.

At first he had found it difficult to decipher the handwriting, since Gaddy wrote mostly in the field, in the short breaks between drill periods, on his pack or his helmet, by the light of sunsets, moonshine, or perhaps by the stars alone. Soon he grew accustomed to the cramped, crooked writing, read it with a practised eye, and even picked out a few spelling mistakes here and there, when the training got tough.

The pretext for the letters—that play in which they both had appeared and whose rehearsals, coinciding with the mathematics hour, had drawn them so close. What performance had been put on there? Tamara had mumbled something on his first night back, on the ride from the airport. He had not heard then. He must ask her.

Apparently she had been the true love of a brave underground hero who throws himself under the wheels of a train he has dynamited. Quite a daft story no doubt, seeing that Tamara could not even recall the author's name.

But Gaddy would sing paeans to the play:

Little is left of our play; nevertheless at night, in my tent, I repeat parts to myself; mine, yours, others. Something has caught in me and will not be resolved.

At times he would even sit down and quote whole passages, in order to wake up memories.

"Run to the river and wait for me there, by the big dam. Don't open fire any of you . . . Be very still . . . Hold back . . . I alone shall wait here for the train. You too, my beloved. Go with them. Do you hear me? That's an order! Leave me by myself."

He asked Tamara to let him see the full text. It turned out that, careless child, she had thrown it away after having learned her own lines by heart.

Apart from that, Gaddy would write at length about camp, tedious accounts of his tentmates, conjectures to the ounce about the weight of the equipment laden on his back, complaints about his shoulder bruised by the recoil of the rifle butt. The smell of brushwood. His denunciations of the platoon commander, stray reflections, words.

As though he were writing himself a diary.

Just out of high school and still reluctant to part with his pen, Gaddy.

From time to time he hinted at her silence, but forebearingly, without taking offence, figuring that the little girl needed time to digest his ideas. Sometimes he would blame himself, in his despair. "I am boring you," he would write again and again on the small military pages smelling of rifle oil. For all that he would not stem the flow of his words, would still add his reflections about death, as though he were wandering behind enemy lines and not in a rifle range set among orange-grove country. "What, after all, is so fearful about death?" he would write with the matter-of-fact simplicity of the soldier-savant, wishing at any price to soften the heart of a girl who never even received his letters.

In one of the letters he suddenly remembered to inquire after her father, ask about his illness. Hoping, he wrote, that he had not had to enter the hospital again.

That same evening, at supper, he put her through a cross-examination. Ruth followed it with amazement.

What had gone on at the play? What had her part been exactly? How much of it had she been onstage? Just in what way had she been involved?

It turned out that in one scene she had been embraced, had even had to be kissed.

He was stunned.

How had it gone?

Ruth intervened, said that, as far as she was concerned, the scene had been perfectly natural, a mark of the director's talent. Tamara on her part blushed a deep red, her pupils dilated, she told with an uncertain smile about a big ado at rehearsals, about the others' glee. She herself hadn't been able to control herself either, would burst into laughter right in his face.

"And how did Gaddy manage?"

A hush followed this outright mention of the name. Even Ruth was taken aback. Does he know him? demanded Tamara tensely, very flustered.

He is surprised: She's talking about him all the time, isn't she?

"Me . . ." Tamara wonders at herself, and gradually she calms down.

And after a brief silence:

"Oh, he was quite all right. So serious always."

Just so, his seriousness, that's what's frightening. Each day at noon he resolves to destroy the passionate letters, but by evening he has changed his mind again. In another few years Tamara will be older, he'll let her read them.

To make her laugh.

A pack of nonsense, the whole affair. He is wandering around, at a loose end all day, else would it ever have occurred to him to waste time over it? And so he spends his white nights huddled in his car, huddled over the letters. There is quite a pile of them by now.

The boy is in love, after all, lonely. All these words of his are a kind of fraud, though not a big one. If Gaddy knew that only I read his letters, he thinks, and he is sick at heart.

With the temperature soaring, the sky swept bare of clouds, the air turbid with the intensity of the light, the effect of the letters aggravated. And the letters themselves, filled with despair, sadness, grew shorter and shorter.

"Nothing is left of our play," he would write, soldier baking on a hill in the Negev sands.

And suddenly the letters stopped.

Though he felt certain that the kid hadn't got himself shot on manoeuvres, he grew restless. Besieging the letter-box, pursuing the postman.

A number of days now.

His much-blighted car, his crippled steed, overheating, gasping uphill, drowsing in the morning. Even on that first drive home from the airport, in the stillness of the night, by Ruth's side, he had realized that the car was on its last legs.

Ominous throbs in the gearbox, creaks in the clutch, rattles in the engine.

Ruth's verdict: sell it, get rid of it fast.

He said: fix it. There's still hope. Why be left without a car? Look, he'd fix it himself.

After his return from hospital he had appropriated the car from Ruth. And each blue sun-charged moming he puts on some old rags, approaches the silent car, throws open door and bonnet and worms his way in between the wheels.

However, he lacks the tools.

Every few days, therefore, he descends on the garage to look for what he needs. The people there put up with him patiently. Hadn't he bought the car at this very garage? And though many years have passed since, he still repeats to them with half a smile: It's you who are responsible.

In any case, it is a complex relationship.

He appears just before the noon break, when all eyes are down, faces averted from the harsh sun. Softly he edges the car in, parks it in the yard, out of the way; walks leisurely into the dim garage like a man with all the time in the world. He saunters among the mechanics, from pit to pit, watches the work in progress, bends over a stripped engine here and there, collecting gear as he goes. Back to the car in a wide arc, and with harsh jerks he disconnects, say, the whole electric system, hauls it over to a dark corner and takes it apart.

Moving among them, he is quite at home. The workers are tolerant with him. The boss himself, a veteran mechanic always under pressure of distant business and rarely to be found on the premises, had come over to him on one of the first days for a cordial handshake, had even received a little story from East Africa. Since then he has left him to his affairs, unrestricted.

From time to time, reaching a dead end, he will talk one of the mechanics into coming to listen to the engine, step on the pedals, turn switches. They will say whatever they say, invariably adding that the car is going to pieces anyway, better get rid of it.

And he, stung, will retort that indeed, that much he knows himself. How much would he get for her, by the way?

He is taken aback by the low figure.

For the time being he isn't losing money, inasmuch as these wanderings through the garage don't cost him anything. Only rarely does he pay a few pennies for a screw or a little tube. Sometimes, in the noon break, when the garage is empty, he may coax one of the apprentices to stay behind and together, in the still garage, they hoist the car up on a winch and investigate its underside.

The boy will always be eager to give his opinion, trying to figure as an expert. And he listens without a word. In these peaceful hours he would sometimes contrive to get to the heart of the engine, to the cold twisted steel.

Finally he began to renounce even the boy's services. He would arrive exactly at the mid-morning break, tie a grey apron around his middle, and start to work. A great plan was taking shape in his mind: to take the whole car apart and put it together again.

But today, in the silent garage, with him crouching greasily in a corner, fussing over a tiny screw, a heavy hand suddenly grips him and there is the boss in person, quiet, easy, at leisure, giving his shoulder a fatherly squeeze, asking gently: "Trouble?"

And the engineer gives a sad nod, lets go of the tools in his hand. To his great surprise the boss offers to take him out for a run in the car so that he can sound her out himself.

The boss at the wheel, he by his side, they set out at a snail's pace, the mechanic steering with one hand, with the greatest of ease, as though he were driving a toy. He had expected them to take a turn around the block and back, but apparently the boss has a longer drive in mind, makes for the main road, lunges through the burning noon hour, in the very face of the sun, aiming for the sea. At first they both keep silent, intent on the engine. Then the boss

begins to talk. He is speaking of Ruth: "She's basically sound. After all, I've seen older cars than this one keep going. But when a car gets to be this age she takes on a personality of her own. She gets capricious, has whims. Say, one of the gears will get obstinate, will have to be shifted just so, with a certain twist, say. Well, that's not so terrible, the driver must just be a bit gentler, a bit more patient. Being an engineer, you know what I mean. But your wife, let me tell you, she took this car while you were away and drove it like it was, oh, the latest make Jag or something. Hell for leather she rode it. Look, I'm sorry, I'm not talking of the pedestrians, that's not my affair. But the car suffers. She would slam her foot down on the accelerator in one go and so hard as to bust the whole car up. About once a fortnight we'd have to clean the carburettor for her and then she'd still put the blame on my lads. I myself, with my own hands, took hold of her foot and laid it down the way it should be. I even took her shoe off and joined her bare foot to the pedal so she'd feel the proper motion. Nothing doing. A question of reflexes, that's what it is. And me, I have no patience with women. The more so as she didn't seem to get my meaning. She would keep arguing with me, like all of them. Hasn't the faintest grasp of machinery. Doesn't even know how to change a wheel, your wife doesn't. Sorry, I don't want to speak ill . . ."

"No, that's all right, go on."

"You see, every fortnight or so she'd bring the car in for repairs. I'm not thinking of the expense, that's your affair. But the nuisance, the phone calls, the times she got stuck. And it wasn't always the car's fault either. The craziest things would happen to her. The clutch would get jammed, wouldn't disengage, particularly in winter, on cold days. Time and again I'd have to send someone after her to get her out. At nights I'd go myself and tow her. Look, we even scratched my private phone number here on the wheel . . . so she'd remember."

He looks, and there it is. Tiny figures scored into the steering wheel. All at once his heart swells with pain.

"Didn't she tell you? Must have been ashamed. Yes, some nights, right in the middle of the night she'd call for me."

"In the middle of the night?" he whispers, stunned, his eyes on the sea that has suddenly appeared in front of them.

"One time she called me to come for her at two in the morning on the main road to Jerusalem. I found her by the roadside, shivering in the car. Wouldn't turn to anyone else at such an hour. I

trust no one but you, she said. Thank you very much, I said, and towed her to the garage, and then I still had to take her home. Those weeks I never went to bed without checking the fuel in my tank. In a state of alert, I used to be . . . ha-ha, up in arms. All it lacked was for me to sleep in my clothes . . . ha-ha, in my shoes . . . ha-ha-ha, I said to my wife: Right here's the reason I'll never let you drive. So you won't get like her."

His heart heating hard. Sweat drops blinding his eyes. His head swimming. Suddenly his old pains seem to well up in him. The sight of the calm sea, blue and pretty, drives him mad, makes him sick.

He smiles.

The boss, utterly serene, cruises down a deserted side road alongside the beach, like a youngster delighting in his first turn behind the wheel. All of a sudden he swerves the car and takes a steep dive, down a slope and straight on to the sea, drives along the beach, very close to the water line. He is driving in zigzags, pulling the wheel from side to side in a slow dizzying roll. Meanwhile he chatters on, drivel about other women, other cars giving him trouble. At last by way of finale, he points the car with its nose to the sea, makes headlong for the waves, stops, makes a wide U turn. Back up the steep slope and the car is screaming with the strain, strange high wails, and nevertheless she obeys the quiet unperturbed mechanic, makes the climb in a single rush. Then they are on the road once more. The way back seemed short, suddenly.

The mechanic falls silent, thoughtful, increases speed a little to cut the time short.

The engineer sits and stares into the sweltering air that is making the road wave and contort.

He has already calmed down.

He even considers speaking about Africa.

Furtively he draws a few sheets of Gaddy's letters from the toolbox under his seat, glancing over familiar lines.

By the time they arrive at the garage the work there is in full swing, workers and clients milling through the yard. The boss parks the car at the entrance, goes out without a word and beckons to one of the apprentices. He orders him to tighten one nut in the engine, turns to the engineer, gives him a little absent smile.

"Well, you've seen for yourself. Nothing wrong with the car, is there. That's what I always say: it depends who's driving her . . . Leave her alone. Better not take her apart every day. She'll do fine. Just keep your wife away from her."

And suddenly he extends a hand, shakes his to indicate a final goodbye, disappears into the garage. And left there, stunned, the engineer hasn't even managed to thank him.

He leaves the garage and it is already after two with the sun exploding silently, breaking up into a thousand sparks. Splinters of light quiver between his feet, and over his head a canopy of coals. But he is still convinced this isn't a real heat wave. Not as bad as yesterday, anyway.

He starts the car and inches it slowly into the stream of traffic, crawls towards the centre of town. The car trembles, the gear lever rattles under his hand. He makes his way through the heavy traffic with the utmost courtesy. Patiently, politely, he waits to give dashing cars, jaunting pedestrians, the right of way.

Drivers of fast cars swear at him.

He reaches a narrow alley in the shopping quarter, mounts his car on to the pavement in front of an old poulterer's shop stuffed with coops containing live chickens. The shop is empty of customers and the fat proprietress ambles over to help him in his choice of a victim—a chicken that had looked enormous in its cage and small now that it is struggling in the woman's strong hands. He nods his consent and at once they transfer the bird to the slaughterer who has been standing there looking at them with vacant, insolent eyes.

A few minutes later they are wrapping the pale naked body in layers of evening paper, handing it to him. He pays.

He places the chicken on the passenger seat beside him, and for a moment he imagines it fluttering under the newspaper. When he lays his hands on the wheel he lets out a gasp. The wheel has grown searing hot, so hot that even the figures inscribed for his wife have become obscured. He finds a rag to swathe around the wheel, and drives that way.

Back into the traffic again, in the trembling car, against the white-hot glass of the windscreen (yes, a heat wave), bound for the white apartment houses, through swooning streets; arrives, runs the car backwards into the shed, its nose pointing at the sandy slope. He rushes to the box to dig for letters and finds, to his amazement, a postcard in English, from Kenya, in the Dutchman's hand: "Many thanks for your card. I'm delighted to see that you haven't forgotten me yet, and that everything is OK with you. Your successor is a fine man. We are greatly enjoying ourselves together. Regards to your unknown family. Yours . . ."

Flushed, he enters the darkened house. Blinded after the glaring light, he fumbles his way between doors. The chicken corpse is warm in his hand, with sun or with its own life. He goes to the kitchen, lays the parcel on the draining board, goes out and sheds his sweaty clothes one by one, strewing them over chairs; then he is naked again, goes to the bathroom, rinses his body with water, dries it. He puts Ruth's white work coat on over his nakedness, returns to the kitchen and switches on the light. He finds a large knife in one of the drawers, whets it till the wrinkles around his eyes are reflected in the blade. He relieves the chicken of its newspaper wrapping, which he spreads out on one side. He stands and ponders, looking at the doubled-up body withdrawn into itself. He bends and sniffs at it. Then he cuts off head and legs swiftly, throws them into the garbage can, lays the knife down and washes his hands. He takes the knife, sticks it into the bottom of the belly, carefully cuts a long slit, puts the knife aside and thrusts his fingers through the incision, probing its insides. His fingers get entangled, blood splatters on him. He lets go, washes his hands, goes to fetch a lamp from the living room to cast its strong light upon the mangled, headless body. And once more he begins to stir his hand inside, cutting with the other hand, separating slippery organs, separating unknown, tortuous, inedible from the known, the familiar, the eaten. Finally he carves off whole sections, piles them into a heap that has no relation whatever to the complete image. He cleans, plucks, rinses with quantities of water, places everything in a large pan and lights a flame.

Now he loosens the strings of his coat, sits on a chair, his excitement subsides, he picks up the old evening paper and, amid the bloodstains, the sticky feathers, he reads of curious happenings.

The door opens. Tamara enters, drops her bag on the doorstep. Her uniform is crumpled, she is hot, wet, golden, her face flushed, drooping lashes, dark eyes. As though home from a battle. Softly, musingly, she comes over to him, into the darkness, rises on tiptoe, drops a sudden damp kiss on his face, passes her hand lightly through his hair, absently, and without a word goes to the bathroom to wash her face. He follows her, stands in the doorway.

"Well?"

"Well, what?"

"The test?"

"Lousy. I'm sure I made it though."

She goes to the kitchen, opens the refrigerator. He is still behind her.

"What are you looking for?"

"A drink."

"Water . . ."

"No, something fizzy."

"There isn't anything fizzy."

She shuts the refrigerator with a despairing gesture, makes a little pirouette, and becomes aware of the darkness as though for the first time.

"This darkness. What's the point of it?" And she opens a window, raises a shutter, and hot light flows in to them.

He sits her by the table, puts a drumstick on a plate before her. She picks with her fork at a sliver of meat. Her slim fingers are stained with ink. She chews without relish, cursorily. Soon she will go to her guitar lesson.

"Any letters for me?"

"Letters? Who from?"

"Oh, nothing . . ." resigned, a little disappointed.

"The test. How did it go?"

"Don't remind me."

"Still."

She rises, goes to the front door, bends over her schoolbag, rummages, brings back a crumpled, stencilled page strewn with figures, drops it into his hands, flops back on her chair.

He runs through it quickly.

So?

She got one question right. Two others she muddled up completely. As for the fourth one, there are several different versions.

What are they?

She raises her eyes to his face, gives him a searching look. Then she bursts out laughing.

What does it matter?

A woman already. Ruth. Longing chokes him. Mature wisdom. She, blossoming before him. The scent of her flesh. Her head leaning against open palm; the fork dances between her fingers.

What is her version?

She tells him. Completely wrong. He grasps her error at once and explains it to her. Her lashes droop. She is listening with closed eyes. This whole business of mathematics doesn't in the least penetrate her hot summer being.

"Yes," she mumbles at last "that's more or less what some of the others claimed too." All the same, it's a fact— two boys got exactly the same result she did.

"What result?"

"Seven."

"Seven?" he mocks, roused.

"Exactly."

"That's another two morons."

She isn't offended. On the contrary, she smiles, shrugs her shoulders. Well, what can you do. She isn't made for this. She'll be an actress. She had thought, frankly, that if the answer had come out so simple it must be right.

He lectures her.

She's not listening. She steals a glance at the morning paper lying on a chair. He flares up, snatches the paper away. Her failure at the test makes him furious. He starts pacing around her. At least let her listen to what he's telling her. If she had listened to him before she wouldn't have failed to begin with. His voice grows harsher, he grasps her thin shoulder with a hard hand. Wishing to shake this dreamy child slouching on a chair, at ease, smiling, bathed in a square of light. A woman outright. Beloved. A maiden. And yet before his trip, when tired in the evening, she would still climb on his knees and snuggle into his lap, Ruth's smiles regardless.

He takes a sheet of paper, sits at the table to do the test, joyfully polishes off question after question. When he lifts his eyes he finds the door open, guitar and child gone.

And suddenly he feels giddy and escapes to Tamara's room, lies on her bed, closes his eyes. In no more than five or ten minutes he is awake again, dragging himself up from a hot abyss, his head bathed in sweat, and he panics. He can't make up his mind whether he has been asleep or unconscious, takes all his clothes off, examines his body, sits down gingerly on a chair, very faint. There is no light in the house except that streaming unchecked through the window torn open by Tamara. Suddenly it comes to him that he has had a dream, that the dream was set in Africa. Never since his return to Israel has he had a single dream about Africa, though he had prayed for it.

Now he is trying to recall its details when the doorbell sounds, a sharp ring, and he throws on some clothes and, preoccupied, his hair dishevelled, goes to open the door.

Standing there is a sunburnt person who asks for Tamara.

He replies that Tamara isn't home and wants to shut the door.

The young man, lanky, bespectacled, bows his head, takes a slight step backwards and asks in a low voice when she will be back.

And he understands suddenly that here is Gaddy.

And wakes up.

Outside the air stirs, a faint pink: artificial air, product of a flaming day. Maybe high up near the tree-tops there still hover some last wisps of cool air, but the road, the pavement, the balcony, the house, Gaddy himself, exist in an oxygenless air, the air of a dream. And the huge sun that has fused into a ball once more seems to float in a vacuum.

At last he speaks: "She's at a guitar lesson. When will she be back? One never knows. She will, though. Because she hasn't even started her homework yet. You are Gaddy."

And the young man, the boy, very flustered: "That's right."

And winningly, with a rush of joy and fear, eager to gain his friendship on the uncertain doorstep:

"How did you know?"

And a ray of light shatters on his glasses.

The father does not reply. He watches the boy who sadly, reluctantly, is planning his retreat. Dropping his arms by his sides, moving them slightly, shuffling his feet, his head thrown back inviting sorrow upon himself, the sorrow of a creature in love who even though receiving no answer to his letters will still go on hoping.

"Please . . . if you could tell her that I came and shall return later. Maybe I'll phone up first. Okay? Thanks. Goodbye."

But the father comes to with a start, decides at once that he must not let the boy escape. He opens the door wide.

"You may wait inside. As long as you're here. She'll be back. Homework. Besides, she failed a mathematics paper."

"I wouldn't like to be in the way."

"That's all right."

He moves aside for him, lets him by, and shuts the door behind them. And Gaddy can't know that he will suddenly be plunged into the dark, into a trap of darkness.

He leads him straight to Tamara's room, raises the shutter a bit to let in more light. The room is stifling very untidy. It is still a child's room through and through, a nursery almost with traces of the baby. Here, the little stool of doubtful purpose (there's a pot inside), tiny dolls dressed in frills lined up on a shelf, a few gaily coloured dwarfs dancing on one wall. There are times when, mysteriously, a smell of nappies will waft through the room.

Gaddy hesitates in the doorway. Worried about his nailed boots, overcome with the rapture of finding himself in the room of his beloved. His eyes rove hungrily from wall to wall, come to rest on the rumpled bed.

He is offered a cold drink.

No, thanks, there's really no need to go out of one's way for him. His face is flushed with heat, his shirt clinging damp to his back.

"All the same, it's hot today."

"That's true. Terribly."

"So what'll you have?"

"Okay, some water then, suggests Gaddy as the easiest way out.

The father goes to the kitchen, fills a large glass of water, returns to the room and finds the young man looking at the bookshelf, with grave attention, by the weak light that filters in between the slats of the shutter, studying the colourful books of childhood—encyclopaedias, the titles of novelettes and nursery tales. He offers him the glass. Gaddy thanks him so much, is so respectful. He takes the glass with a solemn air, raises it almost as though for a toast, takes a tiny, a very polite sip. But when he notices the father still standing waiting there he brings the glass quickly to his mouth and drains it in one go. Drops trickle on his shirt, splash on the floor and evaporate at once. He hastens to return the empty glass.

He hadn't expected that the father, instead of leaving him to himself, would drop on the dishevelled bed, would bid him into a chair opposite.

A small squashed pillow on the bed still retains the shape of the father's head and perhaps also the scraps of the dream that came and went here moments ago. He picks up the pillow, smooths it with his hands, hoping to remember that dream whose smell is fading. The room is ablaze. It isn't light streaming in through the slits in the shutter but thin jets of fire. The water that Gaddy has drunk is even now breaking out on his forehead, dribbling gently on his face like tears. Gaddy does not move. His eyes are still raised to the encyclopaedia volumes as though his fate were written there.

Such silence.

The two smouldering hot.

He is amazed that Gaddy wears glasses. It had never occurred to him that the boy might be shortsighted. Especially since Gaddy

himself had never given a hint of it in any of his many letters. Apart from that, nothing surprises him: neither the long face, the pimples, nor even the somewhat protuberant lips.

He had realized that someone writing that kind of letter would be no Adonis.

"This sun, wasn't it the end of you?"

"Where?"

"Oh, I don't know . . . On manoeuvre, in the field, in the desert . . ."

"No," a surprised smile. "Got used to it."

And after a brief silence, Gaddy, too, sets out to startle.

"All this sun must be child's play to you, after Africa."

But he, strangely enough, is not at all inclined to talk about Africa. Resentment flares up in him, he mutters: "All you know about Africa is fairy tales. Not at all hot there. On the contrary, it's cool."

At first Gaddy is daunted by the sharp reply, then considers embracing this chance, which is still only a chance in his mind. If he is doomed to be shut up with the father in the dark and sweltering room of his love, he will gladly listen to any stories about cool Africa.

He had not imagined that the father, stretched out flat on the bed would subject him at once to a brief interrogation:

About target practice, about the equipment, kinds of weapons, time of training, the commanders, the penalties, the dreams at night.

Gaddy, his face in shadows, pupils dilating, is amazed and fascinated by the accuracy of the questions. Seated on the edge of his chair, stiff, ready to shoot bolt upright.

And replying with devotion.

At last the questioning is over. In the renewed silence Gaddy is striving to catch Tamara's footfall. Then he removes his glasses, wipes them with the edge of his shirt. Large beautiful eyes exposed for a moment. He glances at his watch. Contemplating escape? His eyes, with nowhere to go, resume their diligent study of the bookshelf.

The intensity of the light in the room dims a little. A lost cloud wandering past the sun, no doubt. The eyes of both of them stray through the room, meet for a moment, part, rest on Tamara's desk to discover, both at the same instant that stuffed among the books and papers are some of her clothes: a thin blouse, shorts, a tiny, sky-blue brassière.

They are embarrassed. But, no doubt of it, Gaddy is filled with happiness.

He resolves, therefore, to feed him some chicken.

"Like a bite of something?"

"Oh, no. Thank you."

"Come, now. Have something."

"No, thanks. I swear I'm not at all hungry."

"Just something. So you won't say later they didn't receive you nicely here."

"Good God, no, why on earth would I say such a thing?" Gaddy laughs, a troubled laugh, thinking there is some wretched joke in all this somewhere.

Silence.

Gaddy lowers his eyes.

"Still, what'll you have?"

Now Gaddy's alarm is up.

"No, I swear. Nothing."

"Now you're being stubborn. And I had thought we might be friends."

The kid gives in straightway.

"Okay . . . But what?"

"Meat."

"Meat?"

"A piece of chicken."

"Chicken?"

"Don't you like chicken?"

"No . . . I do . . ." Incapable of lying right now.

Silence.

"Well?"

"How about waiting for Tamara," the boy offers desperately, not hungry.

"She'll be late. Besides, she doesn't like chicken."

That is something Gaddy couldn't have thought of.

"Okay, then. But please, just a tiny piece. I'm really not hungry."

"As you like."

He heaves himself off the bed, goes to the kitchen, picks up Tamara's abandoned plate, returns to the room and finds Gaddy on his feet again, stretching his legs, wandering round the room like a caged animal, the African statuette clutched in his hands. He holds out the plate. Gaddy thanks him profusely, as though it had been he who had asked for food. He imagines, Gaddy does, that now at last the father will leave him alone, but he installs himself on the bed

again, facing him, watching how Gaddy takes hold of the drumstick gingerly, brings it to his lips and takes a bite. On the one hand, Gaddy would like to get the whole business over with fast, on the other he is careful not to appear ill-mannered. Gradually his appetite revives, he chews the meat off neatly, nibbles a little at the bone, places it carefully on the plate, licks his lips.

"Thanks," he whispers, vainly searching his pockets for a handkerchief.

The father smiles at him.

The cloud that had darkened the sun's face is past and gone, the light has grown a little stronger, but now it is no longer the same hard desert glare. A faint reddish languor has seeped through.

Gaddy stretches his legs in front of him. He has suddenly begun to feel at home. The drumstick settling in his stomach has thawed him. He bends, picks up the African statuette again, strokes its skull.

"This from Kenya?"

The father nods, is startled anew by the resemblance between the figurine and the young doctor.

He inquires whether Gaddy wants to be a doctor.

No.

An engineer?

No, nothing in that line.

An officer, then.

No, that's the last thing he'll be, he detests the army.

Well, what then?

He has his dreams, smiles Gaddy, hugging his sweet secret, stammering a bit now that it is coming out. Something between an actor and a director.

The father would like to know whether he thinks he could live on that, support a family.

Gaddy laughs, excited. He hadn't thought that far yet. It's all way into the future. And all of a sudden he thinks he understands. See, he's considered a suitor, weighed as a prospective husband. He blushes with fervour, his heart swells. In the rosy light trickling through the shutter, glowing on Tamara's tumbled bed, he has visions of a wedding. Seized by a new sense of freedom he jumps up from his chair, paces back and forth in front of the father, blurts out a confused ramble about the theatre, about a play that he has read or written himself, about lights, stage sets. He brandishes the statuette wildly in his agitation, holds forth about truly primitive art.

After a few minutes he falters, realizes that the father is not listening, only watching. He goes back to his chair, replaces the statuette, sits down and is silent.

A very long silence.

Gaddy stares intently at his watch, devours the numerals with his eyes.

"It's you writing these letters?"

"Letters?" Gaddy goes pale. "Who to?"

"Tamara."

"Yes . . ."

And the father smiles at him kindly, bounces off the bed, stretches himself.

"I've read them."

And without looking at the boy he leaves the room, brushes through the corridor, takes leave of the darkness, slips out of the house, crosses the yard, glances into the letter-box, scans the black surface of the road, then the passers-by, the children riding their bicycles, shifts his glance to the end of the street, to the reddening strip of sky skirting the horizon, searches for Tamara. Slowly he retreats at last, goes to the car, gets in, opens the toolbox, collects all the pages, shuffles them into a bundle, looks for a piece of string, finds one, ties it around the bundle, turns in his tracks, lingers awhile by the front door, airily swinging the bundle, watching the world prepare for night, breathing in coolness, enters his dark house at last, crosses the corridor, returns to Tamara's room, is surprised to find Gaddy sitting peacefully on his chair, leafing through a volume of the encyclopaedia, which he has finally dared pluck from the shelf.

On the father's entry he closes the book and sits up.

He'll go now. He's been in the way. Tamara must have been held up on the way. He knows her: such a chatterbox.

And he gives a nervous laugh.

But at once goes rigid when the father presents him with the bundle of letters. He takes it and, unexpectedly, as though he needed to see his own handwriting straightaway, he tears with his fingers at the knot, the bundle bursts into bloom, leaves float over his hands.

The light in the room collects into puddles.

Gaddy really does not understand.

It is explained to him: Tamara hasn't read them. She wasn't given them. She wouldn't have understood anyway. She is only a child, after all. And they are difficult, unintelligible. Shall they say goodbye now?

How Gaddy remains so quiet even if very pale; look, his tan has all faded. The lovesick boy is reluctant to part from the father now. More than that, he turns defiant. Perhaps he is grieving for the little pages written in vain.

"Just what was unintelligible?" very embittered, obstinate, sitting down unexpectedly on his chair again.

Tamara is very late, thinks the father anxiously, and sits down himself, takes a few pages from Gaddy's lap and runs his eyes over them by the faint light. Gaddy draws near, glances at the writing together with him. And now, second by second, the light fades from the room.

On the plate beside them, in the twilight, the naked bone shines, remnant of a forgotten meal. The father reads a sentence here, a passage there, skips, searches for the unintelligible, and Gaddy takes hold once more of the little warrior, drives his nails into it.

"It's the play . . ." mumbles Gaddy all of a sudden.

"Yes, the play," he pounces upon the words eagerly. "All that, it isn't clear. Tamara has lost the text, and you go quoting here out of context."

And Gaddy, maddened, tears in his throat, begins to reconstruct the whole course of the performance.

Tamara came very late; the sun was down by the time she arrived. First they heard the sound of her bicycle, the bang when it hit the ground, then she appeared in the doorway, guitar slung on her back, sticking out over her shoulder like the barrel of a gun. She finds them facing one another wearily, a snowdrift of paper; and on the window-sill, under the window that she herself had opened to the light so long ago, a new darkness shines.

She is very much agitated, very much confused to discover Gaddy in her room. Too young to bear such emotion she may break out in a wail, like that other time, at night at the airport. The boy avoids even glancing at her. His head stays bent, eyes kissing her feet.

Suddenly it seems to the father that his daughter is beautiful, ravishing.

"Gaddy, what're you doing here?" she exclaims, approaches him, completely oblivious of her father. "Why haven't you come in uniform?"

Gaddy picks himself up, rises like a mature man, heavy and final, his head touching the ceiling.

With long steps the father crosses to the doorway, pushes Tamara out of his way, mutters something vague, very silly, about a wedding.

He fled outside. As soon as he shut the door behind him he was thinking of no one but himself. For a few minutes he wandered around the dark yard, lingered among the orange trees, touched the rotten, shrunken fruit, chased some frogs. Their little patch of soil did not even have a smell any longer. An arid waste, dust, wilted lawn. How those two had neglected the garden. If he had the energy he would fetch the hose buried somewhere among the weeds, attach it to the tap and squirt water over everything, over the house itself, over the hot dry air.

Still two hours to go before Ruth comes back.

All these university courses, utter madness.

He turns his back upon it all with an abrupt movement and goes to the car standing at the end of the yard, on its little slope. He approaches, mechanically opens the bonnet, drops his head in among the black greasy iron, touches bolts, fingers the pistons, tugs lightly at some wires. Then he slams the bonnet shut, enters the car and settles behind the wheel, turns the engine a long time till it springs into life at last with a scream. He winces, bends over in his seat, his face tormented, listens with closed eyes to the false breathing of the car. Whatever the mechanic said, he knows, this car is done for. If he had stayed on another year in Africa he would have traded it in. He extends a hand and switches the engine off.

A non-silence. A compound of tragic sounds wafting through the air with a faint hum. Lights in the neighbours' home, and children's voices. He listens: stubborn arguments between them and their parents. Demands, protests, shrilling cicadas. A hint in the air of the scent of citrus groves. Here, nearby, behind the houses, the boom of an old water pump which he himself installed fifteen years ago, and ever since—those low thuds day and night, like a giant heart beating.

To wait two hours for Ruth's return.

A strange hush has descended on his house. He turns a swift glance. The whole place is lit up. They've decided to celebrate, or maybe Tamara is reading all the letters, and Gaddy, bespectacled, is waiting and being ravaged meanwhile.

Ruth will come, and Tamara, well he knows, will blubber to her, then start breaking things. He knows that as soon as he raises voice or hand she turns into a wild animal, attacking anything that is his, sometimes even hammer in hand. She had already smashed the car lamps, once, and his slide rule, and on top of that she would then come and bring him the pieces, still sobbing hysterically or perhaps already stifled with laughter. But tonight he has no intention of being steered into an argument, nor will he have supper. Tonight he won't eat. Won't open his mouth. Will beat Tamara if she opens hers, yes, will snap at Ruth if she drags him into an argument. He's a sick man, after all, and irritable, and it is he should be pitied and not Gaddy.

He ought to be treated gently.

He beats his head against the wheel.

Besides, he ought to go off somewhere.

He means to start the car but changes his mind, pulls the Dutchman's postcard out of his shirt pocket, switches on the little car light, runs his eyes over the few words again.

Dutchman—

He always used to say: I'm a roving man.

He switches the light off, hunches up on his seat, his arms around the wheel, his head drooping. He will sleep here till Ruth comes.

At this hour, hour when babies are put to bed, his fatigue becomes unbearable.

He dozes off.

Towards evening the car stores up a curious coolness. Ruth says: if you'd stop going to sleep in the car every evening you'd not have to beat about in your bed at night to find sleep. But he knows that if it weren't for this doze snatched here each evening he would drop off on his feet.

About half an hour later he wakes out of a deep sleep, his arms aching, his mind over-wrought. Long minutes go by before he recovers. How deep the darkness seems to him. He looks at his house. The lights are out, except for Tamara's room. Gaddy has gone, slipped past him softly. Perhaps he has even taken the letters with him. As for the world—it is as it was, no change. The street sounds, children's clamour, lights in the neighbours' houses, the pump throbbing. Only the Dutchman's card has been squeezed between his fingers. Again he turns on the little light, reads, turns the card over to look at the picture. A native village in the mountains, the peaks of the Kilimanjaro in the distance. True, he hadn't managed to see much of Kenya. They've plucked him from there, uprooted him. He knows nothing but the road between Nairobi and the dam. He had planned the great tour for his vacation. Yes, one night the African foremen had invited the Dutchman and himself to a wedding feast in some out-of-the-way village, inhabited by one of the most primitive tribes of the region. What does he remember from the trip, though. They had set out at six in the evening after work, and had travelled four hours through the darkness before reaching some dark huts.

The foremen had been very embarrassed, had thought that there must have been some muddle and they had brought the white men all this way for nothing. Only after a long and wearisome confabulation with one of the hut dwellers, who spoke an entirely different dialect, did it appear that a celebration would indeed take place, but not before midnight, and that till then the villagers were all asleep. The party had settled down to wait, therefore, in the silent village square, had nested in the crevices of a giant rock that towered in the centre of the square and was considered sacred. Black night all around pressing down on the outline of high heavy mountains. The entire village lay submerged in a tangle of fragrant greenery. Even the native foremen looked somehow alien here in their Western dress, sat sniggering among themselves, chattering in English. The Dutchman sat smoking his pipe in one cranny and he went and lay down at his feet. Lay looking at the stars. In the cold of night his fatigue had changed into a kind of patient tenderness. Towards midnight the village began to stir to life, people's voices were heard in the darkness. On one of the mountain slopes a bonfire was lit. Shadows began to flit by.

From one of the dark gaps of the sacred rock a stranger suddenly appeared, a white man, a young American anthropologist who was wandering by himself in this region, and had come here especially for the occasion, armed with his tape recorder. After mutual introductions the American had sat down with them and began to speak in a rapid, baffling flow about the significance of the feast, about wedding customs among the various tribes. He had made an effort to listen but had not taken in much and he had thought the young man's enthusiasm very much overdone. Little by little the low voice of drums had risen. Bare-breasted tribesmen began to stoke up a huge bonfire beside them. The anthropologist jumped up to help, staunchly determined to talk to them in their vernacular. New bonfires were springing up all around. People were constantly emerging from the huts, and all at once the square was full, the mountainside humming with crowds. Someone made the party alight from the rock, led them to a place of honour beside the bonfire. People pressed close around them. Little children, mere infants, would be propelled out of a darkness astir with faces towards the light, would crawl around the fire, circle around them, put out a hand to touch the white men. Cries sounded and a kind of singsong chant began to ripple through the gathering. Nocturnal hullabaloos. Little by little a dance sprang into life. Skinny men, bearded, their hair wild, buttocks bare, were jumping about in one corner. Bare-breasted young girls, girls Tamara's age, began to sway gently, disjointedly, each girl dancing alone. A great weariness came over him. He wasn't a folklore enthusiast. It all seemed pointless to him. Those witch doctors with their painted faces and their straw ribbons, jumping up and down with would-be threatening gestures. The Dutchman by his side began to doze off too, the constantly fanned fire was numbing them. The girls danced on and on, always with the same movements, only their pace growing faster. Possibly these were the brides themselves. One Negro, an odd character, cheerful, grey-haired dressed in jeans, speaking a very crude English, was doing duty as a kind of intermediary between the guests and the performance, explaining, speaking non-stop, dancing and singing himself too. He was trying to arouse the white men, make them happy. The anthropologist was hanging on his words, clapping his hands and frisking about elated, dragging his micro-phone around, tearing off to record the drums. The native foremen, who had kept themselves aloof at first, began to come to life as well, grew enthusiastic. Memories were stirred in them and all of a sudden they turned tribal, joined in the general bawling. He was bored, had all but stopped watching. He took it upon himself to feed new tapes into the recording machine and was growing immersed in its workings. Into the circle, meanwhile, an important witch doctor had entered, completely decked in rags and straw. The roar of the drums swelled. The girls, still each one by herself, increased the pace of their dance. The grey-haired Negro joined the witch doctor, danced beside him, spun around the girls, threatening to catch them. The girls shrieked. At a certain moment he started catching them in earnest, gripping them around the waist, swinging them up in the air and pitching them one by one into the arms of the guests; he gave the first to the anthropologist, woke the Dutchman and placed the second in his lap, the third he dropped into his own arms, and so on to all the foremen. He, who had grown sleepy again, woke with a start, dumbfounded. In his lap, like a giant bird, a black native girl, nude, soft and moist with perspiration. Velvet skin, odd smell, small breasts all pressed against him. The dance went on. Other girls replaced the abducted ones. Hundreds of faces all around were watching them with a smile. Cries of joy sounded. He, steeped in sweetness, was petrified. Afraid to make any movement before the crowd lest it be misinterpreted. He held his breath. The Dutchman, on the other hand, had been kindled into life. He surprised him, this pale bachelor. He had removed the pipe from his mouth and placed it on the ground and gently he began to caress the girl in his lap, bending to kiss her shoulder, moving his lips over her breasts, and all of it with a light smile, with very delicate gestures. The whole affair had taken less than five minutes, and when he himself made ready to move, the happy Negro appeared and took them back, one by one; and the girls returned to their dance, were swallowed up by the circle. The drums beat on in the same fierce rhythm. Again the fire was fanned.

The time came for them to return. They emerged from the ring of fire, took leave, shivering with cold, climbed into the van and were once more tossed about for nearly five hours through the darkness, over the mountain track. Most of them fell asleep at once but he had stayed awake all the way, seated beside the Dutchman who had wrapped himself in silence, giving no sign whether he was asleep or awake. From a snatch of conversation picked up he had discovered that this whole act with the girls was by no means part of the ceremony but had been a piece of initiative on the part of that jolly native who, it seemed, wandered from one celebration to another and acted as a kind of *compère*.

By the time they arrived in camp the first streaks of dawn had already shown in the sky. They had all been exhausted. They had gone to their huts, he walking close to the Dutchman. They had not said a word, had arrived at his own hut, the first on their way, and the Dutchman, pipe in mouth, had nodded his head in parting; but he, without knowing why, had blindly refused to part from the Dutchman, had cleaved to him, accompanied him to his hut lingered by the entrance. The Dutchman had smiled and entered the hut wordlessly. He had gone back. He had fallen asleep as soon as he lay on his bed, but half an hour later, just before sunrise, he had wakened in pain. That was how it had begun.

An hour and a quarter to go before Ruth comes back.

He is gnawing his fingers now at the sudden thought that perhaps he has cancer after all.

Impossible. The cold, nerves.

And the pains are gone, aren't they? But if he persists, shuts his eyes, concentrates deep into himself, he can feel the old pains again.

No, they can't be lying.

The child would know at least and he would have sensed her knowledge.

He must make a move.

He will drive to the centre of town, buy an evening paper, cigarettes, cruise around and make the time pass till Ruth returns.

He tries starting the car. For a long time the engine grates and doesn't fire. He decides to start it in motion, releases the handbrake, and the car, its headlights dead, starts rolling down the little sloping path. The wheels turn with a faint rustle, a crackling of dry leaves; they gain speed. Suddenly the car jolts, the wheels swerve, slither. He brakes. Rocks, by God, rocks and timber in his yard still. Damn! He gets out of the car to look what it is that has got itself entangled there and is struck, appalled, to make out a figure lying there close to the wheels. A man, crawling, shaking off dust; Gaddy, rising, his face creaking with tears, without glasses, grimy, holding his arm with pain, bending to pick up the broken frame of his glasses. And without a word, without a glance, he goes, half limping, silent, down the slope to the street.

He is shocked, stares after the boy, resolves to overtake him, but the other has already vanished around a corner.

Now he is truly shattered. Hopelessly he kneels beside the still car. Not a sound comes from the house and it is dark now. The light shining in Tamara's window has gone out too. He glances at his watch: an hour and ten minutes to go. He slumps on the ground, lies down full length, arms thrown wide, as one already vanquished by death. Thus, on the ground, he thinks, on this path, he will wait; and Ruth will return and, tired or no, this time she will crush him indeed.

The Yatir Evening Express

THE isolated north winds, the infuriated north winds, burst into a reckless dance along the mighty Gazeeb mountain range, wailing among the wadis, rushing up onto boulders and dropping suddenly. These winds of prey that leave no corner unvisited, they alone know the small village of Yatir, hidden on a craggy slope overhanging the Saukin Valley that winds its lengthy way into fathomless chasms, dense with mystery, at the foot of the white village.

Only then, with the winds rumbling through the village, gushing in a rage among the houses, destroying our little gardens, and crashing into our quiet lives, only then do we feel that someone has come to visit us, the remote people of Yatir. Hearts would drain, then pound with heavy excitement, and we would wander through the village in a daze, buffeted by the gusts, a quiet sorrow seeping through us, impelling our eyes, blurred by the swirling winds, to seek the distances, in vain: the lost distances stopped short by the massive ridge, the peaks of a winding, weary range, tangled and taut, among the mountains of Gazeeb.

But on ordinary days, when the still sky is a deep dark blue, and a tired local wind drifts along alone, tranquillity reigns in the village and, outwardly calm, we await the persistent whistle of the fast train, the train which flashes by and pierces the mountain: the Yatir evening express.

Whose idea was it to build this village in the wilderness of Gazeeb? No one knows. Tradition has it that in the early days, when the railway bed was being dug from the Biram plain to distant Pamias—a long track equal to the toughest of Gazeeb's terrain—some of the quarriers resolved to make themselves a home in these wild wadis, secretly hoping to create a new life here.

The legends say it was the workers' families who settled in this place, then fertile and promising. They built small houses, ploughed the rich fields that skirted the mountains and, as their crowning glory, built a railway station, believing it would become a major junction in the complex of tracks that was to cleave this rocky land.

Soon enough, when the excitement over the railway died down and the wars broke out overseas, the village remained alone and forlorn. Suddenly it turned out that Yatir was an appalling distance from any other settlement, and its only link was the complex network of mountain passes. The railway station, the focus of their fondest hopes, became a little mountain stop devoid of all importance. Only two trains passed through the village each day. One that stopped before dawn—an old, creaky freight train from the Lesha mines, and another that passed by before dark—a gleaming luxury train, among the company's best, a train that crossed two countries on its way. The Yatir evening express.

Then came the days of disruption, the grey days. Each day was reduced to that narrow, shrunken strip of sunset, when the train sped madly by, accompanied by the softness of the last rays of light. The day was subjugated to this hour, and only at this hour was it affirmed. Each day was split into before-the-appearance-of-the-train and after-the-moment-of-its-disappearance. Those few noisy seconds when it appeared at the foot of the lofty mountain facing the watching village were time—"time-angst", as every member of succeeding generations called that vague feeling of fervent anticipation and impotent fury—restrained and subdued, that accompanied the train gliding on its secure tracks towards destinations unknown.

The greater the solitude and the clearer it became that the village would be isolated forever, the more intense was that mysterious devotion to a repetition both fastidious and surprising. Obedient and attentive, every single day, every evening, we followed the run of the fast train.

On the train timetable it said: the fast train passes Yatir station at 18.27.

At four-thirty, the first of the children who had finished their lessons would go down to the village well, at the foot of the huge mountain, and by five o'clock the rest of the village children would be there too. At five-thirty Mrs Sharira would open the shutters of her window overlooking the wide bridge that spanned the wadi, and bring a few chairs out on to her balcony. Five minutes later, her neighbours and friends would arrive. By six o'clock, all the small windows overlooking the track would be open, with heads peering out of them. At five minutes after six a jaunty group of young people would noisily gather at the fig tree near Mrs Shauli's house. Mr Tarawan would almost certainly turn up at the same moment, stand there gaping and confused, and look around expectantly. At exactly six-ten the daily meeting of the village council would end, and the members of the council and its secretary would adjourn to the square in front of the building. Dardishi would come a few minutes later, inebriated, and look for the rock he would sit on with a grunt. At six-fifteen the wagon of the vintner Parnassi would start to climb the road up to the village and, walking behind it, would come the five labourers who had been working for years on the construction of the huge dam. Slowly they would trek up the narrow mountain path east of the village, to get a better view of the speeding train. At that moment the window of Ehudi, the invalid, would open, and his pale head lean out, whereupon Meshulam the orphan would gallop wildly down to the bridge and line up hunks of scrap iron on the track. Immediately thereafter would come a shout from his aunt, issued in his direction, and always too late.

As early as six-twenty-two there wasn't a single person not shading his eyes from the sun, which was setting and flooding the bridge with its brilliant last rays. At sunset, I would get up from my seat at a leisurely pace, with two flags in my hands—the green one unfurled and the red one rolled up—and position myself to greet the train. At six-twenty-four Ziva would hurry over from her adjacent house and stand next to me, quiet and excited. At precisely six-twenty-five, the old stationmaster, Mr Arditi, would come out of the station. He always walked hurriedly, stooped, aware that the entire village was silently observing him. He went over to the two long grey levers of the track switch and pulled them towards him. He thus created a smooth iron line for the wheels of the train and cut all contact with the auxiliary track—a shunt line to the station that was rusty and moss-covered, running parallel to the main track, with a pretence of accompanying it along the length of the bridge, but which in fact came to a dead end: a sudden, sad finish to stifled ambitions. Arditi concluded his brief task and, drawing his eyebrows together, remained waiting, his body leaning on the two levers as though to reinforce his act.

Six-twenty-six. The train's whistle was heard in the distance, and a mute anxiety descended upon us. I would hurriedly drop the red flag and raise the green unfurled one diagonally in the air. At exactly six-twenty-seven the train would emerge from the mountains, approaching with a rhythmic growl. Clamourous and chugging, it shrieked past us, the thunder of its engines disrupting the quiet world that wrapped itself in light among the window panes. Its wheels were rhythmic and its movements uniform, as it streaked by.

Mrs Sharira, wide-eyed Meshulam and Parnassi's workers, except for one, were the regular wavers-of-hands. Sometimes a few people from the train would wave back as they took in the village in the midst of this wilderness. All eyes accompanied the train along the length of the bridge, until it disappeared at the first bend. After that the people would look at each other stealthily, wordless, with an uneasy sense of gravity. A moment or two passed and they all dispersed, as twilight descended.

So it was every day. So it is every day. So it will be forever.

But she did not think that way, that was not the way Ziva thought, Ziva who came of age waiting for the racing train, who grew lovely in the long daily anticipation of the twilight hour, who stored up her stratagems during the same sad and tiresome repetition, Ziva in whom a burning restlessness seethed, inciting her eyes to seek distant resolutions in the winds from the north, the winds of fury. This was the Ziva whom I loved with all my heart, in secret; and she, knowing this, evaded and hid from me. Ziva, who was so good at keeping silent—until today, when she suddenly shook off her silence.

Today, after the last carriage of the train disappeared amongst the mountains and the night air cleared in anticipation of a huge storm brewing beyond the peaks, I was watching her standing there in the dark, in my usual way, the green flag dangling in my hand. Ziva approached me, which was unlike her, picked up the red flag, carefully loosened the tie that bound it, and slowly, dreamily, spread it out on the ground, holding it with both hands. Her face bore a strange expression, and her blue eyes sparkled. Suddenly, seeing me lean over her, she flashed me a look both fearful and grave, summoned up her courage and said: "The red flag... It's brand new..."

I looked at the red cloth and suddenly realized that I had never seen it unfurled like that.

"Has anyone ever waved this one?" she inquired in a cunning voice.

"At whom?" I wondered.

"At the express train," she retorted, adding softly, "of course."

I was speechless. In the village no one had ever uttered the name of the express train. She sensed my anxiety, but would not let up.

She stood up quickly and asked, all innocence, "Is there really any need for the red flag?"

I gave her a loving smile, but her solemnity persisted. She hastened to explain her words—stubborn, determined to have her way.

"What good would it do to wave the red flag if the train is so fast that there's no chance of ever stopping it?"

Her directness only increased my embarrassment and unease.

"Have you thought about it?" she probed, insistent.

"No..." I stammered absent-mindedly. "No..."

She paused a moment.

"There's another storm coming tomorrow," she said moodily, gesturing towards the darkening sky. "So many things happen during our mountain storms..."

Seeing me standing there lost and confused in contemplation of her words, of this unnecessary concern, she stepped up blithely, stretched out her fingers and tousled my hair. Her face was enveloped in darkness.

"Don't you see? Don't you feel a storm coming?" she said, and concluded in a charming voice, "I'm simply worried about the train."

And I, trying to check my delight at her touch and her sweet deceit, looked on attentively, eager for her every utterance.

"We'll go to the village secretary, to Barradon," she said with a new-found brazenness. "We'll go to him and tell him what's on our mind. He'll certainly understand."

I didn't protest at her use of the plural; artless and entranced, I walked with her to the village, which was just switching on its lights.

Barradon, the energetic secretary, was sitting as usual on the balcony of the council building—his home—and smoking his evening pipe, puffing out numerous white smoke-clouds from his bushy moustache, looking up into the light blue clearing that lingered in the nakedness of the sky after sunset. Silently we edged over, until we were standing in front of him. He didn't even look at us. In a quiet voice, both articulate and bold, the girl began to tell him our fears, our thoughts, leaving Barradon the option of filling in whatever was vague. While she spoke, he didn't budge from his place; tranquil and focused, he looked straight ahead, smoke pouring out of his whispering pipe. When she fell silent at last, he paused a moment, took the pipe from his lips and said simply, "Why don't you both go to the old stationmaster, to Mr Arditi himself, and ask him to allay your fears?"

Undaunted, Ziva would not retreat. With the courage and impudence that had welled up in her earlier, she said to him, "We had already planned to go to the old man, and even set a time to talk to him. But we told ourselves, Barradon is a talented man, a secretary who makes things happen and who is close to village affairs. He must certainly worry about the express train, the whole village is anxious about it; day after day, after the train disappears, the village is sad and depressed. And this approaching storm will certainly increase our fear. Perhaps the secretary will come with us to old Arditi, and together we'll tell him what is in our hearts, before we wander about tomorrow, helpless, in the storm."

She concluded her audacious speech and folded her arms. Barradon was not angry, did not protest, did not even seem surprised. But suddenly he got up from his seat and, a gleam in his eye, went up to Ziva and pressed her shoulder with a strong hand.

"Yes, I'll come with you..." He paused and reinforced his words. "Of course I'll come with you..."

At the appointed hour the three of us went down the white path, through the village now quiet and in darkness. Wisps of thin mist floated down from the mountain ridges, and clouds intermittently dimmed the chill, glimmering moonlight that poured over the wadi. Barradon, short and broad, took the lead, striding with his habitual vigour, looking straight ahead, his thoughts on future achievements. In his footsteps, came Ziva, carefree, her bold, light feet on the sloping path restraining a fanciful urge that was growing within her. And I trailed after the two of them, with icy webs of sleep clinging to my half-closed eyes.

It was the eve of a storm. Gusts of prodigious cold cleaved the air. I hunched my shoulders and kept my eyes glued to the large, familiar rocks of the path.

The station was completely dark and we stopped near the iron door, wondering whether we had the right to knock and disturb this silence. Barradon slid his hand over the two levers, damp with dew, which the stationmaster had restored to their previous position. Then he lifted his eyes questioningly to Ziva. She quickly made up her mind, stretched out a thin white hand and gently knocked on the door. The station's calm was undisturbed. Ziva redoubled the knocking, until there was a muffled stir from within, and the sound of Arditi's shuffling feet.

"Who is it?" came the wary question.

"Us," Ziva replied in her pleasantly throaty voice. "Hurry up and open."

Arditi opened the door and shone the small torch, which he was clutching in his shaking hand, in our faces. At the sight of Barradon, he started and cleared his throat.

"Oh... Barradon," he said apologetically. "It is so late and I didn't even expect... No one has ever come... after dark."

Barradon, confident in the face of the old stationmaster's embarrassment, extended the broad hand of a free man, caught Arditi's arm and pumped it in a friendly fashion, then proceeded into the station, with Ziva hurrying after him. When Arditi noticed me, his staunch assistant, his face clouded, but he didn't say a word. Silence had long since been decreed between us: boredom and repetition had overcome everything there was to say, and we could fairly assume that we had exchanged all words possible regarding this petty, paltry job that we did together for the railway company.

Arditi looked ridiculous in the short, tattered night-shirt he was wearing. His hunched back stood out under the thin gown and his white legs were all too evident. His eyes were still blurred with sleep, red and watery. With trembling hands he lit the big kerosene lamp near his bed which, rather than giving light, sent up shadows in the large room. Barradon immediately took a seat at the desk—the stationmaster's seat. Ziva placed a chair opposite the bed and sat down, hugging herself. I remained standing near the door, leaning my back against the thick wall. Having completed the lighting, Arditi sat down on the bed, hugging his bare legs to protect them from the subtle chill that could be felt in the room. His eyes, wide with surprise, waited for someone to speak. Barradon surveyed the room with a discerning eye, then favoured him with a question.

"There's no electricity in the station?"

"None," Arditi promptly replied. "The railway company has no desire to spend any money on this forgotten place."

Ziva and Barradon exchanged a glance of complacent under-standing, and Barradon even nodded to Arditi as if confirming his words. Then he started to fiddle with the papers on the desk. No one spoke and Arditi's perplexity grew. When the silence became unbearable, he ventured, "What brings you here?"

"The train," Ziva replied. "The fast train... of course..." Her voice choked.

A shadow fell over Arditi's face. Barradon nervously curled his thick moustache then, with a faraway look, he turned to Arditi.

"We came at this late hour, as we were anxious to find out whether the red flag could avert any danger that might happen to the evening train."

"The red flag?" Arditi gasped.

"The red flag! Of course," Ziva cried out, her eyes flashing.

Shocked, Arditi looked in my direction, but finding me hidden in the shadows by the door, he slowly turned his head back to Barradon. He was overwhelmed, beside himself.

The secretary took care to spell things out. "Don't you think that disaster could befall the express train?"

The stationmaster blanched.

"After all, it rushes by at full speed," Barradon continued in a whisper to expound Ziva's marvellous idea, "and the flag would be useless in time of danger. Thus do we abandon our beloved passengers, so trusting of their trains, when in fact they are liable to plunge on to the rocks at any time, without our even being able to warn them."

Arditi sensed that things were leading in a very peculiar direction, to something else entirely, and that Barradon was stalling in his usual mild manner. He bent his head, which was in the shadows and thought awhile. Then he answered, simply, "You were troubling yourself over that, Barradon? Don't you know? Trains don't come off their rails any more. Disasters no longer happen. The train is secure on its long runs; the wheels skim very nicely along the smooth rails. All that waving of flags is only a tradition from the distant past, a kind of ceremonial greeting, you might say, which is superfluous in itself, definitely superfluous."

Barradon's and Ziva's faces brightened, and the secretary enlarged upon his ideas with increasing confidence.

"Well spoken, Arditi, well spoken. Superfluous, it's all super-fluous. We too stand at the sidelines, watching; we too are superfluous. Because this is nothing but a remote station... a fleeting landscape... everything is therefore as it should be. The train passes by, strange and distant, and we mountain villagers, out of a stubborn devotion, stemming from ignorance, turn our attention to this fine hour at the end of the day, and watch the train. Indeed," there was a tremor in the voice of the secretary, who was now convinced of his argument, "indeed, everything is lovely."

A horrible silence filled the room. Arditi did not know how to respond. In terror, he folded his arms tight against his chest and lowered his eyes. Ziva was in the throes of the magic. She sat there quite still, her head between her hands, and her blue eyes rivetted on Barradon.

Suddenly Barradon leant across the desk, shot out a short, powerful arm towards Arditi and whispered menacingly, "Have you ever considered, Arditi, what we are waiting for evening after evening?"

Arditi was quiet. Barradon sat bolt upright, and his outline, cloaked in darkness, intoned, as if to itself, "Well, the answer is simple..." Here he paused a bit. "For a disaster."

"For a disaster..." Ziva murmured to herself, beaming and tender.

"For a disaster..." I responded from the direction of the door, my eyes fastened on the white nape of the girl's neck.

"For a disaster..." The stationmaster bent his grey head, then started, "For a disaster?"

"Yes, Arditi," the secretary responded with growing enthusiasm. "Why, no other hope remains; no other hope was left to us by the honourable railway people. And our mountains are perfect for disasters. The craggy slopes... the deep wadis... the winding track... and, above all, the bridge, the bridge that spans the abyss..."

Barradon's words were choked by the very enthusiasm that inspired them.

Arditi was flustered.

"But why?" he cried out, squinting as if he were going blind. "Why?"

Barradon leaned over him.

"We are so alone here, dear Arditi, so out-of-the-way. The big wars overseas passed us by. We have never known true sorrow, honest-to-goodness disaster..."

"And the passengers? The people themselves...?" Arditi was terror-stricken and bewildered.

The brave secretary cut in, "Those are the very people we want, those who pass so close to our houses evening after evening, the strangers who fly by. And what do we want if not to make their acquaintance, to know them, to mourn their fate?"

"New people," added Ziva, gaping in wonder. "New people, Arditi, whole new worlds."

The room fell silent once more. The exhausted stationmaster hugged his legs fiercely. For a moment his eyes searched for me, his speechless assistant, but I had flattened myself inside the archway of the huge door. Submissively, he shifted his grey eyes back to Barradon. "And so?"

Barradon was being put to the test. He got up, went to the window and opened it wide. Our eyes followed his confident movements. Clear moonlight poured into the room, thin strands of mist drifted around us. The village was in total darkness by then, merging with the mountainside. A fragile silence settled over the room, enveloped in a new chill. Barradon began to speak, meandering.

"Once again, a large storm is brewing... And tomorrow, once more, we will be alone here with the mountain winds..."

Ziva's hands slackened and dropped to her sides, so entranced was she by his words.

"A storm is a perfect time for disasters," continued Barradon, his face turned towards the open window. "How horrible it would be to see the train plunge into the wadi... and what a responsibility to rescue people from such a catastrophe..."

He turned quickly to Arditi, entreating him conspiratorially, "You will not go out tomorrow to change the levers. There will be a mistake... And our express train will be shattered on the hillside, the passengers awaiting our rescue..."

The secretary's secret was out.

Arditi jumped from his seat as if bitten by a viper, furious and incredulous, his battered soul overwhelmed with disgust for the tranquil Barradon.

"How is that possible, Barradon? How? How?" he screamed.

The stationmaster paced about the room. "That is wickedness," he shouted at Barradon and Ziva, who was sitting calmly. "Am I going to be the cause of a terrible tragedy? I who have worked here all my life, who never missed a day, and faithfully saw to the running of the train?"

Here he paused, giving us a strange look, his eyes bloodshot.

"No! No!"

Barradon's head was slightly bowed, and a mocking smile played at the corners of his mouth. Arditi's pleading eyes had searched in vain for support. Ziva's eyes were lowered, filling with tears over her lost dreams. And I, modest and good, was alight with desire for her, for the girl over there with her hunched shoulders.

Our silence was much more than Arditi could bear. With a jolt, as if suddenly remembering, he leaned towards Barradon, his eyes shining, and said, "The gentleman is coming tomorrow, the supervisor-general of the railways. Whenever there's a storm he visits Yatir. This will be of particular interest to him, this new idea..."

Barradon and Ziva shuddered at the news. The supervisor-general of the Gazeeb district was known for his tremendous severity and unstinting dedication to railway matters. Arditi lived in apprehension of every sound he uttered, and there was no doubt that he would turn them in.

Barradon got up and moved towards Arditi, who was now resolute. He put his hand on Arditi's shoulder, pressing it in a fury of concealed despair. Then he spoke in a clear, even voice:

"Are we looking for adventure? We are mountain people, and this wilderness is ours. This is a beloved land, truly beloved, and because it is beloved, and because we want to hold on to it, not to leave it, we want that sorrow, that responsibility which will fall on our shoulders."

He concluded his speech. The kerosene lamp was spluttering and the light gradually dimmed. It was very late. Arditi remained in his seat, aghast: neither he nor we had ever seen the secretary in this agitated state. Ziva got up slowly, as if reluctant to part with this shadowy room; boldly she cast an accusing glance at Arditi. I opened the door.

Without a word, we went out into the night, our eyes searching for the path that led up to the village. Barradon walked first, rapidly, his stride recovering its strength. Ziva and I lagged behind, strolling with the easy stride of youth. Suddenly I turned to her, caught her small, feverish hand and murmured, "My love..."

But she ducked away from me with the ease of her considerable cunning, demurring tenderly:

"Not now... not now... we haven't finished yet..."

Shamed, I accompanied her along another stretch of the path.

The morning was marked by the beginnings of the storm; a gathering haze thundering at the high wall of mountains, conspiring to flood the rocky land. The storm was amassing powerful winds at the edge of the northern mountains, with their projecting cliffs, in preparation for the moment of fury. Sometimes a surge of wind would gust through the village, groaning fiercely as it herded together flocks of loose and tattered clouds, worrying them towards the grey southern horizon, and disappearing; the forgotten sun bursting through breaks in the clouds.

Since dawn Arditi and I had been sitting on the stone bench in the station square, nervously waiting for the supervisor-general, Mr Kannaout. As usual, we sat silently and at a distance from one another, withdrawn into ourselves, and listened to the station's tin roof clattering angrily at every small gust. My eyes were inflamed from the rising dust cloud, and the stinging in my throat was agony, but I did not budge from my seat; I slouched on the bench, my head sunk inside the raised collar of my tattered coat, and stared at the pile of dry leaves collecting in the station square.

Arditi was extremely agitated. It was obvious that he wanted to talk to me, but since we had already said to each other whatever could be said, he kept his words to himself. He began pacing around the square, shrunken and bent, using his hand to shade his wrinkled forehead, and straining his burning eyes to see if the longed-for supervisor-general was approaching. Finally, in the late morning, there in the distance, down the track blurred by dust, a red spot was seen shifting rapidly, disappearing and reappearing amongst the mountain curves. It was this same red spot that came to us only on stormy days. Arditi's features took on a look of tremendous pleasure, and he strode up and down in the small square, muttering excitedly to himself, "Here he comes... here he comes... at long last..."

Without a word, I got up slowly, wiped my watery eyes with my fist, and ambled towards the edge of the square.

The supervisor-general, Mr Kannaout, was a very well-known figure. He had served in his present capacity for many years, and everyone in the mountains knew that he had always known his own mind. He was regarded by the villagers as all-powerful, though some had been known to doubt him. He was thorough in his work, and nothing escaped his sharp eye; he ruled with a firm hand, and remained completely aloof from the villagers. He behaved both strictly and honourably and spoke formally to them all, though when necessary he did not refrain from cursing and swearing. His insistence on order and procedure was legendary, and his ways, they said, were just.

He came to Yatir only infrequently, since it was so remote. And whatever feelings he had for Arditi, he would find nothing to say to him—so routine and tiresome was the business he had come for. Hence he was accustomed to dozing at the big desk throughout his visit, with Arditi and me sitting silently before him. This was the usual behaviour of Kannaout who, out on the railway lines was alert, active and dedicated, but, when he chanced upon a desk with people in front of it, was immediately overcome by a deep fatigue...

The little red car slowed as it approached the station. With precision the supervisor-general drew up right next to us. Deftly, he turned off the engine and, bundled in a coat too wide for him, stepped lightly from the car. A large, peculiar top hat was ensconced on his somewhat flattened head which contrasted with his short round body. Fresh and ruddy from the mountain winds, he extended his two small thick hands in greeting, and while Arditi and I bent to take them, ingratiating in our enthusiasm, he mumbled thickly to himself and rolled his squinting, damp eyes in our direction.

"What a day, what a dreadful wind... phew, what an isolated station, what a distance!"

Then he suddenly pulled his hands away from us, and skipped towards the station building, the sleeves of his coat flapping in the wind. We followed him with great excitement.

His hand trembling, Arditi shut the door behind us, and turned his desperate eyes on the supervisor, who had thrown himself, just as he was in his coat and hat, on to the wide chair behind the stationmaster's desk. Whilst Arditi nervously fetched the station register, the supervisor took from his pocket a battered black pipe and lit it with great effort, inhaling and exhaling through his huge nostrils. Then, having succeeded in expelling from his mouth a number of thick, smelly smoke clouds, and finding pleasure in the odour that met his nose, he left the pipe in his mouth and, already half asleep, began to examine the station register, leafing slowly through the large pages. Arditi did not take his eyes off him. Attentive and tense, he sat rigidly on his narrow iron bed, as if awaiting his sentence. Soon enough the supervisor wearied of his work, pushed the register away, leaned back comfortably in his chair, gave us an amiable smile and prepared himself for a nap. Little by little, his lids drooped over his glassy eyes. The wrinkles of his fat face began to sag, and his soft outstretched hand slipped, depressingly flaccid, on to his small belly.

The windows rattled intermittently and the station's tin-roof clattered in the wind. The supervisor's heavy breathing rose and fell rhythmically, and we sat still so as not to disturb his sleep. Though

Arditi wanted to express his fears, he did not dare to open his mouth. He quietly chewed his fingers, and restrained himself with the same discipline which usually kept him in check.

A short time later, the sleeping figure stirred and the supervisor began to rouse himself from his slumber. He opened his weary, leaden eyes, shifted them around the room, then brought them back to Arditi—who was sitting quietly, open-mouthed in expectation—and asked in a tone of sombre authority, of lordly benevolence, "And so, Mr eh, Mr Ar...diti."

He immediately closed his eyes again, knowing as he did that Arditi had nothing to say. Arditi stole a panicked glance at me, then summoned his courage and, his face radiating excitement, burst out: "Sir... Mr Supervisor! They're plotting against the express train... last night... wicked thoughts..."

The old man fell silent with a restrained sigh, in a state of tremendous agitation.

The supervisor didn't budge. This surprising show of hysteria was not to his taste. His eyes still shut, he raised one limp hand as if seeking to stop the old stationmaster's outburst.

"What has happened to Mr Arditi?" he asked heavily. "What is the reason for his lack of moderation?"

Arditi swallowed, composed himself, then whispered in a rush, "There is a plot in the village. Perhaps it has been brewing here for years. The people of the village want a disaster... They want sorrow... that same sorrow they were denied in the wars overseas. They feel bored and abandoned and therefore want to derail the express, derail our beautiful train!"

A hush fell over the room. The supervisor slowly raised his heavy head, inclining an ungainly ear, and inquired in his melli-fluous voice, as one who would resolve these new issues, "To derail, Mr Ar...di...ti?"

"Yes, yes," the other responded. "To destroy!"

The supervisor leant forward.

"To destroy? Mr Ar...di...ti?" he continued to inquire in his slow sing-song, a small spark of interest rising in his dark eyes.

"Yes, in point of fact," said the eager old man in total confirmation. "They are trying to bring it down where the big bridge is. They're asking me, *me*,"he struck his chest with sunken fists, "they're asking me not to go out this evening to switch the tracks..."

The supervisor closed his eyes and settled into a heavy sleep. His head dropped on to his chest and his mouth fell open with a sigh. Suddenly the shadow of a smile began to spread over his crude mouth. He stretched out one arm and placed it on the desk as a support, then rested his weary head on it, opened his two crooked rheumy eyes, and looked at Arditi, who was waiting, full of admiration, and hoarsely declared: "Aren't those fine words... Mr Ar...di...ti ... those are fine words... How many years have I yearned to hear such excellent phrases...?"

Arditi was so surprised he struggled to understand what had been said and his grey eyes gleamed with the effort.

"Fine...?" his lips barely moved.

"Why certainly," said the other slowly, examining Arditi with an impenetrable expression. "And is it any wonder? This beautiful machine travels such a distance and here we have a mere isolated village, no more significant than the white rocks along the way..."

Arditi seemed on the verge of collapse.

The supervisor again pondered on their plan and declared dreamily to himself, "A great idea..." He immediately fixed me with a discerning look. "And this young man, is he the brains behind this?"

I smiled at him modestly, until a repulsive grin rose to my lips. But the gentleman properly grasped my meaning. He waved his short, fat finger in my direction.

"Great things... He is destined for great things."

I lowered my eyes, tremendously pleased, then stole a glance at Arditi who was still overwrought and muttering out of despair, in a cracked voice, "And I thought of telling him... the supervisor-general... he who knows everything... he who is so fastidious... he alone, who... and our faith in him grows from day to day."

Mr Kannaout was visibly pleased at this flattery but, huddled inside his coat, he burst out, interrupting, "If you would kindly let me be... if you would have the courtesy..."

And he settled back into his nap. Again the room was utterly still, as Arditi and I worriedly observed our master. Finally Mr Kannaout opened his eyes, peered at his large wrist watch, and readied himself for action. Aware of the old stationmaster's chastened look, he took pity on him and gave him a tired but sympathetic smile. Arditi shuddered from head to toe, simpering in gratitude for this expression of warmth and, still nervous, insisted on revealing what else was on his mind.

"And the register, sir? Is it correct?"

The supervisor raised himself out of his seat and, shaking off the last webs of sleep, walked over to the old man—who rose quickly out of respect—and put out a clumsy hand that landed on a faded button of the threadbare coat which was the uniform of Arditi's office. Pulling Arditi towards him, he began to whisper to him, as the old man stooped submissively.

"And what was my good man thinking of when he mentioned the register? Can he not see that it has already become exceedingly tedious? And however devoted and faithful he may be, he is likely one fine day to find himself dying by the station door, with not a soul by his side. And this express train will flash right by, without a single glance of pity, after he guarded and protected it day after day..."

Arditi ran his hands through his hair and let them slide limply down the sides of his face. A stifling silence filled the air; then the supervisor's face took on a grave expression and, turning to the door, he opened it wide. Outside, the storm was raging. We had a difficult day before us. I shielded my face against the wind with my arm. Arditi was staggering in the storm. Only the supervisor stood still and firm in the gale, gazing merrily at the empty square. Suddenly he turned to Arditi and though he shouted at the top of his voice, his words were lost in the wind.

"What a storm... I will rush back here this evening, my dear Arditi!"

He seized Arditi's hand, shook it heartily, waved in my direction and set off into the storm, towards the waiting car, his coat trailing after him, buffeted by the wind. With great agility, the supervisor climbed into the vehicle, started the engine with a confident hand and, seconds later, disappeared around a bend.

I closed the door with great effort. Arditi was rooted to the spot, bound in chains of devotion to his master. I glanced towards the empty chair behind the desk. I walked carefully towards it, and lowered myself into the chair which was still warm from the supervisor's body. Slowly I made myself at home in it and stretched out both legs, feeling a sense of abandonment. Then a chill went through me, and my teeth chattered. Slowly, seeking a little warmth, I pulled the chair up to the desk.

Arditi watched me in quiet sorrow. He wanted to speak to me, and perhaps I too wanted to tell him something, but we did not speak. Again, I stretched out in the chair, closed my watchful eyes and dropped my head on to my chest. Before long I was dozing to the whine of the wind.

Bundled into bulky coats, the first of the children who had finished their lessons were already going down to the village well. With considerable effort Mrs Sharira managed to open the shutters of her window overlooking the bridge, as the winds knocked over the light straw chairs she had put out on her balcony. By six o'clock the other windows with a view of the tracks were open, and covered heads peered out of them. The group of young boys and girls arrived at the appointed hour, and Dardishi had already sat down next to them. At six-ten the village council meeting was over, the door burst open with a bang and Barradon marched out first. The exhausted horse pulling Parnassi's wagon pushed its way through the raging storm until it was forced to stop at the last turn. Through the fog it was possible to discern the five dam construction labourers as they slowly made their way up the hill. Ehudi's window banged open, crashing against the side of the house. Meshulam the orphan had already padded down barefoot to the bridge and laid his scrap iron on the damp tracks. His aunt's scolding was swallowed in the wind.

Now, they were all waiting in their places. The hands of the clock crept slowly towards the moment when Arditi made his routine appearance. Ziva was skipping quickly towards me, wearing a thin dress and shivering in the cold. The two levers of the switch had not been moved, Arditi was not yet there, and a restrained murmur rose from the villagers. All eyes were on the station square, which looked deserted. Everyone was looking excitedly at the two levers of frozen steel. The sun, troubled by sailing clouds, bathed the whole mountain in a red glow. Beyond the storm, beyond the winds, beyond the torrents, a quiet, distant sunset was in progress. The light poured on to Ziva's face, and she shielded her eyes with her hand as she watched the villagers.

"Arditi hasn't come! Arditi hasn't come!" Joy burst through, relieving them of their burden of responsibility. Six twenty-five. There was no turning back.

Ziva hurried eagerly towards the red flag which, as usual, had been thrown on the ground; she quickly untied the string and unfurled it. I watched anxiously for Arditi, but silence prevailed at the station building. The train's whistle could be heard in the distance, echoing through the mountains as if the train were not destined to arrive here. Ziva put the red flag in my hands. I quickly dropped the old flag, the green one, and with both hands raised the new one and waved it towards the people of the village. A murmur of satisfaction rose amongst them, but no one moved from his place. Their eyes gleamed through the storm, determined not to miss a single inch of the flashing rails. The sky suddenly clouded over, as if foregoing the moment of sunset. The approaching darkness and the fog that dropped relentlessly from the sky, saturating the air, evoked a melancholy at the last moments of light. The sound of the train noisily advancing through the mountains, the echoes preceding the train. Departing from my usual procedure, I got up on a boulder and summoned all my strength to raise the red flag in warning.

All at once the locomotive split the screen of mist, rushing around the last bend. It came straight towards us, rhythmically pounding the glittering tracks, surging powerfully, with the carriages following obediently after. Two dim beams were cast by the locomotive's headlights, confidently seeking out the fixed path. Ziva's eyes were wide open and a smile froze on her face. The red flag was nearly torn out of my hands by the force of the gale.

The bored locomotive engineer noticed me and was slow to react to what was happening. He quickly blew the whistle at me, but I was stubbornly waving the red flag—an inexplicable response, peculiar, remote. The sun breaking suddenly through its barricade of clouds gleamed on the locomotive's windows. The engineer's terrified face turned towards me as the train moved with a strange new clatter, on to the rails of Yatir, our own short track. The sound of wheels on the rusty rails was unfamiliar, but the carriages passed, one after the other, on to the track thick with moss, the horrible clatter repeated over and over. The intolerable suspense gave way to stifled delight: "They're coming to us! They're coming on to our track!" But the villagers were unable to express their joy at this gift. The train was trying to brake its mad flight but it blasted through the last barrier in its way and went swerving off the rails, its huge wheels—polished, rhythmic, faithful—leaving the track one after the other. It plunged into the dense mist of the abyss.

The villagers shrieked hysterically, their arms outstretched towards the train disappearing before their eyes. The carriages were latched together, lest they uncouple, and the fate of one was the fate of all. And this was happening on our cliffs, on our granite boulders in the wadi below our miserable houses.

The terrible noise of metal smashing subsided and a delicate silence ushered in a new evening. The people of the village rushed down the slope. Panic-stricken, they clambered down the slopes of the wadi, risking their lives, eager to do what they could. They reached the last carriage, from which passengers were emerging, lost and in pain, and tried to comfort them. The dark night rose up from the foot of the mountain, and the first torches were lit in the village.

Ziva was still standing near me. The red flag drooped in my hand and I looked at her with longing. She stood pale and trembling, shocked at the disaster. I stretched out my hand and gave her a gentle smile.

"And now, my love..."

But she looked at me like a stranger, her lips moving wordlessly; clasping her hands in despair, she dashed nimbly towards the wadi, now swarming with people.

I shuffled slowly towards the dark station and, reaching the door, went in anxiously. I dropped the unfurled flags near the entrance and very quietly closed the iron door behind me. Arditi sat in his seat behind the desk, his head downcast and propped on his hand. I dragged over a broken crate and set it on end in front of the desk. Arditi was not watching me.

The silence was relentless, to the point of suffocation. I violated it in a choked voice:

"A new day has dawned for us, Arditi... We will never forget..."

The stationmaster's frail shoulders shuddered with the horror of it all; his glassy eyes were painful to see.

"The supervisor..."—his words were a charged whisper—'When will he get here? Has he arrived?"

"He'll certainly come," I answered enthusiastically. "After all, he's at the scene of every disaster. He will take everything in hand... after all, he is experienced."

Arditi put his head down on the desk. His age weighed heavily on him. A calloused hand fell on to the desk, dangling over the front. Carefully, I put out my hand and took his gently.

A pale moon rose from the east. Sounds of confusion from the scene of the disaster echoed faintly but persistently. I spent a long time with the old stationmaster before leaving him and slipping out to the scene of the disaster.

Dazed and staggering, I went down into the wadi. I stepped through the wreckage of the train and, feeling defeated and clumsy amongst the splintered trees and overturned carriages, I searched in vain for Ziva. All the villagers were there; no one had stayed behind.

Burning torches were held by the children, grave and tense as they followed their parents who were intent on rescue. These burdened souls spoke little but fulfilled their humane duties solemnly and with scrupulous care and self-control. In groups, by turns, they worked with ropes and tools, with an agility not seen before in the village. A few individuals were still putting out smoky fires with wet sacks, as the enthusiastic children put all their energy into lifting the torches to assist as fully as possible, illuminating the faces of those at work. From time to time a scream would be heard in the dark, accompanied by the comforting voices of the villagers. At one place, where smoke was coming from an overturned carriage, I made out the powerful figure of Barradon presiding over the activity, poised and intelligent. It was obvious that for him a dream had been fulfilled.

I took a flaming torch and started circulating amongst the people, looking around in the darkness for Ziva. The village people respectfully made way for me; my stature had grown today. At last, far down in the wadi, next to one of the steep walls, I spotted her bent over one of the dying passengers. A torch stuck between two rocks flickered, casting wavering shadows on her lovely face. Her mouth was pursed in deep sorrow and her deep-set blue eyes were full of tears. Her hand gently stroked the bandaged face of the dying man, as she drank the pain into her youthful being, totally devoted and eager to absorb the terrible disaster. I stood silently for a time, the dying torch in my hand. At last I roused myself in a burst of anger and seized her shoulder. She glanced at me, her eyes radiant with tears, and whispered, "Look..."

But my own eyes were cold and dry, and a kind of fury seized me—lingering, smouldering. I threw the torch down and put my hands on her face, her neck, demanding repayment of the debt.

"Come with me!" My voice trembled.

"Now?" she asked, anxious, unwilling.

"Come!" I repeated, stubbornly, supporting her, holding on, pulling her up. She let go of the passenger and dragged reluctantly after me. I refused to let go of her, and with a firm, eager hand pulled her up the path towards the mountain.

We picked our way nimbly amongst the rocks. Rid of the day's storm, the night was still and cold. Panting and fearful, we stepped over the black rocks, the granite rocks, as if on our way to the peaks that were crowned with the tender radiance of night, to the ridges, somewhere above our heads. The lights of the village had long ago vanished and we were immersed in pure solitude.

I stopped near an ancient olive tree and grabbed Ziva in my arms, gathering her bowed head towards me, feeling in every inch of my body her resisting youth. Her exposed white shoulders aroused in me a fury of desire I had never known. I embraced her madly, kissing her neck, and I fell with her to the ground, oblivious and happy, stroking, savouring, possessed.

Hungrily we lay at the foot of the low tree, on the black earth, sheltered in the dense shadow. At ease in my arms, she rested, her eyes closed; she was full of thoughts. Then she opened her eyes, caressed my hair with her soft hand, speaking as if in recollection: "The disaster... the disaster... how horrible..." And her eyes assumed a new tinge of sorrow. I was silent.

"Hundreds killed..." she continued slowly. "We'll work all night by torch-light."

A shudder went through me. I released her, as if trying to escape her glance, blue and penetrating. But she moved the side of her hand over my chest, slowly considering a new idea: "And him, what should we do with him?"

"Who?"

She didn't hear. Dreamily, she continued to spin thoughts.

"We'll turn him in... He can't go free any longer..."

A horrible suspicion stole into my heart.

"Who?" I shouted in a suffocated whisper. "Who?"

She looked at me compassionately.

"Old Arditi, of course."

She lifted her eyes to the expanse of darkness that suddenly opened before her. I drew her close to me, drunkenly inhaling the scent of the night on the rocky, tortuous terrain of this beloved land.

Galia's Wedding

"There was once a man whose beloved compelled him to
marry her. He went and assembled all the lovers with
whom she had debauched before her wedding, in order
to remind her of her wrong-doing, and to take revenge on
himself for having agreed to marry this woman. How
ugly that man was, and how ugly his deed. But I found
him quite likeable, and the deed was a fine one in my
eyes."

S. Y. AGNON

IT came upon me suddenly, before I could brace myself. I
didn't know what and how, and began reeling under the weight of
it. I writhed and squirmed, but it was already too late. My blood
wept in its terrified veins. All was lost.

The announcement in the paper was tiny:

"Galia and Danny getting married. Bus from main station at 3
p.m. to Kibbutz Sdot-Or in the south."

It was the letters that created the bitter fact, not Galia's deep
eyes. The letters that were assembled with such finality, put the seal
on this evil—the white space of the paper repeatedly, endlessly,
reaffirming their truth.

I got up, left the house and cut through the yards of the new
buildings towards the open field. I climbed to the top of the small
rise, and assumed my eternal position beside the wasted, solitary
olive tree. With leaden eyes I surveyed the southern suburbs,
wrapped in a blue vapour of afternoon. Tatters of distant autumn
clouds dimmed the eye of the weakening sun. In the cooling ground,
yearnings were checked and silently shattered. I stood a long time
without thinking, until, suddenly, I closed my eyes, dropping my
arms in despair, and swivelled towards the charred olive tree,
gasping, "My Lord God, this is the end."

A light tremor passed through the top of the tree. It held its
breath. I stepped limply towards it, and thrust my head under the
tangle of branches, laden with rotting olives.

"Yes, my Lord, this is the end."

He always hid from my torment.

I stepped inside the tree.

"I'm not angry... I'm not crying..." My voice broke. "Only know, my Lord, that I am at the lowest ebb of happiness. The lowest."

He dodged, hid himself in a black olive, distorted and mute. I beat my head against the trunk.

"Will you tell me? Will you tell me?"

But the wind blew, shunting my cry into the distance.

I rose on my toes and stretched the tips of my thin fingers towards the olive. I touched it.

A scream slashed the sky. The afternoon train was on its way back to town, skimming like a toy through the yellow wadi. My gaze followed it faithfully until it stopped at the station.

Sdot-Or is a small, remote settlement in the south. I saw Galia there a year ago, and have not been back since.

At the grimy bus station, not a soul knew where the bus to Sdot-Or was. The drivers maliciously sent me from one to the other, to keep me guessing. I stumbled between the huge wheels of the buses on their way in and out of the station. In the whole jostling crowd, not a single person seemed to want to go to Galia's wedding.

"I'm dreaming," I thought, with a glimmer of hope. "Nothing has happened..." But I continued to wander around, weak and lost, among the iron railings that marked the bays.

"What are you looking for?" people asked, taking pity on my stumbling feet.

"The bus to Sdot-Or."

No one knew what Sdot-Or was.

"There's no such bus," they would conclude with authority.

"There's one today." I lowered my eyes.

"Why today?"

"Special run..."

"What for?"

"There's a wedding..."

"A wedding? Whose?"

"Someone's..."

"Whose?"

"Danny..."

"And who?"

"Galia," I whispered.

"Which Galia?"

They were trying to trample her with their bored feet, while waiting impatiently for their bus. I resumed my prowl about the terminal.

It was three o'clock.

I began pacing desperately along the brick fence that surrounded the dusty white parking lot. I passed the huge buses one by one, lined up with their faces to the wall. An elegant blue bus was the last in the row, its metal gleaming in the sunlight.

Spotting it, I edged over slowly, sliding my exasperated hands over the glittering chrome.

The bus sat high on its enormous wheels. I clambered heavily onto the front bumper, gripping the side mirror, till I was half-hanging, half-standing, embracing the squarish bonnet. Before my eyes was the raised red emblem of a roaring tiger. I leaned down and pressed my fervent, dry mouth to the little carved beast. The great noise of the city became, in my ears, a solid muffled hum.

Suddenly I remembered, and a wave of terror passed through me. She's his! He kisses her mouth. He fondles her small breasts.

Who is he?

I lifted my head towards the cloudy sky.

"My good Lord, how have I sinned?"

Lowering my eyes, I saw it. There, pasted on the windscreen in front of the driver's seat was the announcement clipped from the morning's paper. My eyes widened in astonishment at seeing the same tiny letters here, clustered at the centre of the glass.

They were following me.

I dashed quickly around the bus, but no one was there. Hesitantly, I mounted the iron steps and entered the empty bus, clacking along the nail-studded floor to one of the back seats. All the windows were closed. I opened mine and looked out wearily at the chaotic station. Slowly my head eased back against the seat.

Some time later, a rustling sound awoke me. Up the steps came an earth-encrusted individual, looking as though he had just been yanked from some copse among the rocks. Dressed in light green safari clothes full of pockets, buckles and snaps, the terrific size of this intricate outfit made it bunch away stiffly from the squat body, appearing for all the world like a twisted tree-trunk.

His head was gigantic, poking forward, and over his forehead hung a green driver's cap. Dark glasses with frames shaped like long narrow leaves were fixed over his eyes. From his shoulder hung a bulging drivers' pouch made of charred leather. In his bearlike paws the creature was seizing fistfuls of fresh olives, tossing them into his open mouth and lustily spewing the pits at the gleaming windscreen.

I was barely aroused from my warm sleep, rubbing my eyes, when the repulsive creature dropped himself into his seat; the doors of the bus closed with a hiss of compressed air, as the engine gave out a mighty roar. The vehicle jerked forward, nosing aggressively past the other buses.

"To Sdot-Or?" I shouted from my seat, trying in vain to outdo the growl of the engine. But the driver paid no attention. With a firm hand he guided the bus out on to the main street and gradually accelerated.

So I was the only one.

I leaned my drowsy head on the window sill. An autumn breeze caressed my eyes.

To Galia's wedding... To the wedding of my beloved...

My eyelids slid shut against my flushed face. The passing city sank into my slumber.

We drove with the sun resting in the hills.

I—my head leaning dreamily against the bars of the window, in the corner of my eye, the warm light wavering and dying somewhere in the distance; and the little monster—ensconced, silent, in his deep seat, and wholly bathed in the brilliant light shattering on the glaring windscreen.

We left the city from the south, on a road winding through the mountains. Alongside us, in the narrow wadi, ran the railway track, a thin black line, disappearing, reappearing. The huge wheels eagerly gulped the desolate road that extended, rising and falling, from the mountains to the southern plain.

I held my head in my hands and fixed my eyes on the road hurrying towards us.

The drops of rain that fell a few days earlier had awakened the exquisite fragrances now hovering over the rocks in the foothills. Sweet memories surged in veils of fine mist, floating with us above the ground. How long had it been since I'd walked in the fields? How many years had drained away since those days when I would return at twilight and climb back alone to the kibbutz?

My God!

The nights in the vineyards. Sharing dreams and visions at the end of a day's work. Stretched out on the moist earth, drinking in the silence—a world unto ourselves. And a dull pang in our hearts—was this our home? Was this the last stop? Ungrudging but uneasy, we kept track of those who were leaving, who were returning to their homes in the city. We felt abandoned there.

Just a handful remain, and new training groups arrive at the kibbutz—an endless cycle. Then you're already counting the days, keeping your own imminent desertion to yourself, and here comes a new training group, with Galia in it. Frail, blue. Blue work-clothes, blazing blue eyes. Alone, and all the world lowered on to her narrow shoulders in a way that makes you worry. She's wild, careless, tormented—but whole in a separate universe.

It's as if you've been struck by lightning. Suddenly you're face to face with your other half, which grew and ripened, mysterious and wondrous, somewhere far away. They were for her, the melodies that stirred you, intent and intense on those clear nights. It was she in the stems you held between your lips.

Now we were gliding down the last slope towards a sun emerging, entire, at the edge of the opening vistas. The driver seemed to be dancing at the steering wheel, his body swaying with each turn. The orb of the red, blazing sun was suspended in front of his face, and he pursued it, as if trying to catch it up and plunge in.

Then had come the madness of my awakening heart. The slender figure blocked out the entire world. Somewhere—so they said—she had a distant lover, and I never exchanged a word with her. My last days there passed by despairingly. And then I left the small houses, the hill, the vegetable patches. And once you leave, you never come back.

A year of illusions. A year of wild anticipation. Bound by my love and helpless to speak of it aloud. From crumbs of information, I followed her throughout her training—solitary, faithful to the strange being that had unwittingly crossed my path. Then, courageous and full of hope, I suddenly broke my silence and exchanged a few peculiar letters with her. Until I went to her at Sdot-Or.

There, in her small and horribly messy room, she heard me out, silent and shaken.

I was not her other half.

The heavens were being sucked in towards the setting sun. Among the clouds, purple figures formed and flowed. The bus filled with elongated shadows. We were speeding now through wide meadows, dotted here and there with brown, fragrant patches. The autumn plough had already been there. All the days of winter, of spring, of summer, had sunk into the weathered stubble spread like a golden, rustling carpet across the land. A whole year would be turned under and swallowed up in the depths of the ranging furrows. What would remain in the silent, quivering air?

At a wide fork in the road, shaded by a few large flowering olive trees, three figures, indistinct in the twilight, seemed to be gesturing excitedly towards the approaching bus. They were three young men trying to flag it down, shouting anxiously one after the other:

"To Sdot-Or?"

"To Sdot-Or?"

"To Sdot-Or?"

The complacent bus driver merely stepped on the accelerator, whizzing delightedly through the shouts, which lingered behind like a wake. But some way past the turn-off, he suddenly stopped the bus, killing the engine while it was still in motion. The wheels rolled on out of momentum; then their drone diminished into thin silence. The bus stopped. The driver's head sank on to the steering wheel.

The three now sprinted towards the bus. Panicking, they pounded on the closed doors.

"Does this bus go to Sdot-Or?" The tallest of the three, looking morose, addressed me through the window.

"Yes," I murmured.

"To Galia's wedding? ..." he added, still panting, looking for confirmation.

"Galia?" I wondered, remote.

The other two continued to pound at the closed front door, trying to get a response from the heedless creature leaning dreamily over the steering wheel.

"Tell him to open up!" one of them shouted at me.

I gave him a vague and distant smile.

They were on their way around the bus to wake the catatonic driver when suddenly the engine started and the bus began to inch down the road. Infuriated, the three of them ran alongside, still pounding on the closed doors. They raced like that for a short distance, shouting and protesting, until there was a sudden whistle of compressed air and the rear door slowly opened. They had barely climbed up, one after the other, when it hissed shut again. Furious and confused, they stood staring at the strange driver, who was by then spurring the bus on in a new burst of enthusiasm.

They hesitated inside the empty bus, then sat themselves down on adjacent seats, away from me, and looked about suspiciously. They didn't recognize me, but I knew who they were.

They were Galia's lovers. Ardon, Ido and Iti. Her first loves.

The three became increasingly intermingled, merging into one thick silhouette. Odd! All three had already married.

When Galia and Ardon were young, and students at their school in the pine grove, they loved each other to the point of madness. When she left him, he slashed his wrists. He was found bleeding and was revived, but Galia never came back, so he went off and sought her in many other young women, until he finally took one of them for a wife.

Ido was Galia's scout leader, a member of a kibbutz in the north. On meeting nights, in the midst of stormy ideological discussions, he would go down to the beach with her, where they'd exchange the kisses of an innocent love. When he returned to his kibbutz, he wanted to take her with him, but she didn't go.

Iti arrived in a whirlwind. Somewhere or other he happened into Galia's crowd; he was good-looking and popular. He took Galia one night during a summer work camp, imagining that this would be just another of his many conquests. But by morning he was in love with her. Miserable, he returned to her night after night, increasingly helpless. Galia slaked her thirst and slipped away from him, to the training programme at the young kibbutz.

That's where I was.

The big silhouette was watching me with its three heads. Dark glances were thrown in my direction, hunting me down. I drew in my shoulders and hunched down in my seat.

Now the bus was gliding along an open plain dotted with the lights of tranquil settlements. The chill of night rose from the cultivated fields. The last pale remnants of blue in the sky faded slowly into the smooth horizon. On a distant hill, outside the bright circle of the many settlements, a few faint lights glimmered. That was Sdot-Or. The whole illuminated plain suddenly shrank behind the bus as it drove towards the lights up on the hill, guided by the slouching driver. We shifted on to winding dirt roads for the short ascent to the kibbutz. The bus started chugging heavily on the rise, but the driver made no effort to ease it into a lower gear. The engine groaned in agony, but the driver cruelly flooded it with fuel. Stupidly oblivious, he continued to goad the poor vehicle on, as it jerked and spluttered, until the engine finally breathed its last in mid-ascent, slid backwards down the slope and stopped.

A rustling emanated from the vicinity of the steering wheel, and we all peered into the darkness. The dwarfish driver had opened the nearby door and immediately disappeared under the bonnet.

The large, clear lights of the kibbutz were before us. I got up and left my seat, nonchalant, my steps echoing in the bus. I came to the folding door and, with my fingers, prised it open. The three followed me. We started walking up the road in silence. Suddenly Ardon came abreast of me and asked, with an open expression, "You, ... going to Galia?"

The black heavens collapsed on my head. The gloom of the trio slid over me like a shadow; my jaws were clenched.

"Yes ..." I admitted soundlessly, my shoes crunching along the road. They sized me up with stares until I trembled.

At the kibbutz the party appeared to be under way, and everyone was gathered at the celebration. The odours of the chicken coops and the cow barns wafted towards us in nauseating waves. There were voices in the distance, and as one we turned our steps towards them. The lights of the dining hall appeared, and our steps quickened. We focused on the light streaming from the windows as we came closer. We pushed the wide door open with our feet; in an instant we were in a small hall, and burst into the dining room.

The light blinded us. All eyes turned in our direction. Shabby, bleak, we stood stiffly in a corner as the last shouts of merriment lapped across the dirty floor and died at our feet. Dozens of anonymous eyes were anxiously fixed on us. No one knew who I was but they all recognized the other three.

Galia stood in another corner, talking with a girlfriend. I closed my eyes tightly. All the forgotten contours of her face, all the careless, revered gestures returned and rushed through me, taking my breath away. My God—my heart wept—how much I love her.

Her blue eyes swept in distracted surprise over the faces of her friends, as if she sensed that the party had stopped, until her startled gaze came to rest on the four of us. Her words died on her lips, her eyes darkened and a pallor spread over her face. Quietly she left her place, floating through the stillness that prevailed in the dining room, and soundlessly approached us where we stood together, each alone with his thoughts. She paused a moment, uncertain who to address first. Finally she lifted her eyes and stepped towards me—the most foreign of all. I was, after all, the only one who had never enjoyed her favours, I who had loved her unrequitedly. She extended her slight hand, which I took, feverish and faint. In a fading voice she said, "How nice of you all to come to my party."

A grape vine, tangled and leafy, criss-crossed the rear wall of the dining room and sheltered a cold stone bench. The four of us sat in this rustling hideaway, seeing and unseen, with our backs to the wall that still trembled slightly with the joy of the merry-makers.

The moon was rising, ripe and full, sending out ripples of light through the clearing skies. Soft and tender. The other three sat next to me, mute and tense. Though it was clear that they didn't know each other well, there was something mysterious that stirred them all. They were on their guard, watching the narrow path that meandered down the slope from the dining room to the darkened houses. The hours dragged on. Finally there was a restrained silence in the dining hall and the gentle singing of a girls' chorus wound its way slowly into the air. Suddenly, the hearty laughter of another group could be heard, then again silence and the song of tender passion.

I stroked my face with my hands.

Stillness. A voice read ancient love-poems in honour of the couple. Simple words, drawn out, resonant with the warmth of the reader's voice, filled the night. A sweet, intoxicating fragrance.

My eyes grew dim. The swell of muffled voices through the thin wall had begun to hurt my ears. I tried to distinguish words, but the desperate effort set my head spinning. Weariness overtook me. The small kibbutz houses blurred before my eyes. Time crawled in the heavens above me, and at my side—*them*, strange in their laboured breathing, in their silent anticipation. Slumber took hold of me, and my head fell on to my chest. Trying to stay awake, I focused on the full moon, floating in space, but its yellow aura closed in on my eyes. I would sink into a doze, wake with a start, and fall asleep again. My legs weakened, my arms were slack. A huge moon wandered through my dreams, and I didn't know if it was the moon before my eyes or another one, unknown. With eyes wide open, I dreamt of sky and heavens. Huddled in a cold web of sleep, I suddenly awoke to the gleaming eyes of the trio. They, persisting in their stubborn, silent vigil, regarded my dozing with pity.

A new wind rustled the foliage of the vine that covered us, the big dusty leaves moving in the darkness against my face as in an enchanted world. A chill went through my limbs, which had warmed in my troubled sleep. My head slipped on to the thigh of one of the trio on the bench. From time to time I pulled myself upright, sightless and sleepy, but would slide down again, fearful, on to the thigh.

How many hours had passed? Where was I? Where was Galia? On the other side of the wall: she was there. She was getting married today. What was I doing here? Why was I stretched out like this? How did I ever meet up with this trio? What were *they* waiting for?

The gleaming hands of my watch indicated that it was already past midnight. The door of the dining hall opened; there was a burst of light and a roar of laughter. A figure moved quickly down the winding path. The three rose from their seats, hunched and suspicious, and set off in pursuit. I followed them.

The figure passed two or three buildings before entering a room in another and turning on the light. They followed the light. One of them silently opened the door. One after the other they pushed their way into the room; I was on their heels.

A young man stood there, changing his shirt. When he saw us enter, his hands froze on the buttons.

"You're Danny..." they slowly pronounced.

My look engulfed him. Danny was me. I was dreaming.

His eyes were frank, with long lashes. His hair tumbled on to his narrow forehead and he cleared it with a charming toss of the head. His features were coarse, healthy and filled with a deep tranquillity. In vain I searched them for something extraordinary.

They closed the door gently. Slowly the trio approached him, surrounded him, moved in on him with voracious eyes.

"We came here to get to know you," Ido intoned in the deep silence that had fallen over the room.

The prisoner's lips parted in a bemused smile, but the stark gravity of the three men wiped it away. The circle closed in on him.

"The three of us have come a long way to see Galia's husband... not Galia," Ido added in a sing-song voice.

Danny threw me a questioning glance, wondering why I'd been left out, looking gloomy and desolate in the corner. Like everyone else, he knew who the other three were, but had heard nothing about me. It hadn't occurred to Galia to even mention my existence.

"We've come to see who the last one is," Ido continued

stubbornly, his face hard, as the other two remained mute at his side. "We came to see who's staying on."

Danny's eyes quivered for a moment, but his customary tranquillity was immediately restored. Ido shifted towards him slightly, pushed his face up to Danny's and whispered excitedly, "On your wedding night, you'll be with us." He paused. "We'll all sit here together."

I felt a surge of affection for that man standing there, rather unexceptional, bashfully bowing his head. He didn't protest; he merely surveyed the surrounding trio meekly and said, with sorrow in his voice, "You're still in love with her..."

Ido winced angrily.

"No," he snarled, his mouth awry in an evil grin. "We've forgotten her. Only the insult of her desertion still eats at us. Her nights have blended in by now with all the other nights, but our wounded pride..."

My eyes sought out the ugly scar on Ardon's wrist, the evidence of his attempted suicide.

A hush fell over the room. Suddenly, as one man, they reached for him, grabbed at his trousers, snatched at his shirt, and lifted him off the floor. His legs trembled in the air, but he remained calm; he fixed them with wide eyes.

The only sound to break the silence was the tearing of his shirt. Slowly the trio heaved him through the air and on to the bed—his marriage bed. They leaned over him solicitously, as if he were deathly ill, then sat down around him.

He lay there without moving, resigned to this amazing fate. Iti bent over him, scrupulously inspecting his face: "You're not very good-looking," he said regretfully. "Your features are crude..."

From his lofty height, Ardon leaned over the head of the prostrate figure: "You're not exactly a genius."

Little Ido placed his head on Danny's chest, listening to the heartbeats.

"You're ordinary," he said, with mock surprise. "Nothing special at all..."

All the while Ardon was passing his scarred wrist over Danny's hair, caressing him compassionately.

"Do you see things as she sees them?"

Danny was speechless with despair.

"Does she understand everything, with you?"

"How is it she didn't leave you in the morning? How is it

she didn't run away from you into her weird dreams?"

Ardon passed his red scar, with its many stitches, over Danny's fluttering eyelashes.

"You're not even miserable enough to please her." Here his voice grew smaller, "And it's you she's chosen to be the father of her children?"

His long fingers slid round Danny's throat, gently choking him. Ido was already draped over the prostrate figure, pressing his body against him.

"Could it be that she took pity on you?" he mumbled. "But she knows no pity..."

Danny's eyes filled with terror.

As if they'd suddenly been struck blind, the three began to grope, touching him all over with their hands. Slowly they lowered themselves on to the body beneath them, wearily squirming all over him. They turned into one great knot of limbs, swishing and rolling on the bed. And Danny was suffocating, lost somewhere beneath them.

"They'll kill him," I exulted in my corner.

But with his last reserves of strength, he sprang out of the heap, away from the cruelly clutching hands and into the centre of the room, his hair unkempt, his shirt torn, his buttons undone, and on his neck, the imprint of Ardon's strangling fingers. He looked at the trio, entangled on the bed; his eyes darted over them, back and forth.

"Took pity on me..." he recalled, and burst into cynical laughter. "*I* felt sorry for *her*."

The three froze in their places. My blood pounded.

He's lying!

I approached him, as the frenzy of his intoxication mounted in him.

"Did *I* ask to marry her?.."

He came and stood facing me, staring in bemusement at me, at the stranger. He recoiled and began mumbling: "Who.. are you?..."

And gliding towards his destruction he added mockingly "Are you another of the rejected ones? Did she give you too a few nights, and flee?..."

My hand was stretched out to kill him. It was suddenly strong, desperate. I slapped him hard on the face until his whole body tensed. With heavy fists I began beating him. He didn't try to defend himself, he understood. Under the hail of blows he stooped, sank to his knees, clinging dumbly to my legs. I struck again at the wounded face that was raised to me, weeping softly, until he fell at my feet, and lay still.

The trio looked at me, dreamy-eyed.

Galia burst into the room. She stopped short at the door, as if turned to stone, her eyes drawn towards her husband, lying at my feet. Beaten and bloody. His eyes were lifted towards her from the floor, and there was a gentle smile on his mutilated mouth. He clumsily wiped the blood from his mouth and tried to sit up, but didn't have the strength. His lips moved: "How they love you . . ."

They exchanged silent, brimming glances, fastened lovingly on each other. Suddenly I saw in his eyes the same sunken look as in hers, the strange, penetrating spark. He was hers. She was his. They had already been joined in an earlier, other existence. It was only a question of finding each other again, to merge once more.

And where had I been then?

I had to get away. Lucid, I turned towards the night, which was visible beyond the open door. They all looked at me with sympathy. Danny tried to get up and the three rushed to his aid.

Galia came after me.

The two of us walked out into the shadowy night, both of us quiet. I wanted to speak, but her silence subdued me. Powerful and assertive, she led me outside the kibbutz. She wanted to abandon me in the middle of the fields, to banish me.

Her blue dress was draped about her. Her hair flowed like waves of desire at the side of her beautiful, elusive face. Her white stockings shone in the darkness, rising and falling with the stride of her sweet feet, trampling my shadow. She took me out to the dirt road beyond the kibbutz fence, stopped short, lowered her head and said softly, "From here it's a straight walk to the road."

I didn't budge.

"Goodbye."

She turned to go. Slow, thoughtful.

I stood there, silent, rooted to the spot. She walked off into the distance, but suddenly turned her head. And when she saw that I was still standing there, watching her, she took pity on me and turned back. My eyes filled with tears. She came and stood before me.

"Get out of here. For God's sake."

"I love you."

Pain crept into her eyes.

"I love you," I repeated stubbornly. "I love you."

She stepped back.

I was terrified. Blood rushed into the empty wells of my soul, and was lost in the depths. I danced wildly across the path, into a field of thistles.

"This is where I'll put up my tent."

Gesturing madly, I showed her its dimensions.

"Not big, Galia, but I will live in it."

I loped about like a lunatic, dragged over a large rock and set it by the door of the tent.

"I will sit on this rock. Day and night I will sit, fold my arms, and look at the hill."

I sat on the rock, folded my arms, and gazed at the glittering lights.

"The rock will grow moss and the moss will be long and fine. It will cover me, weave around me, grow out of me."

Suddenly I pressed my body towards her and murmured, "No one will blame me. No one will fault my love."

The slight figure was reeling with grief.

I hugged myself. I hunched my head down between my shoulders.

"He'll die, in an accident... from some dread disease... none of his doing, of course... and you will be mine."

Her mouth fell open, her eyes were filmy.

"I'll wait for the news. I'll be so patient my eyes will turn to stone. And they'll arrive with the news: 'Your Galia is coming to you. Her husband is dead, all her lovers have left her. She's on the hill, she's coming down, here she comes...'"

"Today is my wedding day. *My* wedding day."

I stood up, thrust my hands into the pockets of my threadbare trousers and sauntered up to her, my eyes devouring her beautiful face.

"I've never done you any harm."

Her head nodded in mute confirmation.

"I never claimed what wasn't mine."

I moved closer, the breath of my desire caressing the beloved features.

"I have never reached out a hand to you except in greeting."

I reached out with both hands and clasped her hips. Her slender body shuddered, warm and soft. I bent my head and whispered,

"You have never touched my lips except in dreams."

I pressed my mouth against her deep-set eyes. She sank into my arms.

"My brother... my friend..." she gasped, running her fingers quickly through my hair. I took her hands and kissed them one at a time. The wedding ring gleamed on her finger. Wearily, I bit the thin gold band. Something greater than me groaned with all my soul.

"Galia, my sweet Galia... The three of them will go back home and wear down their wives, but I'll go back to die by the hollow olive tree."

Her face was bathed in tears. A terrible exhaustion suddenly crept through my limbs. I released her and sat down heavily on the rock.

"Enough..." I closed my eyes, and when I opened them I saw her standing by me.

I hung my head.

Galia's bent frame vanished among the glittering lights at the top of the hill and I remained looking up at the stars.

A chill wind was moaning across the plain. I sat, shuddering, on the rock. Forever. Till my bones turned to dust. The field of stubble showed me no mercy. Alone, my legs rustled among the dry stalks. I wanted to lose myself, to wander through these strange expanses under the pale moon.

Something darkened on the track in front of me, and I saw the bus that had brought me. Confused, I quickened my steps towards it, my head heavy and spinning. I continued for some time, but the distance never seemed to lessen. Then I realized that the bus was moving slowly along the dirt road. I started running to catch it up. Now I was actually getting closer. My footsteps were swallowed up in the noise of the engine. Then it was obvious that the bus, too, was picking up speed. Sweat started streaming down my forehead, dripping on to my drying tears. My legs were giving out. I started shouting and my shout fluttered after me, lost in the expanse.

"Driver! Sir!"

But the dark mass in front of me only answered with a burst of white smoke in my damp face.

"Stop!" I screamed into the heavens, and with all the fury of my broken heart, I lunged at the bars of one of the rear windows, and hung on. The bus took off like a shot. My body was tense, my legs dangling, thudding against the metal of the bus.

"Wait... Wait..." I cried, choking.

I tried to hoist myself up through the window, but my arms had succumbed to exhaustion and fear. The whole day's weariness flooded my eyes. My arms were about to break. I lifted my head and suspended myself by my chin from the iron bar. I thrust my aching arms inside, feeling for the arm of the seat, and pulled myself through, head first, legs flailing outside. The bus swayed and gave me a fierce shove backwards, but my face had already met the seat, and my moist lips slipped against the leather.

The bus accelerated.

"Sir," I whispered, upside-down and in agony, from the back seat.

My head was bleeding, and my feet were hooked over the window-bars. With some effort I released them and tumbled on to the soft seat, breathless.

The bus was completely dark; only a small red light flashed among the shiny dials on the dashboard. The dark figure sat there, ponderous, steadfast, merciless, his driver's cap flattened down on his shaven head. Silhouettes of the trees lining the road flitted by mysteriously, getting lost in the coloured advertisements along the inside of the bus. I got up, my legs shaky, and started to make my way down the bus, lurching between the empty seats. I stood, mute, behind the driver's wide, plump back.

He showed no sign of having registered my presence. His eyes in their dark glasses were glued to the road ahead. Only then did I notice that the headlights were not on and that we were gliding with increasing speed along the rough road. A shout died in my throat.

He certainly must have known the road well, since the bus was flying in the dark, taking every twist and turn as it came. But gradually he lost control, as his memory betrayed him. From time to time he would turn around needlessly, going off the road, and the big bus would bump along the edge of a ditch, almost falling apart.

"You'll turn us over yet," I yelled nervously above his head.

But he was unaware of my existence.

I put a warning hand on his back, but he felt nothing. He was focused on his driving, his hands firm on the shiny wheel.

"Don't go on!" In a panic I gripped his thick, smooth hand. But he didn't budge. Fat, oblivious, he continued to goad the bus on. I started clawing at his hot hand in despair, pulling at his shoulder, but he threw me off and sent me sprawling.

"Driver, you are going to kill us," I whispered bitterly.

My arms had fallen against the gearbox, and I tried to pull the gearstick, but I couldn't. I crawled to the pedals underneath, but his legs were like iron—short and horrible iron stumps. I tried to bite them but he, feeling nothing, continued to floor the accelerator as the bus swayed perilously to the sides of the road.

"Driver, sir," I wailed at his feet, rolling exhaustedly in the dark. "Have pity..."

I blacked out.

When I came to, the bus was still, flooded with light. My head was glued to the metal floor, and I could see the white bulbs alight up and down the bus. I passed my hand over my eyes, which burned from the intense glare.

The fat driver rose to his full dwarfish height, keeping an eye on me. Slowly he lifted a hand and removed his dark glasses, revealing his face for the first time. It was right up close to me—a lustful face, red and bloated, with huge, bulging brown eyes set into it, and the whites exposed down to the swollen roots. The face of an ancient pagan god, with a small slash of a mouth.

I recalled the burnt-out olive tree near my house.

He sized me up attentively. Crumbled me into fragments, sucked me into the abyss of his rolling eyes, expelled me small and pitiful. Suddenly his compassion was awakened. He leaned heavily over me, grabbed me by my thin arm and pulled me up, frightened and filthy, from the floor. He brought me closer, right up to his huge forehead, ploughed with thousands of wild circular wrinkles. He puzzled over me for a long time, then finally opened his mouth and announced in a deep, shattered voice, "Galia's wedding is over..."

The words came out strangely, unexpectedly.

I returned a steady gaze to the face in front of me.

"Yes," I said, beaten, broken, in my sorrow.

A light went on behind my closed eyes.

"Shall we continue?" He asked my permission with docile gravity.

I rolled my eyes, as though dreaming. The bus stood in the centre of the huge, dark plain. The road in front of it was illuminated well into the distance by the bright headlights, a quiet asphalt road.

I turned to him, my silent lips awaiting a sign from the eyes waiting for me.

"Shall we continue?" he repeated, interrupting my sob.

I let my head fall on the driver's chest, and emotion guided my lips: "I beg you to."

Flood Tide

A storm has been raging over the Southern Islands for the past fortnight, and day by day it grows more violent. In an instant everything will go misty and a mass of clouds will come to rest on the plain like piles of dirty cotton wool. A burst of hard clear hail will sweep the wasteland and batter the grey prison house. Is it any wonder that tonight, in the dead of night, with the storm at its wildest, the Chief Warder should suddenly order the sentry to my cubicle to wake me from my wide-eyed sleep and summon me to the office, to receive startling midnight instructions?

The words of the messenger are still echoing around the dark walls when I, and I alone, crawl naked from under the rough blankets, and all the other actors in my dream perish among the wrinkles of the sheet. Shivering with cold I don the stained service overall, and while my hands race down the long, long row of buttons my face is turned to listen to the mounting gales. I am newly come to this jail and still a novitiate in the service. Hence I am awake to everything about me and eager to excel in my work. If it wasn't for the dreams unsettling me at night I would consider myself an exemplary jailer. It is but a month since I graduated from the stiff course for jailers; there I was taught to shoot a submachine gun and never miss, to leap high hurdles, to wrestle in hand-to-hand combat, and to understand the tersely worded Manual of Regulations. Was it my taciturnity that made them think I could restrain my passions too, and made them send me to serve at this small jail on its remote island? True, the men confined here are real criminals, murderers reprieved from the gallows and sentenced to life imprisonment; but they are few, and they are very old.

I fumble for my shoes in the dark. I do not light a candle for I am sparing of property belonging to the King. Does there exist a regulation that permits jailers to let their thoughts wander while on duty? I do not know. As long as I haven't studied every last dot in the Manual of Regulations and made certain either way, I can grant myself the benefit of the doubt. But I know that, though silent, my face betrays me, at least to this Chief Warder for whom I am bound now, proud and thrilled, correctly dressed though it is the middle of the night. I cross the eternal twilight of the cell-lined corridor, dimly lit over its whole length and into the deepest corner of the prisoners' cells ranged along both sides, ascend the three steps to the office and present myself, saluting as laid down in the rules.

He is sitting behind his desk, alert and watchful whatever the hour. A middle-aged officer, short, his hair greying, his face dry and strikingly severe; a member of the old school, which I venerate. The curtains are drawn over the barred windows, and the huge red emblems of the kingdom are displayed on them in all their glory. His two long-legged dogs squat on the carpet and look at me with mournful dignity. Only the hail lashing against the windows disturbs the grave imposing silence that graces our prison. My commanding officer turns his eyes full on my face, and his eyes burn, bold with lust, in utter contradiction to the grim lines of his face. He starts to speak in his blunt manner and the essence of his words is one wondrous message:

The sea is about to rise and flood our island.

How did the Chief Warder learn of this? Not from any doubtful weather forecasters, who know nothing of our island, nor from any urgent call from the Central Prison authorities in the capital who scarcely remember our existence. The fact has come to the Chief Warder's knowledge solely through his own exhaustive studies, his poring day and night over the old diaries of our prison that stand volume by volume, massive and tall, in his locked bookcase. The jailers of old who died at their post (they could have known no other death) and whose bleached skeletons lie buried at the bottom of the sea took care to write a daily chronicle of all that occurred on the island. It is from these chronicles that the Chief Warder has learned about the flood tide, about the signs in nature portending it and about the destructive force of the water. Three times the prison house has been flooded, completely destroyed and built anew. Even I, the novice, knew this from my studies in the History of Prisons. Yet I had never imagined that it would be this tempest, this wild wind hurling itself against our walls, that would bring us the ancient flood tide once again.

Unthinking I take a few short steps nearer the desk, kindled by a new interest. Is it happiness, this glow inside me?

The Chief Warder lays his hand on the neck of one of his beloved dogs and starts stroking its fur voluptuously. In a low voice he tells me about the Regulations that require the Chief Warder to escape from the island on the fateful day together with his men, to lock up the prisoners in their cells and to leave one or two jailers in charge, volunteers, worthy of the task. The little officer lowers his eyes. Who else should offer himself if not I, the young jailer who is so very eager to distinguish himself in the service?

Emotion grips me whenever the Regulations are spoken of in my presence, but on this occasion, when I hear that the Chief Warder has chosen me of all his men, I am stunned, I nearly fall at his feet. I bite my lip to contain a shout of exultation.

Do I wish another man to stay with me, inquires the Chief Warder, and his eyes show a glint of cunning. Serving in this jail, beside the two of us, there are a cook, a barber, an armourer and a locksmith. But I know what is in his mind.

"I want no one with me, sir," I reply softly.

No, I think, I want none of those functionaries, those trying to evade the pure naked function of jailer. And even as my eyes are watching his fondling hands and the pampered dogs at his feet, an idea flashes through my mind.

"Leave only your dogs with me, sir."

This time I have managed to take the little man by surprise. He cherishes those two dogs of his, is so attached to them as to arouse suspicion. He is a solitary man, childless, his wife away in the distant capital and none but the dogs left him. They are dog and bitch, and he has bred and pampered them from puppies. Now I shall take them from him and turn them into proper prison dogs, fierce. How can he refuse me now that I am going to be left alone in this dark prison, left to face the rising sea? His hands tremble, he makes no reply. Softly he tells me of an ancient boat found on the island. It had been the jailers of old who had built it to save their own lives. It has recently been fitted out with a new engine brought over from the capital. This boat will avail me when the waters rise and flood the building—then I, too, shall escape. For thus say the wise Regulations: "When the waters shall prevail upon the earth, then shall the last jailer leave his prisoners and shall escape. Generations of prisoners come and go, but jailers are few and shall abide forever."

He hands me the key of the engine, tiny and bright. Tomorrow I shall be given all the heavy keys of the prison house.

Where will my master, the Chief Warder, flee to? To the mountains, the mountains of course. Even through the bars of the narrow prison windows you can see them, right to the dense growth bristling at their summits. There my master will flee with his men. Perhaps he will find a dry cottage. They say there is a hamlet there, low in a wadi between mountains. Who knows? His fate may yet be worse than mine. I, at any rate, have already raised my arm in parting salute. To my surprise he does not return it but rises from his chair, and a look of sorrow comes into his face. He leaves his dogs, sails around the desk, puts himself in front of me, rises on tiptoe and places both his small hairy paws on my shoulders in such a fatherly manner that a shiver runs through my body. His words, his obscure parting words, cut deep into the silence of my mind:

"Restrain your passions with the rising water, resist temptation and stand the test. Find it in yourself to escape, you and the dogs with you."

Good for you, Master.

At dawn, during a brief pause in the rain, the dogs thrust their heads through the two windows of the office where they have been locked up and howl at the little master who is deserting them. The fugitives with their luggage file in gloomy procession through the building; locking door after door, adding key after key to the heavy bunch jingling merrily in my hand. In the courtyard they show me the boat fastened with a rope to the building, and I give a careless nod. Barely patient, I accompany them to the gate, go outside with them, out to the plain, and lock the gate behind me. My eyes fly at once to the horizon, but I see nothing. The prison house is quite a distance from the sea, and it is only on golden days that one can make out a blue strip on the horizon. The fugitives climb into the barred prison van and crowd with their luggage on to the prisoners' seats. They measure me with their eyes. Are they glad to have escaped? Our parting is brief, unemotional: relationships are stiff within the framework of the Regulations. Presently the car drives off into the sandy plain surrounding us, accompanied by the dogs' wild barks of despair. The car is swallowed up by the heavy fog.

Now I am sole ruler in this house of stone. How wise to have built it on the plain, enabling me to see from afar all that may come and go, all that may attack or escape. I open the gate, enter the courtyard. Every time I open a door I lock it behind me at once. I am familiar with keys and fond of handling any of them, let alone the huge prison keys, their bare teeth frozen in an eternal gape. I have to pass many doors in order to reach the second storey, the cell-lined corridor. The prisoners have risen from their aimless sleep. They are already seated on their stools beside the doors, doors that are not made of solid sheets of iron but of grating, that the prisoners may always be visible through the bars and not be hatching plots. They resemble apes in cages, except that they are always silent and they do not move. Their crimes were committed long ago, even perhaps before I—their new young warder—saw the light of day. Now they are old, and their shaven skulls mask their baldness. The prison barber takes pains never to leave a single hair on their head. He mows off everything with his shears, out of boredom. Most of them are heavy and fat. All these years they are gorging on the state's food and drink, and they do nothing. There is no telling whether they are violent or wasted.

They watch me with tranquil eyes. They always they sit facing the corridor, as though waiting. What are they waiting for now? Their breakfast, of course. The whining of the dogs imprisoned in the office is also changing tune from a whine of lament to one of hunger. I therefore hurry and unlock the kitchen, set myself at once to cook a meal according to the instructions pinned on the wall. Afterwards I load everything on a trolley and start rattling dishes through the dim windowless corridor. A small hatch opens between the bars of each door, and through it I am handed a bowl with the remnants of the previous meal congealed at the bottom and hand back a fresh, full one. They are used to this back-and-forth exchange of bowls, and the whole routine is accomplished in utter silence. They must be aware that I am now their only guard. All that happens in this place is known to them even though, according to the Regulations, they are not allowed to talk among themselves, let alone talk to the jailers. What should we talk to them for? We are not interrogators, nor are we judges; only jailers guarding them lest they escape. The Law has been laid down, the sentence pronounced, and if they have not been brought to the gallows—that is their fate, and one does not discuss fate. I may have forgotten to mention that a loaded submachine gun hangs at all times suspended from a strap over my shoulder.

The food distribution is over. The dogs' howls are rending my ears. I unlock the office door and they burst out and leap at me, mad with joy, lick my face and hands. With great difficulty I manage to calm them down. From now on I am their master. I put their daily meat ration before them, the largest ration of all distributed in this place. They fall upon the meat, chew voraciously with their large molars, in rapture, their eyes rolling. I look on in silence at this gluttony, stand frozen on the spot till they have devoured everything. Then I prepare my own austere, frugal portion. Swiftly, indifferently, I gulp the tasteless food and go down to the courtyard to look at the storm.

Fog. I strain my eyes to make out water and see nothing. I prick up my ears to catch its murmur as one waiting for a beloved step, but the savage howling of the wind through the fog erases all sound. Impossible to learn anything about the progress of the sun. The world is grey from end to end. I return to the corridor. Silence; only the sound of the prisoners bent over their bowls, chewing on the last of their food.

My day is filled with activity. I wash the dishes, sweep the floor. From time to time I pick up the submachine gun suddenly, burst out of the kitchen and go wandering along the corridors. The inmates of the cages do not look at me. They are common people and the spiritual is beyond their ken. They have now opened their books and begun their daily reading. Ageing assassins with thrillers in their hands, tales of murder and obscenity out of the prison library, with their last pages torn (or ripped out maliciously), so that the readers never know about the capture of the criminal and linger to their satisfaction over the futility of the detectives in pursuit. Once a month we traverse the corridor with a trolley and collect the twenty-one books, shuffle them, and return with the trolley from the other end of the corridor. Some prisoners happen to get back their own book, some get a new-old one to read. It stands to reason that each of them knows all the books. Yet even now they sit there, their dim eyes straying over the tattered pages. Don't they know that their death is near? Don't they sense the rising tide? If they were to hoist themselves up a little to the slit high in the wall of their cell, they would be able to see the horizon stretching to the sea, or lift their eyes to the mountain tops.

Noon. A few lost rays of sunlight wander suddenly through the two narrow windows over the kitchen sink. I am warming up the midday meal. The dogs crawl into a corner for their daily copulation. Deplorable habits they have acquired in this jail. I stand watching them and a great sorrow fills my heart. The hours of the afternoon are once more spent in drudgery. Again I wash dishes, sweep floors, polish the doors. I am a servant to the prisoners, not their master. But when evening comes and darkness fills the building, and I have finished my work—then a sweet weariness spreads through my limbs and I realize again with wonder that I am sole master of this entire building, without intermediaries, without commands. I and the Law alone. With hands rough from the day's work I take up the bunch of keys that accompanies me always and go rambling among the silent stones of my castle. I feel my way through the dark, the dogs ahead of me sniffing every corner. When I pass through the corridor I see that the eyes of my prisoners are tired, as though washed by a sombre sea. Yet they haven't lifted a finger all day. I light the dim corridor lamp. The prisoners are never left in darkness, always in twilight. My eyes stray to the yellow pages tacked to the front of each cell. A blurred list of its inmate's crimes. It is decreed by the Chief Warder that their felonies should be recorded for us to see and never pity them. Pity is dangerous on so remote an island.

The hours of the night come to me like giant birds—each blacker than the one before. The prisoners do not raise their eyes, are still poring over their books. Nearly all of them have grown short-sighted from years of reading in bad light , and they sit with their faces on top of the print, their lashes grazing the page. Who cares about them going blind in jail? I enter the office, fill in the day's forms and lock the door on the dogs crouching among the piles of old documents and chronicles. Then I go to my cubicle, lock my door and secrete the keys beneath my pillow. I light a candle and by its feeble rays start taking my weapon apart in order to clean it. Hail lashes against the building, but not a single drop leaks in. Three times they built this place anew, and every time they improved upon the last. Now they will build it a fourth time. Except for the wind howling, the silence is absolute. Could any man wish for a silence deeper than this? True happiness comes and floods my heart again. I am alone here, but my solitude does not frighten me. For it is not a personal solitude but one ordained by the Regulations, and the Regulations are from the King. With a final click I attach the butt to the body of the submachine gun and lay it shining and steely on my bed, between the sheets. Then I lie down in my clothes on the hard narrow mattress, a jailer's mattress precluding deep sleep. The taut sheets, the folded blankets, the gun lying like a cruel child by my side—everything bears the monarchal emblems imprinted upon it. I pick up the Manual of Regulations. My master, the Chief Warder, no longer reads the Manual of Regulations, only the diaries left by the jailers of antiquity. But I know that the diaries are but commentary and the Manual is the main thing. I read only it, therefore, read slowly, thoroughly. After an hour or two fatigue makes the lines start humming within me like a soft chant, a lament.

At midnight I force myself to shut the Manual, lest I be tempted to read all night. I am a member of the Prison System and I know that the prison needs my sleep, in order that my head be clear at all times. I blow out the candle and remain lying with my eyes open to the darkness. Everything is locked, no one will break through the heavy doors. And who would go wandering on this bleak plain?

In the morning the sheets are twisted. Everything is in wild confusion. The gun has dropped to the floor, the keys crept deep into the pillow, and the monarchal emblems have slipped, limp and crumpled, from under my head down to my nakedness. What dreams came to me? I do not wish to remember, I must not remember. I hasten to smooth the grey sheets and fold the blankets, efface the night's memory, shamefaced, and rush to see if the waters have come.

The two days preceding the flood tide pass like a grey dream filled with soft happiness and work. Every free moment I fly to the windows to look at the wide open world. Amazedly I discover that the storm is abating. The wind has completely died down and only a thin soft rain is drizzling from grey skies. A hush lies over everything. Can the Chief Warder have been mistaken? Is all this really but a prelude to the flood that will come? The silence of the far sea tells me nothing. Slowly my eyes travel to the other side of the island, to the great mountains, their impervious summits. No doubt the fugitives have arrived there by now. I do not in the least regret being here, waiting here still.

Faithfully I perform my daily labours, changing the prisoners' bowls and feeding the dogs, the tall dogs on heat who follow me with their long-legged tread, meek and faithful like a couple of foolish aristocrats come down in the world. In the evening I fill in the forms and write a few words of my own about the grey universe. And at night, in my locked cubicle, I become engrossed in the Manual once more.

The second day is also amazingly, excitingly grey. The skies are calm now, not a drop of rain. The plain lies still, suffused by an expectant hush, the whole universe in attendance. The temperature has risen with a sudden leap. But the sun has not broken through the grey shroud, and the day has gone by without any change in the light. Late in the afternoon, when the light began fading from the sky at last, I collected the two dogs, locked door after door behind me, descended the staircase, opened and locked the large iron gate, crossed the square prison yard, opened the gate

in the outer wall and left the precincts, locking the last gate behind
me like a man locking up his home. The dogs raced about madly in
the open space. I began walking over the monotonous plain where
there is no road, no mark—nothing but a dry sandy waste. The
evening drew across the sea to meet me, passed through me and on
to the darkening island. No wind, not the slightest whiff. I walked,
drawing further and further away from the locked prison, the keys
on my belt jingling softly, like bells. The dogs romped about me.
They would dash off far ahead into the distance, then suddenly
come tearing back to me in a furious rage, lick my hands and go
roaming again. Sometimes they would stop, puzzling over some
anonymous sandstone, sticking their damp muzzles into it, searching
for the traces of some mysterious smell known to them alone. They
had spent all their life in prison and were delighted with this
unexpected outing. I, too, was gratified. I was going to see whether
the sea was coming, and the prison house was transformed in my
sight—by darkness or by distance—into a blurred shadow. Some
may think that I could have gone, taken myself and the two dogs
away and beyond the plain, and left the old prisoners locked in the
silence behind me. The slight advantages we have in being at liberty
to move about the corridors and wander of an evening into the plain
around the prison may cause some people to believe that we jailers
are free. But we are not. We, too, are imprisoned, but of our own
accord. As yet we are innocent.

Perhaps that will explain why I stopped at last in my slow
peaceful journey across the endless plain. No, I had not found the
sea yet, but I had found everything dry and waiting for it. Darkness
descends. The prison is an insignificant speck on the plain, but I
know it is part of me. The soft hazy air fills my eyes with longing.
The dogs have stopped their ferreting about and come to stand by
me, their ears cocked, listening too. I turn and start walking back.
The dogs wonder why, without having achieved any purpose,
reached any point, I suddenly stop midway and turn in my
tracks. They defy me, continue in the direction of the sea till they
vanish in the dusk; but in the end they come running in a wide arc
back to me, and then once more they scamper merrily before me as
though nothing had happened. Now the sun is setting. I can tell by
the crimson streaks erupting over the mountains. By the time I
reach the prison, darkness has covered everything. Flushed with
happiness I open the gate in the wall. I am at peace. I find my
prisoners seated in their cells, in complete darkness, their books

trailing in their hands, patiently waiting for the dim light which I now turn on in their corridor. Everything is as it was. They are incapable of even thinking about flight. Only now do I realize how attached I have grown to this place. I shall not speak of the passion with which I fill in the day's forms.

At the break of dawn, in my dream, I hear the distant thrust. The first of the water is come. The invisible sea has hurled itself at the land and started its headlong advance. The dogs are restless. They have wakened and together with me they look out of the high windows and bark for no reason. The water appears to frighten them, somehow. For the time being the flood tide is nothing but a faint bluish line, as though the horizon itself were coming here, that same horizon that would never be visible except on the clearest of days. These are only playful waters as yet, casually they conquer the unresisting plain, as though surprised at themselves. These are only explorers, advancing in a crooked line and ready to yield to the first stone in their path, adapt themselves to the land for the sake of its conquest. So that when they reach the prison wall they halt respectfully before it. They mean no harm, they have only come to lick at the island, just lick it the way one of the dogs is licking my arm now in a dumb request for food.

I fling him away with a blow of my fist. Instead of savage, blood-thirsty animals, these two have been bred here into senti-mental lap dogs with sad soulful eyes. I doubt if they are capable of attacking a man. Anything but a little grunting and growling is beyond them, and even these shows of menace will soon turn into snivelling.

A rhythmic banging of bowls against bars sounds from the corridor. The prisoners are demanding their food. The water has been distracting my attention and breakfast is long overdue. The prisoners have heard the water as well, but the limp bodies by the cell doors have not tensed; not a spark of excitement in their vacant eyes. I respect their silence and perhaps they, too, respect mine. I have heard it said that there were times when they would never stop talking and shouting among themselves, but over the years they had grown weary of each other and had limited themselves to strict necessities; before long they had found out that the only necessity was silence.

They have no contact with each other now, except through me.

As soon as I can spare a minute from my work I rush to the windows, stand staring at the waters, spellbound. Irresistibly the sea is urging its horizon on. Those first surprised explorers have already passed the prison house and are moving leisurely ahead, toying with every stone and conquering the entire plain in their offhand manner. Thus they will roll on till they reach the mountains, and there surprise will turn to adulation and their easygoing, playful domination will turn into a helpless fawning. But around the prison house the water is already swirling, endlessly flowing. Not a thin line any longer but a torrent, a close surging body of water turning the plain into a deep lake. Now it is reaching the top of the wall, towering, surmounting it, and in numerous sparkling cascades it drops into the courtyard, floods the tiles and rapidly approaches the prison house itself, licks the grey stones of its wall, plotting its evil and sure of victory. Caressed by the water, the boat rocks a little on its mooring.

The hours of the day go swiftly by. I look and look at the water and marvel. The prisoners do not raise their eyes from their books and sit wallowing in their stories. But in my brain the waters bore with a thin persistent wail. I do not think that the sound of the water can reach the distant mountains. I serve supper to my prisoners, amazed and hurt. Why will they not raise their heads? I collect the dirty bowls, wash the dishes. This is the third day that I have not eaten, just tasted my food. I am startled by the fast pace at which the tide is rising. Alone and deserted I wander about the corridors and suddenly my heart pines for all the people of the distant kingdom who are taking their pleasures and know nothing. Self-pity fills me, floods me. Joy and sorrow mingle and I crawl into a dark corner and cry a little. But soon my eyes dry, and once again I am a cruel guard bullying the frightened dogs. When I cross the corridor once more, and when I see my prisoners bent over their books, rage mounts in me and I cock my gun as in a dream and fire a long volley, piercing the twilit wall. Dust, smoke and a smell of sulphur. The prisoners are rigid in their cells. My Sovereign Liege, I am here, in this dark and distant corridor, lead me not into nto temptation. Again tears well up in my eyes: when shall I, too, go out into the mountains?

It is but a slight flutter. I pull myself together at once and return to work, clean the blackened gun. Afterwards I pass along the cells, collect the prisoners' buckets and empty their excrement into the sea.

Deep grey night, and the swirling of the water does not cease. A deadly silent world. This flood tide is nothing but the sea coming home. The sea will always come back and retake what it conquered once before. Let no one bear it malice for returning to trace its ancient crime. I look through the high windows. Softly the water has risen, has reached the windows of the ground floor. A black object sways near the wall—it is my escape boat slowly mounting towards me with the rising sea.

Are the prisoners growing alarmed? They must hear the howling of the water, they can see the rising water between the bars of their windows as well as I. Yet perhaps they are too old to scramble up the walls of their cells. A mere glance at my face would tell them everything. I lock up the dogs, who have been following me—sad, their tails between their legs—wherever I go. For a moment I stand listening to the water, then I enter my cubicle, lock the door and light the candle. Tomorrow is the last day, no question about that. I shall escape with the keys. The building will crumble in the water and I shall have the keys—that is the way it happens in the old legends. It is the perfect escape, the right one. Afterwards they will build a new prison here. Indeed, it would be a waste to relinquish this deserted plain where the sea comes from time to time and drowns the ageing prisoners. But I shall escape with my life. With doorless keys I shall walk in front of the King's palace—a faithful servant, who may yet be honoured in the capital.

I lie down in my clothes; always in my clothes. I take up the Manual of Regulations and settle down to read, but I am too agitated still. The small cracked mirror by the wardrobe reveals my pale face, the black rings under my eyes, the bloodless lips. When I declare that I sleep at night, it is only lest it be said of me that I violate the sleeping rules prescribed for jailers to promote vigilance by day. Actually, however, I lie wide-eyed hour after hour during most of the night. I lie clutching the thick square Manual, looking at its close print. It is divided into chapters and verses: instructions, laws, commandments. Yet there are times when I fancy that the Lawgiver is toying with me and has written nothing but obscure poetry. There is no explicit mention of the flood tide, but perhaps it is conveyed between the words. Fatigue envelops me. The figure of the teacher who used to instruct us in the Manual of Regulations looms before my eyes. He was a strict, profound man, ever dressed in black. It was he that kindled my passion for the dry words. I lie lost in reverie, brooding over his figure till the flame dies out. I cannot sleep. The ceaseless gurgling of the water. Whenever I doze off the water rises in my dreams. In the middle of the night I start up, awake with sudden terror. I open the doors and see that the water has invaded the ground floor and is flooding the rooms. When I drag myself back through the corridor, I see the prisoners slouching on their stools, some reading by the faint light, some nodding over their books. One of them is always awake, to warn the others. Sometimes I have a desire to enter one of the cells and sit on a stool, like them, peacefully bent over my book.

Morning of my day of escape. The water is climbing sluggishly up the staircase. My head feels heavy. I trail along the corridors, draw near the two windows and look out. A grey sea stretching under grey skies. Wisps of fog floating. We are in the middle of the sea. Far, far into the distance the restless waters have swept, flooding the whole plain on their way to the mountains. Overnight the boat has risen an entire storey and is now floating up and down under the office windows. All I have to do is break through a window and jump into it.

There is a smell to the water, and the smell intoxicates me. Between the walls of the house the water is coming at me, a strange, alien mass. I descend to the last dry step of the staircase and the dogs follow me down with cautious tread, hesitating, slipping on the steps, their ears drooping; they lap a little at the water. Their lascivious passions have faded.

I spend all morning cleaning the house and making my preparations for escape. I intend to take nothing with me except the dogs, my weapon and, of course, the Manual of Regulations; it is the copy presented to me upon my graduation from the course, and is inscribed with a splendid dedication from the kingdom. The dogs sense that I am about to escape and do not let me out of their sight. The water is rising very slowly now. The flood tide has spent its impetus; now the sea is only finding its level in the plain, and it is due to flood the building in the process. I see a small puddle even now (and there is no knowing where it came from), collecting against the corridor threshold. At noon I divide all the food that is left in the house among the prisoners. Better that they die by drowning.

Afterwards I shut myself up in the office with the day's forms. I cannot recall what it was I wrote there, but I do know that I stayed a long time by the desk and that a strong emotion gripped me when I found the right words. Now I am scrubbing every corner of the house and arranging everything in its proper position. Actually, a strict order reigns in this place always, yet even this order may appear deceptive set against the severe demands of the Regulations.

A swift glance at the windows covered with a thin haze tells me that dusk is hovering over the sea. I do not hurry myself on that account, not at all; it suits me well, departure in the black of night.

Out of the wardrobe in my cubicle I take my black costume with the monarchal emblems imprinted on its lining. It is the formal attire for grand occasions, executions and such. The costume is creased here and there, but is still new. I have not worn it since the graduation ceremony of the course. I slip out of the dirty service overall, stride naked through the corridor, in full sight of the prisoners. I am not ashamed. I wash my limbs in the cold familiar water of the faucet, return to my cubicle and put on my clean clothing, smooth out the creases, pull on the high boots; I am ready for a journey into night. I shall light my torch and ford the darkness.

The water has flooded the top stair, arrives at the second landing like a guest sure of himself and his welcome. A single rivulet gushes forward suddenly, drawing a blind, timid line along the corridor, meandering over the crack between the tiles till it comes up against the wall. Soon the water will grip my hand in a cold wet salute. How strange to see it here, the flood of the distant sea here in this dim corridor. The moment has come to escape. The dogs wriggle joyously at my feet, their tails thumping hard against the floor; they, too, are excited at the thought of meeting their little master again. I don my coat, lash the dogs to my belt with short, tough straps, attach the keys to my buckle, hitch the gun on to my shoulder and take the Manual of Regulations in my hand. I cannot deny that I am sorry to leave this dark prison house sinking in the sea. For three days I was sole ruler here, and I have grown attached to the long corridors.

Slowly I move along the cells and softly the keys jingle. One last inspection of my prisoners. They do not raise their heads from their books, some are dozing. Is that how they will part from me? They stay motionless, rooted to their stools with the placidity of very old, jail-hardened men, their striped prison garb emphasizing the drab ordinariness remaining here, in contrast to my festive clothes. The dogs are jerking at the straps attached to my belt, dragging me on. One of the prisoners is gnashing his teeth. Which one? I scan the cells with angry eyes and he falls silent. Are they really placid, or is the calm feigned? I am deserting them now. In my imagination I see my little boat steering swiftly for the mountains, and this deserted building with its prisoners caught between bars and battering sea. All that I leave here will remain outside the Law. I look at the small volume in my hand with surprise. Softly the Regulations have come, have flocked unnoticed from all corners where they belong and folded themselves back into the Manual; and with me, inevitably, they will go away from here.

Anarchy—I suddenly think of it, and I tremble.

I stop, pull back the panting dogs bent on escape. The Chief Warder has fled and has entrusted this place to me. Now I am about to escape. Whom shall I entrust the prison to? For a moment I consider leaving the beloved Manual here, in the middle of this dim corridor, at the heart of the flooded building, but I know that the water will sweep it away like a lifeless object. Suddenly the walls seem naked. I look at my prisoners, their bowed heads, and imagine them breaking into howls, tearing up the doors, breaking through secret tunnels, wrecking the whole crumbling prison in their rage and shattering the silence, this hard-won silence.

I could rip out the pages of my little book and paste up the Regulations on these walls, fuse them with the iron of the bars, knead them into the prisoners' food—but it will all be in vain, I think in despair. The prisoners see that I have stopped. Their eyes narrow as though in wonder: You still here? Our glances cross. Is there one among them worthy to receive the Regulations from my hand?

In a flash I make up my mind, boldly, as befits the personal (personal!—I could weep with joy) representative of the King in this jail. And then I have taken the keys from my belt, raised the gun to my waist and cocked it, and I turn on my heels and start opening the cells, one by one. The locks creak in amazement. Even the dogs appear shocked at the unthinkable deed. All the doors are unlocked. Twenty-one heavy iron doors. I command the whole length of the corridor with my short barrel. In a strong voice I order them out. The doors shriek, they open. The prisoners emerge, nearly all of them tall, their shaven heads bent; the dogs growl, terrified. A shiver of hatred passes through their bodies at the sight of the prisoners. The smell of ancient crimes is in their clothes still. With difficulty I manage to hold them back by their straps lest they break loose and attack them. The long line of prisoners passes before me in single file, splashing barefoot through the puddles. They climb the three steps to the office. They have not forgotten to take their books along, just in case I should bore them, the scoundrels.

Next I am seated like the Chief Warder in the chair behind the desk. The two dogs chained to my belt stand like haughty beasts of prey, one at each side of me. The gun is on the desk, its muzzle facing the prisoners. Instead of a young jailer all of a flutter I have twenty-one heavy, burnt-out prisoners before me. The smell of their sweat reaches my nostrils. An unbearable stench. I swing the oil lamp up over my head and the walls fill with long-faced shadows. I open the Manual of Regulations. Where ought I to start? Can I teach it all to them? Every sentence in the Manual has some bearing upon another, no Regulation stands on its own. I therefore begin at the beginning. In a clear, eager voice I read out the first fairly simple Regulations. I make no attempt to explain, trusting to the power of the written word. It is brief, the time I can afford to linger here without endangering my life. I sense that they, lined up before my desk, are listening with startled attention. My voice is rapt with exaltation. All I want is to make them understand the Law that is abandoning them to their lot. Page after page turns under my fingers as I read, enunciating clearly, giving myself up to the words. Time passes. Their attention flags. They are feeling behind them for walls to lean against. A few even make bold to lower their eyes to their books and continue reading. I ignore them and accelerate my pace. I dare not raise my head from the book and see the utter incomprehension surrounding me. I know that the speed I am reading at makes it impossible for them to take in anything, but I would rather go over as many Regulations as possible. Indeed, even if I were to read slowly they would grasp nothing. The eagerness is there in my voice still. A whole hour passes. My hand holding the oil lamp is sagging with fatigue, my voice growing hoarse. The dogs have lain down on the floor. I skip whole pages, seek out only my favourite Regulations now. But the text is growing involved. I am coming to Regulations that are unfamiliar even to me. My speech is growing careless and confused. The flame is fading in the lamp. Still my prisoners stand before me, a dark mute mass. A few are asleep on their feet and I hear their soft snores. The letters are dissolving into the darkness and I fill in the missing words with the aid of my imagination, rapidly creating new regulations. They won't notice the difference. When my voice breaks at last, and the flame dies, I raise my eyes.

They show no reaction. I jump up to examine their faces. Now I see that some of them are standing there with their mouths sagging, lips trembling. I feel a momentary surge of pity; such old men. But in an instant I collect myself, move swiftly to the door and whisper a command. They file past me, close, so close. In a long shuffling

line they descend the three steps to the corridor and slip quietly into
their cells. They are disciplined to the core, obedient to the muzzle
pointing at their backs. I follow them down the steps, halt at the
mouth of the flooded corridor and listen to them dragging their
stools back into place, settling down. Now I shall go and lock their
cells, and flee to save my life. But what have I done? Have I tarried
too long? I lower my hand to my belt to take the keys, and I do not
find them. Madly I search through the pockets of my coat, turn my
clothes inside out, go down on the floor, but the heavy bunch has
vanished. I glance along the corridor. A deep hush. The water is
caressing my boots.

My keys are stolen.

Sick with panic, in torment, I rush back the three steps to the
office. The dogs are dragged behind me on their straps. In vain I
search the floor, the spot where I have been standing, hunt over the
desk, snatch up the Manual that has remained there to look
underneath. No doubt about it: the keys have been stolen from me.

I turn back to the corridor at once, tear down the three steps
with the gun raised in my hand. If I find that they have come out of
their open cells I shall mow them down to the last man. But when I
reach the threshold of the corridor and pull myself up I find dead
silence. Not one of them has left his cell. As yet they are lurking
within, plotting their evil unseen by me, not seeing me. I cannot
advance into the corridor to search for the keys lest they attack me
from behind. I have no choice but to stand here on the threshold,
tense, my gun ready. They stay mute. Impossible to tell which of
them is holding my keys. How skillfully they manage to communi-
cate among themselves without speech, with invisible signs. An hour
goes by, then two, I lean a little sideways against the wall. The dogs
are lying at my feet. No, I am not miserable. On the contrary, this
new and unforeseen trial rouses an intense excitement in me. I am
still too determined to be miserable. Only a few times in my life
have I been tested, and each new trial enriches my spirit. I have
forgotten the boat rocking under the windows, forgotten the
mountains. Open-eyed I stand, listening. The dogs too prick up
their ears, absorb my excitement. I could roar commands into the
dark void, but who would obey me now. I do not want to make a
fool of myself at this difficult hour.

The current has slowed down, the water is almost, marvellously,
still. I slacken the dogs' straps a little and they crawl up the three
steps to find themselves a dry spot. Their eyes are sad now. They

never really loved me, but this time I have plainly disappointed them. My apprehension grows from moment to moment. I am afraid to leave my place lest the prisoners break out and overrun the whole building, I am afraid to draw deeper into the corridor lest they attack me from behind.

The evening hours go quickly by. I feel hungry when my prisoners munch the food I have given them. By midnight my legs give way and I stumble against the steps. At last the water is touching my flesh. I sit on the floor and my new costume is stained by the black water. The muzzle of my gun is still pointing zealously at the cell openings, but I have to admit that, strained beyond bearing, my limbs are overcome by fatigue. For a moment I consider rising, going from cell to cell and shooting the inmates. Yet I am unable to call up a single Regulation that would in any way justify such an act. I am a jailer, and I may be called upon to die for the Manual of Regulations.

My eyelids are as rocks upon my eyes. I who could master my sleep so well am crumbling with exhaustion. The dogs, too, are nodding by my side. They have crowded me against the wall and spread themselves over the entire floor space. Their tension has relaxed and they are sprawling in an ugly pose, their tongues lolling wet on the floor, their legs stuck out, giving off a repulsive smell. But I am awake, my Liege. I am awake here in this remote house of yours that the sea is flooding. Are your prisoners awake as well? Certainly they are, for they do as I do—subject to my behaviour and awaiting my collapse. Softly I repeat passages from the Manual to myself to ward off sleep. My tired brain can only recall the first Regulations, the most simple, most basic ones. For an instant the idea to rise and run, run away from here with the last of my strength, crosses my mind. But I still have the power to banish such weak thoughts.

The dogs' slumber is infecting me too. Who would have thought that these dogs would betray me so in an hour of need? I try shouting, beating them, but I cannot bring out a sound. I have lost my hold over them. I am falling, sinking. Remember that I am in the middle of the sea, and the sweetness of the water is enveloping my heart. I seem to see shadows gliding through the corridor. Everything grows confused before my defeated eyes. Am I asleep already? My finger remains on the trigger. This much I know. I might even put a bullet through my brains, but what good would that be. Is that what is demanded of me? Will that stop them from fleeing to the mountains?

The gun is slipping. It is pointing at the floor now and I haven't the strength to raise it. I lift my hand from my lap to look at the time, but even if I could discern the dials I would not take in anything. It is obvious now. I am asleep. I dream. It is my soul that is stretching like a long dim corridor before me, it is from me that the shadows are breaking forth.

Dawn, first light. The doors are open. The water is turning grey again. Slow, so slow is the flood tide now. Imperceptible. Clearly a kind of lull has set in, a moment of grace, of peace. I doze awhile and wake, doze and wake. What is the trial I am failing? Only a trial of wakefulness, of resisting sleep.

Dim light, shadows. The sound of water and the sound of steps. All is lost.

They attack me in my dream before they attack me in the flesh. Their hands are shaking with the exhaustion of a sleepless night and with the long years of waiting. Many many hands, gnarled and cool. They numb my head with fists that are not strong, that hurt but little. They are frail. With little effort they slip the gun out of my hand, haul me sleepy and lost along the corridor, lift me up and cast me into one of the cells. Me, and the two dazed animals pulled behind me. Through the feeding hatch they mockingly fling the Manual of Regulations in after me, then lock the door with the stolen keys.

I maintain my calm, the superiority of my position. Don't you take notice of the tears in my eyes. They are not tears of sorrow but of joy. The blows hurt no longer. Imprisonment does not frighten me. I am not in despair. Here, perhaps, I shall gain insight into the real significance of the laws, here better than anywhere else. Here I shall understand the importance of imprisonment to the morality of the state. I am young still and need to perfect my personal knowledge of the Manual of Regulations. Dank cell and bleak cold of dawn—have I made myself clear?

The fugitives stampede about the building. They do not speak but snarl at each other. They break through the windows, search for the boat. I hear their shouts as they fight for a place in the crowded boat. In no time some of them are being pushed overboard and rend the air with their drowning screams. Eternal prisoners, and even if they knew how to swim in youth they have forgotten over the long years. I hear the boat cutting its moorings. None of them knows how to start the engine and they throw it overboard and use the oars. They move off. A tiny, overloaded boat.

I dismiss them from my mind.

Yes, I fall asleep; and when I wake the sun is high in the sky and true silence enfolds the empty building. The water is rising no longer. Birds fill my window with gay twitter. I am happy once more. The tide has abated. The flood, surprisingly, has not turned out to be long-lasting. The birds know it is safe to come back, but not so the humans. They think I sailed my boat to the mountains long ago.

I fling myself down on the soiled mattress. The food left in this cell will last me for a time. Presently I shall sit on the stool and read the Manual of Regulations. Now I realize the greatness of the Lawgiver who composed it as a book of verse, to be read psalm by psalm and grow truly serene, grow close to all that is far and beyond. But the dogs in my cell, the dogs are unquiet. They pace round and round the cell, hugging its walls with their heads down, hunting for a hole to escape through. They pay no attention to each other, only to the search for an outlet. Their passions have all condensed into the single passion for liberty. What shall I do with them? I cannot get them out of here.

I thought I had found peace but there is no peace. They race madly around me, the little cell is full of their long bodies. Even if I sit hunched in my corner they still bump into me on their restless circuits. From time to time they go straight for me, throw themselves hopelessly upon me with the full length of their bodies, lay their paws on my shoulders, lick my face with their long rough tongues, sometimes even biting a little. Their eyes are sad, tearful. I shut my book, stroke their heads. All the warmth that is left in me I lavish on them.

But they do not calm down. From time to time they hurl themselves at the bars of the door and break into a long wail for their real master. Their wolf-like cry sends a shiver of pain through my heart. Who will carry my wail to my master?

They start circling me again. Caged, hungry, two disciplined dogs reverting into wild beasts. Will they rise against me? I place food before them—husks and salt herring. It is all I have. They sniff at it, nibble a piece and spit it out in disgust. It is not this food that they claim. Once more they pounce upon me, their temporary master, their hated master now. Lightly they bite me, lick my blood, intoxicated. A new passion is roused in them, a grim passion throbbing in their jaws. I try tying them up but they manage to slip their heads out of the straps. I try to soothe them, suffer them with infinite patience. My heart goes out to them. Tears are blinding my eyes.

The world is radiant with light. The glory of it. Still and smooth lies the water, joyously the sunbeams splinter. It is from this narrow window alone that one can see how vast it all is, how wide open. Nothing, no one from end to end. Over in the mountains they all must think that the sea has flooded the whole prison by now. No one will imagine that the last guard is imprisoned here in one of these cells, and is still alive. The dogs are hurting me, but the pain is sweet as yet. This, apparently, is my last trial. As yet, it is not much.

Facing the Forests

ANOTHER winter lost in fog. As usual he did nothing; postponed examinations, left papers unwritten. He had completed all his courses long ago, attended all the lectures, and the string of signatures on his tattered student card testified that all had fulfilled their duty, silently disappeared, and left the rest of the task in his own limp hands. But words weary him; his own, let alone the words of others. He drifts from one rented room to another, rootless, jobless. But for an occasional job tutoring backward children he would starve to death. Here he is approaching thirty and a bald spot crowns his wilting head. His defective eyesight blurs many things. His dreams at night are dull. They are uneventful; a yellow waste, where a few stunted trees may spring up in a moment of grace, and a naked woman. At student revels he is already looked at with faint ridicule. The speed with which he gets drunk is a regular part of the programme. He never misses a party. They need him still. His limp figure is extremely popular and there is no one like him for bridging gaps between people. His erstwhile fellow students have since graduated and may be seen carrying bulging briefcases, on their way to work every morning of the week. Sometimes, at noon, returning from their office, they may encounter him in the street with his just-awake eyes: a grey moth in search of its first meal. They, having heard of his dissipations, promptly pronounce the unanimous, half-pitying half-exasperated decree: "Solitude!"

Solitude is what he needs. For he is not without talent nor does he lack brains. He needs to strengthen his will power.

He, as a rule, will drop his arms by his sides in a gesture of pious despair, back up against the nearest available wall, languidly cross his legs and plead in a whisper: "But where? Go on, tell me, where?"

For look, he himself is craving solitude. He plainly needs to renew his acquaintance with words, to try to concentrate on the material that threatens ever to wear him down. But then he would have to enter prison. He knows himself (a sickly smile): if there should be the tiniest crack through he would make it a tunnel of escape at once. No, please, no favours. Either—or.

Some content themselves with this feeble excuse, shrug their shoulders wryly and go their way. But his real friends, those whose wives he loves as well, two budding lecturers who remember him from days gone by, remember him favourably for the two or three amazingly original ideas that he had dropped at random during his student days—friends who are concerned for his future—these two are well aware that the coming spring is that much more dangerous to him, that his desultory affairs with women will but draw zeal from the blue skies. Is it any wonder then if one fine day they will catch hold of him in the street, their eyes sparkling. "Well, your lordship, we've found the solution to your lordship's problem at last." And he will be quick to show an expectant eagerness, though cunning enough to leave himself ample means of retreat.

"What?"

The function of forest scout. A fire watcher. Yes, it's something new. A dream of a job, a plum. Utter, profound solitude. There he will be able to scrape together his crumbled existence.

Where did they get the idea?

From the papers, yes, from a casual skimming of the daily papers.

He is astonished, laughs inordinately, hysterically almost. What now? What's the idea? Forests . . . What forests? Since when do we have forests in this country? What do they mean?

But they refuse to smile. For once they are determined. Before he has time to digest their words they have burned the bridges over which he had meant to escape, as usual. "You said, either—or. Here is your solution."

He glances at his watch, pretending haste. Will not a single spark light up in him then? For he, too, loathes himself, doesn't he?

And so, when spring has set the windows ajar he arrives early one morning at the Afforestation Department. A sunny office, a clerk, a typist, several typists. He enters quickly, armed with impressive recommendations, heralded by telephone calls. The man in charge of the forests, a worthy character edging his way to old age, is faintly amused (his position permits him as much), grins to himself. Much ado about nothing, about such a marginal job. Hence he is curious about the caller, considers rising to receive him, even. The plain patch of wilderness on top of the head of the candidate adds to his stature. The fellow inspires trust, surely, is surely meant for better things.

"Are you certain that this is what you want? The observation post is a grim place. Only really primitive people can bear such solitude. What is it you wish to write? Your doctorate?"

No, sad to say, he is still at the elementary stages of his study.

Yes, he has wasted much time.

No, he has no family.

Yes, with glasses his vision is sound.

Gently the old manager explains that, in accordance with a certain semi-official agreement, this work is reserved for social cases only and not for how-shall-I-put-it, romantics, ha-ha, intellectuals in search of solitude . . . However, he is prepared, just this once, to make an exception and include an intellectual among the wretched assortment of his workers. Yes, he himself is getting sick of the diverse social cases, the invalids, the cripples, the cranks. A fire breaks out, and these fellows will do nothing till the fire brigade arrives but stand and stare panic-stricken at the flames. Whenever he is forced to send out one such unstable character he stays awake for nights thinking what if in an obscure rage, against society or whatever, the fire watcher should himself set the forest on fire. He feels certain that he, the man in front of him here, though occupied with affairs of the mind, will be sufficiently alive to his duty to abandon his books and fight the fire. Yes, it is a question of moral values.

Sorry, the old man has forgotten what it is his candidate wishes to write? A doctorate?

Once more he apologizes. He is still, sad to say, at the elementary stages of his study. Yes, he has wasted much time. Indeed, he has no family.

A young secretary is called in.

Then he is invited to sign an inoffensive little contract for six months: spring, summer (ah, summer is dangerous!), and half the autumn. Discipline, responsibility, vigilance, conditions of dismissal. A hush descends while he runs his eyes cursorily over the document. Manager and secretary are ready with a pen, but he prefers to sign with his own. He signs several copies. First salary due on the 5th of April. Now he eases himself into his chair, unable to rise, tired still. He is not used to waking so early. Meanwhile he tries to establish some sort of contact, display an interest. He inquires about the size of the forests, the height of the trees. To tell the truth—he runs on expansively, in a sort of dangerous drowsiness—the fact is that he has never seen a real forest in this country yet. An occasional ancient grove, yes, but he hardly believes (ha-ha-ha) that the authorities in charge of afforestation have anything to do with that. Yes, he keeps hearing over the radio about forests being planted to honour this, that, and the other personage. Though apparently one cannot actually see them yet . . . The trees grow slowly . . . don't gain height. . . Actually he understands . . . this arid soil . . . In other countries, now . . .

At last he falters. Naturally he realizes, has realized from the start, that he has made a bad blunder, has sensed it from the laughter trembling in the girl's eyes, from the shocked fury colouring the face of the manager who is edging his way to old age. The candidate has, to use a tangible image, taken a careless step and trampled a tender spot in the heart of the man in charge of forests, who is fixing him now with a harsh stare and delivering a monologue for his benefit.

What does he mean by small trees? He has obviously failed to use his eyes. Of course there are forests. Real forests. Jungles, no, but forests, yes, indeed. If he will pardon the question: What does he know about what happens in this country anyway? For even when he travels through it on a bus he won't bother to take his head out of his book. It's laughable, really, these flat allegations. He, the old man, has come across this kind of talk from young people, but the candidate is rather past that age. If he, the manager, had the time to spare, he could show him maps. But soon he will see for himself. There are forests in the Hills of Judaea, in Galilee, Samaria, and elsewhere. Perhaps the candidate's eyesight is dim after all. Perhaps he needs a stronger pair of spectacles. The manager would like to ask the candidate to take spare spectacles with him. He would rather not have any more trouble. Goodbye.

Where are they sending him?

A few days later he is back. This time he is received not by the manager, but by an underling. He is being sent to one of the larger forests. He won't be alone there but with a labourer, an Arab. They feel certain he has no prejudices. Goodbye. Ah yes, departure is on Sunday.

Things happen fast. He severs connections and they appear to come loose with surprising ease. He vacates his room and his landlady is glad of it, for some reason. He spends the last nights with one of his learned friends, who sets to work at once to prepare a study schedule for him. While his zealous friend is busy in one room cramming books into a suitcase, the prospective fire watcher fondles the beloved wife in another. He is pensive, his hands gentle, there is something of joy in his expectations of the morrow. What shall he study? His friends suggest the Crusades. Yes, that would be just right for him. Everyone specializes in a certain subject. He may yet prove to be a little researcher all in his own right just so long as he doesn't fritter his time away. He ought to bring some startling scientific theory back from the forests. His friends will take care of the facts later.

But in the morning, when the lorry of the Afforestation Department comes to fetch him out of his shattered sleep, he suddenly imagines that all this has been set in motion just to get rid of him; and, shivering in the cold morning air, he can but console himself with the thought that this adventure will go the way of all others and be drowned in somnolence. Is it any wonder that Jerusalem, high on its hills, Jerusalem, which is left behind now, is fading like a dream? He abandons himself to the jolts and pitches of the lorry. The labourers with their hoes and baskets sit huddled away from him in the back of the car. They sense that he belongs to another world. The bald patch and the glasses are an indication, one of many.

Travelling half a day.

The lorry leaves the main road and travels over long, alien dirt roads, among nameless new-immigrant settlements. Labourers alight, others take their place. Everyone receives instructions from the driver, who is the one in command around here. We are going south, are we? Wide country meeting a spring-blue sky. The ground is damp still and clods of earth drop off the lorry's tyres. It is late in the morning when he discovers the first trees scattered among rocks. Young slender pines, tiny, light green. "Then I was right," he tells himself with a smile. But further on the trees grow taller. Now the light bursts and splinters. Long shadows steal aboard the lorry like stowaways. People keep changing and only the driver, the passenger and his suitcases stay put. The forests grow denser, no more bare patches now. Pines, always, and only the one species, obstinately, unvaryingly. He is tired, dusty, hungry, has long ago lost all sense of direction. The sun is playing tricks, twisting around him. He does not see where he is going, only what he is leaving behind. At three o'clock the lorry is emptied of labourers and only he is left. For a long time the lorry climbs over a rugged track. He is cross, his mouth feels dry. In despair he tries to pull a book out of one suitcase, but then the lorry stops. The driver gets off, bangs the door, comes around to him and says: "This is it. Your predecessor's already made off—yesterday. Your instructions are all up there. You at least can read, which makes a change."

Laboriously he hauls himself and his two suitcases down. An odd, charming stone house stands on a hill. Pines of all sizes surround it. He is at a high altitude here, though he cannot yet see everything from where he is. Silence, a silence of trees. The driver stretches his legs, looks around breathes the air, then suddenly he nods goodbye and climbs back into his cab and switches the engine on.

He who must stay behind is seized with regret. Despair. What now? Just a minute! He doesn't understand. He rushes at the car, beats his fists against the door, whispers furiously at the surprised driver.

"But food . . . what about food?"

It appears that the Arab takes care of everything.

Alone he trudges uphill, a suitcase in each hand. Gradually the world comes into view. The front door stands open and he enters a large room, the ground floor. Semi-darkness, dilapidated objects on the floor, food remnants, traces of a child. The despair mounts in him. He puts down the suitcases and climbs absent-mindedly to the second floor. The view strikes him with awe. Five hills covered with a dense green growth—pines. A silvery blue horizon with a distant sea. He is instantly excited, forgetting everything. He is even prepared to change his opinion of the Afforestation Department.

A telephone, binoculars, a sheet covered with instructions. A large desk and an armchair beside it. He settles himself into the chair and reads the instructions five times over, from beginning to end. Then he pulls out his pen and makes a few stylistic corrections. He glances fondly at the black instrument. He is in high spirits. He considers calling up one of his friends in town, say something tender to one of his ageing lady-loves. He might announce his safe arrival, describe the view perhaps. Never has he had a public telephone at his disposal yet. He lifts the receiver to his ear. An endless purring. He is not familiar with the proceedings. He tries dialling. In vain. The purr remains steady. At last he dials zero, like a sober citizen expecting a sober reply.

The telephone breaks its silence.

The Fire Brigade comes on with a startled "What's happened?" Real alarm at the other end. (Where? where? confound it!) Before he has said a word, questions rain down on him. How large is the fire? What direction the wind? They are coming at once. He tries to put in a word, stutters, and already they are starting a car over there. Panic grips him. He jumps up, the receiver tight in his hand. He breaks out in a cold sweat. With the last remnant of words in his power he explains everything. No. There is no fire. There is nothing. Only getting acquainted. He has just arrived. Wanted to get through to town. His name is so-and-so. That is all.

A hush at the other side. The voice changes. This must be their chief now. Pleased to meet you sir, we've taken down your name. Have you read all the instructions? Personal calls are quite out of the question. Anyway, you've only just arrived, haven't you? Or is there some urgent need? Your wife? Your children?

No, he has no family.

Well, then, why the panic? Lonely? He'll get used to it. Please don't disturb us unnecessarily in the future. Goodbye.

The ring closes in on him a little. Pink streaks on the horizon. He is tired, hungry. He has risen early, and he is utterly unused to that. This high commanding view makes him dizzy. Needless to add—the silence. He picks up the binoculars with a limp hand and raises them to his eyes. The world leaps close, blurred. Pines lunge at him upright. He adjusts the forest, the hills, the sea on the horizon to the quality of his eyes. He amuses himself a bit, then lets go of the binoculars and eases himself into the chair. He has a clear conception of his new job now. Just watching. His eyes grow heavy. He dozes, sleeps perhaps.

Suddenly he wakes—a red light is burning on his glasses. He is bewildered, scared, his senses heavy. The forest has caught fire, apparently, and he has missed it. He jumps up, his heart wildly beating grabs the telephone, the binoculars, and then it occurs to him that it is the sun, only the sun setting beyond the trees. He is facing west. Now he knows. Slowly he drops back into the chair. His heart contracts with something like terror, like emptiness. He imagines himself deserted in this place, forgotten. His glasses mist over and he takes them off and wipes them.

When dusk falls he hears steps.

An Arab and a little girl are approaching the house. Swiftly he rises to his feet. They notice him, look up and stop in their tracks—startled by the soft, scholarly-looking figure. He bows his head. They walk on but their steps are hesitant now. He goes down to them.

The Arab turns out to be old and mute. His tongue was cut out during the war. By one of them or one of us? Does it matter? Who knows what the last words were that stuck in his throat? In the dark room, its windows ablaze with the last light, the fire watcher shakes a heavy hand, bends to pat the child, who flinches, terrified. The ring of loneliness closes in on him. The Arab puts on lights. The fire watcher will sleep upstairs.

The first evening, and a gnawing sadness. The weak yellow light of the bulbs is depressing. For the time being he draws comfort only from the wide view, from the soft blue of the sea in the distance and the sun surrendering to it. He sits cramped on his chair and watches the big forests entrusted to his eyes. He imagines that the fire may break out at any moment. After a long delay the Arab brings up his supper. An odd taste, a mixture of tastes. But he devours everything, leaves not a morsel. His eyes rove hungrily between the plate and the thick woods. Suddenly, while chewing, he discovers a few faraway lights—villages. He broods awhile about women, then takes off his clothes, opens the suitcase that does not hold books and takes out his things. It seems a long time since he left town. He wraps himself in blankets, lies facing the forests. A cool breeze caresses him. What sort of sleep will come to one here? The Arab brings him a cup of coffee to help him stay awake. The fire watcher would like to talk to him about something; perhaps about the view, or about the poor lighting perhaps. He has words left in him still from the city. But the Arab does not understand Hebrew. The fire watcher smiles wearily in thanks. Something about his bald crown, the glint of his glasses, seems to daunt the Arab.

It is half-past nine—the beginning of night. Cicadas strike up. He struggles against sleep engulfing him. His eyes close and his conscience tortures him. The binoculars dangle from their strap around his neck, and from time to time he picks them up, lifts them to his eyes blinded with sleep, glass clicking against glass. He opens his eyes in a stare and finds himself in the forest, among pines, hunting for flames. Darkness.

How long does it take for a forest to burn down? Perhaps he will only look every hour, every two hours. Even if the forest should start to burn he would still manage to raise the alarm in time to save the rest. The murmur downstairs has died down. The Arab and his child are asleep. And he is up here, light-headed, tired after his journey, between three walls and a void gaping to the sea. He must not roll over on to his other side. He nods, and his sleep is pervaded by the fear of fire, fire stealing upon him unawares. At midnight he transfers himself from bed to chair; it is safer that way. His head droops heavily on to the desk, his spine aches, he is crying out for sleep, full of regret, alone against the dark empire swaying before him. Till at last the black hours of the first night pass; till out of the corner of his eye he sees the morning grow among the hills.

Only fatigue makes him stay on after the first night. The days and nights following revolve as on a screen, a misty, dream-like screen lit up once every twenty-four hours by the radiant glow of the setting sun. It is not himself but a stranger who wanders those first days between the two storeys of the house, the binoculars slung across his chest, absently chewing on the food left him by the unseen Arab. The heavy responsibility that has suddenly fallen upon his shoulders bewilders him. Hardest of all is the silence. Even with himself he hardly manages to exchange a word. Will he be able to open a book here? The view amazes and enchants him still and he cannot have enough of it. After ten days of anguish he is himself again. In one brief glance he can embrace all the five hills now. He has learned to sleep with his eyes open. Lo, a new accomplishment; rather interesting, one must admit.

At last the other suitcase, the one with the books, gets opened, with a slight delay of but a fortnight or so. The delay does not worry him in the least, for aren't the spring, the summer, and half the autumn still before him? The first day is devoted to sorting the books, spelling out titles, thumbing the pages. One can't deny that there is some pleasure in handling the fat, fragrant, annotated volumes. The texts are in English, the quotations all in Latin. Strange phrases from alien worlds. He worries a little. His subject—"The Crusades". From the human, that is to say, the ecclesiastical aspect. He has not gone into particulars yet. "Crusades," he whispers softly to himself and feels joy rising in him at the word the sound. He feels certain that there is some dark issue buried within the subject and that it will startle him, startle others in him. And it will be just out of this drowsiness that envelops his mind like a permanent cloud that the matter will be revealed to him.

The following day is spent on pictures. The books are rich in illustrations. Odd funny ones. Monks, cardinals; a few blurred kings, thin knights, tiny, villainous Jews. Curious landscapes, maps. He studies them, compares, dozes. On the hard road to the abstract he wishes to linger awhile with the concrete. That night he is kept off his studies by a gnat. Next morning he tells himself: "Oh wondrous time, how fast it flies upon these lonely summits." He opens the first book on the first page, reads the author's preface, his grateful acknowledgements. He reads other prefaces, various acknowledgements, publication data. He checks a few dates. At noon his mind is distracted from the books by an imaginary flame flashing among the trees. He remains tense for hours, excited, searching with the binoculars, his hand on the telephone. At last, towards evening, he discovers that it is only the red dress of the Arab's little daughter who is skipping among the trees. The following day, when he is all set to decipher the first page, his father turns up suddenly with a suitcase in his hand.

"What's happened?" the father asks anxiously.

"Nothing . . . Nothing's happened. . ."

"But what made you become a forester then?"

"A bit of solitude . . ."

"Solitude . . ." he marvels. "You want solitude?"

The father bends over the open book, removes his heavy glasses and peers closely at the text. "The Crusades," he murmurs. "Is that what you're engaged on?"

"Yes."

"Aren't I disturbing you in your work? I haven't come to disturb you. . . I have a few days' leave."

"No, you're not disturbing me."

"Magnificent view."

"Yes, magnificent."

"You're thinner."

"Could be."

"Couldn't you study in the libraries?"

Apparently not. Silence. The father sniffs around the room like a little hedgehog. At noon he asks his son:

"Do you think it is lonely here? That you'll find solitude?"

"Yes, what's to disturb me?"

"I'm not going to disturb you."

"Of course not. What makes you think that!"

"I'll go away soon."

"No, don't go. Please stay."

The father stays a week.

In the evening the father tries to become friendly with the Arab and his child. A few words of Arabic have stuck in his memory from the days of his youth, and he will seize any occasion to fill them with meaning. But his pronunciation is unintelligible to the Arab, who only nods his head dully.

They sit together, not speaking. The son cannot read a single line with the father there, even though the father keeps muttering: "Don't bother about me. I'll keep myself in the background." At night the father sleeps on the bed and the fire watcher stretches himself out on the floor. Sometimes the father wakes in the night to find his son awake. "Perhaps we could take turns," he says. "You go to sleep on the bed and I'll watch the forest." But the son knows that his father will see not a forest but a blurred stain. He won't notice the fire till it singes his clothes. In the daytime they change places—the son lies on the bed and the father sits by the desk and tries to read the book, which lies open still. How he would like to strike up a conversation with his son, stir up some discussion. For example, he fails to understand why his son won't deal with the Jews, the Jewish aspect of the Crusades. For isn't mass suicide a wonderful and terrible thing? The son gives him a kindly grin, a non-committal reply, and silence. During the last days of his visit the father occupies himself with the dumb Arab. A host of questions bubbles up in him. Who is the man? Where is he from? Who cut his tongue out? Why? Look, he has seen hatred in the man's eyes. A creature like that may yet set the forest on fire some day. Why not?

On his last day the father is given the binoculars to play with.

Suitcase in hand, back bent, he shakes his son's hand. Then—tears in the eyes of the little father.

"I've been disturbing you, I know I have. . ."

In vain does the son protest, mumble about the oceans of time still before him—about half the spring, the whole long summer, half the distant autumn.

From his elevated seat he watches his lost blind father fumbling for the back of the lorry. The driver is rude and impatient with him. When the lorry moves off the father waves goodbye to the forest by mistake. He has lost his bearings.

For a week he crawls from line to line over the difficult text. After every sentence he raises his head to look at the forest. He is still awaiting a fire. The air grows hot. A haze shimmers above the sea on the horizon. When the Arab returns at dusk his garments are damp with sweat, the child's gestures are tired. Anyway you look at it, he himself is lucky. At such a time to be here, high above any town. Ostensibly, he is working all the time, but observing could hardly be called work, could it? The temperature rises day by day. He wonders whether it is still spring, or whether perhaps the summer has already crept upon the world. One can gather nothing from the forest, which shows no change, except thorns fading to yellow among the trees perhaps. His hearing has grown acute. The sound of trees whispers incessantly in his ears. His eyes shine with the sun's gaining strength, his senses grown keen. He is becoming attached to the forest in a way. Even his dreams are growing richer in trees. The women sprout leaves.

His text is difficult, the words distant. It has turned out to be only the preface to a preface. But, being as diligent as he is, he does not skip a single passage. He translates every word, then rewrites the translation in rhyme. Simple, easy rhymes, in order that the words should merge in his mind, should not escape into the silence.

No wonder that by Friday he can count but three pages read, out of the thousands. "Played out," he whispers to himself and trails his fingertips over the desk. Perhaps he'll take a rest? A pensive air comes over the green empire before him each Sabbath eve and makes his heart contract. Though he believes neither in God nor in all his angels, there is a sacredness that brings a lump to his throat.

He combs his beard in honour of the holy day. Yes, there is a new beard growing here along with the pines. He brings some order into the chaos of his room, picks a page off the floor. What is this? The instruction sheet. Full of interest he reads it once more and discovers a forgotten instruction, or one added by his own hand, perhaps.

"Let the forest scout go out from time to time for a short walk among the trees, in order to sharpen his senses."

His first steps in the forest proper are like a baby's. He circles the observation post, hugging its walls as though afraid to leave them. Yet the trees attract him like magic. Little by little he ventures among the hills, deeper and deeper. If he should smell burning he will run back.

But this isn't a forest yet, only the hope and promise of one. Here and there the sun appears through the foliage and a traveller among the trees is dappled with flickers of light. This isn't a rustling forest but a very small one, like a graveyard. A forest of solitudes. The pines stand erect, slim, serious; like a company of new recruits awaiting their commander. The roaming fire watcher is pleased by the play of light and shadow. With every step he crushes dry pine needles underfoot. Softly, endlessly the pines shed their needles; pines arrayed in a garment of mingling life and death.

The rounded human moving among trees whose yearning is so straight, so fierce. His body aches a bit, the ache of cramped limbs stretching; his legs are heavy. Suddenly he catches sight of the telephone line. A yellowish wire smelling of mould. Well, so this is his contact with the world. He starts tracing the yellow wire, searching for its origin, is charmed by its pointless twists and loops between the trees. They must have let some joker unwind the drum over the hills.

Suddenly he hears voices. He wavers, stops, then sees the little clearing in the wood. The Arab is seated on a pile of rocks, his hoe by his side. The child is talking to him excitedly, describing something with animated gestures. The scout tiptoes nearer, as lightly as his bulk will permit. They are instantly aware of him, sniff his alien being and fall silent. The Arab jumps up, stands by his hoe as though hiding something. He faces them, wordless. It is the Sabbath eve today, isn't it, and there is a yearning in his heart. He stands and stares, for all the world like a supervisor bothered by some obscure triviality. The soft breeze caresses his eyes. If he did not fear for his standing with them he would hum them a little tune, perhaps. He smiles absently, his eyes stray and slowly he withdraws; with as much dignity as he can muster.

The two remain behind, petrified. The child's joy has shrivelled halfway through her interrupted story, the Arab starts weeding the thorns at his feet. But the scout has retreated already, gone forth into the empire. He has been wandering in the woods for all of an hour now and is still making new discoveries. The names of donors, for example. It had never occurred to him that this wouldn't be just some anonymous forest but one with a name, and not just one name either. Many rocks bear copper plates, brilliantly brushed. He stoops, takes off his glasses, reads: Louis Schwartz of Chicago, the King of Burundi and his People. Flickers of light play over the letters. The names cling to him, like the falling pine needles that slip into his pocket. How odd! The tired memory tries to refresh itself with these faceless names. Name after name is absorbed by him as he walks, and by the time he reaches the observation post he can already hold a little rehearsal. He recites the assorted names, a vacuous smile on his face.

Friday night.

A wave of sadness wells within him. His mind happens to be perfectly lucid at the moment. We'll clear out on Sunday, he whispers suddenly and starts humming a snatch of song; inaudibly at first, the sound humming inside him, but soon trilling and rising high to the darkening sky. A hidden abyss behind him echoes in reply. The light drips, drips. Strings of light tear the sunset across and he shouts song at it, shrills recklessly, wanton with solitude. He starts one song, stops, plunges into another without change of key. His eyes fill with tears. The dark stifles his throat at last, he hears himself suddenly and falls silent.

Peace returns to the forest. Relics of light linger. Five minutes pass and then the Arab and the girl emerge from the cover of the underbrush and hurry to the house with bent heads.

The Sabbath passes in a wonderful tranquillity. He is utterly calm. He has begun counting the trees for a change. On Sunday he is on the verge of escaping but then the lorry brings him his salary, a part of the job he had forgotten. He is amazed, gushes his thanks to the mocking driver. So there's a prize in the whispering world, is there? He returns to the books.

Hot summer. Yes, but we have forgotten the birds. Presumably the observation post stands on an ancient crossroads of bird trajectories. How else to explain the mad flocks swooping in from the forest to beat their wings against the walls, drop on the bed, dive at the books, shed grey feathers and green dung, shatter the dull air with their restlessness—and vanish on their circuitous flight to the sea. A change has come over him. Sunburned, yes, but there is more to it than that. The heat wells up in him, frightens him. A dry flow of desert wind may rouse the forest to suicide; hence he redoubles his vigilance, presses the binoculars hard against his eyes and subjects the forest in his care to a strict survey. How far has he come? Some slight twenty pages are behind him, thousands still before. What does he remember? A few words, the tail end of a theory, the atmosphere on the eve of the Crusades. The nights are peaceful. He could have studied, could have concentrated, were it not for the gnats. Night after night he extinguishes the lights and sits in darkness. The words have dropped away from him like husks. Cicadas. Choruses of jackals. A bat wings heavily across the gloom. Rustlings.

Hikers start arriving in the forest. Lone hikers some of them, but mostly they come in groups. He follows them through the binoculars. Various interesting ages. Like ants they swarm over the forest, pour in among the trees, calling out to each other, laughing; then they cast off their rucksacks all at once, unburden themselves of as many clothes as possible and hang them up on branches, and promptly come over to the house.

Water is what they want. Water!

He comes down to them, striking them with wonder. The bald head among the green pines, the heavy glasses. Indeed, everything indicates an original character.

He stands by the water tap, firm and upright, and slakes their thirst. Everyone begs permission to go upstairs for a look at the view. He consents, joyfully. They crowd into his little room and utter the stock formulae of admiring exclamations. He smiles as though he had created it all. Above everything, they are surprised by the sea. They had never imagined one could see the sea from here. Yet how soon they grow bored! One glance, a cry of admiration, and they grow restless and eager to be away. They peep at his notes, at the heavy books, and descend the staircase brimming with veneration for him and his view. The group leaders ask him to give some account of the place, but there is no account to give. Everything is still artificial here. There is nothing here, not even some archaeology for amateurs, nothing but a few donors' names, inscribed on rocks. Would they be interested in the names? Well, for instance . . .

They laugh.

The girls look at him kindly. No, he isn't handsome. But might he not become engraved on one of their hearts?

They light camp-fires.

They wish to cook their food, or to warm themselves. A virtuous alarm strikes him. Tiny flames leap up in the forest, a bluish smoke starts blowing gaily about the tree-tops. A fire? Yes and no. He stays glued, through his binoculars, to the lively figures.

Towards evening he goes to explore his flickering, merrymaking empire. He wishes to sound a warning. Softly, soundlessly he draws near the camp-fires, the figures wreathed in flames. He approaches them unnoticed, and they are startled when they discover him beside them. Dozens of young eyes look up at him together. The leaders rise at once.

"Yes? What do you want?"

"The fire. Be careful! One spark, and the forest may burn down."

They are quick to assure him. Laying their hands on their young hearts they give him their solemn promise to watch, with all their eyes shining in a row before him. They will keep within bounds, of course they will, what does he think?

He draws aside. Appeased? Yes and no. There, among the shadows, in the twilight of the fire, he lingers and lets his eyes rove. The girls and their bare creamy legs, slender does. The flames crackle and sing, softly, gently. He clenches his fists in pain. If only he could warm his hands a little.

"Like to join us?" they ask politely. His vertical presence is faintly embarrassing.

No, thanks. He can't. He is busy. His studies. They have seen the books, haven't they? Now there is nothing for it but to withdraw with measured tread. But as soon as he has vanished from their view he flings himself behind the trees, hides among the needle branches. He looks at the fire from afar, at the girls, till everything fades and blankets are spread for sleep. Giggles, girls' affected shrieks, leaders' rebukes. Before he can begin to think, select one out of the many figures, it will be dawn. Silence is still best. At midnight he feels his way through the trees, back to the observation post. He sits in his place, waiting. One of the figures may be working its way in the darkness towards him. But no, nothing. They are tired, already sleeping.

And the same the next day, and all the days following.

Early in the morning he opens his book and hears wild singing in the distance. He does not raise his eyes from the page but his hand strays to the binoculars. A dappled silence. Flashes of light through branches. His eyes are faithful to the written page, but his thoughts have gone whoring already. From the corner of his eye he follows the procession threading through the forest—sorting, checking ages, colours, joys of youth. There is something of abandonment about them from afar, like a procession of Crusaders; except that these women are bare. He trembles, choking suddenly. He removes his glasses and beats his head against the books. Half an hour later they arrive. Asking for water to drink and the view to look at, as usual. They have heard about the wonderful view to be seen from up here. Perhaps they have heard about the scholar as well, but they say nothing. The group leaders take them, a batch at a time, into his room turned public property. No sooner have they scattered about the forest than the camp-fires leap up, as though that were their prime necessity. In the evening he rushes over the five hills, from fire to fire, impelled by his duty to warn them or by an obscure desire to reveal himself. He never joins any of the circles though. He prefers to hide in the thicket. Their singing throbs in his heart, and even more than that—the whisperings. Warm summer nights—something constantly seeping through the leaves.

Gradually the groups of hikers blend. One excursion leaves, another arrives. By the time he has managed to learn a few outstanding names their owners are gone and the sounds alone survive among the branches. Languor comes over him. No longer does he trouble to caution against fire. On the contrary. He would welcome a little conflagration, a little local tumult. The hikers, however, are extremely responsible. They themselves take care to stamp out every dying ember. Their leaders come in advance to set his mind at rest.

The birds know how much he has neglected his studies; the birds whom he watches constantly lest they approach his desk. A month has passed since he last turned a page and he is stuck squirming between two words. He says: let the heat abate, the hikers be gone—then I shall race over the lines. If only he could skip the words and get to the essence. From time to time he scribbles in his notebook. Stray thoughts, speculations, musings, outlines of assumptions. Not much. A sentence a day. He would like to gain a hold upon it all indirectly. Yet he is doubtful whether he has gained a hold even upon the forest in front of his eyes. Look, here the Arab and the girl are disappearing among the trees and he cannot find them. Towards evening they emerge from an unforeseen direction as though the forest had conceived them even now. They tread the soil softly. They avoid people, choose roundabout ways. He smiles at them both but they recoil.

Friday. The forest is overrun, choking with people. They come on foot and by car, crowds disgorged by the faraway cities. Where is his solitude now? He sprawls on his chair like a dethroned king whose empire has slipped from his hands. Twilight lingers on the tree-tops. Sabbath eve. His ears alone can catch, beyond the uproar of voices, beyond the rustling, the thin cry of the weary soil ceaselessly crushed by the teeth of young roots. A hikers' delegation comes to see him. They just want to ask him a question. They have argued, laid wagers, and he shall be their arbiter. Where exactly is this Arab village that is marked on the map? It ought to be somewhere around here, an abandoned Arab village. Here, they even know its name, something like . . . Actually, it must be right here, right in the forest . . . Does he know anything about it perhaps? They're simply curious.

The fire watcher gives them a tired look. "A village?" he repeats with a polite, indulgent smile at their folly. No, there is no village here. The map must be wrong, the surveyor's hand must have shaken.

But in the small hours of the night, somewhere between a doze and a slumber, in the face of the whispering, burgeoning forest, the name floats back into his mind of a sudden and he is seized with restlessness. He descends to the ground floor, feels his way in the dark to the bed of the Arab, who lies asleep covered with rags. Roughly he wakes him and whispers the name of the village. The Arab does not understand. His eyes are consumed with weariness. The fire watcher's accent must be at fault. He tries again, therefore, repeats the name over and over and the Arab listens and suddenly he understands. An expression of surprise, of wonder and eagerness suffuses all his wrinkles. He jumps up, stands there in his hairy nakedness and flings up a heavy arm in the direction of the window, pointing fervently, hopelessly, at the forest.

The fire watcher thanks him and departs, leaving the big naked figure in the middle of the room. When he wakes tomorrow, the Arab will think he has dreamed it.

Ceremonies. A season of ceremonies. The forest turns ceremonial. The trees stand bowed, heavy with honour, they take on meaning, they belong. White ribbons are strung to delimit new domains. Luxurious coaches struggle over the rocky roads, a procession of shining automobiles before and behind. Sometimes they are preceded by a motorcycle mounted by an excited policeman. Unwieldy personages alight, shambling like black bears. The women flutter around them. Little by little they assemble, crush out cigarettes with their black shoes and fall silent—paying homage to the memory of themselves. The fire watcher, too, participates in the ceremony, from afar, he and his binoculars. A storm of obedient applause breaks out, a gleam of scissors, a flash of photographers, ribbons sag. A plaque is unveiled, a new little truth is revealed to the world. A brief tour of the conquered wood, and then the distinguished gathering dissolves into its various vehicles and sallies forth.

Where is the light gone?

In the evening, when the fire watcher comes down to the drooping ribbons, to the grateful trees, he will find nothing but a pale inscription saying, for example: "Donated by the Sackson children in honour of Daddy Sackson of Baltimore, a fond tribute to his paternity. End of Summer Nineteen Hundred and . . ."

Sometimes the fire watcher, observing from his heights, will notice one of the party darting troubled looks about him, raising his eyes at the trees as though searching for something. It takes many ceremonies before the fire watcher's wandering mind will grasp that this is none other than the old man in charge of afforestation, who comes and repeats himself, dressed always in the same clothes, at every ceremony.

Once he goes down to him.

The old man is walking among his distinguished foreign party, is jesting with them haltingly in their language. The fire watcher comes out of the trees and plants himself in front of him for the inevitable encounter. The distinguished party stops, startled. An uneasy silence falls over them. The ladies shrink back.

"What do you want?" demands the old man masterfully.

The fire watcher gives a weak smile.

"Don't you know me? I'm the watchman. That is to say, the fire watcher . . . employee of yours . . ."

"Ah!" fist beating against aged forehead, "I didn't recognize you, was alarmed, these tatters have changed your appearance so, this heavy beard. Well young man, and how's the solitude?"

"Solitude?" he wonders.

The old man presents him to the party.

"A scholar . . ."

They smile, troubled, meet his hand with their fingertips, move on. They do not have complete faith in his cleanliness. The old man on the other hand, looks at him affectionately. A thought crosses his mind and he stays behind a moment.

"Well, so there *are* forests," he grins with good-natured irony.

"Yes," admits the scout honestly. "Forests, yes . . . but . . ."

"But what?"

"But fires, no."

"Fires?" the old man wonders, bending towards him.

"Yes, fires. I spend whole days here sitting and wondering. Such a quiet summer."

"Well, why not? Actually, there hasn't been a fire here for several years now. To tell you the truth, I don't think there has ever been a fire at all in this forest. Nature itself is harnessed to our great enterprise here, ha-ha."

"And I was under the impression . . ."

"That what?"

"That fires broke out here every other day. By way of illustration, at least. The whole machinery waiting on the alert, is it all for nothing? The fire engines . . . telephone lines . . . the manpower . . . For months my eyes have been strained with waiting."

"Waiting? Ha-ha, what a joke!"

The old one hurries along. The drivers are switching on their engines. That is all he needs, to be left overnight in this arboreal silence. Before he goes he would just like to know the watchman's opinion of the dumb Arab. The lorry driver has got the idea into his head that the fellow is laying in a stock of kerosene . . .

The watchman is stirred. "Kerosene?"

"Daresay it's some fancy of that malicious driver. This Arab is a placid kind of fellow, isn't he?"

"Wonderfully placid," agrees the fire watcher eagerly. Then he walks a few steps around the old man and whispers confidentially: "Isn't he a local?"

"A local?"

"Because our forest is growing over, well, over a ruined village . . ."

"A village?"

"A small village."

"A small village? Ah—(Something is coming back to him anyway.) "Yes, there used to be some sort of a farmstead here. But that is a thing of the past."

Of the past, yes, certainly. What else . . . ?

One day's programme as an example.

Not having slept at night, he does not wake up in the morning. Light springs up between his fingers. What date is today? There is no telling. Prisoners score lines on the walls of their cell, but he is not in prison. He has come of his own free will, and so he will go. He could lift the receiver and find out the date from the firemen bent over their fire engines, waiting in some unknown beyond, but he does not want to scare them yet.

He goes down to the tap and sprinkles a few drops of water over his beard to freshen it up. Then he climbs back to his room, snatches up the binoculars and makes a pre-breakfast inspection. Excitement grips him. The forest filled with smoke? No, the binoculars are to blame. He wipes the lenses with a corner of his grimy shirt. The forest clears up at once, disappointingly. None of the trees has done any real growing overnight.

He goes down again. He picks up the dry loaf of bread and cuts himself a rough slice. He chews rapidly, his eyes roving over a torn strip of newspaper in which tomatoes are wrapped. It is not, God forbid, out of a hunger for news but so as to keep his eyes in training lest they forget the shape of the printed letter. He returns to his observation post, his mouth struggling with an enormous half-rotten tomato. He sucks, swallows, gets smeared with the red trickling sap. At last he throws a sizeable remnant away. Silence. He dozes a bit, wakes, looks for a long time at the treetops. The day stretches out ahead of him. Softly he draws near the books.

Where are we? How many pages read? Better not count them or he will fall prey to despair; for the time being he is serene, and why spoil it? It isn't a question of quantity, is it? And he remembers what he has read up to now perfectly well, forwards and backwards. The words wave and whirl within him. For the time being, therefore, for the past few weeks, that is, he has been devoting his zeal to one single sheet of paper. A picture? Rather, a map. A map of the area. He will display it on this wall here for the benefit of his successors, that they may remember him. Look, he has signed his name already, signed it to begin with, lest he forget.

What is he drawing? Trees. But not only trees. Hills too, a blue horizon too. He is improving day by day. If he had coloured crayons he could have added some birds as well; at least, say, those native to the area. What interests him in particular is the village buried beneath the trees. That is to say, it hasn't always been as silent here. His curiosity is of a strictly scientific nature. What was it the old man had said? "A scholar." He strokes the beard and his hand lingers, disentangles a few hairs matted with filth. What time is it? Early still. He reads a line about the attitude of the Pope to the German Kaiser and falls asleep. He wakes with a start. He lights a cigarette, tosses the burning match out into the forest, but the match goes out in mid-air. He flings the cigarette butt among the trees and it drops on a stone and burns itself out in solitude.

He gets up, paces about restlessly. What time is it? Early still.

He goes in search of the Arab, to say good-morning. He must impress his own vigilant existence upon the man, lest he be murdered some morning between one doze and another. Ever since the fire watcher has spoken the name of the vanished village in his ears the Arab has become suspicious, as though he were being watched all the time. The fire watcher strides rapidly between the pines. How light his footstep has grown during the long summer months. His soundless appearance startles the two.

"Shalom," he says, in Hebrew.

They reply in two voices. The child—a voice that has sweetness in it, the Arab—a harsh grunt. The fire watcher smiles to himself and hurries on as though he was extremely busy. Chiselled stones lie scattered among the trees, outlines of buildings, ruins and relics. He searches for marks left by humans. Every day he comes and disturbs a few stones, looking for traces.

A man and a woman are lying here entwined, likes statues toppled from their base. Their terror when the bearded head bends silently over them! Smile at them and run, you! A couple slipped away from a group hike, no doubt.

What is he looking for? Relics of thoughts that have flitted here, words that have completed their mission. But what will he find one fine day, say even the day that we have taken for a sample? Small tins filled with kerosene. How wonderful! The zeal with which someone has filled tin after tin here and covered them up with the girl's old dress. He stoops over the treasure, the still liquid on whose face dead pine needles drift. His reflection floats back at him together with the faint smell.

Blissfully he returns to the house, opens a tin of meat and bolts its contents to the last sliver. He wipes his mouth and spits far out among the branch-filled air. He turns two pages of a book and reads the Cardinal's reply to a Jew's epistle. Funny, these twists and turns of the Latin, but what a threat is conveyed by them. He falls asleep, wakes, realizes he has nearly missed an important ceremony on the easternmost hill. From now on the binoculars stay glued to his eyes and he mingles with the distinguished crowd from afar. He can even make out the movements of the speaker's lips; he will fill in the missing sound himself. But then the flames of the sunset catch his eye and divert his attention, and with a daily returning excitement he becomes absorbed in the splendour, the terrible splendour.

Afterwards he wipes the dust off the silent telephone. To give him his due—he bestows meticulous care on the equipment that belongs to the Afforestation Department, whereas his own equipment is already falling apart. The loose buttons shed among the trees, the frayed shirt, the ragged trousers.

A private outing of joyriders arrives with a loud fanfare to spend the night in the forest. Wearily he chews his supper. Nightfall brings the old familiar sadness.

The Arab and his daughter go to bed. Darkness. The first giggle that emerges from the trees is a slap in his listening face. He turns over a few dark pages, swats a gnat, whistles.

Night. He does not fall asleep.

Then it is the end of summer. The forest is emptying. And with the first autumn wind, who is blown to him like a withered leaf but his ageing mistress, the wife of the friend who sent him here. Clad in a summer frock she comes, a wide-brimmed straw hat on her head. Then she clicks her high heels around his room, rummaging through his drawers, bending over the books, peering through the papers. She had gone for a brief vacation by herself somewhere in this neighbourhood and had remembered him. How is it when a man sits solitary, facing the forest night after night? She had wanted to surprise him. Well, and what has he come up with? A fresh crusade perhaps? She is awfully curious. Her husband speaks well of him too. In this solitude, among the trees, says the husband, he may yet flower into greatness.

The fire watcher is moved. Without a word he points at the map on the wall. She trips over to look, does not understand. Actually she is interested in texts. What has he written? She is very tired. Such a time till she found this place and she's more dead than alive. The view is pretty, yes, but the place looks awfully neglected. Who lives downstairs? The Arab? Is that so! She met him on the way, tried to ask him something and suddenly—the shock! Dumb, his severed tongue. But the Afforestation Department—hats off to them. Who would have imagined such forests growing in this country! He has changed, though. Grown fatter? This new beard of his is just awful. Why doesn't he say something?

She sinks down on to the bed.

Then he rises, approaches her with that quiet that is in his blood now. He removes her hat, crouches at her feet, unbuckles her shoes; he is trembling with desire, choking.

She is shocked. She draws back her bare tired feet at once with something of terror, perhaps with relief. But he has already let go, stands holding the binoculars and looks at the forest, looks long, peering through the trees, waiting for fire. Slowly he turns to her, the binoculars at his eyes, turns the lenses upon her mischievously, sees the tiny wrinkles whittled in her face, the sweat drops, her fatigue. She smiles at him as in an old photograph. But when the moment drags, her smile turns into protest. She draws herself together crossly, holds up a hand: "Hey, you! Stop it!"

Only towards sunset does he finally manage to undress her. The binoculars are still on his chest, pressed between their bodies. From time to time he coolly interrupts his kisses and caresses, raises the binoculars to his eyes and inspects the forest.

"Duty," he whispers apologetically, sending an odd smile to the nude, ashamed woman. Everything mingles with the glory of the crimson sun—the distant blue of the sea, the still trees, the blood on his cracked lips, the despair, the futility, the loneliness of the act. Accidentally her hand touches the bald crown and flinches.

When the Arab returns it is all over. She is lying in the tangle of her clothes, drowsy. A beautiful night has descended on the world. He sits by his desk, what else should he do? The dark transforms her into a silhouette. The forest bewitches her. Suddenly she rouses herself. The soft voice of the little Arab girl sends a shiver through her. What is she doing here? She dresses rapidly, buttons, buckles. Her voice floats on the darkness.

Actually, she has come out of pity. No one had thought he would persist so long. When does he sleep anyway? She has been sent here to deliver him, deliver him from this solitude. His silence rouses suspicions. Her husband and his friends have suddenly begun to wonder, have become afraid, ha-ha, afraid that he may be nursing some secret, some novel idea, that he may outshine them all with some brilliant research.

A sudden dark breeze bursts into the room through the gap where there is no wall, whirls around for a little and dies out in the two corners. He is kindled. His eyes glow.

"Pity? No, unnecessary. When do I sleep? Always . . . though different from the city sleep. Leave here now, just like that? Too late. I haven't finished counting the trees yet. Novel ideas? Maybe, though not what they imagine . . . not exactly scientific . . . Rather, human . . ."

Does she wish him to accompany her on her way back through the forest, or would she go by herself perhaps?

She jumps up.

They cut diagonally across the hills. He walks in front, she drags behind, staggering over the rocks in her high heels, hurt and humiliated. Though thickset, his feet are light and he slips through the foliage swift as a snake, never turning his head. She struggles with the branches whipping back behind him. The moonlight reveals them on their silent trip. What do you say now, my autumn love? Have I gone completely out of my mind? But that was to be expected, wasn't it? Out of my round of pleasures you have cast me into solitude. Trees have taken the place of words for me, forests the place of books. That is all. Eternal autumn, needles falling endlessly on my eyes. I am still awaiting a conflagration.

Wordless they reach the black main road. Her heels click on the asphalt with a last fury. Now he looks at her. Her face is scratched, her arms bloodstained. How assertively the forest leaves its mark. She contains the thin cry rising in her. Her silence grants her dignity. After some minutes a sleek car driven by a lone grey-templed man halts at her waving hand. She joins him in the car without a parting word. She will yet crumble between his fingers on the long road.

He turns in his tracks. After a few paces the Arab pops up in front of him. He is breathing heavily, his face is dull. And what do you have to say, mister? From where have you sprung now? The Arab holds out her forgotten hat, the straw hat. The fire watcher smiles his thanks, spreads his arms in a gesture of nothing we can do, she's gone. But how amazing, this attention. Nothing will escape the man's eye. He takes the hat from the Arab and pitches it on top of his own head, gives him a slight bow and the other is immediately alarmed. His face is alert, watching. Together, in silence, they return to the forest, their empire, theirs alone. The fire watcher strides ahead and the Arab tramples on his footsteps. A few clouds, a light breeze. Moonlight pours over the branches and makes them transparent. He leads the Arab over roads that are the same roads always. Barefoot he walks, the Arab, and so still. Round and round he is led, roundabout and to his hideout, amid chiselled stones and silence. The Arab's steps falter. His footfalls lag, die and come alive again. A deathly cold grips the fire watcher's heart, his hands freeze. He kneels on the rustling earth. Who will give him back all the empty hours? The forest is dark and empty. No one there. Not one camp-fire. Just now, when he would like to dip his hands in fire, warm them a little. He heaps up some brown needles, takes a match, lights it, and the match goes out at once. He takes another and cups his hands around it, strikes, and this one too flares up and dies. The air is damp and traitorous. He rises. The Arab watches him, a gleam of lunatic hope in his eyes. Softly the fire watcher walks around the pile of stones to the sorry little hideout, picks up a tin of clear liquid and empties it over the heap of pine needles, tosses in a burning match and leaps up with the surging flame—singed, happy. At last he, too, is lit up a little. Stunned, the Arab goes down on his knees. The fire watcher spreads his palms over the flame and the Arab does likewise. Their bodies press in on the fire, which has already reached its highest pitch. He might leave the flame now and go and bathe in the sea. Time, time wasting here among the trees, will do his work for him. He muses, his mind distracted. The fire shows signs of languishing, little by little it dies at his feet. The Arab's face takes on a look of bitter disappointment. The bonfire fades. Last sparks are stamped out meticulously. Thus far it was only a lesson. The wandering mind of the fire watcher trembles between compromises. He rises wearily and leaves. The Arab slouches in his wake.

Who is sitting on the chair behind the book-laden desk? The child. Her eyes are wide open, drinking in the dark. The Arab has put her there to replace the loving fire watcher. It's an idea.

Strange days follow. We would say: autumn; but that means nothing yet. The needles seem to fall faster, the sun grows weaker, clouds come to stay and a new wind. His mind is slipping, growing unhinged. The ceremonies are over. The donors have gone back to their countries, the hikers to their work, pupils to their study. His own books lie jumbled in a glow of dust. He is neglecting his duties, has left his chair, his desk, his faithful binoculars, and has begun roving endlessly about the forest, by day and by night; a broken twig in his hand, he slashes at the young tree trunks as he walks, as though marking them. Suddenly he slumps down, rests his head against a shining copper plaque, removes his glasses and peers through the blurring foliage, searches the grey sky. Something like a wail, suddenly. Foul fantasies. Then he collects himself once more, jumps up to wander through the wood, among the thistles and rocks. The idea has taken hold in his dim consciousness that he is being called insistently to an encounter at the edge of the forest, at its other end. But when he plunges out of the forest and arrives there, whether it be at night or at noon or in the early dawn, he finds nothing but a yellow waste, a strange wadi, a kind of cursed dream. And he will stand there for a long time, facing the empty treeless silence and feeling that the encounter is taking place, is being successful even though it happens wordlessly. He has spent a whole spring and a long summer never once properly sleeping, and what wonder is it if these last days should be like a trance.

He has lost all hope of fire. Fire has no hold over this forest. He can therefore afford to stay among the trees, not facing them. In order to soothe his conscience he sits the girl in his chair. It has taken less than a minute to teach her the Hebrew word for "fire". How she has grown up during his stay here! She is like a noble mare now with marvellous eyes. Unexpectedly her limbs have ripened, her filth become a woman's smell. At first her old father had been forced to chain her to the chair, or she would have escaped. Yes, the old Arab has grown very attached to the negligent fire watcher, follows him wherever he goes.

Ever since the night when the two of them hugged the little bonfire the Arab, too, has grown languid. He has abandoned his eternal hoe. The grass is turning yellow under his feet, the thistles multiply. The fire watcher will be lying on the ground and see the dusky face thrusting at him through the branches. As a rule he ignores the Arab, continues lying with his eyes on the sky. But sometimes he calls him and the man comes and kneels by his side, his heavy eyes wild with terror and hope. Perhaps he too will fail to convey anything and it will all remain dark.

The fire watcher talks to him therefore, quietly, reasonably, in a positively didactic manner. He tells him about the Crusades, and the other bends his head and absorbs the hard, alien words as one absorbing a melody. He tells him about the fervour, about the cruelty, about Jews committing suicide, about the Children's Crusade; things he has picked up from the books, the unfounded theories he has framed himself. His voice is warm, alive with imagination. The Arab listens with mounting tension and is filled with hate. When they return at twilight, lit by a soft autumnal glow, the fire watcher will lead the Arab to the tree-engulfed house and will linger a moment. Then the Arab explains something with hurried, confused gestures, squirming his severed tongue, tossing his head. He wishes to say that this is his house and that there used to be a village here as well and that they have simply hidden it all, buried it in the big forest.

The fire watcher looks on at this pantomime and his heart fills with joy. What is it that rouses such passion in the Arab? Apparently his wives have been murdered here as well. A dark affair, no doubt. Gradually he moves away, pretending not to understand. Did there used to be a village here? He sees nothing but trees.

More and more the Arab clings to him. They sit there, the three of them like a family, in the room on the second floor. The fire watcher sprawling on the bed, the child chained to the chair, the Arab crouching on the floor. Together they wait for the fire that does not come. The forest is dark and strong, a slow-growing world. These are his last days. His contract is drawing to an end. From time to time he gets up and throws one of the books back into the suitcase, startling the old Arab.

The nights are growing longer. Hot desert winds and raindrops mingle, soft shimmers of lightning flash over the sea. The last day is come. Tomorrow he will leave this place. He has discharged his duty faithfully. It isn't his fault that no fires have broken out. All the books are packed in the suitcase, scraps of paper litter the floor. The Arab has disappeared, has been missing since yesterday. The child is miserable. From time to time she raises her voice in a thin, ancient lament. The fire watcher is growing worried. At noon the Arab turns up suddenly. The child runs towards him but he takes no notice of her. He turns to the abdicating fire watcher instead, grabs him between two powerful hands and—feeble and soft that he is and suffering from a slight cold—impels him towards the edge of the observation post and explains whatever he can explain to him with no tongue. Perhaps he wishes to throw the abdicating fire watcher down two storeys and into the forest. Perhaps he believes that only he, the fire watcher, can understand him. His eyes are burning. But the fire watcher is serene, unresponsive; he shadows his eyes with his palm, shrugs his shoulders, gives a meaningless little smile. What else is left him?

He collects his clothes and bundles them into the other suitcase.

Towards evening the Arab disappears again. The child has gone to look for him and has come back empty-handed. Gently the hours drift by. A single drop of rain. The fire watcher prepares supper and sets it before the child, but she cannot bring herself to eat. Like a little animal she scurries off once more into the forest to hunt for her father and returns in despair, by herself. Towards midnight she falls asleep at last. He undresses her and carries the shabby figure to the bed, covers it with the torn blanket. What a lonely woman she will grow up to be. He muses. Something is flowing between his fingers, something like compassion. He lingers awhile. Then he returns to his observation post, sits on his chair, sleepy. Where will he be tomorrow? How about saying goodbye to the Fire Brigade? He picks up the receiver. Silence. The line is dead. Not a purr, not a gurgle. The sacred hush has invaded the wire as well.

He smiles contentedly. In the dark forest spread out before him the Arab is moving about like a silent dagger. He sits watching the world as one may watch a great play before the rising of the curtain. A little excitement, a little drowsing in one's seat. Midnight performance.

Then, suddenly—fire. Fire, unforseen, leaping out of the corner. A long graceful flame. One tree is burning, a tree wrapped in prayer. For a long moment one tree is going through its hour of judgment and surrendering its spirit. He lifts the receiver. Yes, the line is dead. He is leaving here tomorrow.

The loneliness of a single flame in a big forest. He is beginning to worry whether the ground may not be too wet and the thistles too few, and the show be over after one flame. His eyes are closing. His drowsiness is greatest now, at this most wonderful of moments. He rises and starts pacing nervously through the room in order to walk off his fatigue. A short while passes and then a smile spreads over his face. He starts counting the flames. The Arab is setting the forest on fire at its four corners, then takes a firebrand and rushes through the trees like an evil spirit, setting fire to the rest. The thoroughness with which he goes about his task amazes the fire watcher. He goes down to look at the child. She is asleep. Back to the observation post—the forest is burning. He ought to run and raise the alarm, call for help. But his movements are so tranquil, his limbs leaden. Downstairs again. He adjusts the blanket over the child, pushes a lock of hair out of her eyes, goes back up, and a blast of hot air blows in his face. A great light out there. Five whole hills ablaze. Flames surge as in a frenzy high over the trees, roar at the lighted sky. Pines split and crash. Wild excitement sweeps him, rapture. He is happy. Where is the Arab now? The Arab speaks to him out of the fire, wishes to say everything, everything and at once. Will he understand?

Suddenly he is aware of another presence in the room. Swiftly he turns his head and sees the girl, half naked, eyes staring, the light of the fire playing over her face. He smiles and she weeps.

Intense heat wells up from the leisurely burning forest. The first excitement has passed. The fire is turning from a vision into a fact. Flames are mobilizing from all the four winds to come and visit the observation post. He ought to take his two suitcases and disappear. But he only takes the child. The lights of the neighbouring settlements have become so pitiful, so plain. They are no doubt sure, over there, that the fight against the fire is already in full swing. Who would imagine that the fire is still being nourished here, brooded over? Hours will go by before the village watchmen come to wake the sleepers. The nights are already cold and people not disposed to throw off their blankets. He seizes the trembling child by the hand, goes down and begins his retreat. The road is lit up till far into the distance. Behind his back the fire, and in his face a red, mad, burning moon that floats in the sky as though it wished to see the blaze as well. His head feels heavy, the road stretches ahead. They drag along, dipping in light and in darkness. In the lanes the trees whisper, agitated, waiting. A fearful rumour has reached them.

The observation post can be seen from afar, entirely lit up. The earth is casting its shackles. After a long walk the trees start thinning out at last, they grow smaller, then disappear. He arrives at the yellow waste, the wadi, his dream. A few dry, twisted trees, desert trees, alien and salty; trees that have sprung up parched, that the fire has no hold over. He sits the barefoot girl on the ground, slumps beside her. His exhaustion erupts within him and covers them both.

With sleeping eyes he sees the shining fire engines arrive at last, summoned by another. They too know that all is lost. In a dream the Arab appears—tired, dishevelled, black with soot, his face ravaged—takes the child and vanishes. The fire watcher falls asleep, really asleep.

At dawn, shivering and damp, he emerges from the cover of the rocks, polishes his glasses and lo, he is the little scholar once more who has some kind of future before him. Five bare black hills, and slender wisps of blue-grey smoke rising from them. The observation post juts out over the bare landscape like a great demon grinning with white windows. For a moment it seems as though the forest had never burnt down but had simply pulled up its roots and gone off on a journey, far off on a journey, far off to the sea, for instance, which has suddenly come into view. The air is chilly. He adjusts his rumpled clothes, does up the last surviving button, rubs his hands to warm them, then treads softly among the smoking embers, light of foot. The first rays of the sun hit his bald patch. There is a sadness in this sudden nudity, the sadness of wars lost, blood shed in vain. Stately clouds sail in the cold sky. Soon the first rain will fall. He hears sounds of people everywhere. Utter destruction. Soot, a tangle of charred timber, its wounds still smoldering, and a residue of living branches unvisited by fire. Wherever he sets foot a thousand sparks fly. The commemorative plaques alone have survived; more than that, they have gained lustre after their baptism of fire. There they lie, golden in the sun: Louis Premington of Chicago, the King of Burundi and his People.

He enters the burnt building, climbs the charred stairs. Everything is still glowing hot. It is as though he were making his way through hell. He arrives at his room. The fire has visited it in his absence and held its riot of horror and glee. Shall we start with the books burnt to ashes? Or the contorted telephone? Or perhaps the binoculars melted to a lump? The map of the area has miraculously survived, is only blackened a bit at the edges. Gay fire kittens are still frolicking in the pillow and blankets. He turns his gaze to the fire smoking hills, frowns—there, out of the smoke and haze, the ruined village appears before his eyes; born anew in its basic outlines as an abstract drawing, as all things past and buried. He smiles to himself, a thin smile. Then abruptly it dies on his face. Directly under him, in the bluish abyss at the foot of the building, he sees the one in charge of forests who is edging his way to old age, wrapped in an old windbreaker, his face blue with cold. How has this one sprung up here all of a sudden?

The old one throws his grey head back and sends up a look full of hatred. Looking down upon the man from his high post, his own eyes would be faintly contemptuous in any case. For a few seconds they stay thus, with their eyes fixed on each other; at last the fire watcher gives his employer a fatuous smile of recognition and slowly starts coming down to him. The old man approaches him with quick mad steps. He would tear him to pieces if he could. He is near collapse with fury and pain. In a choking voice he demands the whole story, at once.

But there is no story, is there? There just isn't anything to tell. All there is, is: Suddenly the fire sprang up. I lifted the receiver— the line was dead. That's it. The child had to be saved.

The rest is obvious. Yes, the fire watcher feels for the forest too. He has grown extremely attached to it during the spring, the summer and half the autumn. So attached, in fact, that (to tell the truth for once) he hasn't managed to learn a single line.

He feels that the old man would like to sink to the ground and beat his head against some rock, would tear out the last of his white hair. The late fire watcher is surprised. Because the forests are insured, aren't they (at least they ought to be, in his humble and practical opinion), and the fire won't be deducted from the budget of the old man's department, will it? Right now (this morning has found him amazingly clearheaded), he would very much like to be told about other forest fires. He is willing to bet that they were quite puny ones.

Except that now, ghost-like through the smoke, the firemen appear, accompanied by some fat and perspiring policemen. Soon he is surrounded by uniforms. Some of the men drop to the ground with exhaustion. Though the fire has not been completely tracked down as yet, they have already unearthed a startling piece of intelligence.

It has been arson.

Yes, arson. The smell of morning dew comes mingled with a smell of kerosene.

The old man is shattered.

"Arson?" he turns to the fire watcher.

But the other smiles gently.

The investigation is launched at once. First the firemen, who are supposed to write a report. They draw the fire watcher aside, take out large sheets of paper, ornate ballpoints, and then it appears that they have difficulty with the language, with phrasing and spelling. They are embarrassed. Tactfully he helps them, spells out words, formulates their sentences for them. They are very grateful.

"What have *you* lost in the fire?" they inquire sympathetically.

"Oh, nothing of importance. Some clothes and a few textbooks. Nothing to worry about."

By the time they are through it is far into the morning. The Arab and the child appear from nowhere, led by two policemen. If he will be careful not to let his glance encounter those burning eyes he may possibly sleep in peace in the nights to come. Two tough-looking sergeants improvise a kind of emergency interrogation cell among the rocks, place him on a stone and start cross-examining him. For hours they persist, and that surprises him—the plodding tenacity, the diligence, page upon written page. A veritable research is being compiled before his eyes. The sun climbs to its zenith. He is hungry, thirsty. His interrogators chew enormous sandwiches and do not offer him a crumb. His glasses mist over with sweat. A queer autumn day. Inside the building they are conducting a simultaneous interrogation of the Arab, in Arabic eked out with gestures. Only the questions are audible.

The old forest manager dodges back and forth between the two interrogations, adding questions of his own, noting down replies. The interrogators have their subject with his back against the rock, they repeat the same questions over and over. A foul stench rises from the burnt forest, as though a huge carcass were rotting away all around them. The interrogation gains momentum. A big bore. What did he see, what did he hear, what did he do. It's insulting, this insistence upon the tangible—as though that were the main point, as though there weren't some idea involved here.

About noon his questioners change, two new ones appear and start the whole process over again. The subject is dripping with sweat. How humiliating, to be interrogated thus baldly on scorched earth, on rocks, after a sleepless night. The tedium of it. He spits, grows angry, loses his temper. He removes his glasses and his senses go numb. He starts contradicting himself. At three o'clock he breaks in their hands, is prepared to suggest the Arab as a possible clue.

This, of course, is what they have been waiting for. They had suspected the Arab all along. Promptly they handcuff him, and then all at once everything is rapidly wound up. The police drivers start their cars. The Arab is bundled into one of them and there is a gratified expression in his eyes now, a sense of achievement. The child clings to him desperately. Autumn clouds, autumn sadness, everything is flat and pointless. Suddenly he walks over to the forest manager and boldly demands a solution for the child. The other makes no reply. His old eyes wander over the lost forest as though in parting. This old one is going mad as well, his senses are growing confused. He stares at the fire watcher with vacant eyes as though he, too, had lost the words, as though he understood nothing. The fire watcher repeats his demand in a loud voice. The old man steps nearer.

"What?" he mumbles in a feeble voice, his eyes watery. Suddenly he throws himself at the fire watcher, attacks him with shrivelled fists, hits out at him. With difficulty the firemen pull him back. To be sure, he blames only this one here. Yes, this one with the books, with the dim glasses, with that smug cynicism of his.

The policemen extricate the fire watcher and whisk him into one of their cars. They treat him roughly, something of the old man's hostility has stuck to them. Before he has time to say goodbye to the place where he has spent nearly six months he is being borne away at a mad pace towards town. They dump him on one of the side streets. He enters the first restaurant he comes to and gorges himself to bursting point. Afterwards he paces the streets, bearded, dirty, sunburnt—a savage. The first dusty rain has already smirched the pavements.

At night, in some shabby hotel room, he is free to have a proper sleep, to sleep free from obligations for the first time, just sleep without any further dimensions. Except that he will not fall asleep, will only go on drowsing. Green forests will spring up before his troubled eyes. He may yet smart with sorrow and yearning, may feel constricted because he is shut in by four walls, not three.

And so it will be the day after, and perhaps all the days to come. The solitude has proved a success. True, his notes have been burned along with the books, but if anyone thinks that he does not remember—he does.

Yet he has become a stranger now in his so familiar town. He seems to have been forgotten already. A new generation is breaking into the circles. His waggish friends meet him, slap him on the back, and with ugly grins say, "We hear your forest burned down!" As we said, he is still young. But his real friends have given him up in despair. He drops in on them, on winter nights, shivering with cold—wet dog begging for fire and light—and they scowl and ask: "Well, what now?"

The Last Commander

> "The Gnostics, who were the contemporaries of the Jewish Tannaim of the second century, believed that it was necessary to distinguish between a good but hidden God who alone was worthy of being worshipped by the elect, and a Demiurge or creator of the physical universe, whom they identified with the 'just' God of the Old Testament."
>
> GERSHOM SCHOLEM
> "Redemption Through Sin"

I

AFTER the war there we were in murky offices, pushing pencils, and sending form letters to one another on matters which seemed important to us. Had we lost, we would have been in a real mess now. We would have been accounting for murder, for robbery, committed by our dead comrades. Since we had won—we brought liberation, but they had to give us something to do, otherwise nobody would vacate the fast, murderous jeeps, full of machine guns and rounds of ammunition.

Now our clothes are clean; no grime on our faces. Only adding machines are softly humming at our side, and at night, in the crazy city, we rush from place to place to avoid loneliness. We run from light to light, clinging to our jaded women. Our eyes grow weak.

Each year when summer comes around, the reservists go off for military practice. The commands flutter around the offices like white soft bullets, but they don't touch us—the veterans. At first we felt slighted, but we consoled ourselves: no doubt this world needs us and our sharp pencils. Seven years we fought without stopping. Our nights have become hollow with fear. Now they ask us to rest on our withered laurel wreaths. So we barricaded ourselves behind piles of letters.

But this year when summer came around, strange to say, we too were caught. Our good brothers, the officers in charge of sending out the summonses, remembered us. And the call-up summonses landed on our desks to our amazement. No escape.

One fine day they loaded us dodgers, former military men, on to freight cars, and sent us off to the south, to clamber up the hills.

And now, who knows, we might have picked up the weapons, unfamiliar to our hands by now, and stormed off; carried packs and fought until our strength gave out in new, imagined battles; attacked, retreated, returning again to conquer the wind and ourselves—had it not been for Yagnon—a swarthy, angular character, who was appointed at the last moment and with some trepidation, to substitute for the Commander of the Company who was suddenly called away on some business.

Already at the point of departure near the desert crossroads we could see that the new Commander tarried. While the rest of the companies were very busily engaged in loading equipment to go off to some place of action and trouble, and the commanders were running back and forth, this one went up on a small hill at the side of the road, and there he dozed off all by himself, bared to the sun. I remember our men hanging around idly by the silent machines— grunting and grumbling. The other companies disappeared one by one, and the square quietened down. But that black dot on top of the hill didn't move. No one knew the reason for this delay. Fed up with one another, scorched by the heat, we hadn't yet realized that from now on time was not our own. Darzi and Hilmi, two Division Commanders, approached me, their limbs moving restlessly. In the war they had served as sappers, and they had blown up whole villages together with their inhabitants, and since then they don't move without one another, out of fear.

I could see that the hours were passing, so I climbed up the hill and went over to him. This was the first time that I really saw him. He was lying at my feet—an elongated form with limbs stretched out, sporting a huge broken nose in an ugly face. With bifocals perched on his nose and a long scar deeply imprinted on his forehead. He was sleeping in a state of deep fatigue, but his breathing was barely audible. I knew that he, too, had served in the lower echelon in one of the offices, but he was a bachelor, and in the war he had displayed bold leadership on the southern front. I bent over and touched him. I remember his look—tear-veiled from sleeping in the sun. If death is very close to life, then death had been caught in his eyes. He lifted his head slowly, calmly, like one who had experienced an eternity of death. An old khaki shirt hung limply on his body. No military stripes.

"The other units have already left," I said, bending over him. "Isn't it time for us?"

He shot me a look out of another world.

"What?" His lips broke out in a strange drawl.

I repeated what I had said.

A weak smile lit up his mouth.

"You're in a hurry?" he said in a kind of mocking surprise.

Only when the heat subsided and a breeze came up from the desert did he rouse himself, glide weakly down the hill, get up on an old bullet-ridden jeep which had been given to us, a survivor of the war years. The whole column followed in his footsteps.

We travelled for many hours, slowly, with long stops. It seemed as though lead had been poured into the wheels of the cars that were crookedly wending their way at the bidding of the drowsy officer. We pressed deeper and deeper into the heart of the desert, getting ever farther away from any shadow of a settlement. Nobody knew where we were going. In the north, we had fought for every house, for every clod of earth; but in this desert only a few small scattered units were roaming about, without direction and without reason. The whole wide expanse was conquered in a swift, seven-day campaign. Anything wider than a narrow parcel of dust cutting through the length of the desert was beyond our ken.

The sun beat down on the cars that wormed their way around in the menacing chalk-white region, somberly, through sand dunes glistening with fool's gold, oceans of wasteland whose gentleness belied the eye. In the evening we found ourselves ascending a strange mountain, a formidable reddish ridge of Hymettian stone and reddish-black rocks. The wheels of the cars were caught in the steep rise little by little, until finally the spluttering motors gave out and stalled in the middle of their ascent, halfway up the mountain, next to a wide, deep rut with desert brush sticking out of it, their branches twisted as though demented.

We jumped out of the cars, weakened and confused, and a dim, ghostlike twilight encircled us. The drivers unloaded the cases of army rations, unfastened the trailing water tank, and disappeared to the rear down the slope. Like sleepwalkers we began going around among the piles of equipment that were thrown around, among the heaped weapons, coming to a halt and standing at the mouth of the abyss that was but a chain of extinct volcanic craters; their bases either cooled off or still smouldering. Every step opened up long and gaping canyons, small craters that dropped—crookedly—to deep layers of chalk, broken up in a mysterious way. We were still wandering about when the officer who looked now like a dark brown hawk stepped down into the rut, spread out a blanket for himself on the ground, curled up, and without a word, fell asleep. We were still bunched together here and there, looking for food, but the utter chaos confused everything. One after another we followed him into the rut, hungry and tired. Soon all had fallen asleep around the new officer, after a day in which nothing had been accomplished.

The camp was asleep and silent until late in the morning. The slow crawling rays of the sun added slumber to slumber. A strange, paralyzing heat flowed beneath us all the time, from hidden sources in the mountain itself, as if we had been placed inside a giant furnace. Darzi and Hilmi crept over to me, drowsily and heavily, and snuggled up next to me, among the smouldering rocks. From their mumbling I figured out that they wanted to know whether to awaken the men, since the new officer didn't seem to show any signs of life.

The heat of the sun was now more intense and there was a burning sensation which weakened everybody. From between the slits of our aching eyes, the rocks looked like trembling molluscs, formations of sandstone running amok in a riot of colours. The blue of the sky disappeared and in its place there remained only a stark white heat. No soldier moved a muscle. Here and there somebody would try to move around, but immediately his legs would buckle and he would collapse to the ground. Only the youngest amongst us, the Commander of the fourth unit, an officer of the youth corps, who at the time of the war was still a child and collected bags of bullets, he alone got up and wandered around, ready for a day's work. He glanced apprehensively at his slumbering Commander, then he settled at the edge of the abyss, and cleaned his weapons.

The morning hours passed. The bellies of the soldiers of the Division stretched out around me were glued to the ground. At noon Yagnon suddenly turned over from one side to the other, opened his eyes and gazed at the world while lying on his back, took a cigarette from his shirt pocket, and lit it. The whole camp lay in wait for his every move. We got up, bent over, and came near him; the youth joined us. We knelt, all together, at the side of the officer, who tossed his ugly head in our direction.

"What's to be done today?" the young officer burst out. Yagnon didn't answer. A queer grimace twisted his mouth. The scar on his forehead was gleaming like a long, bloody stain.

"Today," repeated the youth, almost angrily, "what's to be done today?"

Yagnon didn't move from his place. His slim, tanned hand was thrown over his sack, between his mussed-up blankets. Papers rustled. A smile came over his lips.

"There are plans," he whispered tiredly. "They gave me plans," he repeated.

The young man tried to seize the practice plans.

"So then what's to be done today? One just can't keep on lying around like this."

He was aflame with the heat, and it seemed that he was right.

Yagnon's tiny eyes glided along Hilmi and Darzi's palpitating bellies, lying criss-crossed, at least that is the way I saw them. His lips mumbled drowsily.

"Today—rest . . . at night perhaps . . . the heat will subside . . . now—rest."

Darzi bent his head towards the figure bundled up on the ground.

"Rest," he repeated with an inward smile.

We looked at each other, all three of us. The young officer wanted to open his mouth, but we had already disappeared, stooping down over the rim of the shadow under the scrawny trees, returning to our sweaty slumber. When the heat subsided, when it started to get dark, Yagnon again woke up, and sucked on a cigarette. It was clear to all of us that he was not setting aside the approaching night for anything but sleep. Again, one after the other, we succumbed to heat-ravaged slumber, riddled with disturbing fantasies. And in the morning we were still lying down, only more tired than we were before.

On the third day we had already removed our clothes. Rank disappeared. We wondered suspiciously what schemes the sleeping man was devising. But, after the hours passed without anything happening, we knew that he had decided to lie low on the rocks until the end of the practice period.

We were struck with terror when we realized his clear, simple purpose. We attacked the deceiving shrubs, we uprooted and reduced them to splinters. We made a fire and nibbled without appetite on some dry rations we had at hand. Now there was not even the slightest bit of shade left.

On the fourth day, at noontime, we woke up. A hot wind whispered through the clefts of the rocks. Sun-scorched papers were flying around us, we made weak attempts to catch some of them. Yagnon had let fly away the practice plans. The wireless was cracked, and the sleepy liaison officer had tied it up with blankets, and had placed it under his head. The only possible connection with other units was severed. At twilight the young officer suddenly jumped up, got on the jeep that was left with us, to escape this hell. The roar of the engine shattered the silence. They all opened their eyes, but no one got up from their place. They hoped it would alarm the sleeping officer. The jeep started gliding down the incline; suddenly the dry brakes snapped, and it rolled down to the edge of the abyss and got stuck between two rocks. He was saved by a miracle. He returned shamefacedly to us, his eyes on fire. That night we saw neither the moon nor the stars. Complete darkness covered the mountains.

On the fifth day the sound of a car was heard in the mountains, horn blowing noisily, and the men inside it shooting in the air, looking for us. Perhaps letters were coming from the cold, far-off city, our memory of which had completely disappeared. Again the young man straightened up, like a roe-deer—his blue eyes flustered. The sun scorched his skin, he was all aflame. He cocked his weapon, shot into space, pierced the silence. The dialogue of shots continued for a long time, but the abyss scrambled the echoes. The car went further away. The young man started running among us like a madman, yelling and pleading. Drowsy and indifferent, we observed his thin shadow gliding around us. After the car had disappeared and silence was restored, he was still standing like a hurt child, his fist releasing his weapon, until at last he sank down near Yagnon, who smiled at him tiredly. During the night he disappeared and was not seen again. Perhaps he is still lost among the craters.

We are getting confused as to the number of the days, but already the sixth day has arrived, and as our skin has blackened, so has our human image faded. People who used to pray have stopped praying. The six working days passed in idleness, and on the Sabbath our capacity for sleep doubled. By now we know only the rocks hanging over our heads. We are lying in a group but each one is alone. Our hearing is clearer in the silence, and when we make an attempt to speak, we whisper. Nobody is looking for us, nobody ever gets up here. At times in the winding wadi below there are what appear to be three tiny figures, swathed in black, one in front and two in the rear, in a fixed order. These are our silent, bitter, vanquished enemies, but no one wakens to the danger that it is possible to slaughter all of us with just one dagger—without a single outcry.

Only occasionally, at night, would somebody's mind become lucid, and he would toss around, unable to fall asleep. He jumps up all by himself and sees the mountain very clearly with all its sharply edged outlines. He circles the sleepy camp crying softly to the sleeping men. He too feels like sleeping. When he reaches the ugly face of Yagnon he halts, he seems to think that he hears cries of pain from the neighbouring mountain, into which those black-swathed ones are disappearing. With nothing else to do, he feverishly piles up rocks. Then his passion suddenly subsides, and a dry, ashen look returns to his lips. He sinks down on the spot where he is standing, and returns to forgetfulness. On the next day, in the light, between one fit of sleep and the next he discovers next to him only a pile of rocks.

For seven days we have been captives in this realm in the power of this skinny magician who can't get enough sleep. But there is a kind of bewitching delight in having leaden legs that keep getting entangled, in the waning consciousness.

"God Almighty," a mumbling cry is heard at times, "why didn't we come here after the war?"

And at night, again and again, one dreams about the war.

II

Was this Sunday? We were lost in reverie when suddenly we heard a faint rumbling sound over our heads. We lifted our eyes. In the white expanse of brightness a grey dot fluttered over us. We rubbed our eyes, when a roaring, bellowing helicopter in a whirlpool of dust and wind hovered like a bird over the furrow in the earth. Suddenly its flight was arrested in mid-air, a rope ladder unfurled, bags were thrown out, a sturdy figure descended and waved a hand to the pilots who were disappearing in flight like blue angels. Perplexed and tired, we raised our heads from the dirt. He gathered his bags and came towards us with firm strides we could no longer match. Flushed, human, heavy-framed, silver-haired, blue, paternal eyes, and hands that knew how to praise. Insignia gleamed on his shoulders. He held back for a second, surveyed the bunch of shadows that peered at him—black, lean, bare.

We gazed at him. We knew—that was our enemy.

He made a firm decision, stepped over to a soldier who had straightened up in shock, and said curtly:

"I am the Company Commander . . . where is my deputy?"

We led him to Yagnon, who was sleeping, as always. His heavy shadow completely covered the slim figure. We sank down by the side of the slumbering man, we touched him. He opened his small, crafty eyes.

"Yagnon," we whispered, all bent over and frightened.

The Company Commander measured him with his eyes, undecidedly.

"You are my deputy?"

He nodded his head as he lay on the ground. Our hearts went out to his ugly face.

"What happened? Someone killed?" The sturdy Commander turned his eyes on us.

Our tongues moved without a sound. The words got choked. We are dead, we tried to tell him. But he wasn't looking for an answer. He had already stopped listening. He wiped away his sweat and spoke: "Why did you come to this furrow? I hovered in the sky for a long time looking for you . . . and it was only with difficulty that I found time to come to you . . . They say that since the end of the war you haven't done a thing."

No one blinked an eyelash. He surveyed the furrow wonderingly.

"How in the world . . . utter chaos . . . so one lies, like this, naked?"

His voice was sharp like a whip. We kept silent. Yagnon shut his eyes tiredly, his head still lying on the ground. The officer cocked his ear, demanded an answer.

"Today: rest." Darzi's voice rose at last as if from beyond the grave.

"Rest?" roared the Company Commander, and his roar awakened the remaining sleepers.

"Rest," uttered Hilmi naively and with frightened eyes, "Sabbath today?"

A threat rent the officer's mouth. Even I murmured apologetically.

"The days have got mixed up."

They all nodded their heads with me. Our souls were already sold to the man who lay on his back, and gazed quietly with dead eyes.

The Commander was taken aback. He was an officer of high

rank, and he was not used to insolence. Even during the war they uttered his name respectfully, though he was a civilian. At that time he used to travel around the world, and he was the one who used to bring ammunition to the depleted arsenals. He could have been resting now in his huge office, but he always kept looking for the main action. When he heard that they were conscripting the war heroes, the dodgers, he made himself a Company Commander, and though it had seemed that he would not appear, here he was.

From then on he didn't utter a sound. He bent over his bags and rummaged around in them. Solitary and strong, a white figure. He pitched a small tent outside the furrow and shut himself in it. When evening came he crept out of his tent, and roamed a bit among the piles of equipment that were thrown about until he found a broken lamp. He fixed it and lit it. For the first time we had light. All night the lamp glowed next to him and from behind the canvas of the tent his outline was silhouetted devising schemes and bent over plans.

On the following day he got us up before dawn, before light. With dictatorial anger he delivered us from the furrow, and soon we were standing before him in sleepy formation, armed and ready. The tardy ones he sent to the mountain peak to light a fire for the rising sun. He dispatched the officers to put on insignia. When the skies lit up with golden rays, and the fire died down, the tardy returned, and then we all climbed after him in a long file, with Yagnon trailing along at the end like a black shadow. It was a difficult climb but we eventually reached the mountain peak, where the blue sky was spread out, a vast expanse. All day we fired into the abyss, until our shoulders were fractured with pain. In the evening we ran after him down the slope, and he did not allow us to eat or drink until we had put up a high flagpole. At night we again climbed up the mountain, under star-studded skies. Until midnight we fired in the darkness, hitting and missing, with the echoes rolling all around us. The remaining half of the night we had alternate guard duty with the commander-who-knew-no-sleep awakening the guards.

We had only slept a few hours, and here it was Tuesday, and he was standing over us—clean, alert, and cross. In the morning twilight, heavy and weak, we fell in to raise the forgotten war flag which he had brought with him, and to hear the order of the day which he composed, a biblical psalm. All that day we dug ditches, camp sites, and pits. Our hands were blistered, as though leprous. There was no rest. From trench to trench he passed, and upbraided the lazy ones. Our eyes searched desperately for Yagnon, but he found himself a deep pit and slept on, and while we were striking the rocks in vain he was in his pit, dozing off. Smoke from his cigarette curled up from time to time. In the evening we dug out holes for lavatories, we covered them with tin, and gathered our scattered excretions into one place. From now on we walk to the edge of the canyon to relieve ourselves. With the setting rays licking the burning rocks, he was the first to go there. The whole company hung around feebly, icy eyes glued to the sturdy figure crouched over there by itself.

At night—a bonfire. He assembled us in circles and talked about the war. About the war that was, about the war that will be. Is there ever a moment without a war? Is there ever rest? He stood before us and read from the book of wars, in a clear, flat voice, as though giving orders. Our heads were nodding and drooping, but he shot pebbles at the dozers and kept them jumping. As midnight approached he demanded all of a sudden that we sing the battle songs that had long since sunk into oblivion. We looked at one another fearfully, as if we were having a nightmare. But he kept right after us. We sang. Hesitating at first, hoarse, but little by little our singing turned into a terrible wail, drunken and wild. Exhausted from a burning hot day of toil, we yelled and bellowed out the old bloody battle songs. He was standing, arms crossed over his heart, a trace of a smile on his lips. After which he turned serious, silenced us by raising a firm hand, and sent us off to our blankets, to our guard duties. There will be a big day tomorrow, he said.

And on Wednesday we charged. The whole art of fighting that we had forgotten came back to us in one day. From hill to hill, from mount to mount, he collected us and showed us where to charge, where to win. Afterward, we would spread out on the rocky hills, running, shooting, and falling until winning as he said. At noon, after we had been running in the wadi, and our eyes were blurred with the heat and dust, there appeared before us, a short distance away, the three figures clad in black. We stopped for a moment, gazing, but the roaring Commander, who was running after us with his helmet falling over his hot face, noticed them, cocked his gun, and fired at them. And immediately they disappeared light and swift into one of the canyons, like a mirage.

Where is Yagnon?

At times it seems to us that we see him treading soundlessly at the side of the Commander, a dark, shadowy figure. But mostly he would appear to be going around alone in the mountain chains. The Commander could keep the whole company under control by himself, and it seemed that he was afraid of his strange adjutant, the tired officer, who throughout the war was busy with the dead.

In the evening, in a period of slight rest, the Commander busied himself with a car. He was wonderfully capable and he fixed it right away. At night its two headlights shone, strange, large lights. The whole night we charged back and forth within the beams of the light that it threw over the surrounding hills. Terror gripped us again. The smell of sulphur that stuck to our clothes brought the war back to us. The morning chill found us at the foot of the mountain, fainting with fatigue, but still alert enough to hear with the last ounce of strength his comments on the methods of a war that he had never fought. At dawn we returned to the deserted furrow, to the flag, after a sleepless night. He fixed his blue eyes upon us, smiled to himself, and said: "It's Thursday."

In the morning a new drill was set up. He stood on top of the mountain, and it was up to us to reach him, without being noticed. The whole mountain was full of soldiers crawling like insects, trying to hide from him. It was hopelessly impossible. Whenever we thought we had got to the top and reached him, his alert eyes would stop us in time, and turn us back again to the starting point, to the place where Yagnon was lying, smiling and blowing clouds of smoke. Before this we had intended to fall asleep in one of the passes between the great rocks, but since yesterday we hadn't had a drop of water in our mouths, and the water was beside him at the top of the mountain. Crazed with thirst, we were creeping, scratched and dry, until noon. No one succeeded in reaching him. He won.

In the afternoon, no one paid any attention to the sound of the car wandering around the mountains, carrying letters. But he heard. He assembled us at once and commanded us to go and meet it. We marched a great distance and found it stuck in one of the small wadis. We freed its wheels from the pits, we cleared the path before it, we split rocks, and as a reward we received crumpled and yellowed letters from those who remained in the city. They wrote to us about their petty worries. We wanted to throw the letters away. He stood there and demanded of all of us that we send our answers, as in the war days, so that they would know that we were still living, and wouldn't mourn. We leaned over and scrawled large letters on top of the rocks, staring at him with open hostility. We returned to the camp in a trot around the mountain.

On Friday he was feeling good. He said: "I haven't done anything yet . . . I haven't accomplished half of what I want." All day he spread out and rolled up maps and coloured diagrams which he had brought with him to demonstrate to us what was going tp take place, what was still to happen. When he saw that we were dozing off in front of him he dispatched us to pitch tents outside the furrow, in precise squares. There will be a shade over your head, for your damned tiredness.

In the evening he instructed those who prayed to pray. Even the agnostics—it is better for them to pray, to ease their troubled minds. He stood and looked at them until their hurried prayer ended. At night he took out of his pack a box of broken, dried-up biscuits that he had brought with him, and divided them fairly and evenly with us. He was glad, so he said, that he had accomplished a great change in six days; no longer do we crouch dejectedly in the dry furrow. He rubbed his strong hands together, slowly and firmly. And isn't everything all right? We didn't answer. He doesn't really want an answer. And anyway has anybody except him said anything throughout these six days?

A gleaming night is spread over us. A strong dark sky. A deep rumble grows in the distance. The canvas of the tent is flapping in the wind. The mess has disappeared under the precisely folded blankets. We had said: Tonight we shall rest, we shall sleep. But he did not favour that. He wanted to sum up, to give himself credit. Since the war we hadn't done anything. All night he spoke to us about the fighting man.

Sabbath. Stones in our skulls instead of eyes. Hush. Quiet. As in the days when we first came here. Now it seems that we are permitted to sleep, but we can't. We keep opening our leaden eyelids to see what he is doing. How does he relax? Does he rest? The tiny tents are suffocating us. The shade is hot and dirty, not much of a shade. We are dying to close our eyes, we must. We have had a week of terror, and another week of terror is yet to come. The hours were passing, but sleep did not come. Painfully awake, like driven dogs we groped around on the ground to find a place for ourselves.

Yagnon. We remind ourselves of that one individual deep in sleep in the deserted furrow—why has he abandoned us?

And out of the corners of inflamed eyes, against our will, we keep seeing the Company Commander who is making the rounds among the tents, alert and awake, smiling at our drooping faces.

"Why don't you sleep? You say you're tired. At night I hear you crying."

III

In the evening, at the end of the Sabbath, he assembled the officers and Yagnon in his tent in order to give directions for a taxing march of seven days' duration through the Wilderness of John and its plains, up to a distant well of water at the desert crossroads, where cars will wait for us to take us back home. All night he kept us in his tent and spelled out for us every item of the march with maddening attention to detail. Plans for assaults, charges, entrenchments, retreats, complicated night raids. With his swift red pencil he encircled on the map places where he wanted to stage battles with an imaginary enemy, and the point of his pencil cruelly indicated the many kilometres that we would be carrying the imaginary wounded. He wanted to conduct the march under military conditions, with packs and ammunition, with meagre rations of food and water, without rest. He ordered us to take the tents with us, and to drag along the boxes of ammunition; so that no trace of our existence be left in the furrow.

We bit our lips in anger, looked up at Yagnon who was sucking on a cigarette in the darkness of the tent, but he didn't raise his head. We exchanged hopeless looks. Darzi took heart, extended a weak hand towards the officer, who was bent over the map, his voice wavering.

"Why the tents?" he said sarcastically. "At any rate there will be no time to fall asleep in them."

The Company Commander directed his blue gaze at us. Darzi was awed, waiting for the scathing anger of the Commander.

"In vain . . ." Another word died on his lips. The Company Commander controlled his temper, but rage made his quiet voice quiver. Once more he spoke about the war that was, the war that will be. About the blood, about those who would be killed, about the crying, about the need to learn how to win. Suddenly he turned to the silent spark that was lighting one cigarette with another, as though he knew that in that one's silence lay all the trouble. Yagnon removed the cigarette from his mouth, lifted his eyebrows in mock amazement, and said in his warm, quiet voice :

"Of course these are the plans."

And he put the live fire back into his mouth. The Commander's eyes softened. He passed his glance over the men who were sitting bent and crushed. He knew that the march would be taxing, but was there really any other choice? Are we the masters? Years ago, in the war, battles took place here, and through the arid Plain of John men went out on offensive marches. He bent his body towards us; his eyes were glistening. Perhaps we would find remains of equipment, or even skeletons of fighters who were killed in the passes. He looked sternly into the gloomy space that was visible from behind the folds of the tent. With unconcealed sorrow. What a pity that he wouldn't be able to lead us on that march.

The last sentence that was swallowed up in the darkness made our hearts leap with sudden joy. We didn't believe what our ears had heard. Only Yagnon didn't bat an eyelid.

"You aren't coming with us?" we asked with unconcealed joy.

"No . . . I only came here for seven days . . . no more."

We lowered our heads so that he wouldn't notice the relief that engulfed us. Only slow-witted Hilmi slipped in with a delighted voice, "Who will take you, sir?"

He smiled with sovereign condescension. "Those who brought me . . . tomorrow morning."

We shook hands thankfully.

After he finished speaking, we went out of the tent. A desert breeze was blowing. Only a few hours remained before sunrise, and although we were exhausted after a night of planning, we weren't looking for sleep. Hilmi and Darzi lit a small bonfire at the edge of the abyss, and the four of us sat around the fire. The heat enveloped our drowsy limbs. The star-strewn sky was hazy, and the shadows of the mountains long. From time to time we would smuggle a look at Yagnon who was sitting with us. This was the first time that he looked wide awake and his eyes were inwardly twinkling with a strange smile.

The fire attracted the Company Commander. He came over to say goodbye to us in a nice, friendly way, reminding us to carry out his orders. At the edge of the abyss he stepped towards us, somewhat cautious. He came, he seated himself near us, he warmed his strong hands in the fire. The light fell on his handsome face. His eyes lifted up beyond the Plain of John, whose border points to the north, a place where the ridges end. After that he examined us with a steady gaze. No bashfulness in his eyes, no perplexity. He kept looked relentlessly at

Yagnon, trying to tear apart the curtains that he was wrapped in. But he kept smoking peacefully away, and his eyes kept lapping up the fire. Suddenly the Commander jerked his head back, partly stating, partly asking:

"You fought here . . . in these mountains."

Yagnon raised his eyes to him. For the first time they gleamed with interest.

"Yes."

"They say that some bitter fighting took place here."

"Yes."

"Why?"

"We were surrounded."

"Surrounded?"

"Yes."

"Where?"

"Here . . . around this very mountain. We hid in this furrow . . . we were hiding."

"And after that you broke out and beat the enemy." He wasn't asking. He was stating facts.

"No . . . we fled. We escaped through the Plain of John."

"The Plain of John," we whispered.

"Yes," answered the quiet, somewhat slovenly voice of Yagnon. "On the road they murdered us all. The retreat lasted seven days."

"Seven?" We recoiled.

"Seven."

At dawn the watchmen awakened the camp. The men got up in fear. Already word had leaked out about the long and tiring journey that was arranged. They packed their bags and grumbled, tied up the tents and grumbled, they removed the crates of ammunition from the pits and divided them among themselves, and the grumbling rose to the very heavens, wan in the light of the dawn. They nibbled on their dry rations, formed subordinate groups, and already the packs were on their shoulders, and the polished weapons in their hands. The sun's rays that streamed from the mountain, like broken arrows, lit up the company that stood in formation laden and weighted down with iron helmets, weapons and ammunition, and with the tents rising like squashed towers from the stooped shoulders. Sixty pairs of eyes intent on evil searched for Yagnon. The Commander passed in front of the soldiers, his bag in his hand. The grumblings fell like sheaves.

Seven days he was with us, and each day was branded with a hot iron. He tried to impose order, and what he brought was terror. Now he is trying to clear us out of here to bruise our feet for seven days with the rocks of the arid Wilderness of John. What for? Is there anything we need here? Is there anything we search for here? The ugly vulture, the corpse, spread out here. He didn't demand a thing. We are tired. We have gazed open-eyed into the abyss. The sun has scorched us.

The Commander spoke to the soldiers, described the way, talked about the drills. If we should complete the journey before seven days we could return to our homes earlier. His smile lit up his face. Would we indeed be strong enough to complete the difficult journey in less than seven days? No one stirred. Not a sound. He didn't even want an answer. He finished his short message, and his eyes looked for Yagnon; he crept out from the rear of the company, saddled with a helmet, and a cane in his hand. In that same instant a faint buzzing noise was heard. They all lifted their eyes to the sky. A grey dot was moving on high.

The Commander said to Yagnon, and his voice cut the air :

"Take your men and get on your way!"

Yagnon raised his dark eyes to him, but did not stir. All were glued to the manoeuvring plane in the sky, looking for us. Our feet stuck to the ground. If we should go down the slope we wouldn't ever come back here.

The Company Commander bristled with a stern look.

"What are you waiting for?" he roared at the bunch of platoon officers, who were standing at the side and were looking intently at him, petrified. They shifted unwillingly from foot to foot. The men lifted the crates of ammunition, ready to march. But the pupils of their eyes didn't budge from the plane that was getting bigger, flying like something from outer space. Suddenly Yagnon picked up his feet, marked time slowly, and came and stood in front of the Commander, bending over with a sort of slight bow. The scar on his forehead looked like a dark, wide-open hole.

The Commander gaped in astonishment.

"Mister," his lips stammered out the civilian term, and his eyes narrowed, "they want to see how they're going to take you out of here . . . so that we will remember . . . please, mister . . ."

The noise of the plane turned into a frightening blast. A whirlpool of winds went wild all around us, a smarting and very fine dust covered us. The helicopter, agitated and stormy, started to come to a stop very slowly on to the ground. Now to our joy we couldn't understand a word of the shoutings of the Company Commander. We only saw his moving lips. A door opened in the helicopter, and a rope ladder unfurled. The pilots, wearing sun visors and earphones, smiled at us who were standing laden with arms and packs.

Yagnon poked among the rocks with his cane. Everybody was waiting in hushed silence. Only now did the Company Commander understand what we were planning, burdened and silent as we were. Like a madman he ran between the lines, but the awesome vehicle drowned out his voice. Tears stood in his eyes, his hands trembled all of a sudden. The pilots accelerated the noise impatiently, laughing. Strange and removed—from a blue, swift world.

He waved his fists at them, alone under the sky and on the earth, his back bowed, for the first time we saw him at a loss, helpless. He climbed the rope ladder, then stopped suddenly and turned his chiselled head to us. His lips twisted in a sort of shudder. He murmured a few quiet, mute last words. Curses. We bowed our heads. His body was swallowed up inside the helicopter which at once ascended from its place. The noise was dying down, the clouds of dust settled on the ground. The plane melted into the sky, and calm returned to the everlasting mountains.

Without a word, each man turned full circle. We unloaded the packs, we threw down the arms. We threw away the crates of ammunition. Quietly, on tiptoe, like someone walking with the fear of God, light-footed and intoxicated with the light. Spellbound we made our way to the kitchen tent and threw it to the ground, someone kicked the lamp until it fell apart. The toilets that we had put up were smashed in a twinkling, the tins were flying in the air. Two tackled the deserted flagpole and broke it in two. Everything returned to its former state, and before much time had elapsed, we were again sprawled out inside the furrow, exposed to the morning light, to the growing heat of the sun rays. Yagnon had already shut his eyes.

The horror of white heat is burning on us. The sun does not leave us alone. We are tired and we are growing wearier by the hour. We have returned to the tender mercies of Yagnon's bony hands. Many days are still left for us to sleep here.

Day after day passes. A sleepy, paralyzed camp. Only from time to time does one of us lift his eyes to the gleaming expanse of white, which is called sky, in case a grey dot is fluttering, trying to come down to us and bring him back again.

Early in the Summer of 1970

I believe I ought to go over the moment when I learned of his death once more.

A summer morning, the sky wide, June, last days of the school year. I rise late, faintly stunned, straight into the depths of light; don't listen to the news, don't look at the paper. It is as though I had lost my sense of time.

I get to school late, search the dim green air in vain for a fading echo of the bell. Start pacing the empty playground, across squares of light and shadow cast by the row of windows, past droning sounds of classrooms at their work. And then, surprised, I discover that the Head is running after me, calling my name from afar.

Except that I have nearly arrived at my class, the Twelfth, their muffled clamour rising from the depth of the empty corridor. They have shut the door upon themselves not to betray my absence, but their excitement gives them away.

Again the Head calls my name from the other end of the corridor, but I ignore him, open the classroom door upon their yells and laughter which fade into a low murmur of disappointment. They had by now been certain I wouldn't show up today. I stand in the door waiting for them to sort themselves out, wild-haired, red-faced, in their blue school uniforms, scrambling back to their desks, kicking the small chairs, dropping Bibles, and gradually the desk tops are covered with blank sheets of paper, ready for the exam.

One of them is at the blackboard rubbing out wild words—a distorted image of myself. They look me straight in the eye, impudent, smiling to themselves, but silent. For the present my grey hairs still subdue them.

And then, as I walk softly into the room, the exam paper in my hand, the Head arrives, breathless, pale. All eyes stare at him but he does not even look at the class, looks only at me, tries to touch me, hold me; he who has not spoken to me for the past three years is all gentleness now, whispers, pleads almost: Just a moment . . . never mind . . . leave them . . . you've got to come with me. There's some notice for you . . . come . . .

It is three years now that no words have passed between us, that we look at each other as though we were stone. Three years that I have not set foot in the common room either, have not sat on a chair in it, not touched the teapot. I intrude into the school grounds early in the morning, and during break I wander up and down corridors or playground—in the summer in a large, broad-brimmed hat, in the winter in a greatcoat with the collar up—floating back and forth with the students. I pay my trips to the office long after school is out, leave my lists of marks, supply myself with chalk.

I hardly exchange a word with the other teachers.

Three years ago I had been due to retire, and had indeed resigned myself to the inevitable, had even considered venturing upon a little handbook of Bible instruction, but the war broke out suddenly and the air about me filled with the rumble of cannon and distant cries. I went to the Head to say I was not going to retire, I was staying on till the war would end. After all, now that the younger teachers were being called up one by one he would need me the more. He, however, did not see any connection between the war and myself. "The war is all but over," he told me with a curious smile, "and you deserve a rest."

No rest, however, but a fierce summer came, and flaming headlines. And two of our very young alumni killed one a day after the other. And again I went to him, deeply agitated, hands trembling, informed him in halting phrases that I did not see how I could leave them now, that is to say, now that we were sending them to their death.

But he saw no connection whatever between their death and myself.

The summer holidays started and I could find no rest, day after day in the empty school, hovering about the office, the Head's room, waiting for news, talking to parents, questioning them about their sons, watching pupils in army uniform come to ask about their exam results or return books to the library, and sniffing the fire-singed smell in the far distance. And again, another death, unexpected, an older alumnus, much liked in his time, from one of the first-year classes, killed by a mine on a dirt-track, and I at the Head again, shocked, beaten, telling him: "You see," but he straightaway tried to brush me off: he has given instructions to prepare the pension forms, has planned a farewell party—which of course I declined.

A week before the new school year I offered to work for nothing if only he would give me back my classes, but he had already signed on a new teacher and I was no longer on the roster.

School starts. I arrive along with everyone in the morning, carrying briefcase and books and chalk, ready to teach. He spotted me near the common room and inquired anxiously what had happened, what was I doing here, but I, on the spur of the moment, did not reply, did not even look at him, as though he were a stone. He thought I had gone out of my mind, but in the turmoil of a new school year had no time to attend to me. And meanwhile my eyes had been searching out the new teacher, a thin, sallow young man, in order to follow him. He enters the classroom, and I linger a moment and enter on his heels. Excuse me, I say to him with a little smile, you must be mistaken, this isn't your class, and before he has time to recover I have mounted the platform, taken out my ragged Bible. He stammers an apology and leaves the room, and as for the dazed students who never expected to see me again, I give them no chance to say a word.

When after some moments the Head appears, I am deep in the lesson, the class listening absorbed. I do not budge.

I did not leave the room during the break, stayed planted in a crowd of students. The Head stood waiting for me outside but did not dare come near me. If he had I would have screamed, in front of the students I would have screamed and well he knew it; and there was nothing he feared as much as a scandal.

By sheer force I returned to teaching. I had no dealings with anyone but the students. For the first few weeks I scarcely left the school grounds, would haunt them even at night. And the Head in my wake, obsessed by me, dogs my steps, talks to me, appeals to me, holding, stroking, threatening, reproaching, speaking of common values, of good fellowship, of the many years of collaboration, coaxes me to write a book, is even prepared to finance its publication, sends messengers to me. But I would not reply—keeping my eyes on the ground, or on the sky, or on the ceiling; freezing to a white statue, on a street corner, in the corridor, in the empty classroom, by my own gate, or even in my armchair at home, during the evenings when he would come to talk to me. Till he gave up in despair.

He had meant to drag me into his office, but I did not wish to move out of the students' range. I walked a few paces out into the corridor and stopped, and before the attentive gaze of the students I wrung it all out of him.

Some five or six hours ago . . .

In the Jordan Valley . . .

Killed on the spot . . .

Could not have suffered . . .

Not broken it to his wife yet, nor to the university . . .

I am the first . . .

He had put my name on the forms and for some reason given the school for address.

Must be strong now . . .

And then the darkness. Of all things, darkness. Like a candle the sun going out in my eyes. The students sensed this eclipse but could not move, weren't set for the contingency of my needing help, whereas the Head talked on fluently as though he had been rehearsing this piece of news for the past three years. Till suddenly he gave a little exclamation.

But I had not fainted, only slumped to the floor and at once risen to my feet again, unaided, and the light was returning to me as well, still dim, in the empty classroom, seated on a student's chair, seeing people throng the room, teachers rushing in from nearby class-rooms, curious students, office workers, the caretaker, people who had not spoken to me these three years. Here they were all coming back, some with tears in their eyes, surrounding me, a whole tribe, breaking my loneliness.

He had returned from the United States three months ago, after an absence of many years. Arrived with his family late in the night, on a circuitous flight by way of the Far East. For six hours I waited at the airport, thinking at last that they wouldn't arrive, that I would have to go back as I came. But at midnight, when I was by then dozing on some bench in a corner, they approached me, emerged from the obscurity of the runway, as though not coming off a plane but back from a hike; rumpled and unkempt, heavy rucksacks on their backs and in in one of them a white-faced toddler who looked at me with gentle eyes.

I hardly recognized my son in him. Bearded, heavy, soft, my son's hair was already sprinkled with grey, and, in his movements, some new, slow tranquillity. He, whom I had already given up for a lost bachelor, coming back a husband, a father, nearly a professor. I was dazzled by him. And he bringing his wife forward, in trousers, a slim girl, enveloped in hair, dressed in a worn-out tasselled coat, one of his students presumably; and then she is leaning towards me and smiling, her face clear. Very beautiful. At that moment anyway I found her so beautiful, touching me with cool, transparent fingers.

And I, my heart overflowing, rise at once to touch them, kiss them, kiss the child at least, but he is too high for me, hovering up there in the rucksack, and as soon as I touch him he starts chattering to me in English, and the thin student girl joins in as well, a shower of words, in two voices, pouring their incomprehensible English out over me. I turn to my son for illumination, and he listens with a smile as though he, too, could not take it in at first, then says they are amazed by the resemblance between us two.

And afterwards the customs inspection, a long, remorseless affair, as though they were suspected of something, myself looking on from afar, watching all their parcels being taken apart. And when at last we embark on the journey home, in a dark taxicab, through a gradually lightening spring night, the baby is already drooping with sleep, like a plucked flower, huddled in his rucksack between the two of them on the front seat; while I, behind them, among the luggage, among a guitar, typewriter, and rolled-up posters, watch the loosely tied parcels softly disintegrate.

My son fell asleep at once, enfolding his sleeping son, but my daughter-in-law was surprisingly wakeful. Not looking out at the road, not at this land she had never seen, not at the stars or the new sky, but her whole body turned towards me sitting in the back, her hair tumbling over my face, she was shooting questions at me, speaking of the war, that is, what do people here say, and what do they really want, as though accusing me of something, as though in some furtive manner I were enjoying this war, as though there existed some other possibility . . .

That or thereabouts, I mean, since I had much difficulty understanding her, I who was never taught English, and what I know is what I caught from the air, just so, from the air, from English lessons sounding out of adjacent classrooms when the hush of an examination is on mine, or when I pace the empty corridors waiting my turn to enter the class.

And I am straining to understand her, exhausted as I am from the long waiting hours in the night. And my sleeping son on the front seat, a heavy mass, his head wobbling, and I alone with her, observing the delicate features, the thin glasses she has suddenly put on, such a young intellectual, maybe this New Left thing, and for all that a trace of perfume, a faint scent of wilted flowers coming from her.

In the end I open my mouth to answer her. In an impossible English, a staggering concoction of my own make, laced with Hebrew words, lawless, and she momentarily taken aback, trying to understand, falling silent at last. Then, softly, she starts to sing.

And we arrive at my place, and though worn out they show the sudden efficiency of seasoned travellers, shed their sandals by the door and start walking about barefoot. Swiftly they unload their luggage and send the driver away. They pick up the sleepy child and quickly, both together, undress him, put him into some kind of sewn-up sheet like a little shroud and lay him on my bed. Then, as though suddenly discovering the immensity of their fatigue, they begin to undress themselves, right in front of me, move half-naked through the small flat, and dawn is breaking. They spread blankets over the rug, and I glimpse her bare breasts, very white, and she sends me a tired smile, and all at once I lose my own sleep, all desire for sleep. I shut the door upon them and start wandering through what little space is still left me, waiting for signs of the sun itself. They had sunk into a deep sleep, and before I left for school I went and covered up their bare feet. At noon I returned very tired and found them still sleeping, all three of them. I thought I'd burst, I who was aching to talk to them. I had lunch by myself, lay down beside the child who was wet by now and tried to get some sleep, but could not. I got up and began to search through their luggage, see what they had brought, a book perhaps, or a magazine, but after a few minutes my hands flagged.

Towards nightfall I could bear their silence no longer. Softly I opened the door and came upon them. They lay slumped each to himself, submerged, catching up on the time they had lost in their journey round the world. Once again I bent down to cover my daughter-in-law's feet, but I turned back the blanket under which my son lay.

Little by little he awoke, naked, hairy, heavy, his breath catching, opened his eyes at last and discovered me in the half-light standing over him, looking down. He gave a brief start as though for an instant not recognizing me. "What's with you?" he whispered from the floor.

"At school still, every morning, the Head keeping silent still," I whisper at him in one breath.

For a moment he is puzzled, even though I used to write to him about everything, devotedly, all the details. Perhaps he did not read my letters. The silence grows, no sound except the breathing of the young woman by his side who has thrown off her blanket again. Little by little he recovers his composure, slowly pulls the blanket over himself. His eyes lift in a smile.

"And you're still teaching Bible there . . ."

(Already he has nothing to say to me.)

"Yes, of course. Only Bible."

"In that case"—still smiling—"everything's as usual."

"Yes, as usual"—and another long silence—"except of course for my pupils getting killed," I spit out in a whisper straight into his face.

He shuts his eyes. Then he sits up, huddled in his blanket, his beard wild, picks up a pipe and sticks it into his mouth, begins to muse, like an ancient prophet, to explain that the war won't go on, haven't I noticed the signs, can't go on any longer. And now his wife wakes up as well, sits up beside him, likewise drapes the blanket about her, sends me a smile full of light, ready to make contact, join the conversation, explain her viewpoint, straightaway, without going for a wash, coffee, her eyes still heavy with sleep, in the shimmer of spring twilight, in the littered room filled with their warmth.

Striding through the corridors to the office, a little mourning-procession, I in their midst, like a precious guest, like a captive. And classroom doors open a crack as though under the pressure of studies, and teachers' faces, blackboard faces, student faces, the entire school watching me as though discovering me anew.

. . . And we never knew he was back, you never told, your silence. I didn't think you'd remember him, though in fact he used to be a pupil here too. How old is he, was he? Thirty-one. God, when'll all this stop. So young. Not quite so young any more, took me aback when he got off the plane, aged some . . . And right away the army takes him? Give him no breathing-space? How no breathing-space, three months they gave him, everybody goes these days, and in the Six Day War he didn't take part, not before it either, and he's no better than everybody else, is he? But right away to the Jordan Valley? Yes, odd that, I never thought they'd still find a use for him, he himself was sure they'd send him to guard army stores in Jerusalem. . . .

And we cut across the empty playground simmering in the sun.

. . . And how about his wife? American, doesn't even know Hebrew. And whom has she got here? No one. And the child, how old is the child? A toddler still. About three. Oh, God Almighty, enough to make you cry. Who's going to be with them now? I'll be with them . . .

And another corridor, classrooms, doors, and a flushed student in light-blue uniform running after us.

. . . What's up? Teacher left his briefcase and book behind in class. Oh, never mind, leave them here, I'll take them for him. What are you doing in there now? Nothing . . . I mean, waiting . . . We're so sorry . . . Maybe you could get on with that exam all the same? By ourselves? Yes, why not . . .

And arriving at the office at last, heads bowed.

. . . Been years since I've set foot in your office. Yes, so pointless too, this breach between us, sit down a moment now, rest, a difficult time before you, I'm quite stunned myself, when they told me on the phone, I couldn't believe it. Would you like us to get in touch with the military now, maybe talk to them yourself. No, no need. Hadn't they better come here and pick you up, maybe let his wife know, the university. No, no need, I'll tell them all myself, I'll go to Jerusalem, I don't want anyone else to precede me. But that's impossible, you can't by yourself, must get in touch with the army, they'll pick you up, someone must go to the hospital too . . . that is, to identify . . . you know . . . I'll identify him. Why are you getting up? What can we do for you? The entire school's at your service, say the word, what do you need? I need nothing, just to go, just want to go now. I'll take you, I'll come with you, it's madness for you to leave here by yourself, maybe somebody could drive you in their car. But why a car, I live so near, you're pressing me overmuch, I shall lose my breath again . . .

But he insists on coming along. Abandons the school, his humming empire, and takes my arm in the street, carries my briefcase, the jacket, the ragged Bible. There are tears in his eyes, as though not my son but his had fallen. At every street corner I try to detach myself, that's enough, I say, but he insists on tagging on after me as though afraid to leave me alone. By my gate, under a blue morning sky, we come to a halt at last, subside like two large, grey, moss-grown rocks, and as a vapour above us trail the words of condolence that he does not believe in and I do not hear.

Finally silence, his last word spent. I collect my things from him, the jacket, Bible, briefcase, urge him to go back to the students, but still he refuses to take his leave, as though he had detected signs of a new breakdown in me, in my silence. And I put out my hand and he takes it and does not let go, seizes me in a tight grip, as though I had suddenly mysteriously, gained a new hold over him, as though he would never be able to part from me again.

I leave him by the gate, go in and discover an unfamiliar kind of light in my flat, light of a weekday morning. I let down blinds (he is still standing by the gate), strip, and go to take a shower; knowing people will come close to me this day, touch me. Stand a long time naked under the streaming water, head throbbing, trying to tell his wife of his death in broken, water-swept English. Clean, cleanse myself, put on fresh linen, find a heavy black suit in the wardrobe and put it on. Peer through the blinds and see the Head still by my gate, rooted to the spot, sunk in thought, aloof, as though he had really given up his school. And then I tidy up the flat, unplug the telephone, let down the last blinds and all of a sudden, as though someone had given me a hard push, I fall down sobbing on the rug where they lay that night. And when I get up it is as though the darkness had grown. My temples ache. Softly I call to the Head who is there no longer, who is gone and has left the street empty, accessible.

And afterwards supper, on the porch, on a spring evening filled with scents, under the branches of a tree in flower. And the three of them sit there, pink-cheeked, gorged with sleep, and I, very tired, knees trembling, bring them bread and water. They have brought out cans left from their travels and have spread a meal as though they were still on the road, a halt between inns. And the toddler still in his white shroud, sitting upright, clear-eyed, prattling endlessly, arguing with the crickets in the garden.

And my son is engrossed in his food, betrays a ravenous appetite, rummages among the cans, slices up bread, his eyes moist, and in vain I try to sound him out about his work, what exactly he is researching, what he intends to teach here, and has he perhaps brought some new gospel. He sits there and smiles, begins to talk, flounders, has difficulty explaining, doesn't think I'd understand him. Even if he should give me stuff to read he doubts I'd be able to follow, the more so as it is all in English. It is a matter of novel experiments, something in between history and statistics, the methods themselves such a revolution . . .

And he goes back to his food, his beard filling with crumbs, his head bent, chewing in silence, and I sink down before him, drawn to him, more than twenty-four hours without sleep, begin to speak to him softly, desperately, in a burning voice, about the endless war, about our isolation, about the morning papers, about the absent-mindedness of my pupils, about the bloodshed, about my long hours upon the platform, about history disintegrating, and all the time the child runs on, in non-stop English, babbling and singing, beating his knife on an empty can. And the night fills with stars, and my daughter-in-law, wide-eyed, restless, smiles at me, does not understand a word I say but nonetheless very tense, nodding her head eagerly. And only my son's attention wanders, the absent look in his eyes familiar, unhearing, already elsewhere, alien, adrift . . .

And the night grows deeper and deeper, and every hour on the hour I turn on the radio to listen to the news, and the announcer's voice beats harsh and clear into the darkness. And my son swears at someone there who doesn't see things his way, then gets up and starts pacing the garden. And the child has fallen silent, sits bent over huge sheets of paper, painting the night, me, the crickets he has not seen yet. And my daughter-in-law at my side again, hasn't despaired of me and my English. She talks to me slowly, as if I were a backward pupil, her summery blouse open, her hair gathered at the back, a black ribbon encircling her forehead, all in all very much of a student still, of the kind that many years, eons ago, I might have fallen in love with, pursued in my heart, year after year.

And the night draws on, a kind of intoxication, dew begins to lap us. And she in a sudden burst of enthusiasm decides to sleep outside, fetches blankets from the house and covers up the child who has fallen asleep with his head on his papers, puts a blanket over me as well, and over her husband, and curls up in his lap, and he already puffing at his pipe, he who is thinking his own thoughts, whose heart there is no knowing, exchanges a few rapid sentences with her in English, kisses her with frightening intensity.

And I try to talk them into staying with me another day, but they cannot, must start getting organized, find a flat, a nursery school for the child, and I take leave of them, pick up the radio and go in, go to bed and fall asleep at once. And at daybreak, half in dream I see them load their bundles into a black cab, on their way to Jerusalem.

And without any preparations, without longing, like a bird, you too find yourself on the way to Jerusalem. On a bright morning, a Friday, on a fast, half-empty bus, among newspaper-rustling passengers, and no longer toiling up the old, tortuous road but tearing with a dull hiss through the widened wadi, through trees that have receded, and there is no knowing any more whether one goes up to Jerusalem or down.

And suddenly you cry out, or think you do, and are amazed to see the people around you sink slowly into their tall seats, and for an instant the newspapers freeze in their hands. And you stand up, overcome, start crossing the aisle, and from the stealthy glances thrown at you you understand, they have made you out, you and your grief, but are powerless to help. And you want to vomit over the people, but they motion to the driver and he stops the bus, and you descend the iron steps into the roadside, near a painted yellow stripe, piles of earth and asphalt rubble and you want to vomit over the view, over the mountains, the pines, but it comes to nothing, a fresh breeze plays about you, you recover your breath, and far away in the opposite lane cars rush past on their way to the plain as on a different road. And you climb back into your bus, mumble apologies, and people look up kindly, say: That's all right . . .

And shortly afterwards on the Jerusalem hills, steeped in hard, hurting, almost impossible light, you make your way to the house of your dead son in an erstwhile border slum raised from the dust. Cobbled alleys have been paved over, ancient water holes connected to the drainage, ruins are turned into dwellings and in the closed courtyards new babies crawl. And you find the place at last, touch the ironwork door and it opens, and you lose your breath because the news has caught in your throat. And softly you enter into an apartment turned upside down for cleaning, bunched-up curtains, chairs lifted on to tables, flowerpots on the couch. Broom, dustpan, pail, rag, are strewn about the room. And the radio is singing Arabic in great lilting chorus and drums, heroic songs. And an Arab cleaning woman, very old, is wildly beating a red carpet. And his wife isn't there and nor is the child. And your strength is ebbing, you stumble over the large tiles worn smooth by generations. And from great depths, through the loud singing, you try to dredge up forgotten Arabic words. "*Ya isma'i . . . el wallad . . . ibni . . . maath . . .*"

(Listen . . . the child . . . my son . . . dead . . .)

Amazing that my cry does not frighten her, that she understands at once that I belong here, that I have rights, and perhaps she perceives traces of others in my features. Slowly she approaches me, the carpet-beater in her hand, an old crone (where did they dig her up?), her face crumpled, deaf apparently, for the radio is still going full blast.

Again I shout something, point at the radio, and she goes over to it at once, stoops by an elaborate device with multiple microphones, turns the knobs till the singing fades and only drums still rumble from some hidden microphone. Then she comes back to me, withered monkey, bent, swathed in skirts, her head covered with a large kerchief, waiting.

"*Ibni* . . ." I try again and fall silent, tears choke me, begin moving through the apartment, between upturned chairs, dripping flowerpots, between packing cases (still not unpacked), transformers, records, exploring amid this American clutter the apartment I never knew, and she in my wake, with the thudding drums, barefoot, still holding the carpet-beater, picking up things from under my feet, shifting chairs, letting down curtains, and increasing the confusion beyond repair.

And I reach the bedroom and find the bedclothes tumbled, long dresses strewn about, the imprint of her body on the sheet, the pillow; and in a corner still the inevitable packing cases, one on top of the other.

The place will have to be arranged for mourning . . .

I sit on the bed, study the vaulting lines, begin to perceive the structure of the building, and the old woman by my side, imagines I ought not to be left alone, wishes to help me, serve me, expects me to lie down perhaps so as to cover me, and once more I try to explain very softly.

Ibni maath . . . walladi . . ."

And finally she understands.

"*El zreir?*" (The little one?) she asks, as though I had many sons.

And I stand up, hopeless, try to send her away, but she has already grown attached to me, such faithfulness, my being such an old man perhaps, she awaits orders, apparently used to the fact that she will never understand what is said to her in this house, but totally overcome when she sees me begin to tidy up the room. Folding the bedclothes (discover a telephone between the twisted blankets and unplug it), spreading a rug over the bed, returning clothes to cases and discover nappies in one of them, new, whole stacks of them in transparent wrappings, as though they planned to beget an entire tribe.

And in the next room still the beating drums . . .

And the old woman restless, fidgeting about me, wishing to help and not knowing how, begins to speak suddenly, or to sob, or scream, repeats the same phrase over and over, tirelessly, till I understand. She thought I had meant the child.

"*La, la, la zreir,*" (No, no, not little one). I lean towards her, breathing the scorched smell of dead bonfires in her clothes. "*Abuhu* . . .*" (His father . . .)

But at that she seems ten times worse stricken:

"*Eish abuhu . . .?*" (How, his father . . .?)—stunned, unbelieving, taking a pace backward.

But I am seized with a sudden anxiety for the child, begin to look for him, want to fetch him home, and she grasps my intention at once, pulls me to the door, and on the doorstep, facing the little alleys, gesturing and yelling, she shows me the way to the nursery school.

And in a room drenched in sun, smelling of bananas—the story hour; in a circle, upon tiny chairs, arms folded, all in blue pinafores, I haven't identified him yet, all of them very still, listening tensely to the slow, confident, melodious voice of a little teacher. It is years since I have known so deep a silence among children, had not imagined them capable of it.

And dropping into this, me, in black, flushed, stepping over piles of huge blocks, still trying to spot him, and something cracks in me, here of all places, and I wish to sink down beside the little towels hung up in a row, under the paintings scattered on the wall. And the brief shout of the teacher.

A bereavement in our family . . .

Before dawn . . .

But she, pale, misses the name, thinks I am rambling, thinks I belong at another nursery school perhaps, but then he stands up, rises like a slender stalk from his place, arms still folded, very grave, silently admits to the connection between us, listens to the teacher who has suddenly understood, has gone over to put her arms about him, addresses him in English, picks him up, lifts him out of the circle.

And at once the little lunch box is hung around his neck, a blue cap placed on his head, and he asks for something in his language and is immediately given a painting he has made that morning, and through the mist that veils my eyes I see—the page is filled with a red sun sparking splinters all around. And his little hand in mine, and my fingers closing over it. They have given him to me, even though I haven't told everything yet, could have been any old man entering a nursery school wishing to take away a child.

Back in their apartment. Soundless, barefoot, the Arab woman pads about in the kitchen. The child is with her, eating an early lunch. Now and then a few soft phrases reach me, she talking to him in Arabic, he answering her in English. A distant rustle from the open windows. We are waiting only for her. Everything will be turned upside down here in a day or two, people will fill the rooms. In a month or two nothing will remain. She will stow the child in a rucksack and go back where she came from. I find his study, go in and shut the door upon myself. Dim and cool in here. Stacks of books on the floor, the desk littered with papers. Left everything as it was and went to the army. Confusion of generations. I circle his desk, lightly touch his papers. Who could make order in this chaos. Fifteen years since I have inspected his exercise books. Vainly I try to let in some light. The blind has stuck, won't open. I come back to the desk. What had he been working on, what planned, and how can I link up with this? I touch the first layer and at once telephone bills, electricity bills, university circulars, come fluttering down. He is something of a teacher himself. I peel off a second layer— accounts, thick magazines in English, unfamiliar, pictures of men posing for advertisements, some half-naked, all of them long-haired, fat and lean revolutionaries displaying novel ties or striped trousers, small electric instruments of doubtful purpose. And suddenly I also find a pipe of his, and a smell of unknown tobacco. Tokens of my son's mystery. Son, child of mine. Another spell of dizziness. My eyes grow dim. I return to the window and strain all my powers to wrench the blind loose. Specks of light, a thin current of air; through the slats I discover a novel angle of a teeming wadi, and beyond it new buildings of the university. I return to my rummaging about the desk. Transcripts sent him by colleagues. Diagrams of statistical data. Will have to try and read these as well. Notes in his handwriting, book titles. Promises of new ideologies. I stuff some in my pocket. And now something genuinely his, a sheaf of papers in his handwriting, half in English, half in Hebrew, entitled "Prophecy and Politics." A new book perhaps, or an article. I pull drawers, perhaps there will be a personal diary as well, but they turn out to be almost empty. More pipes, a broken camera, old medicine bags, and snapshots of his girl-wife—by some trees, by a hill, a car, a river. And beyond the pictures, in a far corner of the drawer, I find a small knife, sharp, ornamented, inscribed with the word PEACE.

And the front door opens, and the house fills with the sound of light steps and with her laughter. The child's singsong, then the hectic whispering of the Arab woman. And now light streaming at me from the opening door. And she—in a light dress, still hot and sweaty from walking, her bag on her shoulder, sunglasses on her eyes, such a tourist. Stands there surprised at the depth of my intrusion, tries a smile for me at once, but I am buried in the chair, behind the desk, black-suited, heavy, the knife between my fingers.

She takes a few quick, airy steps towards me but suddenly she halts, has sensed something, dread seizes her, as though she had perceived the marks of death upon me.

"Something wrong . . ." her voice trembles, as though it were I on the point of death, concealing a mortal wound beneath my garments.

And I straighten up, drop the knife, a burst of hot light hits me, begin to move, past her. Mumble the morning's tidings in an ancient, biblical Hebrew, and know she will not understand, the words dart back at me. And I am filled with pity for them, stroke the child's hair, incline my head before the old Arab woman, and am drawn onwards to the hot light in the rooms, through the still open front door, towards the looming wadi, to the university. Will have to enlist their help.

And in a straight line, almost as the crow flies, I cross the wadi towards the university, and in a tangle of thicket, in the depth of a teeming ditch, for a moment I lose the sky. Suddenly I think of you and you alone, ardently, hungrily. My killed, mine only son. Out of the depths I cry, noon is passing, the Sabbath near, and in Jerusalem they still know nothing of your death. Your wife has not grasped the tidings. I was wrong, I should have let the authorities perform their duty.

And here rocks, and a very steep slope, and bushes growing out of an invisible earth tangling underfoot, and who would have imagined that near the university there could be such a wilderness still.

At last I have seen your papers. Vainly you feared that I would not understand, I understood at once, and I am inspired, burned and despairing of you. You came back to preach your gospel, I am with you, my son, I have filled my pockets with your notes, shall learn English properly, shall go up into the mountains and wait for the wind.

And I crash through the barbed-wire fence surrounding the university, behind one of the marble buildings, a gnarled branch in my hand, a long time since I have been here, am confounded anew by the sequence of the buildings. Start looking for your faculty, wander along corridors, between oxygen bottles, dim laboratories, small libraries, hothouses, humming computers, and the campus emptying before my eyes, students receding.

And in the compound of the main library, defeated, I detain a last, book-laden, hurrying professor, but he has never heard your name and, embarrassed, he shows me the way to the offices. And a flock of clerks, just leaving, listen to me attentively, advise me that the telephones are disconnected already, that moreover they are not authorized to handle such tidings, perhaps I had better go to the police. And I realize suddenly: they take me for mad, or for some eternal student, a crank wishing to draw attention to himself. In a black suit slightly earth-caked, and hands holding a branch. It is the branch that makes me so suspect.

And I throw it away at once, in the middle of the square, and hasten back to the faculty building, into a lighted, balcony-tiered lobby. And on the top landing a stout porter moves about, letting down blinds. I, from my depth down below, in a shout, ask him about you, and he *has* heard your name, knows you by sight at least. "That professor with the wild beard"—he says, and comes down to me, jangling his keys, and takes me up to your office at the end of a corridor. And on the door I find a long list of students who want to consult you, and near it a typed announcement of your absence due to reserve duty, and on one side a list of books that you are asking your students to read pending your return. And I turn all these papers over, combine them and write a first death notice, my dearly beloved. And the porter reads it over my shoulder and believes it straightaway, brings me more thumbtacks to pin the paper to the door.

And we descend the stairs, and I tell him all about you, and our steps echo in the empty building. And the dusky light is pleasant, gentle to the eyes, I hang back, my steps waver, I would fain linger here awhile, but the porter is suddenly impatient, resolutely turns me out, back into the sun.

And it blazes with such passion, softening the world for a final conflagration. And I had said in my haste: early summer, and here it is high summer already. And back to drifting, in sweltering clothes, between the white buildings, the locked laboratories of the spirit, tramping across limp Jerusalem grass, drawing, drawn, towards a lone remnant of American students sprawled on one of the lawns, abandoning themselves to the sun, barefoot, bearded, half-naked some of them, nodding over copybooks and English Bibles, playing pop-songs to themselves on small tape recorders. Calling me from afar— "You guy"—as though inviting me to accost them. And I do, I butt in, start walking among them, over them, step on their flabby, diaspora limbs, strike at them lightly with the branch that has reappeared in my hand. I could have been appointed professor here myself if I had really been determined, couldn't I?

And far away, somewhere on the horizon—the Hills of Moab.

They laugh, so passive are they, maybe even slightly drugged, "You old man," they say to me, taking me for who knows what, for some waster, someone come to peddle drugs perhaps. They are pleased with me, "You're great," they say, twisting on the ground, wallowing in the sparse grass, no word of Hebrew do they speak, it is only two days since they were set down at the airport. And I bend over them, am even prepared to examine them there and then, test their Bible knowledge, and I start talking to them in my broken, impossible English, which has all at once become intelligible to them.

"Hear me, children. My son killed at night. In Jordan. I mean, near the river," and I point at the horizon which is fading in a blue haze. And they laughing still, "Wonderful," they say, delighted, slap my back, eager to draw me in, make me join their crowd, assimilate me in the swelling beat of their song.

". . . I am grateful to you, my dear friend and Principal, for letting me address our students on this solemn occasion of their graduating from our school. I know, it wasn't easy for you to cede me this privilege for once. You, after all, haven't given a single lesson for years, not stained your hands with chalk, not touched a red pencil to correct a paper. You no longer stand for hours in front of a class, for you are busy with the administrative part of education, which you much prefer to any education proper. Nevertheless, and precisely therefore, you would always look forward impatiently to this moment when, before our anxious parents, you could hold forth as a guiding spirit to these youngsters; and all the more so in these troubled times.

"And who is not eager to address the young these days? We are all seized with a veritable passion for speaking to you, dear students, long-haired, inarticulate, slightly obtuse students, vague graduates without ideals, with your family cars, your discothèques and pettings at night in doorways. And with all that—with the strength and readiness to die. To burrow in bunkers for months on end, under constant fire, to charge at unseen wire fences in the night, so young, and in fact so disciplined, amazing us over and over with your obedience. Isn't that so, dear parents?

"Ladies and gentlemen, I am not speaking to you as senior teacher, but as one who was a father and is so no more. I came here the way I am and you see me with my beard of mourning, my dark clothes. I have no message, but I want to encourage you. See, I too have lost a son, though he was not quite so young any more. We thought he would go to guard army stores in Jerusalem, but they sent him to the Jordan Valley. Thirty-one years old. An only, beloved son. Dear parents, students, I do not want to burden you with my grief, but I ask you to look at me and guard yourself against surprise, because I was prepared for his death in a manner, and that was my strength in that fearful moment.

"And even on that very Friday I was informed of his death, before going to identify him, very lonely, wandering across lawns, between university buildings, under a fierce sun, even then I began to think of you, of the things I should say to you, how out of my private sorrow a common truth would illumine us all . . ."

From a great distance, beyond the summer clouds, as from a bird's-eye view, I look down upon myself. A tiny speck, abandoning the pale cubes and rolling slowly through a great splash of asphalt. An intersection. And all about—the heart of the dominion, a pile of government offices, reddish Parliament, sheer white museum, pine trees like soft moss, nibbled hills, blasted rocks, ribbons of road one atop the other—a plain attempt to transform the scenery. And a black dot comes spewing smoke from the east, stops beside the speck and swallows it.

It is an old taxi, some charred relic, and I drop on to torn and sweaty upholstery and wave the driver on.

Southwards. Through the stifling air—the stubbornness. Cemetery Hill, twisted lines of graves as a wild scrawl, and on all sides still more buildings, big housing projects, scaffolding, cranes—like rocket pits. Houses copulating with houses. The Kingdom of Heaven by force of stone.

And the driver—an unshaven ruffian, ageless, cracking sunflower seeds, hums under his breath, peers at me constantly through his mirror, ready for contact.

But I shut my eyes.

The taxi worms its way down the slope to a wadi, leaving a thick trail behind it. The hospital comes into view. A red rock dropped there once and turned into a windowed dam, hushed in the midday air, a small helicopter hovering above like a bird of prey.

My clothes are shedding wisps of grass. I doze, dream. The car rattles, its doors shake, windows subside. The hum of the springs sends the driver's spirits soaring and, having given me up, he starts singing aloud, with abandon, vigorously banging his steering wheel.

But I am transcending the heights, dominating the view. Long wadis drawing from Jerusalem to Mount Hebron, pouring, delving into bare eternal hills. Olive groves, stone walls, flocks of sheep, the beauty of it, ancient kingdom changeless for thousands of years, and in the same glance, higher up, the sea appears and the mouth of the desert. Heavily does this fearful land seize me by the neck.

I touch the back of the driver's neck lightly, his singing is cut short at once. I begin to talk. He does not understand at first, thinks I have gone out of my mind. But over the short distance remaining to the hospital I manage to convey the essential.

Yes, at thirty-one . . .

Only son . . .

Before dawn . . .

They were expecting me, as indeed they had said this morning, in the heart of the tiled compound, in the heart of the mountains, an army chaplain, heavy-limbed, his beard red and savage, a khaki-clad prophet, stands with the sun in his eyes, waiting. And when I arrive in my taxi he spots me at once, as though bereavement had marked me already, hurries to catch me before I should vanish through one of the glass doors gaping on all sides.

"You the father?"

"I am the father."

"Alone?"

"Alone."

He is astounded. His eyes burn. How on earth? How could they have let you come alone? For it isn't merely a matter of identification but a last leave-taking as well.

I know, but have no answer. Only cling to him with speechless fervour. At last a real rabbi, a man of God at my disposal. And silently I attach myself to his sweat-stained clothes, lightly touch his officer's insignia, and he, surprised at my clutching hands, surprised too at my weakness stirring at him through my hot clothes, puts his arm about me in embarrassment, his shoulders sag, tears in his eyes, and slowly, in the same embrace, he turns me towards the sun's radiance pouring out of the west, and softly pulls me inside.

Into an enormous and empty lift, and at once we sink slowly to the depths, no longer touching each other now, he beside the panel of buttons, I in a far corner, an empty stretcher between us.

He listens, his head tilted, his face blank, eyes extinguished; I am apparently talking again, not listening to myself, mechanically, probing the pain, the words happening far away, on some vague horizon, words already spoken several times today: thirty-one years old, nearly professor. Only son. Though saw little of him these past few years. A matter of months since he came back from the United States, grown a beard, hardly recognized him. Beloved son. Now he is leaving a wife, American, young, obscure. Leaving me a child. Leaving manuscripts, unfinished researches, packing cases scattered through his house, leaving wires and transformers. Enough to drive one mad. Our children getting killed and we left with things . . .

I am still speaking of him as though he were far away from me, lying in some desert somewhere, as though he weren't a couple of yards away, as though I weren't moving towards him in a slow but certain falling, which is arrested at last with a soft jolt that kindles the chaplain's eyes anew. Automatically the doors tear open before us . . .

He takes hold of me. I must have shown signs of wanting to escape. Leads me through lighted corridors of a basement filled with the breathing of engines. At the crossings between corridors, sudden gusts of wind blow at us. In a little room people rise to meet us, doctors, officials, bend their heads when they see me enter, close their eyes for an instant. Some retreat at once, begin to slip away, some are, on the contrary, drawn towards me, want to touch me. The chaplain whispers: "This is the father who's come alone," and I, terrified, start mumbling again, the familiar formula. And someone at once steps nearer to listen, and a hush all around.

There is a wonderful gentleness in their attitude towards me, in the way they place me in a chair, put a skull-cap on my head, in the swiftness with which they extract the identity card from my clothes, write something down, open a side door; and when they help me up I seem weightless, drawn floating by their hands into a vault, a bare concrete floor, screens everywhere, beating of white wings.

I shiver.

There is an unmistakable sound of flowing water in the room, as though springs were bubbling up in it.

The shed blood.

The child. This curse fallen upon me.

Someone is already standing beside one of the screens, draws a curtain aside, turns the blanket back, and I still afar, swept by a dreadful curiosity, my breathing faint, fading, heart almost still, slip out of the hands holding me, glide softly, irresistibly over there, to look at the pale face of a dead young man, naked under the blanket, at thin lines of blood circling blank half-open eyes. I shrink back slightly, the skull-cap slips off my head.

A deep hush. Everyone is watching me. The chaplain stands motionless, his hand in his waistcoat, any moment now he will come out with a ram's horn, blow us a feeble blast.

"It isn't him . . ." I whisper at last with infinite astonishment, with growing despair, with the murmur of the water flowing in this damned room.

Someone switches on more lights, as though it were a question of light. The silence lasts. I realize: no one wants to understand.

"It isn't him," I say again, say without voice, without breath, gasping for air, "you must have made a mistake . . ."

Amazement comes to them at last. The chaplain attacks a scrap of paper tied to the stretcher, reads the name aloud.

"Only the name is right . . ." myself still in a whisper, and I retreat, and in the deep silence, the murmur of water flowing unseen, the sweet smell of decay, return to the little cabinet which has already grown to be my oasis.

Behind my back the chaplain begins to swear at someone and the little group collapses.

Friday afternoon, and though I see neither sun nor mountains, I know—we are on the outskirts of town, deep in the vaults of a hospital that leans heavily into a wild plunging wadi. The people around me want to go home, the nearer the Sabbath the further the town draws away from them. They had been waiting for me in patience, knowing how brief the ceremony, a few seconds—enter, look, weep, part; sign a paper too perhaps, because somewhere the evidence must be left. I am not the first to come here after all, nor the last.

Now I am keeping them back. How distressing therefore to see the people enter the room with eyes lowered as in guilt. And when they see me sitting in a corner words fail them. Such a terrible mistake. And behind the walls I hear the whirring of bells, frantic telephones. They are trying to sort out the confusion before I should start fanning false hopes.

But I am not fanning a thing. Only straighten up suddenly and stand on my feet, watching the others in silence. It is only a truce, I tell myself, a little cease-fire. But they are dismayed at my rising, believe I am going violent on them, are already resigning themselves to it, except that I am nothing of the kind, only start moving slowly and dazedly about the room, from wall to wall, and, like a dog, find a plate in some corner with a few stale biscuits on it, take one and start munching. I have eaten nothing since this morning.

But it sticks in my throat at once, as though I were chewing dust or ashes, dust mingled with ashes.

I vomit.

At last . . .

They had been waiting for this, had been prepared. Used to it apparently. They sit me in a chair at once, clean up, offer me some smelling salts.

"It wasn't my son . . ." I mumble at them with a face drained of blood.

Again the chaplain appears, looking very sombre, his eyes glowing, desperate, his beard unkempt, cap awry, the badges on his shoulder shining, invites me in a low voice to return to the room of the murmuring water.

Now I am faced with three screens. The light is glaring, they have turned it full on, thinking again that it is a question of light, that it is with light they'll convince me. Never has such a thing happened to them, and they suspect some fearful muddle may be at the bottom of it. And again I stagger, the shed blood. My son. This curse. And again my breathing grows faint, fades, heart still. Glide softly from stretcher to stretcher, lost faces, young men, like faces in my class, only the eyes closed, slightly rolled upward.

Not him . . .

They take me back to the first stretcher again, as though they were really resolved to drive me out of my mind.

"I'm sorry . . ." I falter and collapse against the chaplain, against the open water channels running along the walls that my eyes detect at last.

I believe I must go over the moment when I learned of his death again.

Summer morning, the sky torn wide from end to end, June, last days of the school year. I rise late, languid, faintly stunned, unaware of time, straight into the glare of light.

Climb the school steps after the bell has faded. An echo still lingers among the tree-tops, in the dim green air. Start pacing through the emptying corridors, among last stragglers hurrying towards classrooms, make my way slowly for my class, from afar already sense their nervousness, their restive murmur.

Those huddling in the doorway spy me from afar and curse, hurry inside to warn the others. A last squeal of the girls. I by the door, and they tense and upright by their chairs, the white sheets of paper spread on their desks like flags of surrender, Bibles shelved deep inside.

The tyranny I enforce by means of the Bible.

Each examination takes on a fearful importance.

I greet them, they sit down. I call one of the girls and she comes over, long-haired, delicate, wordlessly receives the test papers, passes softly between the rows distributing them. The silence deepens, heads bend. The frozen hush and excitement of the first rapid survey.

I know: it is a hard test. Never before have I composed such a cruel text.

Slowly they raise their eyes. Their faces start to burn, a dumb amazement seizes them. They exchange despairing glances. Some of them raise their fingers at me, standing over them high on my platform, but I mow them down with a gesture of my hand. They are stunned, fail to see my purpose. They cannot utter a word before I silence them. Each of them forlorn in his seat. And suddenly, as though it were light they lacked, someone gets up and pulls the curtains, but to no avail. The new light trickling in at them only exasperates them the more. They try writing something, nibble their pens, but give up, a few already tearing up the papers. Someone rises and leaves the room with flaming face. Another follows, and a third, suddenly it seems as though they were up in revolt. At last.

And at that moment the quick steps of the Head sound, as though the rumour had reached him. He opens the door and enters, very pale, out of breath, does not look at the class but makes straight for me, mounts the platform, takes hold of me, three years that we haven't spoken and suddenly he clasps me to him hard, before the astonished eyes of the pupils. Whispers at me: Just a moment . . . leave them . . . never mind . . . come with me . . .

One possibility—not to insist. To release these people, give them time; not to struggle against the waning sun, let the Sabbath descend upon Jerusalem in peace, let the rabbi reach home in time. And for the time being sever contact, depart, come down from the mountains, arrive in the evening, steal softly through our shadowy street. Enter the house through the back door, undress, not think, not tell, wait, the telephone disconnected, the door locked. To make the bed, try to sleep; and wait for a new, more authoritative call.

A second possibility—to insist, shout, tear clothes. To assail the chaplain, the others, demand immediate proof. To rout out additional people, organize a search party. A procession through the streets of Jerusalem on the Sabbath eve, wandering from one hospital to the next, to comb the cellars, descend into hell, find him.

Another possibility—not to stir. Do nothing. Go on lying on this stretcher, covered with a blanket, in this hospital, in the little cabinet. There, someone is already holding a glass of water to my lips.

I open my eyes. It is the chaplain, wild and woebegone prophet, surrounded by doctors, who gives me a drink with his own hands and with infinite tenderness.

He feels they owe me some explanation . . .

But he has none.

Groping in the dark.

Has no words even.

Nothing like it ever happened to him.

The people here are baffled as well.

Something very deep has gone awry . . .

Telephone calls will solve nothing, he knows. What ought to be done is to go back to sources: to the brigade, the battalion, maybe to the company itself.

My suffering is great, but who knows, perhaps out of it a new rising may come.

He had not wanted to use that expression, it is too big.

He is very much afraid of false hopes.

There is a wonderful *midrash,* full of wisdom, only loath to trouble me now.

Such violent times, appalling.

Runs from one funeral to the next.

At night sits at home amending funeral orations.

And he bends over me: to stay here, on this stretcher, rolled up in a blanket, serves no purpose. We ought to go to Jerusalem.

If possible before the onset of the Sabbath . . .

Suggests therefore that I collect myself, that is, if I still have some strength left. That I remove the blanket, get off the stretcher. They won't leave me to wander about by myself any more.

Incidentally, my status is dubious from the point of religious law as well—should my garment be rent or not. However, to be on the safe side, to ward off illusions, and again, before Sabbath sets in—

And he takes a small penknife out of his pocket, removes my blanket, and as I lie there, everyone watching, he makes a long tear in my coat.

And we start the ascent, out of the depths, in the same lift and at the same slow speed, stumble out into the same compound and find a different light, different air, signs of a new hush. And climbing up out of the wadi, out of the heart of the mountains, and with us the sun, caught on the roof of the chaplain's small military car. He is driving zealously, sounding his horn to high heaven, his beard blowing, the steering wheel digging into his stomach, hurtles between near-empty buses, trying to overtake the Sabbath, which is descending upon him from the hazy eastern sky.

There is something desolate about the summery streets of Jerusalem vanquished by the Sabbath's might. I think of my house, of our street at this hour, decked in greenery, with a heavy perfume of blossoming, a swish of cars being washed, and the water murmuring along the curb.

And a taste of autumn suddenly, clouds caught in pines and cypresses. And we burst at a gallop into a large, empty military camp scattered through a grove on a hill, and just at that moment the Sabbath siren rises from the town like a wail. The chaplain stops the car at once, kills the engine, drops his hands off the wheel, listens to the sound as though he were hearing some new gospel, then goes to find someone from brigade staff.

But there is no one, only barracks with boarded-up windows, stretches of cracked and barren concrete, and small yellow signs with military postbox numbers. The army has migrated to the firing lines and left only whitewashed skeletons behind, and legends on blank walls: COMPANY A., MESS, Q.M., SYNAGOGUE.

And torn, sagging wire fences, and weeds rustling underfoot, and I still trailing behind the chaplain who circles the barracks, knocks on imaginary doors, recedes from view, is lost and reappears, his beard shining through the trees.

And I, who never served in the army, and in the War of Independence only stood beside road barriers, double up at last upon a rock in the centre of a crumbling parade ground, the torn flap dangling on my breast, and the smell of ancient hosts about me.

Such despair—

Since morning I have been rolling down an abyss.

This sad hush around me.

And then, as though sprung from the soil, people collect round me, hairy half-naked soldiers, their shoelaces untied, carrying towels and tiny transistors purring Sabbath songs, weary drivers emerging from one of the barracks on their way to the shower. They surround me silently in the middle of the parade ground, and once again I, grey and tired, with the same story: Thirty-one. Informed of his death this morning. Lecturer at the university. Left a wife and child. They know nothing yet. Myself come to Jerusalem to identify him, and then find— it's not him. . . .

Their amazement—

The towels crumple in their hands—

How not him?

Not him. Not his body. Someone else.

Who?

How should I know?

And what about him?

That's what I'm asking. Maybe you know someone who could help.

They tremble. Something in the story has shaken them, hairy men with towels and soap dishes, they silence the transistors at once, forget about their shower, take my arms and pull me up, supporting me, cursing the army. Never in their life heard of such a thing happening. It looks as though they would like to beat somebody up, some officer perhaps. And one of them recalls having seen the jeep of the Brigade Intelligence Officer under a tree somewhere, and at once they take me there. And in a coppice, beneath foliage, beside a locked barrack-turned-storehouse, the jeep stands, loaded with machine-guns and ammunition, its front wheels grazing one of the doors. They try to break down the door but fail, break through a window and peer into a dim room filled with ammunition boxes. And in the corner a camp bed. Someone vaults into the room and wakes up a boy in khaki, a lean officer, curled up like a foetus, in his clothes, shoes, revolver on his thigh, fallen asleep amid the explosives.

He wakes up at once, opens his eyes and waits. They tell him breathlessly, shouting, pointing their fingers at me rooted outside, by the window, like a frozen picture. But he does not look at me. Sits bent over on the bed in his crumpled clothes, indifferent to the general excitement. And only when the confusion of voices dies down, and the wind whispering in the pines is suddenly heard, does he begin to talk to me from afar in a slow, quiet voice.

What's your name?

I give it.

What's his?

I give it.

And it's not him.

Not him.

Who brought you here?

The chaplain.

His eyes darken, a lengthy silence, and at last very softly:

And what do you want?

To find him . . .

He makes no response, as though fallen asleep again. Then he gets up, tired, dream-wrapped, but suddenly assuming the airs of a general, folds up the blanket, opens the door which he had barred upon himself from within, goes out and vanishes among the pines, into their soft whisperings. The drivers follow, find him by a rusty tap half buried under a drift of dead pine-needles, holding his head under it and letting the cool water splash over him. Then he steps aside, not looking, letting the drops trickle. Now the drivers are really ready to hit him. But with the water drying, his eyes quickening, his head bent, he has made up his mind already, and in a quiet voice starts giving out commands to the drivers. He sends one of them to find the wandering chaplain, orders another to bring the jeep around and fill it up, and the rest have already seized me, lifted me, as though I were paralyzed. They clear a place for me in the jeep and wedge me in between a greasy machine-gun, cartridge cases, and smoke shells, place a helmet on my grey hairs, and firmly secure the strap around my chin.

And someone switches on the field radio by my side and it stirs into life with a thin shriek. And as though of its own accord, so slow as to be imperceptible, the jeep begins to move, surrounded by drivers half pushing it, half tagging in its wake. And from somewhere, at the last minute, they have fetched back the chaplain as well, sweat-drenched, lost, burnt out, dreaming of his Sabbath, and he too joins the slow procession, lagging a little behind. Notices me driven off, sitting pinioned between machine-guns, and is unamazed. They are taking me away from him and he yields me up, is even ready to give his blessing to the journey. What's to be done? He has found no one at staff quarters, tried to get in touch with front staff and failed. But has left instructions behind, written out the full story.

And still he trudges behind the slow jeep, through the trees, the humming of the field radio. What else? What else is bothering him? It appears that something has turned up after all, the dead man's personal file, lying on some table. And a sudden thought strikes him—maybe it's all a mistake, maybe only the name is identical but it's not my son. And maybe it would be well if, at the last moment, before going down into the desert, I took a glance at the picture at least. And he pushes a brief khaki folder into my hands, and the men crowd around to look at it with me. And I open it to the first page and find the picture of a thin boy, just out of high school, fifteen years back, my son, in khaki shirt, cropped hair, looking at me with obstinate eyes.

The time is half-past five in the afternoon. A tall aerial scratches the last of the sun. A hesitant jeep is crossing Jerusalem as though in search of a missing person, someone to obviate the purpose of its journey, and meanwhile a Jerusalemite orange-red Sabbath is trampled under dusty wheels.

Passers-by stop to gaze at the elderly civilian, dressed in black, helmeted, his eyes red with weeping. There is something in the way

I grip the machine-gun that poses a menace for the Jerusalemites—the Jews in its western half first, then the Arabs; as though I intended to mow them down, I who do not even know where the trigger is.

I ask the little officer.

He shows me—

I finger it—

(So tiny.)

And then the final collapse of the Sabbath beyond East Jerusalem, the last signs of green dissolving, and the stark white of bare stone houses, of pale, powdery soil at the roadside, bluish smoke from invisible fires in courtyards, and near them Arabs, glancing up and away from us.

And then another collapse, of the road itself, towards a grey, sunless desert appearing beyond a bend in a setting of smoky clouds.

At last, my solemn and fully armed entry into the Jordan Valley, where I have never yet set foot.

And to look at once for signs of a dead, distant, biblical deity among the arid hills flanking the road, in the sun-cracked face of an elderly soldier lifting the barrier.

And from here, I have been waiting for this, I knew, I knew, a great burst of speed, a resurgence. The jeep spins forward, and the officer, as though wrestling with someone, his lips set tight, eyes narrowed, starts driving wildly, greedily. And I cling to the gun in the face of a great sweeping wind, thrust my hand into my clothes and start weeding out papers—bus tickets, old receipts, lists of students, notes from my son's desk, the draft of a speech, text of the morning's examination.

And then, at last, the army proper, and in the falling light. The sad, pellucid desert light dying over a camp of tents, barracks, tanks and half-tracks and immense towering aerials, and smoke spiralling from a chimney as though a different kind of Sabbath reigned here. And old, scorched soldiers in outsize overalls opening still another barrier before us, as though the desert were carved up by barriers.

People crowd around us—

They have been expecting us—

They even run after the jeep.

"The old father's arrived," someone shouts, as though I were a sacred figure.

And before long they have unloaded me, detached me carefully from the machine-gun, loosened the cartridge belt that has coiled itself about me, dislodged a bullet which I have inserted into the barrel by mistake, and lower me, dusty and old, the helmet askew, lead me in the gathering darkness to their commanding officer.

And suddenly, deep in the distance, beyond the hills, shots resound.

My heart freezes—

Such warmth in the touch of their hands on my body, their gladness that a really old man has come among them, in a helmet, a civilian dimension in their desert night, that they dare blurt in an initiatory whisper as if it were a sinful thought: "He's not been killed," "It isn't him," "You've been misled . . ."

But the commander's voice asserts itself, carries firmly through the new darkness, and without seeing his face, listening to a voice heard before sometime, an old pupil doubtless, I nearly identify the voice, impossible that I should not . . .

The encounter happened at night and the body was transferred to hospital before dawn. The men hardly know each other. Some of them haven't been with the unit for years. The clerk was only given an identity tag to go by, and from that set the chain of documents moving. He never looked at the dead man's face. They had taken everything to be in order, and then they received a phone call from headquarters in Jerusalem a short while back, someone giving them the whole story, saying we were on the way. And at once they had put their entire radio network into action. The men are scattered over a huge area. They inquired about the name right away, was there anyone answering to this name, and then, just a while back, someone was found. A man of thirty-one, from Jerusalem. And his military number too, corresponding to that of the body's. That is, the tags must have got shuffled somehow. And they'll still have to get to the bottom of that. Anyhow, they asked no more questions, did not want to alarm him, tell him his family had already been informed. But they are certain it is my son. Bound to be. And so long as I'm here, maybe I'd better see him with my own eyes after all. That way everybody's mind will be at ease. And better before the night is through. Look, he's with the patrol, they'll be here soon, and they've already arranged for them to be waiting at a little distance from here, so if I've come as far as this . . . the forward position . . . maybe I'd go on just a bit farther . . . that is, if I have the strength . . . Here, get up on this armoured car . . . The word had got down from command about my pluck, considering . . .

And suddenly it strikes me. He is afraid of me. This silence of mine, the endless patience, the way I stand there facing him, limp, demanding nothing; the passivity with which I still wear the crushing helmet on my head. Something has gone wrong within his sphere of command and he is alarmed by the tyranny of my silence.

And again, from the distance—long volleys, strung out, echoes splintering.

This time it is a heavy half-track they take me to. They open an iron door, install me, seal the armoured slits. Two or three soldiers clamber up and position themselves beside the machine-guns, someone bends over the field radio and starts muttering.

With infinite slowness, with extinguished lights, tracks churning, cooped in an iron hutch dark except for the glimmer of a tiny red bulb—I understand. We are returning to the Jordan, they want to send me over to the other side, take me out unto the source. All that has happened has been but a prelude.

And suddenly we stop. The engine falls silent. Someone lowers himself and opens the iron door from without, releases me. A junction of dirt tracks, desert and yet not-desert, reeds and shrubs in a narrow ditch beside the road. And silence, no shooting, and a light breeze, and a star-studded sky. We wait. Crouched low upon stones beside the track, in the thicket. And once again I find myself delivered into new hands. Someone not young and not old. An intelligent, sympathetic face, watching me intently, smiling. Something about me seems to amuse him, the helmet perhaps, I attempt to pry it loose. The smile persists. It turns out to be my age that bothers him.

"Seventy years old."

Sabbath eve. Matches flicker on the half-track, cigarettes are lit. The soldiers are talking in low voices, cursing softly, calculating the number of Sabbaths still left them here. The field radio splutters feebly, someone distant signalling, "Can you hear me? Hear me?" but no one takes the trouble to reply.

What do I do?

I tell him.

He smiles. He had thought as much.

"It's my Hebrew," I say quietly.

What about it?

"Some rhetoric still left perhaps."

No, he smiles, not at all, but the eyes, the expression in them. He used to have a history teacher with just the same look.

"What history?"

"Jewish history."

"And he looked like me?"

"Yes."

"Despite the difference."

"What difference?"

"Between history and Bible."

"Why difference?"

And I rise, the torn flap drops from my heart, and I begin to explain with quiet fervor.

". . . I am coming to the main point of my speech. All this has been nothing but a prelude. Mr Principal, colleagues, ladies and gentlemen, dear students, forgive me but I feel the need to say a few words to those among us who may disappear.

"On the face of it, your disappearance is nothing, is meaningless, futile. Because historically speaking, however stubborn you are, your death will again be but a weary repetition in a slightly different setting. Another tinge of hills, new contours of desert, a new species of shrub, astounding types of weapon. But the blood the same, and the pain so familiar.

"Yet another, other, glance reverses it all, as it were. Your disappearance fills with meaning, becomes a fiery brand, a source of wonderful, lasting inspiration.

"For to say it plainly and clearly—there is no history. Only a few scraps of text, some potsherds. All further research is futile. To glue oneself to the radio again and again, or seek salvation in the newspapers—utter madness.

"Everything fills with mystery again. Your notebooks, your chewed pencils, each object left behind you fills with longing. And we who move in a circle behind you and unwittingly trample your light footsteps, we must be vigilant, as in a brief nightly halt in the desert, between arid hills, upon barren, unmurmuring soil . . ."

And then out of the vastness a murmur rises, and from the east or west or north—I for one have lost my bearings—the patrol arrives, shining in a cloud of dust, two or three armoured vehicles, with growing clatter, in the dark, now and then sending a strong beam of light at the embankment, then brandishing it about the arid hills, at the sky.

And there, in that booming clatter, my son must be too. A thirty-one-year-old private whose desk is littered with drafts for researches is now stuck in a half-track, beside a machine-gun or mortar, flashing a beacon upon me and aiming his barrel at me.

Their beam hits us—

Someone fires a shot in our direction.

They have forgotten who we are, take us for infiltrators—

Only everyone shouts at once with all their might.

They would have killed us—

They pull up at some distance, two half-tracks and a tank, engines roaring, and the wadi stirs into life. Vague nightly shapes, faces indiscernible. The officer beside me goes to look for the man in charge. And I, in my darkness, planted on my spot, scan the dim silhouettes and suddenly give up, convinced it is all for nothing, tremble in every limb, am ready to admit to the first identification.

A few soldiers jump off to urinate on the chains, and all of a sudden I discover him too, heavy, long-haired, sleep-walking, lonely, he too urinating.

Myself unseen I make no move, watch him from afar; know, his linen must be foul. As a boy he would come home like that from any hike of a day or two, as filthy as if he had crossed a desert.

Meanwhile they have located him. The commander calls his name. He turns, does up his buttons, comes over, a lumbering shape. Strange, he is not surprised to find me, his old father, late in the evening, in a helmet, a few paces from the river Jordan.

Two officers take hold of him. The half-track engines fall silent. And suddenly a deep hush.

"This him?"

"Yes." I touch him lightly.

He smiles at us, his beard ragged, understanding nothing, very tired, stands before me hung about with grenades, the rifle dangling from his shoulder like a broomstick.

"What's happened?"

How to explain it to him.

"Anything wrong at home?"

How tell him that I had already given him up, intruded into his room, ruffled his papers, that I had planned to collect them for a book.

"You were reported killed . . ."

Not I, someone else said that.

He does not understand, how could he, stooping a little under his kit, his helmet pushed back, his face inscrutable, his eyes holding me, like his son's eyes, like mine gazing at him. This is how he would look at me when he was small, when I would beat him.

He is asked to show the tags—

Gradually a crowd of soldiers is piling up about us.

He starts hunting through his pockets with surprising meekness, takes out bits of paper, shoelaces, rifle bullets, white four-by-two flannel, more flannel, sheds flannel like notes, but the tags fail to turn up. Lost them. Thought they were tied to his first-aid dressing.

"Where's the dressing?"

Gave it to the medic after the encounter. It follows that he gave the tags as well. I begin to suspect that he, too, had considered disappearing, here beside the Jordan, or perhaps he just wanted to signal to me.

The medical orderly is summoned—

Out of the darkness they fish up a scraggy little fellow, middle-aged, embittered, smoking hungrily, who does not remember a thing. Yes, some people gave him their dressings, but he doesn't know about tags. Found tags on the dead man and put them around his neck. Was useless dressing him anyway. Halfway through had realized the man was dead. Finished the job anyway. No, didn't identify him. Doesn't know who it was. Knows hardly anyone here. Himself belongs to a different brigade altogether anyhow, attached here by mistake. Wants to get back to his own unit. Why've they stuck him here in the first place? He misses his pals, and besides, they're getting their discharge soon, and then where will he be? . . .

They remove him—

Little by little, in the massing darkness, understanding comes to my son. His face unfolds, his eyes clear, his figure straightens. He adjusts the rifle and comes to life. And I who feel my collapse imminent want to climb on to him.

"This morning, at school, the Head informs me," I speak to him at last, "it's been a mad day . . ."

The ring around us tightens, the men cleave to us. The story of his death and resurrection thrills them. They press jokes upon the two of us, want to hear all the particulars. We both stand trembling, smiling weakly.

The officers start breaking it up, sending the men back to the half-tracks. The night deepens, the patrol ought to be on its way, there is still a war on.

And we are suddenly alone, both of us in helmets but myself unarmed, with only the torn flap on my heart.

"What's with you?" I whisper at him rapidly, with the last of my strength.

And only now he looks at me, stunned, that I have closed with him, come as far as this and by the very border hemmed him in.

"You can see for yourself . . ." he whispers with something of despair, with bitterness, as though it were I who issued call-up orders, "such a loss of time . . . so pointless . . ."

And how to give him some point, some meaning, but quickly, hurriedly, in the shadow of the vehicles which are starting up their engines again, before he disappears to the vague nightly lines of the desert, and before I myself should fall before him into a deep slumber.

Not dreaming yet, but asleep. I mean: my heart asleep. Nod on my feet, with weakness, with hunger, and diminish under a star-tossed sky and a moon rising in the east. Clouds start to move, the setting changes and consciousness fades. Little by little the senses are quenched as well. I do not hear the shots flaring up again in the distance, do not smell these rushes, the desert mallow; and what I hold in my hand drops soundlessly; it is from a blurring figure that I take leave, flutter my hand like a defeated actor to the beam of light cast at me from one of the half-tracks, and yield my body to someone willing to take it (someone different again, very young) and get me back on to some tank, shut the steel plate upon me. And once again beside a red bulb, without headlights, in the dark, I begin the journey back.

And it was then that I noticed for the first time that I had lost the text. Entire chapters. I would not have passed a single test, not the easiest of tests. The last verses were slipping and being ground by the creaking chains.

After this opened Job his mouth and cursed his day—

A prayer of Habakkuk the prophet upon Shigionoth—

A Psalm of David when in the wilderness of Judah—

In the year that King Uzziah died—

To the Musician upon Shoshanim—

The song of songs—

Hallelujah—

Not allowed to dream yet. By the light of a clouded moon, at the forward position, I discover a civilian car, headlights burning, engine humming softly, no one inside. Next they are taking, almost pushing me, towards one of their huge tents, and there, by the light of one pale bulb, between field radios, twisted telephone cables, and nude photographs stirring against the tent-flaps my daughter-in-law, standing between the beds, surrounded by signallers who are gazing enchanted at the young, wind-blown woman who has turned up at nightfall in their tent.

"He not killed," I tell her at once in my broken English, grimy, on the verge of dreams.

But she knows already, and all she wants now is to fall upon me, wild with excitement, having been certain all along it was nothing but a private delusion of mine.

But I forestall her, and insensibly, drowsily, through a thousand veils, I take two steps, getting entangled in cables, rubbing against the pinups, fall upon her, kiss her brow, stroke her hair, and a delicate smell of perfume steals into my first dream, the cool touch of her skin, smooth, lacking warmth.

This New Left—

Surreptitiously perfumed—

Seeking warmth—

And then she breaks down. The signallers are stunned. About to cry, but first she says something in rapid English, repeating it more slowly, unexpectedly casting about for Hebrew words as well, and at last crying, silently, making no sound.

And only now I become aware of an old signaller in a corner of the tent, bent over a field telephone, trying to find out, unhopefully, with someone very distant, the dead man's true identity.

And again someone comes to fetch me, leads me and her to a tent at the far end of the camp and offers us the rumpled beds of soldiers out on ambush, to sleep in till morning. Then they bring food in mess-tins, a bottle with some leftover wine in honour of the Sabbath eve, light a candle on the floor, and leave us to ourselves, my daughter-in-law and me, in the translucent darkness of one quivering candle, in the close air of the Jordan Valley.

And I, crazed and exhausted with hunger, am stupefied by the smell of the food. And thus, seated on the bed, the dishes on the floor at my feet, without looking at her, without strength left to speak

English, I stoop and eat like a savage, crouching over the food, with a misshapen fork and without a knife, sleepily devouring the army food that tastes wonderful to me, mingled with the smells and flavours of gunpowder, saltpetre, desert, dust, sweat; I set the bottle to my lips and gulp down cheap wine, sweet and tepid and reeking of rifle grease and tank fuel, and right away getting drunk, as though someone were striking me with dull inward remote blows that are growing sharper and sharper.

Shots. Human beings shooting at each other again. I wake up, find myself lying on the bed, the helmet that I had grown used to as to a skull-cap taken off my head, my shoes removed. The moon is gone, the candle extinguished and the darkness grown deep. A new wind has set up, gently beating against the tent flaps, bringing in a current of cool desert air. Without lifting myself up, very heavy, my face sticky with food remnants like a baby's, I make out her profile; sitting up on the other bed, her long hair in wild confusion about her, a soldier's battle dress over her shoulders, her face open, feet bare, sitting and sucking upon a cigarette. Half the night gone and she still awake. Hasn't touched the food. Her head turned towards me, gazing at me in fascination, in wonder, and the dread that drove her through several barriers last night in order to reach this place deepens, as though by my power I had killed him, as though by my power brought him back to life, as though I had not wished but to indicate one possibility . . .

The firing does not stop. Single shots, and it is as if they had changed direction. But I feel I am growing more and more used to them. She is not frightened either, does not stir, even though now he might really get killed, somewhere out there, on his half-track slowly grinding down a trail.

I must still go over the moment when I learned of his death.

Summer morning, the sky a deep clear blue, June, last days, I rise late, stunned, as after an illness, straight into the sun.

The bells are ringing and I am swept slowly up the stairs upon the turmoil of students who suck me upwards in their tide, into the corridors. Move along the open classroom doors, past weary teachers' faces, arrive at my class and find them quiet, aloof, long-haired, Bibles dropping to the floor. One of them is by the blackboard filling it with flowers, dozens of white crumbling bowers.

I mount the platform and they raise their eyes at me. The room is dim, curtains drawn. And I realize: I am not important to them any more, have lost my power over them, they have done with me, I already belong to the past.

How well I know that look; yet I never feared it, for I knew—they would come back in the end. In a few years I would find them about, with their wives or husbands, running after their babies with a faint stoop, and when I would meet them—self-conscious, holding shopping baskets—in the street, I would regain my power over them. If only for an instant, for a split second.

But these last years the parting becomes difficult. They are off to the deserts, far away; I mean, this supple flesh, the erect heads, the young eyes. And there are those who do not come back. Several class-years already. Some disappear. And some balance is upset with me. I remain troubled. This pain of theirs, the advantage of an experience in which I have no share. And even those who do come back, though they walk with their children and their shopping baskets, there is something veiled in their eyes, they stare at me blankly, almost ignore me, as though I had deceived them somewhere. I mean, as though with the material itself I had deceived them. As though everything we taught them—the laws, the proverbs, the prophecies—as though it had all collapsed for them out there, in the dust, the scorching fire, the lonely nights, had all failed the test of some other reality. But what other reality? Lord of Hosts, Lord God—*what* other reality for heaven's sake? Does anything really change? I mean, these imaginary signs of revolution.

And I am seized with a feeling of unease, start handing out the test papers, pass between the rows myself and lay them on their desks. And the silence around me deepens. They read, give a little sigh, then pull out clean sheets of paper and start drafting their straight-forward, efficient, unimaginative answers in the bald, arid style that may suddenly, unaccountably, take a lyrical turn, only to dry up again and expire in the desert.

They'll be the death of me—

And there is my son, returned from the United States, clumsy, hair grown, such a gentle professor, no longer so young. Has brought along a campus girl, a slender student, cloaked in a worn and tasselled garment, and on her shoulders, strapped into a sort of rucksack, a small, pale child who speaks only English. And they alight from the plane and look at me as though they had brought some new gospel, tidings of a revolution, of some other reality, wonderful and unknown. . . .

And I suddenly feel tears spring to my eyes. Still wandering between the desks, past Bibles on the floor, stoop and pick one up here and there. The students follow me with their eyes, already longing to crib, or at least pass on a whisper that they believe might help them, might add another fraction to their marks, even though they are abandoning it all soon, leaving empty classrooms behind them, a pile of chairs in a corner, a clean blackboard, traces of their names scored on desks as on tombstones.

And all of a sudden I long for a different parting, one that will be scored on their memories. In a whirl of emotion I cross to the windows and jerk the curtains aside, bespatter them with heavy splashes of sunlight as drops of blood. Go to the door and open it wide, stand on the threshold, half my face to the corridor and half to the class. And I know the suspense they are in. Am I setting them a trap? Am I here or am I not?

And then I see the Head from afar, striding sadly and pensively along the empty corridor. Approaches slowly, heavily, like an obsolete tank. Something deep has aged in him these past few years. In a year or so he too will have to retire. He lifts his head and sees me standing on the threshold, lowers it again as though I were a stone or spirit. He still assumes I do not want to talk to him. As though three years had not sufficed us. And in the room the whispering swells, and the swish of papers. Passing on the answers to each other. But I make no move. My face is turned to the corridor window, its display of summer bright and full. The Hills of Judaea in the distance, the Hills of Moab, and all the rest. And the image of the students behind me is reflected in the window as well, fused upon the scenery, on a patch of blue, on the tree-tops, faraway aerials, the hum of aircraft.

And the Head stops beside me. For the first time in three years. Very pale. And must break the silence at once.

Five or six hours ago . . .

In the Jordan Valley . . .

Killed on the spot . . .

Missile Base 612

I

A ND in the night he knows a brief spell of pre-dawn wakeful-ness, as though someone had pushed him off the mattress on to the rug, seized him by the collar and plucked him off the floor, dumped him in a chair to face the grey TV screen gleaming in the dark, where now a vague reflection of his face begins to shimmer. And sleep-worn but wide awake, he sticks a bitter pipe between his teeth, wants to say something, would even hold a little lecture.

Some minutes pass and he starts prowling about the dark flat, wanders in and out of the kitchen, the lavatory, the child's room; opens the bedroom door and stands in the doorway, casting a shadow over his wife's body which lies aslant the twin bed. He lingers, waiting to hear if she will mumble something in her sleep, moan perhaps, then retreats, turns back to the living-room, goes to the radio and fumbles between low distant music, readings from the Koran, and faraway signals; drops into an armchair and broods on the impending divorce and how he'll have to take the whole place apart, and presently his strength fails him, his breathing grows harsh, he kneels on the rug, tugs at the sheet, smells people's footmarks, and falls into a deep sleep again.

In the morning when the light floods in through the large balcony door, nothing is left of all his early awakening except a red bulb in the radio which has got stuck between two stations.

And then he gets up, puts the kettle on, washes, dresses, folds the mattress, sheets, blanket, removes the traces of the night and goes to wake the kid. These past weeks he has been lifting him out of bed as he is, carrying him still half asleep into the kitchen, putting him on a chair and talking at the drowsy child while he sips his coffee.

He hasn't exchanged a word with his wife for months. The first shots were fired long ago, the cause obscured; now it's open war.

Once they could squabble a whole day long, not letting go of each other, even forgetting to go to work sometimes; and till deep into the night, in hot fury, occasionally smashing a piece of crockery coming to hand. Now it's each to himself. Urgent messages are passed through the child, who has grown older lately, graver, whom the new silence in the house is grinding down.

Each of them cooks for himself, and they take turns to eat. On the stairs, at chance encounters, they stiffen for a moment, bow their heads—the gestures of stubborn knights. If only she would die, he sometimes thinks, late in the evening and she not home yet from one of her unaccountable night journeys, he laying out the mattress for another solitary night in the living-room, waiting in vain for the sound of the key in the front door, falling asleep in a rage and waking before dawn to find her in her bed, sleeping peacefully, slantwise, unstirring. And in the morning he is alone, dressing his son, giving him breakfast, taking him to school, driving to the university, looking for hitchhikers to draw into conversation. But it's the spring holiday now and there are no students at this time of morning, and when he gets stuck in a line of cars at an intersection, two cleaning women from the university spot him, make a dash for the crawling car, and he stops, lets them in, not acknowledging their thanks, and fiercely, almost savagely, he gallops off with them through this freakish spring—a drab spring blowing with dank breezes, hangover of a winter that hasn't been much of a winter either but cold clear skies and sickly buds shrivelling on their branches.

He crosses the university campus slowly, deliberately, looking for someone to accost; arrives at the nearly empty library, spreads his papers over a desk by the window, goes to take out Aristotle's *Metaphysics* from the reserved section, and in utter silence, with unutterable slowness, not concentrating, he starts to read the ancient, difficult text which he will have to explain to his students next year, his eyes continually straying from the lines to the grey world beyond the window. This sabbatical is also crumbling fast, a year without students, adrift in the library. It's been three years since he published anything. His friends say he's finished, dead. He ought to have tackled something long ago. And again he jumps up to look for someone, anyone, to flip newspaper pages in another room, wander through corridors, return to his desk, read another page or two before he is up and out again, walking in a cloud of tobacco smoke to the bursary to see if they've calculated his salary correctly, from there to his postbox to find only a slender volume of poetry sent to him by an old schoolmate who each year, come spring, publishes at his own expense a batch of wishy-washy love poems. He tears off the wrapper, glances at the inscription, turns a few pages and is filled with weariness. Then back to the corridors to resume his aimless rambling, to follow a slight, delicate girl student, stop with her to study the notice board, holding his breath, watching her furtively, it's been a long time, he's ready to fall in love, desperately, at a hint. Eventually he retreats; back to the reading room, to his book, listlessly, with growing reluctance, to discover after twenty pages that he hasn't taken in anything; and he starts anew, forces himself to summarize each passage like a first-year student. His gaze fixes itself on some grains of sand beating against the window; a few miraculously gain entrance, land by his plodding pen.

Towards noon he returns the book to the reserved section.

"Shall I keep it for this afternoon?" asks the elderly woman librarian, already used to seeing him show up suddenly towards nightfall.

"No, I'm flying to Sinai this afternoon to lecture at a missile base," he informs her casually, with a smile, hoping to rise in her esteem.

"So for when?"

"Tomorrow morning, as usual."

She does not even look up.

"Yes, I'll be back tonight . . ." he prods her gently.

But the woman just gives him an absent smile, hasn't listened very closely, or perhaps it doesn't strike her as anything particularly wonderful, these shortened distances.

Yet he himself had been amazed when a girl from the army's lecturers pool rang up a week ago to inform him of this lecture. Be at the airport at three, they'll fly you back after, she had told him. As far as I'm concerned, he had said, I don't mind staying the night. But she insisted: No, they'll fly you back. But I wouldn't mind staying once I've come that far. She had refused to give in, though, as if in all that desert there really was no place for him. Ah well, how could she have known that at home he sleeps on a mattress in the living-room?

II

He had been transferred to this unit of itinerant lecturers early in the winter. Before that they used to call him up twice a year, summer and winter, for a fortnight of guarding two huge electrical transmission towers planted in the middle of some field. The long nights of guard duty had been a growing ordeal, the hours dragging out endlessly till at last, around midnight, time would stop completely. And in a trance of fatigue, his mind vacant, his rifle tossed into the corn, he would slip through the criss-cross of iron bars, sit down inside the tower like a caged ape, listen to the monotonous hum of electric current overhead, and wait helplessly for the frozen sky to start moving again.

One morning a young lecturer on reserve duty had given them a talk about official Israeli policy. After the lecture, which he had considered rather crude, he had made inquiries about the lecturers pool and the qualifications needed to join it. Eventually he had gone there, introduced himself complete with academic degree and a tentative list of subjects, and had been accepted at once, to his own surprise. Now he would be called on to give a lecture once every week or two, wandering between various outfits, training camps, strongholds, remote spots he never knew existed. And the country spreads itself before him as he goes on his wanderings, skipping up hill and down dale and speaking, preaching to soldiers.

And all at once—a different audience; no longer a dozen philosophy students with metaphysical texts in front of them, fencing with him, waging stiff battles over every word, but motley crowds, boys and men who assemble on command and are placed in front of him, his words wafting over them as a gentle breeze. And he is treated with respect, is offered coffee or soft drinks, invited to meals, and when he displays an interest they show him their new weapons too—a bridge-laying tank or a bent-barrel gun. Sometimes, when he happens to arrive at some front-line position in the afternoon and his listeners must be routed out of bed first, he mounts the observation posts on his own initiative, to peer through giant binoculars at the other side, to watch the tiny enemy popping up here and there in the dunes, filling sandbags at leisure.

And he speaks. In field, outpost, mess hall; under a blue sky, under a canvas roof, on the top of a hill or in a bunker underground; early in the morning, at noon, and after supper; repeats the same two or three lectures over and over again, jokes and all. The ease with which the words spout from his mouth surprises even him. He does still preserve a tiny quiver of anticipation, every time anew, but it ebbs swiftly after the first few words. And the soldiers' faces before him—a many-coloured multitude. Dozing, yawning, tense, laughing, irritated. And he always still relishes the thought that presently he'll wind up his lecture, answer last questions and be free to leave them, and it's they who'll be left to the long night of guard duty. In vain he tries to keep a face or two of his ever-changing audience in mind. The landscape, on the other hand, does stay with him—the view of a distant hill, a dry river bed, a mudtrack hugging a security fence. And the weapons too. The tanks, the swivel guns, the infra-red sights of machine guns. And nowadays, missiles as well. He hasn't seen the missiles yet.

III

He leaves the university at midday, and the sky is a grey whirlpool. Mercilessly he cuts through the small flock of girls waiting for a lift, races homewards. All at once it strikes him again as something marvellous that he's going to be in Sinai this very day, and back tonight.

Arriving home, he delves into the postbox downstairs as if in breath-expectation of long-awaited, unknown tidings; inspects his wife's letters and returns them to the box; runs quickly over his own unimportant stuff and tears it up as he climbs the stairs. He enters the silent flat, makes straight for the kitchen, warms up the food he's prepared for himself earlier in the week, its charred flavour getting nastier every day. Then he clears the table, washes up, enters the bedroom to collect his army gear and is startled to find her still asleep in the half-light, at the same nocturnal slant across the bed, her expression peaceful as though time had stood still. What's happened? He feels a fleeting urge to wake her, to ask, but what's it to him, after all? If she were dead and done with, but her deep breaths ripple through the room. A glass of water stands at the bedside and sleeping pills show up white in the darkness. He collects his army clothes—khaki trousers, old leather jacket, grey shirt, high boots; undresses, moves around a little in his underwear, makes some noise, but she doesn't move, her uncovered feet pale marble. Briefly, absently, desire stirs. But the sun piercing the clouds kindles cracks between the lowered blinds, casts arrows of light at him. He raises the blinds partly to see the sky swept clear, glances at the quiet street, at the children returning from school. He waits awhile, and then his son appears around the corner too, alone, trudging uphill, weighed down by the heavy satchel. And with a surge of love for him he lowers the blind softly, puts on his clothes, sticks an old hat on his head, takes his army bag, and rushes out.

He meets the child downstairs, flushed, worn out by his schoolday, bruised here and there with the fights he's been getting into lately. He pulls him close, smooths his hair, adjusts dishevelled clothing and showers instructions upon him. What to eat, what to do, what to tell his mother if she asks about him. He has flown to Sinai to lecture at a missile base and he'll be back tonight. The kid doesn't take in either the flight or Sinai, only the missiles. A smile lights up in his eyes. Real missiles? You bet. But don't wake her up. If anyone phones tell them Daddy's out, Mummy's asleep. That's all. The kid listens, keeps nodding his head, saying yes, all right, all right, already looking forlorn. And now the lecturer takes him in his arms, kisses him, and the boy stands still, lowers his head, odd how he freezes these days, blushes even, when kissed by his father. And now the sky clouds over again too, and a few drops fall and cease at once, as if by way of experiment, and he hurries to his car, on his way to the airport.

IV

He watches Tel Aviv tilt slowly sideways, see-sawing, as though straining to turn over, then clouds dropping swiftly on top of it, and then it starts to sink, is covered by the sea; grey-green, turbulent sea, nipped by winds, whipped to feathery crests. Now it's all sea as far as the skyline. And what is left of the sky? A welter of murky light. A dubious spring.

He opens his old student-case-turned-army-bag and inspects its contents. The poetry volume he has received this morning and stuffed in here at the last moment, headache pills, sleeping pills, pep pills, tobacco pouch, a rotting apple from his previous lecture, razor blades, and finally the pages of his lecture in a crushed roll, notes written in outsize script. "Zionism in Confrontation with Other Ideologies," "The Israeli as Jew," "The Face of Israeli Society under Drawn-out Struggle." He invariably picks his subject at the last moment, going by his mood, by the noise around him, the quality of the light on the upturned faces before him, the distance home. Sometimes he comes, talks fluently for an hour without interruption, and departs as soon as he's finished. At other times he stirs up a discussion, trumps up imaginary problems, and starts arguing with stubborn composure.

And meanwhile the plane keeps steadily on its western course, the engines at full power, the coastline long vanished, as though they were heading for Europe, not for the desert. Yet before long it will veer, start the broad curve backwards, inland.

He is the only civilian aboard. The soldiers have removed their caps, shoved their weapons under the upholstered seats, settled down to rustle newspapers, solve crossword puzzles, converse in low voices. The girl sitting next to him, a small, delicate girl-soldier, huddles against the window with her evening paper, as if afraid he'll touch her, though he has not meant to touch her, just wants to talk a little, exchange a few words, without hope, without expectations. He is still unsure of his liberty. His relations with women are clumsy. He gives up in advance.

Over her head he watches the slow return of the land avidly. Dunes, houses, fields, last orchards strung out over sallow hills. The sky is clear, and the sun which had been hidden all morning is there, sailing ahead of them in its full glory. The throb of the engines and the dry, summery heat are sleep-inducing, and all around him heads drop, eyes glaze over druggedly. He tries to sleep a little himself but is still too eager, his eyes searching the slow-moving desert landscape below him for novelty. The pipe is heavy in his hand. Gently he catches the evening paper slipping at him from the other seat, then the feather-light body of the girl-soldier who seems to have relaxed her guard, leaning against him drowsily as the plane dips; a hairpin drops into his lap, softly his lust awakens, and all of a sudden he conceives a provocative, subversive lecture—at a missile base of all places, before the pick of the army.

And now they are deep into the desert, the soldiers are coming to life, the girl beside him pulls away too, opens her eyes and blinks away a tear. He holds out the paper and she smiles vacantly, touching her hair which has come loose.

"When are we going to get there?" he asks, handing back the hairpin as well.

She throws a swift glance at the aimless, amorphous mass of desert:

"We're there already . . ."

It's true. The roar of the engines is falling off, the plane has begun to lose altitude, and as they hover about the runway he still sees nothing but wasteland, his eyes on the window drinking in every detail, thrilled to discover the row of bright hook-nosed fighter-bombers.

"Phantoms . . ." he identifies them with that curious excitement that all weapons rouse in him these days.

"Just painted dummies . . ." The delicate girl-soldier smiles, stares at him as though only now really noticing him. "Have you never been here before?"

"Well, yes, in '56 . . . just for a few hours . . . somewhere around here . . ."

"In '56? " she repeats, puzzled. "What happened in '56?"

"The Sinai campaign. I was dropped here by parachute, on one of these hills."

The plane comes to a stop and there is a general bustle of rising, donning caps, slinging up of guns, crowding to the exit. A stewardess, who has kept herself well out of sight during the trip, stands by the door dressed in a colourful uniform, bestows a personal smile on each passenger, bids them goodbye as though they were holiday-makers arrived at a holiday-camp. He inches forward behind the girl-soldier, his eyes on the nape of her neck, but once on the field he loses her, as usual, without even a parting word.

V

A desert airfield, people milling about, a kind of Wild West. Dozens of vehicles by the fence like a line of hackney coaches waiting for a fare. Station wagons, jeeps, vans, lorries, half-tracks, even an old tank sent especially to pick up two soldiers.

Tired, needled by a thin headache, his dead pipe bitter in his mouth he wanders about the emptying field, the old briefcase in one hand and in the other the reels of film he's been given at the airport to pass on to the local education officer. It is the picture in the thin black suitcase which attracts the notice of a dark, skinny soldier to him. He approaches at a slouch, carrying a bulky transistor radio held together by string, and intoning an Egyptian hit parade song in a shaky whine. He holds out a scrap of paper with the lecturer's name slightly misspelled in a soft, feminine handwriting.

"Yes, that's me . . ."

The soldier crumples the note and drops it as though relieved of a heavy burden, leads the way to a big empty truck, and with the transistor on the seat between them pouring out its tunes, they drive slowly across a large bustling camp.

And already he is questioning the driver.

"Going straight to the battery?"

"No, only as far as command."

"And where's the battery?"

"Not far . . ."

"Figure I'll make it back tonight?"

"Sure."

"And who're the men there?"

"Regulars."

"All high-school graduates?"

"Not all . . . What you lecturing about?"

"Oh, I don't know . . . I'll make up my mind when I get there . . .
maybe I'll let the men choose . . ."

He always prefers not to reveal his subjects in advance. They
appear old-fogyish at first sight, heavy, off-putting . . .

"Give 'em a talk on drugs," the driver suggests magnanimously.
"Know about drugs?"

"Drugs?" says the lecturer, faintly amused.

"Yeah. Couple of weeks back I brought them a lecturer on
drugs . . . Guys loved it . . ."

"So what do you want another lecture for?"

"Why not . . . it's interesting . . . like maybe about other kinds of
drugs . . .

The lecturer smiles to himself, a trickle of sweet smoke escaping
his lips.

"Do the men take drugs?"

"Bet they'd like to . . ."

And all around a land of great drought, hills and copper mounds
and army rubbish, shacks, structures, and vehicles driving about, to
the left and right of them, crossing in front, overtaking each other
erratically. And from time to time they are made to stop at a rope
barrier, one end held by a dark-skinned fellow, the driver's counterpart,
lolling in a frayed wicker chair, a soldier twisted and paralyzed
with idleness.

"Where you going?"

"Lemme through."

"Where you going?"

"None of your bloody business. Lemme through . . ."

"Where you going?"

"To 612. So lemme through, dammit . . ."

But the other makes no move, sprawls full length, a wicked little
grin on his face.

"What you got there?"

"None of your business. Lemme through."
"What you got there?"
"Lecturer."
And the rope drops before them.

VI

And the truck rolls on, reaches a small service base, passes through a square, and pulls up beside a piece of sculpture hatched by an unequivocal military mind. The torn, rust-eaten tail of an Egyptian aircraft whose dim, slightly furry cracks gape at the missile which smashed into it and which has been resurrected here now, painted gaily and inscribed with biblical verses torn out of context.

"This is where I'm to drop you . . ." The driver bangs the radio to silence it and flits away, drawn like a butterfly to a bunch of soldiers kicking at a ball in a far corner of the camp. Ah well, he is used to being transferred like this, handed on from one person to the other, one car to the next, sometimes left in dim barracks, a communication trench, a store-room, to wait till his listeners are rounded up for him.

He alights from the truck, strolls about the grounds, still with briefcase in one hand and film in the other; wanders between two rows of reddish prefabs in the glaring light, stark summer light from an azure sky; inspects his surroundings as one who doesn't belong to this desert, this dull expanse of low, shapeless hills, the incoherent mixture of a great dead hush and camp noises—the roar of tanks, shouts, and wind-blown commands.

He takes a turn around the sculpture, taps the missile lightly and hears the echoing hollowness, peels a strip of metal from the shattered tail and is amazed at the ease with which the aircraft crumbles up between his fingers. Fifteen minutes pass and he is still alone. No one is coming for him. He approaches the playing soldiers, watches the brown bodies shiny with sweat pursue the ball in silence, in seeming fury. By now he can no longer even pick out his driver, who has also removed his shirt and joined the game. He stands there puffing at his pipe and presently there is a faint stirring on the barren ground between his feet, a thin flurry of sand starts up as though a storm were about to rise from the earth. And, as always in moments of waiting, he already bemoans the time lost, confident that if he were seated in the library now he would be able to concentrate. The outline of the hills sharpens slightly. No one comes. They have forgotten him. Though why should he care, he is going back tonight whatever happens, they'll simply have to get him out of here. Still, he *would* like to deliver his lecture, feels a desire to speak, to speak without interruption, break a silence of several days. He returns to the truck, sounds a few brief blasts on the horn, walks over to one of the barracks, starts knocking at doors, one door, another, a third, and finds himself face to face with a grey, elderly colonel who appears to have surrounded himself with missiles: models of missiles glowing in the afternoon light, diagrams of missiles on the wall, photographs of them in action. An ideology of missiles.

The man hasn't noticed his hesitant entry, sits bent over a manual, absorbed in his reading.

"Excuse me . . ." holding out the call-up order.

The colonel looks up, removes his glasses, reaches for the order with smooth, almost effeminate hands, barely glances at it.

"No, that's not here . . . you want Ginger . . ."

"Ginger?"

"The education officer . . . Lecturers are her domain . . ."

And he points at the barracks across the road, hands back the order.

The lecturer retreats slowly, looking at the little missiles set out like toys on the shelves, longs to touch them, does touch them with his fingertips.

The colonel watches him curiously.

"What do you lecture about?"

And he flounders on the doorstep, sticks his pipe in his mouth, chews the stem, removes it. Well, he hasn't quite made up his mind yet—as though anyone cared, as though there were some intrinsic flaw about his subjects—well, let's say, something about Jewish identity, or some brief outline of Israeli society and its prolonged struggle. Or maybe, for instance, Zionism in confrontation with other ideologies, with the New Left for example. Depends on the audience. He won't mind just letting them ask him questions, anything that may occur to them, and he'll do his best to answer.

The officer appears somewhat taken aback, as though these subjects of his were rather peculiar, as though there were something original or faintly shocking about them to give him some ground for concern.

"Do you still want to get back tonight too?" he asks.

"They promised I would . . ." He is seized by a sudden fear that they mean to detain him. "The last plane . . . Do you think I won't make it?"

"You will."

And now he's in a hurry, shuts the door behind him, crosses the grounds, stops at a door, knocks, pushes it open, enters a darkened, chaotic room, something between an office and a girl's sanctum, and discovers by the light from the door, in the faint musty smell, a bed and a tangle of fiery red hair. A girl, a giant of a girl, a great redhead lying on her stomach under a blanket. Her clothes are all over the place, shirt and blue skirt, underwear in a heap beside a military phone. Filthy coffee cups, an empty wine bottle, a carpet of sunflower-seed shells on the floor.

Wearily he touches her. He could have lifted the blanket and lain down silently by her side till this evening ended and the hour of his departure came, but he only touches her, lightly, embittered.

"You Ginger?" he asks, his own reflection looking at him out of two large blue eyes open on his face, and hands her the crumpled call-up order. "I'm the lecturer. I'm due at 612."

He already says "612" as if it were a familiar place, as if he'd moved among the batteries here for years.

She smiles, takes the order, stuffs it under her pillow unread.

"So you've arrived . . ."

"I arrived half an hour ago. I've just been hanging around here, and I've got to get back tonight. We'll never make it this way."

"We will."

Again she smiles at him, a wide provocative grin, still under her blanket, naked no doubt. He smiles back, embarrassed, unnerved by his own smile. Such a giantess. Even if he had the time she'd be impossible for him. Stuck there in the silence he waits for her to emerge out of her blanket.

But she lies there still, her eyes laughing.

"We will, if you'll let me get dressed."

The blood rushes to his face as he turns to leave the dim room, the carpet of shells whispering underfoot. He leaves the door open, goes to the square, paces up and down beside the sculpture, very excited; and sees the flash and dazzle of white springing up there in the darkness he has left behind. She continues dressing at her leisure while he is already on his way back to her, not taking his eyes off, boldly, openly. And when she appears in the doorway, in a childish, much too short skirt, in sandals, zipping up a wind-cheater with faded captain's insignia, he is already there beside her, eyes raised to her face:

"Mind if I just make a phone call?"

"Homesick already?"

"No . . . something . . . it's just . . . I only . . ."

She puts him on her still-warm bed, gets him a line, and goes out. And at home the child picks up the receiver, and is joined by all the roar of the desert.

"Yoram, it's Daddy," he shouts into the trembling, breathing line.

But the boy fails to recognize the distorted voice.

"Daddy's away, Mummy's asleep," he hears the steady, disciplined voice through the turmoil.

"This is Daddy . . . can't you hear me?" he cries desperately.

But the child is gone and the roaring desert is gone with him and the line goes dead, and someone in the middle of another conversation, very near, apparently, lisps soft cajoling words of love at him.

And the redhead in the doorway, a pillar of fire, stands calmly observing his struggles with the phone.

"Finished?"

VII

Actually he ought to go home at once, to the child wandering about there, ought to shake the sleeping woman who must be out of her mind. Instead of which he climbs into the battered, dirty jeep driven up by the girl, its floor strewn with yet more sunflower-seed shells, mingling with machine-gun bullets, food tins whose wrapping has come off, gummy sweets sticking to military documents, a huge white brassière between cans of lubricant. A mixture of war apparatus and feminine paraphernalia. And only now, sitting close to her, bending to put the briefcase and film between his feet, does he notice that she isn't so young any more; the slightly bowed shoulders, the resignation to her oversize self. Maybe she signed on as a regular, imagining that here, in this reddish desert, she'd be less conspicuous. His glance travels coolly over the large thighs, the pale flesh not tanned, yet attractive. What's growing here? This young generation, he thinks, amazed and faintly repulsed, his eyes on her enormous feet against the pedals. She waits for his eyes to complete their inspection and then smiles at him, sadly, as if all too familiar with herself; lifts a hand to smooth her hair, glowing crown of thorns, then starts the jeep savagely.

But she drives slowly, as though sleepy still, circles the sculpture twice as though lost in thought, then turns on to a pot-holed road that lies straight as an arrow in front of them. And beyond the dusty windscreen lies the dreary desert, low, bleak hills, sand dunes; a stale, vapid landscape with its stubborn bushes growing under a layer of dust. This wearisome, war-worn desert, good for nothing except strategical vantage—even the approaching twilight hour cannot soften it.

"This landscape . . . so depressing . . ." he says, to break the silence, to make contact. For a moment she appears not to have heard, but then the jeep comes to a stop, in the middle of the empty road. She eyes him quizzically.

"You find the landscape depressing?"

This sudden braking, the direct question, as if it were a personal matter—his, or hers; as if there were any particular significance to what he says.

"Why does it depress you?"

He smiles, taken aback, the sun full in his face. They are alone in the sun, in space, all the army camps have long vanished behind them, and only the slow whirring of the engine accompanies the stuttered words he forces out in explanation. She listens tensely, her glance shifting from him to the scenery and back as if something could be done about it, as if the scenery were open to change or amendment.

"I suppose I've got used to it" she says apologetically. "I find it beautiful . . ."

And then softly, with absurd politeness:

"I'm sorry . . ."

"It's not your fault . . ." He laughs, shrinks in his seat, graceless, knowing himself graceless. In his embarrassment he discovers a whole sunflower seed among the debris of shells, picks it up, cracks it, chews absently, waits to be in motion again, and slowly they drive on, still in second gear, crawling along the rough road as though they had all the time in the world, and it is nearly six, and he still has a lecture to give and get home again.

Another silence, and she still smiling at him, as though she wanted something from him, this titanic redhead bent over the wheel, her hair brushing the canvas roof flapping in the wind, while he stares at the hills around him, avoiding her eyes. A distant memory flickers through his mind.

"Have you never been here before?"

Yes I have . . ." he replies quickly.

And once again the jeep stops, as if she couldn't talk while driving, as if his words called for careful study, at a standstill.

"I was here in '56."

"When?"

"In the Sinai campaign."

"Lecturing too?"

"No, of course not!" He grins—the idea! "I was dropped somewhere around here, on one of these hills. Maybe even that one there . . .", pointing at a hill on the near skyline which is slowly turning crimson.

She listens thoughtfully, her hands in her lap. He is never going to give that lecture.

"Every lecturer who comes here goes on about some battle or other he took part in. . . . Once we had one—told stories, talked my head off, in the end it turned out he was talking about the First World War."

"The Second . . ." he corrects her.

"The *First*," she insists. "Me too, I thought he must mean the Second World War. He didn't seem that old . . ."

He doesn't answer, looks away, beginning to lose his patience. The girl's muddle-headed.

"I didn't hurt your feelings, did I?"

Her voice, very gentle.

"No." Startled, he looks at her sitting beside him, hands loose in her lap, smiling sweetly at him. And with a jolt the jeep starts again and the pipe slips from his hand, drops to the floor, rolls under the pedals. He bends but she forestalls him, picks it up, but instead of placing it in his outstretched hand she thrusts it between his lips in an intimate gesture, and he smells her, covertly, the smell of a big queer animal. So that's her game, is it?

And now he is faintly excited. And they drive on in silence at the same slow, nerve-racking pace, approach the crimson hills, and he's afraid to say a word or she'll stop again and this journey will never end, while by now he is bent on giving this lecture, passionately, an ache in his chest. The twilight, the lengthening shadows, the emptiness around. In this desert, this Sinai—this is where he wants to speak. Where are they? The people, the nation. To stand before them, hear the buzz, the murmuring, the creaking of chairs or stones. Briskly to pull the sweater over his head, fling it over a chair or on the ground, remove his wristwatch, place the notes in front of him, and start speaking as a first caress, in a sweet voice soon to harden. To envelop them, penetrate the veil of lethargy and seep through their attention, drive in the words at an ever-quickening rhythm, and see them surrender, eyes shining, mouths opening in surprise, in resistance, then in smiles of pleasure. Till he is quite becalmed, starts retreating, drawing himself out of them, lightly smooth over final questions, dab at the sweat, leave a few question marks, a few vague promises for the future, smile self-consciously, gather up the notes, the watch, pull on the sweater, and get out.

The jeep picks up speed with a humming of air through the wheels. He looks at the approaching hills, first clouds looming in the distance.

"Is the Canal visible from here?" he asks unthinkingly, half to himself, and at once regrets the question. But she hasn't heard, or at any rate doesn't stop but drives on, only turns the wheel a bit, leaves the road, sweeps on to a dirt track and without slowing down, without shifting gear, in one rush, starts climbing a hill, at an ever steeper angle, regardless of any track, straight up as if aiming for the sky. Flintstones catapult from the plunging wheels. A bare waste all around, no sign of a house, a missile, a man.

"This it?" Wearily he climbs out of the jeep, looks for the missiles, but he's already used to finding his listeners hidden behind ridges and down dry river beds.

"Not yet. You wanted to see the Canal."

"Oh, never mind, thanks, it's getting late," and he turns back to the jeep.

"Come here . . ."

Calls him like a dog.

And the sense of freedom gripping him suddenly . . .

VIII

An unexpectedly strong wind is blowing here. He holds onto his hat, bows his head, but the wind tugs at him, winds come from every side and pounce on him as though they had lain in wait. Ten past six already. The sky has darkened, the light grown murky. The last plane back is at nine. She'll have to see that he gets there, this redhead. First he's had to wake her up and now she chooses to go gallivanting about the hills with him. She's taken a fancy to him, apparently. He follows her over the rocky hillside polished by the winds to a pale, sickly pink. Great big strides she takes, bobbing up and down, hunched by a long habit of minimizing her tall stature. Her hair blazes in front of him. But a few hours ago he was still sitting in the university reading-room, a feeble, wool-gathering intellectual; and now here he is—far from human habitation, hundreds of miles to the south, on a hill of stone, clambering after this pillar of fire who does as she pleases. What does she want of him? Could she want him to make love to her in the short time left to his lecture? Perhaps other lecturers before him had made love to her here. He shivers, his eyes on her strong feet, sapphire flashing white over rock.

They reach the top in a few minutes. It isn't a very high hill, there are higher ones around, but it looks out straight at a gap in the mountain-ridge ahead and a wide horizon beyond. Breathlessly he catches up with her, and she points out the Canal to him, far away to the west. A brief, alarming glitter of blue. The sun is going down over the coasts of Egypt. And distant objects—rocks, hillocks, bushes—seem to float in the air by a trick of the falling light. She is standing very close to him, a full head taller, his hair grazing her captain's bars. Her freckled face smiles at him again.

"Still depressed by the landscape?" As to a small child she speaks to him.

"Less so . . ." He laughs, knocks out his pipe hard against a stone. Could he touch her? He steps up on a low rock to poise himself over her, suddenly thinks of his wife and son.

"Maybe it's here they dropped you?"

Maybe.

A brief silence.

"What're you going to lecture about?"

"If we ever get there, you mean?" he asks, irony in his voice, and resignation.

"Why shouldn't we?"

And once again he flounders through his catalogue of subjects. His eyes on the ground, he starts listing the various possibilities in a low voice. The face of society in drawn-out struggle, or The Israeli's Jewishness, or even Zionism in confrontation with other ideologies. To provoke a discussion or something. Occasionally they just ask questions, anything that comes into their mind, and he answers.

She hears him out evenly, her eyes on the setting sun, as though his words didn't touch her, as though they swerved and fell on the rocks about her. He grins, stoops to pluck a leaf from a scorched, dusty balsam bush at his feet, notices a scrap of torn fabric, and farther down a couple of rusted, wind-worn jerry cans, the loose chain of a tank, a soot-blackened square of canvas, empty food tins, smashed munition crates—the relics of a vanquished army camp coming to light on the stony soil as on a strip of exposed ocean floor.

"Have they heard all that stuff before?" he asks with a surge of unreasonable despair.

She climbs up on a rock, looks down kindly at him, acts as though she still had all the time she might want, and all of a sudden he feels as though an eternity had passed since he came here, and he looks at the horizon and a sense of peace comes over him as well. Forget about the lecture and touch her, just touch her and the words will come later. And promptly he is gripped by excitement, stoops over the bush again to break off a sprig, to smell, to chew something, rouse himself, and then he notices that the bush at his feet isn't a bush at all but a heap of half-buried old clothes growing out of the earth. A crumbling tunic, a riddled, rust-eaten water canteen attached to an outworn military belt, a pair of mildewed trousers. He kicks at them lightly and starts, flinches, looks again, appalled. These are the remains of a human body, how come he didn't notice before? An ancient Egyptian soldier hidden in the sand, a hastily buried corpse, pale grey bones marking out a vanished form.

He looks up at her, and she, casually:

"That used to be the lecturer on Zionism . . . didn't hit it off with the men . . . annoyed them . . ."

Vainly he scans her face for a smile. Still grave, she points at the tumble of canvas and smashed crates:

"And that's the lecturer on Israeli society. Failed to convince them. Too sanguine . . ."

And now he laughs—a brief, muffled snort. He glances about him, leans toward her, searches her face for the smile, but she remains grave, only her eyes twinkle. Not muddle-headed after all then. He is drawn to her, points to a large smudge in the dark wadi.

"And who's that?" teasingly.

"That one preached Jewish ethics," she flashes back at once, "put everybody to sleep, including himself, and when he woke up . . ."

She stops, falls silent.

The lecturer puffs at his pipe, and the smoke twirls blue in the light dying on their clothes. He hugs his briefcase closer to him, already grown restless, shivery. A star lights up in the sky and all of a sudden he loses confidence.

"Funny sort of lecturers . . ." he says, trying to keep up the note of banter—here on this barren hill exposed to the vast landscape, to the distant strip of water in the west still glowing with daylight—"dressed in those old ragged greatcoats . . ."

At last she smiles.

"Yes, that's how they always come here, dressed in their oldest clothes. They figure they're being sent to the back of beyond. Show up to lecture in high boots, old briefcases, funny hats . . ."

He touches his own, reddens.

"Yes . . . hat is a bit funny. . . ."

Now he'll take her. Just a little courage. To hold her, suppress the slight nausea and seek the smooth tender place in her flesh, draw her mouth to him for a first kiss. He isn't going to get to that missile base tonight anyway.

He takes his hat off, throws it down, approaches her, but she slips away, starts downhill to the jeep, now a blurred mass in the fast-falling darkness. She bends down beside one of the wheels, picks something up. Stone? Skull?

"And this one imagined he could answer any question . . ."

And laughing wildly she gets in, starts.

IX

And the missile base turns out to have been only a short distance away all along, on a hill dug up as an ant-heap, well camouflaged, none of it visible except a pinpoint of light floating high on top of a tall aerial. But as soon as they halt at the gate in the grey dust he hears the rumble as if the entire ant-heap were throbbing. And beyond the barrier he sees the slowly rotating radar scanners, the huge camouflage nets, and blank, egg-shaped domes from within which one can eavesdrop on the depths of space. And meanwhile the redhead is already scolding the guards for dawdling—impatiently, loftily, as if they were to blame for her wasted time. And then they are driving uphill again furiously, raising a cloud of dust, and the throbbing around them increases, large dug-in generators producing a din and a great blast of air.

And all of it lightless, not a glimmer of light. All the lights are hidden and buried. And here finally are the missile pits, real missiles, not quite as big as he'd imagined. And the girl manoeuvres along twisting roads, always aiming upwards. And now metal screens flow on both sides of them as the jeep gathers momentum, and metal-roofed communication trenches, metal steps dropping down into the earth, and gradually the ground itself becomes plated in iron. They draw up just below the crest of the hill, next to an enormous, thundering generator, and she leaps out nimbly, opens some door, is sucked in by a great spill of light, leaves him standing outside, briefcase in one hand, suitcase with film in the other; and after a few seconds she pops out again, comes and shouts something at him over the fearful racket, but he doesn't catch a word, smiles in utter confusion, draws nearer to her. In the end she leans over him and wrenches the suitcase from his tight grip, takes it away. The CO has gone off somewhere and she's going to look for him. She opens the door again and ushers him into the brilliance now, and all at once the night seems dispelled and he finds himself in the middle of a bright noonday.

X

It is the blue camouflage paint on the windows and the yellow light of bare bulbs reflected in them that has created the momentary illusion of deep, spring-sky noon.

But then it turns out to be nothing but a military office after all, or maybe Operations itself, for the walls are covered with maps and charts. Two sergeants are playing chess, the board on a camp bed between them. They glance up wordlessly as he enters, then look away again, exchange a brief smile but say nothing. Ah well, he is familiar with the slight numbness, the curious embarrassment that comes over soldiers when suddenly confronted with a lecturer. He puts his briefcase on the floor among a litter of old magazines and tattered thrillers, and sinks into a plush Egyptian armchair, piece of loot from one or another war.

Silence. Only the dull roar of the generator outside.

Crushed by the silence again he rises, starts fidgeting about the room, inspecting the roster, the missile set-up, charts marked with black circles and computer codes for every hill and mountain. Arrows point straight at the heart of Egypt, at the Nile meandering on its way into the depths of Sudan.

Now the two men are watching him.

"Won't you sit down . . ."

"That's all right . . . thanks . . .", a little uneasy, as though

caught red-handed, but continuing to look at the charts nevertheless, defiantly, as if to show he takes orders from no one, as if busy
trying to make out some underlying principle there. At last he
retreats, comes over to them, looks down benignly at their
chessboard, stands there. A long silence.

"What's the range of these missiles?" he asks softly.

And they, evidently familiar with the question, "Depends on your
target."

"No, I mean . . . just like that . . . without any target . . ."

"Without a target?"

And he smiles to himself, gives it up, goes on watching the game;
then off again, back to the charts, tries estimating their scale
himself.

And then the CO bursts into the room: a tall young officer,
skull-capped, good-looking, one of those boy-soldiers, lords of the
front line, who rush about the trenches always in a hurry, never
sporting their ranks; comes in and finds a dark, silent, square-set
civilian puffing a pipe before the telltale charts, his fingers roving
about Sudan.

"Yes?"—laying a hard hand on his shoulder.

"I'm the lecturer . . ." says the lecturer, grabbing the officer's
hand and shaking it.

"Do we have a lecture tonight?" the officer exclaims, turning to
the two sergeants questioningly, then dropping into a chair by the
table.

But the pair of them just shrug their shoulders and animatedly
swop knights.

The lecturer, ill at ease, draws on his pipe.

"Who brought him?"

"Ginger did," says one of the men with a knowing little grin at
his fellow, and the lecturer sees the mischievous twinkle in the
officer's eye.

"Ginger? Where is she?"

"Went to see about the movie . . . Probably looking for you."

The officer seems flustered, picks up a short stick and begins to
play with it.

"These past weeks," he tells the lecturer as if in apology, "we're
simply being bombarded with lecturers, and they don't even bother
to warn us ahead. . . ."

"We can drop it . . . as far as I'm concerned . . ."

"No, why? We'll fix something . . . What do you talk about?"

And once again the lecturer, feeling a fool, starts carefully spreading his wares. Something about the situation of our universities, or maybe the Israeli's self-image, or, say, Zionism versus the New Left. He might get some argument going. Or let the men choose, let them ask questions . . . anything . . .

The two chess players bow their heads. The officer listens, reveals some surprise, ponders.

"Pity you can't talk on some other subject . . . drugs, for instance . . . We had a lecturer here not long ago who did. Men were fascinated. What was he called?"

But neither of the two remembers his name, only that he'd really been great. He'd shown them samples of drugs, had burnt a bit of hash here, on this table, given them a sniff too.

"Yes . . . so I've been told . . ." says the lecturer at last, in a cold fury, controlling it. "Sorry, but I'm no expert on drugs . . ."

A silence follows, and for a split second it again seems to the lecturer that night hasn't come yet, that the sky is still blue outside, a sweet clear summer sky.

"The colour of these windows . . ." he says, "so strange . . ."

But the officer sees nothing strange about it. Inspiration has come to him and he is taking charge:

"Had supper? No. Then go and grab something. Don't worry, I'll see you get yourself an audience that'll listen to anything you may say."

And he sends the lecturer back into the night, and himself returns to chase the two chess players off his bed.

XI

And descending the hill, on the way to the mess, alone again, he takes stock of his surroundings, gazes at the missile pits, the radar scanners, the bunker entrances, the huge generators. And as he walks he meets a steady stream of soldiers coming towards him, and knows they will presently gather to hear him, and feels again the tiny thrill of anticipation. And the farther he goes the more people swarm about him—walking, standing about in groups. He looks out for the redhead, his lost pillar of fire, stops now and then at the sound of laughter. For a moment he imagines seeing her, a flash in the centre of a merry crowd, but when he goes over to ask after the mess hall he discovers only a little ginger-headed soldier talking and gesturing, cracking jokes.

A bus is parked in front of the mess hall, and a newly arrived batch of reserve soldiers wander about in their sloppy fatigues, with their outdated rifles, gather to arrange the watch, are already plotting ways to wangle a pass. And the mess is completely deserted, the tables bare, supper over. A greying, tired-faced cook serves him a meal of baby food—a soft-boiled egg, cocoa, and porridge. As always, he devours his food rapidly, hungrily, the used dishes being cleared away as he eats, crumbs swept up around him.

He gets up still hungry, seeks to wash away the bitter taste in his mouth with something sweet, inquires after the canteen, goes and buys some chocolate wafers, a packet of razor blades which he puts in his pocket, starts peeling the first wafer out of its wrapper as he leaves, and drifts slowly back uphill, munching. Three grey-haired reserve soldiers in cartridge belts and steel helmets stop him, wave check lists in his face.

"You . . ." they demand, "when's your watch?"

He smiles:

"I'm not one of you people."

"What do you mean?"

"I mean you're wrong. I didn't come with you."

But they refuse to let go.

"Aren't you here on reserves?"

"Not with you, though. I'm here to give a lecture."

"A lecture? What about?"

But he remains silent.

"What do you lecture about?" they press him, disappointed, cheated out of a guard.

But he does not answer, studies the three crumpled, agitated figures in silence, does not answer.

And they wait, they still haven't grasped that he does not intend to answer them, but he is on his way already, up the slope between the radar station and missile base, eating his wafers one by one, leaving a trail of tinfoil wrappings behind him in the dark, licking his chocolate-smeared fingers. Solitary—he has become a solitary of late, has fallen into the solitary's ways. He has started going to the cinema alone, has been caught talking to himself at traffic lights, to the amusement of people in nearby cars. Slowly he climbs on under the clear star-freckled sky, stops from time to time to peer at the missile pits, inspect them; the staleness of it, the hollowness, the tedium, the imminent divorce, the lone, onanistic nights, the child being ground down between them. And suddenly making up his mind, casting a swift glance to ensure he is unobserved, he slips down into one of the pits to feel the missiles with his own hands. And there they are, pointed at the light horizon, stolid, their colour a rosy pink. Cautiously he touches them, smooths their flanks, is amazed to find them rather slippery, damp, as though covered in a fine film of oil or dew. He lifts a hand to the slender cone, takes hold of the fins. Such poised might. He squats and by the veiled starlight reads the numbers and letters inscribed on them, gently caresses the dark tangle of wires descending to the pad. And all at once a low buzz sounds and the entire platform with all of its five missiles stirs suddenly, veers left towards him as if to strike him. Hurriedly, he flattens himself against the wall of the pit, ready to dig into it if need be, but the platform lets go of him, swivels blindly to the right, then finally erects itself, aims upwards, and stops. The buzzing lasts another few seconds and ceases. Someone is operating the missiles from afar, pointing them straight at the sky as if he meant to fire at the stars.

He picks up the fallen briefcase, climbs out pale and shaken, meets two soldiers coming down the road who look startled at the sight of a briefcase-carrying civilian emerging from a missile pit. They halt, wait for him to come up with them, grimy, his hands besmirched with missile oil.

"Who're you?" They bar his way, suddenly assuming authority, very serious.

"I'm here to give a lecture . . ." he answers, putting on a frank air, a smiling face, suppressing his agitation.

"What were you looking for down there?"

"Nothing . . . just wanted to see what they look like from nearby . . ."

"They might have sent you sky-high, you know . . ."

But that is just what I wish, he wants to tell them. His lips only turn up in a wry smile, however, and he resumes his casual walk, not to excite suspicion; saunters off to inspect other missile pits, lingers here and there, and the two soldiers stay where they are, follow him with their eyes. Gradually he quickens his pace, falls straight into the hands of the officer and the girl who are waiting for him in the darkness.

"Had supper?" they ask anxiously, as if that were what he'd come to Sinai for. "Come on then, they're waiting for you . . ."

And the lecturer gives himself up to them, follows the officer down steep, narrow steps underground, tiny, star-like lamps brushing his hair.

"Duck!" He hears the officer's voice from the depth below him, and he bends his head a little and hits it hard against the ceiling.

A sharp pain stabs him. Gasping, he doubles up on the stairs, head in hands, his eyes filling with tears.

The officer turns, comes back to him, amusement in his voice.

"You too? Every damn lecturer has got to bang his head here. What's the matter with you fellows?"

But he is incapable of replying, chokes on the words, continues the descent at a stoop and enters the bunker, bowing. The place is awash with a purplish light and there are instruments everywhere—a radar screen, control panels, a small computer, sticks, levers, phones, wires, cables—all of it painted a greenish khaki. A low buzzing sounds from one corner.

"Here's your lecturer."

There are only four men in the room—one at the wireless wearing a headphone, the same two chess players still at their game on a camp bed against the wall, and one other soldier, a dull, dumb face.

"Is this all?" the lecturer asks with a little laugh. He has never had such a small audience before.

"This is it."

"Aren't you staying?"

"No . . . I've got to go . . ."

"And that girl . . .", in despair.

"She'll come and fetch you after. You two there, break it up . . ."

One of the players freezes in mid-move.

"What's your subject?" asks the officer, but doesn't wait for a reply. "You tell them . . .", and is gone.

So the moment has arrived. To break the silence at long last, to start speaking. A dull ache throbs in his head. He has waited for this moment all day, has been brought from afar for its sake. Slowly he pulls the notes out of his briefcase, biding his time. Even though it's ridiculous to stand here in this dim mudhole with four soldiers for audience and hold notes in his hand, as if he even needed them, as if he couldn't talk fluently, almost unconsciously, abandoning himself to the sweetness of his own voice, swayed by his own surreptitious, inescapable rhetoric, its slant of distortion growing as he proceeds.

The four of them watch him calmly, wordlessly, no doubt used to having a lecturer drop in on them from time to time, here, between their beds, among the instruments.

Where to begin? Try something entirely new perhaps? Question them a bit about themselves. Personal questions: Who are they? What are they? How long have they to serve still? What are their plans after? Start perhaps precisely with that dumb one, who has a touch of violence about him, who needs a little sympathy perhaps, a kind word.

He takes the chair and places it in front of him, removes his watch, unbuttons his jacket, drops into the inevitable lecturer's mannerisms; rubs his hands, plans to open quietly, in a hush, now, the first phrases already welling up in him, not bearing on anything definite yet, only in due course edging towards one or another subject. What will it be this time? Perhaps the face of Israeli society in drawn-out struggle—a harsh political analysis which suddenly, towards the end, for no good reason, takes an optimistic turn. But then the lecturer catches sight of his own face on the radar screen, like a target in the grid of thin white numbered lines covering the area. Sunken eyes, a face drawn with fatigue, a mass of hair, and blood on his forehead. So there's blood. That's why the pain persists. He touches his forehead lightly, smiles at the dumb soldier. What time is it?

"Can I have some water?"

The dumb one holds out a canteen.

He pours a little water over his head, then drinks some. The water soaks into the earth at his feet. He shivers a little. This silence of theirs. He approaches the instruments, smiling pleasantly. A large switch protruding from the board attracts his attention.

"What's this for?" He points at it as if it were the only one whose function he didn't know.

"To light this here up," the dumb one answers patiently, the only one of the four to respond.

"Light it up?" The lecturer sounds puzzled, unbelieving. "Can I?" And he pulls the switch all the way, secretly expecting a distant explosion, but all that happens is a row of little bulbs lighting up on the instrument panel. He turns them off. Emboldened by this apparent liberty to touch the instruments, his hand roves on, questing.

"Which . . . which one fires the missiles?"

"Why d'you want to know?"

"Nothing . . . just to see which button's pushed . . ."

"There's no such button...you don't exactly push anything either..."

He looks straight into the soldier's blank eyes. Is he being had? He moves back to his papers which have slipped to the floor. Here, in a bunker deep underground, in the middle of the desert, he stands opposite four soldiers and is supposed to speak to them, enliven the boredom of their long days, offer some information, possibly some ideology, best of all some faith. In short—inspire them; in return for which he is exempt from guard duty.

And now he decides to begin. There is no avoiding it any longer—he'll have to give this lecture, come what may. The entire pointless, wasted day drops off him as an empty shell. Softly he embarks on the opening words. And at the same moment the signaller, too, starts speaking quietly into the mouthpiece attached around his neck; looking at the lecturer and talking to some distant person, who answers him now, who in a crisp voice reports the weather forecast, the wind force, visibility, his voice coming from a small loudspeaker fixed to the wall. And everybody strains to listen, while the signaller takes it all down in writing.

And with the return of silence the lecturer moves hesitantly back to the instruments, his embittered smile on his face.

"Can one get Tel Aviv on this tool . . ."

"Now?"

"If I may, just for a moment . . .'

The signaller rises, removes his headset, puts it over the lecturer's head, and instants later the phone is ringing at home, and the child picks it up again and his voice is clear and warm and close as if he were within arm's reach.

"Daddy's away, Mummy's asleep," he says mechanically even before being asked.

"Yorami, this *is* Daddy . . ."

And now the child does hear him.

"Daddy?"

"Yes, this is Daddy here. Isn't Mummy up yet?"

"No."

"Then wake her up. Go wake her up right away, you hear me?"

"Yes."

But the child doesn't go, doesn't want to relinquish the phone, his breaths verging on sobs.

"Yorami . . ." he whispers anxiously. The soldiers' faces are lifted up at him, following the conversation. He fondles the switches in front of him with both his free hands.

"What are you doing now?"

"Nothing."

"Have you eaten?"

"No."

"I'll be home soon."

"Daddy . . . ?"

"Yes."

And all at once the child breaks down, cries from the depths of his abandonment, unable to stop; dry, harsh wails, rising and swelling without interruption; and the men in the room with him smile a little, and only then he remembers they can hear it all over the loudspeaker, and he removes the weeping headset, casts about vainly, not knowing how to break the connection, till the signaller comes to his rescue and slowly the weeping recedes.

And all of a sudden he feels relieved. He abandons the idea of a lecture, collects his notes, replaces the watch on his wrist, makes to say something and changes his mind at once. Not a word will he utter. The chess players watch him briefly, quizzically, then start moving the few pieces still left on the board. The signaller picks up a screwdriver and starts taking the mouthpiece apart. Only the dumb soldier continues to stare at him, but the lecturer avoids his eyes, rummages through his briefcase, pulls out the volume of poetry received this morning, sits down, begins to read, barely taking in the shape of the letters, overcome by boredom. He is familiar enough with this clever-clever romanticism—sentimental stuff notwithstanding the ragged lines. He reads on all the same, turns the pages over wearily, his eyes almost shut. Ought to get the divorce, start a new life.

And still the dumb soldier's eyes haven't left his face. Is he still looking to him for a lecture, a revelation? He applies himself to the poems, skimming pages unhopefully; suddenly finds a wonderful poem, knows it to be so from the first line that is like a blow on the head. He reads quickly, once, then again. Three simple, lucid stanzas, each word in place, pearls on a dunghill. Maybe the fellow's pinched it from someone else? He reads it once more, then a fourth time, and it's as if it was meant for him personally. One more time he reads it, then looks up. The men in the bunker appear blurred, as if seen through a fog. And the radar screen in front of him fills with white scurrying dots, like a rash, like an air attack. "There's something here . . ." he wishes to say to them, but no one is looking at him, each is intent on his own. Even the dumb soldier has despaired of him, has pulled a cheap paperback out of his pocket and sits reading it, his lips parted in excitement.

XII

And at eight a shadow falls across him. The redhead stands in the doorway, has approached without making a sound and stands there tranquilly, a submachine gun over her shoulder, gazes at him seated there in the middle of the bunker, head bowed, the poetry volume on the floor at his feet.

"Finished?" she asks gently.

He makes no reply but gets up at once, stuffs the book in to the briefcase, and without a word to the men in the room follows her up the steps, feeling his way, bent over, careful, but even so fully expecting to bump his head again, except that this time she waits for him beside the obstacle, lays a warm hand on the top of his head, presses it down low.

And then he is up the hill again, near the almost savage-sounding rumble of the generators, is signing a form which the skull-capped officer hands him, is looking stunned and bewildered, his clothes rumpled as though he had slept in them. Ah well, as long as he's *been* here. And a flickering light in one of the barracks reveals the audience they have deprived him of. Dozens of soldiers crowded into a smoke-filled room, absorbed in the movie he has brought. And he wants to lash out at these two here, but under his eyes she approaches the officer, kisses him, and the officer recoils slightly.

And then they are rolling down the slope, and the metal hissing under their wheels becomes earth again, the missiles and radar scanners are wiped out by the darkness as if they had never been. And the guard has changed at the gate too, and it is by elderly soldiers that they are stopped this time. The jeep escaping to freedom rouses their envy and they try to detain it, shine their flashlights into it, take down numbers, inspect papers; grey-haired, wrinkled, they fill in some form with stubborn zeal, gape at the redheaded girl behind the wheel, wink at him, and at last, reluctantly, raise the barrier.

And then they are on the arrow-straight road again, and he looks back and the missile hill is gone, only a red pinpoint floats high on a vanished aerial. And he is well content to have things dissolve like that, fade swiftly behind him. He looks at the silent girl by his side who strains over the wheel, intent on her driving, the submachine gun in her lap, her face illuminated by the glow of the headlights cast back from the road. A pale relic from another existence.

He reaches out and lightly touches her thigh.

"That hill," he waves a hand at the dark landscape, "have we passed it yet?"

"No . . ." she smiles, and soon to his surprise the jeep leaves the road once more, and with the familiar sweep, without slowing down, starts the ascent.

XIII

And again he trails behind her, climbing rocks, wandering through small crevices, stumbling over rusty containers, tangles of canvas. By the feeble starlight he discerns the smashed munition crates, breathes the cool desert air, sees the land opening out to the coasts of Egypt, the distant Canal which even now, in the darkness, still glows with a faint incandescence.

How could he ever have forgotten this place? How come he hadn't recognized this rocky hill at once? This is where they had dropped him. He remembers it perfectly now. It had been on the fourth day of the Sinai campaign, at night. The chief battles were virtually over, the war decided, and they had been spending all four days at a small airfield, sitting around beside an old Second World War Dakota plane. On constant alert, cut off from events, disgusted at missing what seemed from afar like a grand adventure, they lounged on the asphalt at the edge of the landing strip, under the blades of the propeller, and once every few hours or so people would come and bring them yet one more machine gun, another munition crate, an intercom set, a stretcher. Their load grew bulkier and more cumbersome day by day, till, towards dusk of the fourth evening, they were put on the plane which had suddenly come alive, and after a two-hour flight were dumped as a couple of live bundles of equipment in the no-man's-land between the two armies. A soft eastern breeze had carried them gently to this hill. At first they had tried to dig themselves in, then had just sat and waited tensely, shivering with cold, for the advancing troops. Towards dawn they had come under heavy fire from the very unit they were expecting. It took several minutes till contact was made and the shooting stopped. One of them was killed. Presently the riflemen arrived in person, gay and noisy, drunk with their swift advance through the vanquished desert. They took away the supplies and

munitions, bundled him into a jeep with the dead body and sent
him back to the rear. For a long time after he had still gone around
feeling cheated.

"How did the lecture go?" She is standing a few paces away from
him with her gun, watches his excited prowling among the rocks.

He stops, looks at her.

"The lecture?" He grins a little as if in recollection. "There
wasn't any after all . . . I kept silent . . ."

"You did, did you?"

"Yes, why not? I'm sure my predecessors said all there was to say.
What more could I add?"

She laughs, appears relieved.

He approaches her.

"I mean, what's the point? Just talk for the sake of talking?
Invent fake problems? Even though I could have . . ."

And suddenly he slumps on a rock at her feet, knocks his pipe
out on a stone, sick at heart, stubborn.

"And I thought you'd fallen asleep," she says.

He doesn't answer. It's as if a dam had burst in him. Hands thrown
wide he touches a bush, bits of fabric, metal scraps; lies back among
the shapeless debris around him, lowers his head carefully to
the ground, looks at the rapid motion of the sky which is growing
bleary behind a thin mist. Above him the ugly freckled face with
the red crown of thorns. The sadness of it. He closes his eyes.

"This lecturer ought to be buried . . . mustn't leave him lying
like that . . . there aren't going to be any more wars here . . ."

"Are you sure?" she says mockingly.

"I've seen the vast power . . . touched the missiles . . . Who
could ever break through . . . ?"

"We ought to get moving . . ." he hears her say.

But he doesn't want to move, he digs in, clings to the last of
his liberty, is ready to stay the night in the desert, perhaps even
deliver the missed lecture. And she—she does not even know his name.

But she doesn't care about his undelivered lecture, she wants to
get rid of him, approaches the prostrate lecturer, touches him, tries
to raise him, and he, as in a dream, bends and kisses her large foot,
white sapphire no longer immaculate to his lips but filthy, filling his
mouth with sand. And now she recoils, tries to shake him off, drags
him along the ground a pace, pulls him up, and he feels the power
in her, in her strong hands.

"You'll miss your plane . . ."

XIV

The steps are all but dropped away under his feet, and he has no sooner got on the plane than it starts to roll as if his boarding had set it in motion. And once again he is the only civilian, and the soldiers, bareheaded and well behaved, sit quietly rustling their papers, not even glancing at the latecomer. And he sinks at once on a vacant seat in the rear, fastens the seat belt, watches the torches disappear on the runway one by one, and is already growing bored again, jumps up in his everlasting restlessness to find someone to sit by. And towards the front he discovers the grey head of the battery-commander he talked to a few hours ago at the service base. He slips in beside him with a nod and a smile, but the Colonel fails to recognize him, reads on, in the same manual still, with the same absorption. The lecturer waits awhile, then lays a tentative hand on the Colonel's shoulder. The other starts.

"You don't remember me. I'm the lecturer."

"What lecturer?"

"At the battery—612."

The man removes his glasses, stares at him as if he were seeing a ghost.

"You . . . You got back from there . . . ?"

"Yes . . ."

"And they listened to you?"

"Certainly. In perfect silence. I had a hard time getting them to let me go."

"You're lucky. They're pretty tough with lecturers as a rule."

"Not with me, though. They were wonderful. Showed me the view, took me to the missile pits, spread out charts, showed me around the control rooms, the instruments, the radar, everything . . . explained how things worked . . . I nearly fired a missile myself . . ."

The Colonel seems bothered, frowns. The lecturer's hands, which are black with oil, the mud on his clothes, his flushed face and the blood on his forehead, and on top of that the shrill note that has crept into his voice.

"A wonderful experience to see that vast might . . . and the perfect camouflage . . . not a pinpoint of light . . ."

And beyond the window, between sky and dark desert he suddenly discovers himself, sailing serenely through space, his features heavy, weary, the day-old stubble like a greyish vapour on his cheeks, stars entwined in his hair.

"There's just one thing I didn't quite get"—still clinging to the elderly officer—what depth do these missiles reach . . . ?"

"What range, you mean."

"Range. Of course: range."

"Depends what exactly you're aiming at."

"The maximum . . ." says the lecturer with sudden heat.

But the colonel waxes impatient:

"No. What is it you want to hit?"

"No, I mean—just at random . . . not to hit anything."

"If it's not to hit, you don't fire."

The lecturer bows his head. No chance they'll ever understand him. And meanwhile the Colonel is already engaged in getting rid of him, puts his glasses back on, returns to the manual and becomes engrossed in it again. And down below lights spring up from the emptiness, more and more lights. Signs of habitation, villages, lamp-lit roads, intersections, light upon light; and then there is the sea and the shore, and Tel Aviv coming up at them.

And the doors open, everyone gets up, and the Colonel swiftly escapes from him; and he is the last to step off the plane and finds it is raining outside. A spring rain is sweeping the town. And all at once he is reluctant to go home, wanders a little about the wet, deserted airfield, turns to the emptying terminal and finds a telephone in a leaking kiosk, rain slanting in at him.

"It's me," he tells his wife who picks up the receiver, "you hear me?"

"Yes."

And again, the chill.

"What happened? Where's the kid?"

"Asleep."

"Managed to wake you up finally, did he . . . ?"

"No . . . I found him asleep in front of the television set."

The child wandering about by himself all afternoon. In the end they'll kill him between them.

"What happened? What happened to you?" he flares up, rain lashing at him, a headache starting.

"What do you want now?"

Her remoteness, her loathing.

"I've been in Sinai, at a missile base. I rang up several times. What happened to you? What made you sleep like that? Nearly all day . . ."

She remains silent.

"You hear me?" his voice softening all at once.

"Yes."

"Look, is something the matter?"

"What's it to you?"

This endless privation, the unchanging hostility. Perhaps she even attempted suicide. So the war's still on. Whereas he would suddenly be willing to yield, to forgive. The headache mounts. The dead pipe in his hand drips wetly. He sways a little under the leaking roof. But he will go home prepared to do battle.

FOR THE BEST IN PAPERBACKS, LOOK FOR THE

In every corner of the world, on every subject under the sun, Penguin represents quality and variety—the very best in publishing today.

For complete information about books available from Penguin—including Pelicans, Puffins, Peregrines, and Penguin Classics—and how to order them, write to us at the appropriate address below. Please note that for copyright reasons the selection of books varies from country to country.

In the United Kingdom: For a complete list of books available from Penguin in the U.K., please write to *Dept E.P., Penguin Books Ltd, Harmondsworth, Middlesex, UB7 0DA.*

In the United States: For a complete list of books available from Penguin in the U.S., please write to *Dept BA, Penguin,* Box 120, Bergenfield, New Jersey 07621-0120.

In Canada: For a complete list of books available from Penguin in Canada, please write to *Penguin Books Ltd, 2801 John Street, Markham, Ontario L3R 1B4.*

In Australia: For a complete list of books available from Penguin in Australia, please write to the *Marketing Department, Penguin Books Ltd, P.O. Box 257, Ringwood, Victoria 3134.*

In New Zealand: For a complete list of books available from Penguin in New Zealand, please write to the *Marketing Department, Penguin Books (NZ) Ltd, Private Bag, Takapuna, Auckland 9.*

In India: For a complete list of books available from Penguin, please write to *Penguin Overseas Ltd, 706 Eros Apartments, 56 Nehru Place, New Delhi, 110019.*

In Holland: For a complete list of books available from Penguin in Holland, please write to *Penguin Books Nederland B.V., Postbus 195, NL-1380AD Weesp, Netherlands.*

In Germany: For a complete list of books available from Penguin, please write to *Penguin Books Ltd, Friedrichstrasse 10-12, D-6000 Frankfurt Main I, Federal Republic of Germany.*

In Spain: For a complete list of books available from Penguin in Spain, please write to *Longman, Penguin España, Calle San Nicolas 15, E-28013 Madrid, Spain.*

In Japan: For a complete list of books available from Penguin in Japan, please write to *Longman Penguin Japan Co Ltd, Yamaguchi Building, 2-12-9 Kanda Jimbocho, Chiyoda-Ku, Tokyo 101, Japan.*